An Intimate
Deception

By the Author

Unknown Horizons

Savage Horizons

An Intimate Deception

Visit us at www.boldstrokesbooks.com

AN INTIMATE DECEPTION

by

CJ Birch

2019

AN INTIMATE DECEPTION

© 2019 By CJ Birch. All Rights Reserved.

ISBN 13: 978-1-63555-417-5

This Trade Paperback Original Is Published By
Bold Strokes Books, Inc.
P.O. Box 249
Valley Falls, NY 12185

First Edition: May 2019

CREDITS
EDITOR: ASHLEY TILLMAN
PRODUCTION DESIGN: STACIA SEAMAN
COVER DESIGN BY W.E. PERCIVAL

Acknowledgments

Finishing a book is a strange thing, especially one that was almost a decade in the making. This was the first book I ever wrote. It took eight years and at least a dozen major rewrites to complete. Some of it is very similar to that first draft and some of it is miles away. I say it's strange to finish because I spent so long stepping into the familiar world of Flynn County, now that it's done, I don't have much reason to go back, and it's definitely somewhere I'm going to miss.

The only reason this book is even here is because of some amazing people who encouraged me and read the horrible (I think I'd cringe if I ever read it again) first draft. I want to thank those first readers: Jody, Courtney, Liz, Five, and my mom. And thanks also to every person who had to listen to me talk about this book for almost a decade. I can't promise I'll stop now that it's done.

I'd also like to thank the incredible people at Bold Strokes and especially Sandy for (among many other things) always suggesting the right title. I feel privileged to be part of the Bold Strokes family.

And also, I'd like to thank my readers who continue to explore my worlds with me. I hope you enjoy this one; it's one of my favorites.

For Jody, because you read the first chapter and said it didn't suck.

Chapter One

It couldn't have gone more wrong.

All the planning and none of it had happened the way he wanted. Even from the start of the evening, everything had been off.

Now, thrashing deeper into the forest, he began to panic. There was so much blood. He was covered in it. His hands, which he'd wiped down the front of his shirt without thinking, his boots, although the fallen brush was taking care of that, and his favorite shirt.

He stopped and held out his shirt to see how bad it was. The pentagram on the front was marred by two elongated streaks down the front. There was no way he could hide that.

Fuck.

He pulled it over his head, taking care not to get blood anywhere else, and stomped farther in. He needed to find a good spot to stash it. Somewhere no one would ever find it or think to look. Up ahead, the forest opened into a clearing and below a cliff that overlooked the sweeping waters of the Red. The river might wash it away, maybe some of the blood too. But they had tests for that. He'd seen it on TV. No, the river was a bad idea. There was no way to judge where it could end up. Some kid might find it stuck on a branch near the edge and then what?

He had to keep his cool. That was the only way out of this. He stopped at the edge of the clearing and looked up at the night sky. The stars, one of the best things about living in this shit-ass town, sparkled like crystals above. Wind played with his hair, cooling the inner storm that raged. His heart, which had been drumming against his chest, slowed.

He needed to hurry and get back to the truck to meet up with everyone. They'd been counting on him tonight. He had to pull his shit together. Turning back toward the darkness of the forest, he spied a cubbyhole at the base of a nearby tree. Few people came through here. There were no roads that led to the clearing, and the forest was dense in this part. He bent to examine the crevice, rotted out by a previous occupant. It was perfect. He balled the shirt up and stuffed it in as far as it would go. As he stood, he made a silent prayer no one would find it or discover what he'd done. He headed back toward the truck and what promised to be a great night.

❖

The dirt road kicked up tiny pebbles as the cruiser sped by the entrance to the Old Bailey farm. The only lights this far out were the cruiser's. They jumped with each pothole—plentiful on the unpaved back roads of Flynn County.

From the open window, Elle Ashley could smell summer barreling toward Turlough. The small town lay hidden in the southern tip of Illinois's boreal forests. It sat between two rivers: one a raging behemoth, the other a lazy Sunday afternoon stroll.

Pretty soon everything would be covered in a fine dust, from porches, to petals, to people. And then the humidity would come. It would set in, squeezing the town in a wet suffocating embrace. A grasp it held until the waning days of summer late in September.

The cruiser curved around bends, taking corners quicker than the tires or suspension would have liked. The last bordered by Nelly's ravine on the passenger side, a yawning drop to the trickle of the Red River below. The town named the ravine for a young girl who, years previous, had wandered to the edge and lost her footing. She slid to the bottom, only to drown in the two inches of water slopping past.

The red and blue lights atop the car sat dark, and both front windows were rolled down. Elle always kept the windows down in summer, even when the cruiser's air still worked. All three cruisers in Turlough were a gift as far as Elle figured it. They still worked—mostly. Unlike their neighbor county, which had five of its cars repossessed by the bank, they'd paid Turlough's off last year. Even if they were '05s, even if you had to disregard the rust spots for the paint, and even if the sirens only worked half the time, each deputy had their own.

The recession had hit small towns harder. And Turlough was no different. It had been leaking young folks for years. To places like Evansville, Louisville, Nashville, Chicago. The big cities promised jobs. The most you could hope for in Flynn County was trucking or laboring on the roads, or a fat baby and a dusty garden. But it had taken Turlough longer to recover than others. Some said they never would.

Before the noise came the lights, playing with the tree branches in the distance. They'd constructed a bonfire in a small clearing. The harsh powerful colors painted everything around it an orange hue. As the cruiser started up the hill toward the group of teenagers parading around with plastic cups, Elle flicked on the red and blues.

The cruiser's lights created a panic. Fingers loosened, dropping cups to the ground, feet uprooted, the crowd scattered to the trees, leaving the area and refuse behind. A lone officer was not enough to catch and hold an entire party. If they could stay upright long enough to get out of range, they'd get away.

Elle unfurled from her cruiser. She watched as the crowd bounded for the forest, leaving a keg, two young men, and a mishmash of cigarette butts and crumpled red cups behind. The two sipped their beer and eyed Elle from the safety of a far tree.

"Dan, EJ," she said.

In unison they said, "Sheriff."

Clad in the Flynn County uniform of tan pants with a gray stripe up the seam, a black cotton uniform shirt with the gold star-shaped badge of a sheriff and a straight, unwavering tie to match the pants, Elle strolled up to the keg with her thumbs hooked into her Sam Browne belt. She'd left her hat on the passenger seat. Her dark red hair was coiled in a tight bun at the nape of her neck. She kicked the keg. Her boot made a soft metallic thud, indicating the keg was still half full.

"Where'd you get it from?" she asked.

EJ shrugged but kept his eyes on the dirt in front of his worn Chucks.

"Is it Christmas? Because usually I don't get presents like this handed to me any old time." She picked up a cup and sniffed it before setting it down on the keg. "Which one of you knew underage drinkers are my favorite?"

"The pump's mine," said Dan, his eyes level with hers. "We didn't steal it."

Someone giggled close by, a soft feminine noise. The bonfire had slowed without encouragement, but there was still enough light to make out the white faces lining the edge of the trees.

Elle let a slow, long breath escape between her tight lips. "Go home," she said to the trees in general. Silence. "Or I'll call every one of your parents and wake them up." She turned to address the trees full on. "Don't think I didn't see you," and she began trilling off names. "It's a lot of work, but if you piss me off enough I'll do it."

There was a quick and violent rush of noise and the trees were clear. Cracking twigs and branches echoed down the hill.

"Come on." She waved toward the cruiser. "In the back."

"That pump cost me fifty bucks." Dan chugged the last of his beer. He crumpled the cup and tossed it to the ground.

Elle stared.

"Fine. But if someone takes it before I get a chance to pick it up…" He ran his hand over the pump as he passed, stealing a look into the forest, letting the words trail. Then, almost as an afterthought, he picked up a sharp rock and gouged a mark into the hard black plastic of the pump handle.

EJ slouched against the back door, waiting. As the tall and lanky have a way of doing, he always managed to melt into his surroundings. If life were a track, EJ would plod along, taking each step as if the next didn't matter and the last had never happened. A mash of freckles peppered his white complexion. A by-product of his flaming red hair, which sat on his head as it grew, curled and frizzled.

Elle opened the door and watched EJ climb in and slide to the far side. She felt Dan slink up behind her but turned before he could place a hand on her ass.

"You can arrest me anytime, Sheriff Ashley," he said, a blast of his beer-infused breath hitting her in the face.

"Well, thank you, Mr. Baker. I will remember that the next time I pull you over for broken taillights." She ushered him into the back and closed the door, scanned the clearing one more time, then walked to the pit. She circled the fire, spreading the logs out with the tip of her boot, then picked up an empty Solo cup and doused the fire in dirt. It crackled and smoked as it died. She watched it for a couple minutes, letting the boys stew in the back of her cruiser, until it was out.

The inside of the cruiser smelled of artificial apples, a condition of daily scrubbing with scented Lysol wipes. The paint was peeling on the cage separating Elle from her guests, but a recent sand job had removed any chunks that could fall and mar the upholstery. The windows gleamed from Windex, free of streaks and dried water spots.

Dan watched her drive, twisting the white threads on his jeans between his fingers. He oozed confidence the way a half-cracked beer oozed foam. His short butterscotch hair blended with his smooth, tanned skin. His gray, unblinking eyes followed her hands as they moved over the steering wheel. They turned down County Road 12. She slowed the speed of her cruiser to account for the potholes along this belt of road.

"Wait up," said Dan. "Why're you turning here? I'm down number six."

"If I'd told you I was taking you to lockup would you've gotten in voluntarily?"

No response.

"I didn't think so."

"Fuck that!" His body straightened in the back seat. "What about my parents?"

"You can call them. I'm not arresting you. I'm employing a different tactic. Because talking at you about trespassing on private property and underage drinking have no effect. A sparse cell and shared cot, on the other hand…"

"If it smells like disinfectant, I'm out." Dan crumpled down on the back seat.

"And, Dan? If you use that kind of language in my car again, I will bust you for that bag of pot in your pants."

"Your sister has the largest arm of the law stuck right up her ass." He demonstrated with his own arm, then used it to punch EJ's thigh.

EJ turned his gaze to the ditches and roadside hills. He let the cool night air from Elle's window wash over his face. Sometimes he would turn his head toward the wind and let it steal his breath, seeing how long he could go without breathing. He stared as they passed the marker, a red stake he'd stuck in the ground. The paint was fading back into the wood, and the grass stalks obscured more of it each year. He turned to gauge Elle's reaction. Their eyes met, then released. She had noticed it too. A brief smile came to the edge of EJ's lips.

Elle was twelve when EJ came home from the hospital. She'd decided he was a rumpled mess. And from the moment she became the built-in babysitter, EJ was the black spy to her white. The irritant who'd wear himself out to keep up on his BMX as she and her friends sped down the road in their old Buick. Red hair and a chalky complexion were their only comparable traits. EJ's hurdles were walked around. Elle's were leaped over. Where EJ waded, Elle splashed. EJ the underachiever. Elle the valedictorian. Her success was practically assured.

And then one phone call changed it all. In her last semester at the University of Chicago, about to take her finals, Elle got a call from Sheriff Bailey. There'd been an accident out on County Road 12. No details, but she should come home. EJ was staying at the Cases'.

From the moment she saw EJ, only ten, holding on to the porch frame, fighting back tears and waiting for her to come pick him up, they were a team. From that second forward, she would do anything and everything to never see that look in his eyes again. It crumpled her, that look of anguish, of losing everything that mattered. She would matter. From then on, she would be perfect for him.

Elle pulled the cruiser into one of three empty parking spots in front of the sheriff's office. For such a compact building, it also housed the coroner's office and the county morgue, making it a veritable multi-tool of office space. Turlough's main strip came to an abrupt stop next to the sheriff's office. Beside it was a small square that folded into the forest on the other side. Across the street was Dell's Diner, the only restaurant in town open for breakfast, lunch, and dinner. The other two were Finnegan's, the local pub, and Torrini's, an Italian restaurant. It served hard spaghetti and limp baguettes but managed to stay open anyway. They all stood dark, except for the sheriff's office.

As Elle marched the boys past the empty clerk's station, the clock above read 2:11 a.m. The layout resembled an old-style newspaper room. The main floor was open concept with several multipurpose desks, tidy except for a few files in the out-boxes. Only one had a computer—a discolored mammoth from the early aughts—parked in the corner to give a modicum of privacy.

Elle seated the boys in the tiny waiting area outside her office—it was the only one with a door on the first floor—before grabbing two large clear Ziploc bags.

"Dan, you can use the phone if you want to call your parents." She nodded at the phone on an empty desk across from him.

He shook his head.

"You're eighteen. I'm not calling them for you." She placed the two bags in front of them.

"I said I wasn't calling them."

Elle shrugged her left shoulder. "Empty your pockets. And, Dan, I want to see that bag of pot in there."

"I'm just guessing here," he said as he began emptying his pockets and placing the contents in the bag. "But I'm never seeing this pot again, am I?"

"This particular pot?" She lifted the small Ziploc bag containing two large buds from his hand. "No, but I'm sure that won't stop you from buying more."

EJ sat holding his breath, pleading for Dan to stop. His bag contained nothing more than a wallet, a Zippo, and some spare rolling papers. A distant rush of water moving through the pipes indicated a toilet had been flushed somewhere in the building. Stan Carrick emerged from a door behind the workstations, zipping his fly, a newspaper under one arm. He half smiled when he noticed Elle and the boys.

"Hey," he said, a soft pink taking root in his cheeks. "Need any help?" Stan wasn't just thin, he was concave. Underweight in a way that spoke in terms like anorexic or anemic. He had deep, dark pockets under his eyes, and his belt had several extra holes.

"I've got it. But thanks."

"No problem. Want me to start on the report about that dog?"

Elle nodded. "Please. I'll have Neil follow up with the owners in the morning." Before making her rounds she'd been called to a convenience store just outside of town. Someone had broken in and beaten a dog to death. What had started out as a quiet night had turned into one of their busier ones.

Elle motioned the boys to lead the way to the basement.

"You guys are going to smoke that pot, aren't you? I bet you'll be going back for our keg too." Dan handed her his bag.

"You're right. I will be going back for the keg, so I can return it to Finnegan's where you stole it." Elle tucked the two bags under her arm and followed them down the stairs to the basement. The hallway continued for several feet beyond with doors on either side. The coroner's office was through the door on the right, the morgue at the end of the inky, uncarpeted hall. To the left stood a single diminutive cell, complete with a stony cot and staunch bars.

EJ studied the windowless cell with its cement walls and water-stained floor. "Are you really going to lock us up in here all night?"

The floors had been scrubbed with vinegar recently and the pungent smell was prickling EJ's nostrils. This combined with the harsh florescent lights above, and the fact that he was sobering up, made his head begin to throb.

Elle checked her watch. "Not that there's much of it left," she said. But she squeezed his elbow when she was sure Dan couldn't see.

They both turned, Dan with a look of disdain, EJ with accusatory eyes. "Sit, sleep," she ordered, pointing to the lonely cot.

"What if we need to make pee-pee?" Dan asked, folding his arms and kicking the side of the cot with his scuffed shoe. The cot was basic. It had a thin pad as a mattress, an even thinner pillow, and clean sheets. The laundered smell mingled with the vinegar. Like much of Turlough, the cell functioned. Any frills were best left for the cities.

"If you're sleeping, you shouldn't need to go."

Elle closed the door, jiggling it to make sure it was locked. "Stan will be down to check on you in a couple of hours." She turned and walked back down the hall and up the stairs.

They could hear the lock from the door click back into place. The silence was painful. The kind that bounced around in your head, knocking things off shelves to fill the void.

"Well, this is the shits." Dan plunked down on the cot and began taking off his Chucks. "I'd much rather be banging Tully and her big, fat husband than down here, surviving the night with you." He threw one shoe, then the other against the far wall, each with its own loud echo ringing through the basement. It made EJ flinch. "Why's your sister such a bitch anyway?"

Without any warning EJ punched Dan in the arm fast and hard. He stood quickly, with his back to the bars, ready if Dan came at him. "Don't call her that."

But instead of showing anger, Dan laughed it off, rubbing the outer part of his bicep. "Why? What would you call her?"

EJ still hadn't completely relaxed, but his fists were starting to drop.

"Because where I'm from, locking your brother up overnight doesn't inspire the warm and fuzzies." A grin spread across Dan's face, big enough to take up the entire lower half. His teeth were so white they almost managed to brighten the cell. He patted the cot next to him. "I'm sorry, all right?"

EJ nodded and took a seat next to him. Shrugging off his jacket and shoes, he passed Dan the lone pillow. "Where you're from they probably don't worry so much about this kind of thing. I'm guessing big cities have more important things to worry about." EJ crumpled up his jacket to use for himself.

"I wouldn't exactly call Evansville a big city. It's more like a trough for big city runoff." Dan fluffed up the thin pillow. "How come your sister's like that anyway? All stiff like she's got a fire poker up her ass?"

EJ shrugged. "You should've seen her before..." He trailed off, unable to finish.

With their bodies in the fetal position at opposite ends of the cot, they settled in for what was left of the night, awaiting the consequences of what only morning could bring.

CHAPTER TWO

"The mayor's on the line, boss," called a voice from the other side of Elle's office door. Sitting up with a groan, she tied her hair back and stretched out the kinks.

After rejecting the idea of going home around four a.m. last night, she settled for the love seat. Her office wasn't large, or even grand, but it was more of a home than her house as of late.

Elle picked up one of many mugs at random and sniffed, taking a tentative sip she lifted the receiver to her ear. "Ken, what's up?" Her voice echoed into the mug.

Contrary to her sparse cruiser, Elle's office overflowed. Every surface was blanketed with orderly stacks of files rising like saplings from the forest floor. An ancient Cary safe stood stoic in the far corner. With the weight and girth of a cruiser, it acted as the station's evidence locker. The doors were propped open, revealing various size wooden drawers.

"I wanted to talk to you about something that's come up." He had the kind of voice that belonged to game show hosts and radio personalities.

"If this is anything to do with the festival, direct it toward Neil." Elle made an unpleasant face as she took another sip of cold coffee.

"It does, but only indirectly."

"Then talk to Neil. He is the grand poobah of the festival this year." She stifled a yawn and sat down in a huff. Not generally a morning person, this was shaping up to be a bad start.

"There's no such thing as a grand poobah of the festival. That's not a thing."

"Yes, it is. I just made it a thing."

"Elle, this is serious. I need you to be serious."

"When am I not serious?"

A deep sigh drifted through the receiver. Elle didn't even try stifling her grin. She lived for winding Ken Brady's crank.

"Have you ever heard of *Verve Magazine*? They want to send a reporter down and do a story on us."

"Have you ever heard of *Verve Magazine*?"

"It doesn't matter if I've heard of it. It's a Chicago magazine. All that matters is people read it. Their website says it has over a million subscriptions. Just imagine how many people we could potentially reach."

"We're not exactly a tourist destination."

"No, but we could be. The festival is coming up in a little over two weeks. This could be a chance to get people interested, you know, for next year."

"In the Beer and Berry Festival? In Turlough? Ken, you're dreaming if you think anyone wants to trek all the way out here to get bitten by mosquitos and consume flat beer and stale pie." She tried to keep her hands busy by organizing the stacks of files into even taller, less stable piles.

"Goddammit, Elle. It's not like it used to be when the brick factory was still running. In fact, the council is trying to find ways to cut money. We need this. We need to bring in some tourism dollars. And if someone from Chic—" But she didn't let him finish. She calmly replaced the receiver and trudged toward the door.

In the outer office Neil Dell, Elle's senior deputy, perched his considerable bulk on the edge of the reception desk. "Heather's sick today," he said as she swept past. "And Mr. Rutherford's been hounding us to speak to you." But she was already out the station door before he could finish.

It was late spring in Turlough, which meant peach blossoms. They had a way of becoming the next season's carpet. They coated benches and stoops and cars that hadn't moved since the night before. The sun hadn't yet risen over the buildings, adding a sleepy dreamy effect to the morning mist. The sight reminded Elle of a Dr. Seuss book she'd read as a kid. It was like you could take the whole world in your arms and give it a big hug.

Less than a block down, Elle pulled at a large wooden door, rushed past the reception area and through a door in the back. Behind the oversized desk sat Ken Brady, Turlough's mayor. He was still questioning the connection when Elle barged in.

"Ah." He replaced the receiver. "So you did hang up." Brady's golden brown hair appeared glued to his head. Combined with the bronzing moisturizer he wore, it made him look plastic.

Elle stood with her hands on her hips and gave him a let's have it look.

Brady raised his hands in surrender. "Okay, I know I kinda sprang this on you, but let's face it, you'll make a better PR front than me." He placed his hand to his heart. "As much as it pains me to say that." His teeth were fake, covered in veneers that were too white and perfect. When he smiled his face looked fake.

"Don't schmooze me, Ken. You know I hate it when you do that." Without asking, Elle skirted behind Brady and helped herself to a cup of coffee from the sideboard. She inhaled the steam before taking a large gulp.

"I need you to do this interview," he said. "Just show him your smile, flap your gums about community and safety, I'll handle the rest."

Elle took another sip before responding. "Don't you find it kind of odd that a journalist from Chicago wants to come all the way down here to do a piece on us? Some no-name town?"

"City. That's no-name city. We're incorporated."

"Ken, I know how you love your ego stroked and everything, but nine hundred people does not a city make. Get over yourself." Three years ago, Turlough had incorporated. The purpose of which was to leverage more money from the state. It had only succeeded in giving a few people more impressive titles. The county commissioner became the mayor of Turlough, and the board of county commissioners became the city council. The lobbying for this change, of course, had come from Brady himself.

She sank into a seat across from him and eyed the picture frames sitting on his back wall. There were several she knew to be fake. The one with Arnold Schwarzenegger was a Photoshop job, as well as the one with Pat Quinn. The only real photos were the one with his mother the day he moved her into the retirement home in Mason and the one from the breaking ground ceremony for the new hockey arena. It was also the only one with a genuine smile on his face. His arms were in an upward swing as a shovel full of dirt flew over his shoulder. His eyes, which were crinkled at the edges, followed the arc of soil. That was over a year ago and the foundation had yet to be poured.

"I think we should put our past differences aside and focus on being professional. As sheriff, it's your job to schmooze occasionally, throw a little PR voodoo around and make us look good. Besides, I already said you'd do it." He muttered that last line quick. Instead of answering she just eyed him over the brim of her mug. As long as she'd known Brady, the only way to win any argument was to let him do the talking. The longer she stayed silent, the more concessions he'd be willing to make just to get her to leave his office.

He steepled his fingers and leaned back, as the seconds turned into minutes. Elle took another long sip of her coffee, relishing the caffeine coursing through her bloodstream.

"I need you to do this, Elle."

She shrugged one shoulder, continuing to stare.

"Dammit, Elle, this is part of your job."

"Ken, don't tell me my job. I know it may not be as impressive as yours, but it sure as hell doesn't involve kowtowing to some shithead from Chicago who thinks he can poke fun at hicks, 'kay?" She stood, straightening the creases in her pants as she did.

"Elle, come on, they're not here to make fun of you."

"Oh, I didn't mean me." And she left, taking the mug of coffee with her.

❖

"What the fuck are you doing?" Dan asked. He looped around potholes in his '89 Dodge Dakota like he was dancing with an unseen partner. The truck grumbled as it rode the hard back roads.

EJ poked his head out from under the passenger seat. "I'm looking for my knife. I think I dropped it in here last night." The sweat from EJ's hairline was creeping down his face one stream at a time. It invaded the corners of his eyes and the creases around his nose and settled at the edge of his jaw.

"I haven't seen it. We'll have a look when we collect the keg." Dan turned a sharp corner fast.

EJ grabbed for the oh-shit bar. "I told you, Elle would've gone back for it last night."

"Right, like her and Deputy Do-Right could lift that thing into the back of a cruiser."

EJ shook his head. "Elle's stronger than she looks. I've seen her lift a tractor wheel just because someone told her she couldn't do it."

"You think she'll give me my pump back?"

"Doubt it."

EJ grinned as he pulled a tiny silver key from under the seat. He slipped it into the lock of the glove compartment and turned. It gave a groan, then a pop as it flipped open. EJ shoved his hand inside and began pulling things out at random and piling them on his lap. "Ugh! That's disgusting," he said as he pulled out a clump of melted condoms. They had fused together in a congealed mass of latex. He threw them out the window into a damp ditch where they sank to the bottom.

The morning was setting the stage for a brilliant spring afternoon. It was the kind of day people made excuses to be out. The kind of day that made you forget winter existed and carried the promise of summer vacation on the wind.

They'd met Dan's first day of school. He'd moved with his family from Indiana halfway through the year. EJ huddled in a corner near the back of the school, lighting a smoke in the cold November wind. A couple of guys Dan could tell were football players by their bulk and swagger strolled up and started rolling EJ for money.

At first Dan held back, listening, taking stock of the situation, enjoying his own smoke at the edge of the tree line.

One of them laughed loud and punched EJ's shoulder hard enough that EJ slammed back against the brick wall. "What else you got in that jacket? Got any money?" EJ shook his head. "Why? Your sister make your lunch today? She make you a chickenshit salad sandwich?" The group all laughed.

EJ didn't say anything, just stared back at the wall of football players, wary, his eyes darting between faces, waiting for the next blow. One of the bigger guys, the one going through his wallet, pushed him against the wall. "Hey, retard, where's the rest of my money?"

"It's not your money."

"Well, my fist says it is."

"Yeah? Well, my mouth says it isn't, so go jerk off or something."

Before EJ had even finished the sentence, a meaty fist smashed into his face. Blood exploded from his nose and mouth, but he stood up straight again as if he wasn't bleeding and stared at the group.

"You're still not getting how this works, Ashley."

The taller one wearing a hoodie with the J.P. Flynn Cavaliers logo on the back pushed EJ back against the wall. "You going to go cry to your big sister now? Little baby Ashley." They all laughed again.

"She wouldn't give a shit anyway, guys, she knows he's just the retard in the family."

Dan dropped his smoke and it fizzled in the wet grass. Ten strides and he was face to chest with the bulkier one of the group, his fists clenched, jaw tight, ready to go.

They'd all ended up in the office sitting across from the principal's door. Dan was the only one not bleeding on his clothes, and he had a great big smirk on his face. He and EJ had been friends ever since.

They arrived at the clearing to reclaim Dan's pump and, with any luck, the stolen keg. The glade was empty save for a makeshift fire pit and forgotten red cups, left behind as a memento and calling card for future partiers.

"What now?" EJ asked as he foraged along the tree line, scanning for his knife.

"We find your sister and give her a talking-to."

"Come on, she's just doing her job. It's not like she pressed charges."

"Aren't you pissed?"

EJ shrugged his left shoulder, still in search mode.

"You should be. Your sister just locked you up for the night like it was no big deal." He applied a falsetto voice. "Oh, boys, underage drinking is bad. It's my mission to see all you hooligans sent to camps."

EJ laughed. It came in one loud spurt. But Dan's eyes made him stop. He sighed instead. "She's the sheriff."

"That's not an excuse." Dan punched him playfully in the arm. "It's a cop-out. You need to cowboy the fuck up."

"Elle always says I need to put my big girl panties on and deal with it."

Dan stared at him. "No. See? This is what's wrong with being raised by a single woman. They rip your balls off and serve them up for dinner and bitch at you for not having any over dessert." Dan checked the air pressure on his tires for the fourth time that morning.

"Doesn't look like it's here."

"What's the big deal? So we buy you a new knife."

"It belonged to my granddad." EJ desperately tried to remember the last time he'd seen it. He wasn't even supposed to have it. He'd taken it from his dad's toolbox a couple of months ago. Elle had caught him with it a few weeks later and confiscated it. He'd found it hidden in the back of her underwear drawer. Even when they were kids she'd always thought the fear of her underwear was enough of a deterrent. If Elle found out that not only had he been through her private things but he'd lost their granddad's knife, she'd be furious.

His grandfather had been dead long before EJ was born, but he'd seen pictures of the tough Irishman. He looked like someone who didn't take any shit. EJ liked carrying the knife; it made him feel like he didn't take shit either.

Dan smacked him on his back. "Don't worry, it'll turn up."

"We should get going, Tanya's probably waiting for us by now. Maybe I dropped it somewhere over there."

Dan jumped into the cab of his truck. The engine started with a slow sputter. "I've got a better idea. Come on."

❖

The main strip of Turlough reminded Robin Oakes of a zombie movie she'd watched as a kid. It looked deserted in the early morning. There was no traffic and the only noise came from the birds chattering at her from the trees above.

She'd been in town less than an hour and already everything she'd brought was covered in a fine pink dusting. The way it stuck to your skin and clothing was like a fungus.

The walk from the Collard's Bed and Breakfast had been shorter than she'd expected. There wasn't much to the town. It looked more like a strip of houses had attempted to escape the forest, only to give up after a couple of blocks. The forest held the town within a swath of green. Protective or suffocating, she wasn't sure.

As Robin entered the sheriff's office, she brushed her pale blond bangs to the side. A few delicate petals fell to the floor by her heels. She swiped at her clothes, more as an excuse to inspect her shoes for scuffs. Finally she pulled her attention to the inside of the building. It appeared larger on the outside. She'd had apartments bigger than this. And that was in Chicago, where they charged a premium for tiny shit holes.

A rotund officer sat on the edge of the reception desk speaking into the phone. He stuffed half a muffin into his mouth.

"Hold on a sec," said Neil as he pulled away from the phone. "Can I help you?" Bits of muffin dropped from his mouth to his uniform.

"I have a meeting with the sheriff." Robin stood in the doorway, her tall frame blocking most of the sunlight. Robin exuded urban. Like most city dwellers, she wore her arrogance like a shield. A safeguard against any number of embarrassments or misunderstandings.

Neil chewed as fast as he could, moving his right hand in a circular motion as if to speed up the process. "She's out for a sec. You can take a seat by her office and wait if you like." He turned his attention back to the phone, but not before giving her backside the once-over as she passed.

Instead of taking a seat outside, Robin stepped into Elle's office. "An open door is an open invitation," she whispered to herself. Her eyes roved around the room. Busy desk, old safe—open. "So much for security." A pump-less keg. "Interesting." The room was devoid of personal pictures and items.

She felt a buzz in her pocket and slipped out her cell phone. She smirked at the caller ID. "A little light on the content, were we?" She ran her fingers over the spines of the books as she listened. "I know it was a rush job and it looks great. But can you beef it up a little? It's way too flimsy." Her red lips curled into a pleasant smile. "Thanks, you're a doll." She slid the phone back into her skirt pocket.

After getting a brief glimpse of the town, Robin expected Sheriff Ashley to be the female version of the burly deputy stuffing his face in reception. So when Elle marched in, Robin's throat nearly swallowed her tongue.

"Who are you and why are you in my office?" Elle moved around to the back of her desk. She placed her stolen mug of coffee on the blotter and shifted piles of folders around. She was unsuccessful at trying to clear space on her desk.

Robin had to shake herself mentally. The image she'd held in her mind of an oafish woman in her fifties was replaced with this woman and her flaming hair. "I'm Robin Oakes. I'm with *Verve Magazine*." Robin stuck her hand out, but the look of sheer death in Elle's eyes made her pull it back in.

"I haven't even agreed to give you an interview and you're already snooping around." Elle made a quick scan to see what Robin had seen, her eyes landing on the keg. "Why exactly are you writing this story anyway?" She remained standing. So did Robin.

"Oh." Robin's smile was smooth. She was used to coming up against opposition with her job. Very few people were happy to see her. When she showed up, it usually meant something had gone wrong. There wasn't much that ruffled her on a daily basis. "Mr. Brady assured me this was all set up."

"I'm sure he did." Elle's face was stone.

Robin took a moment to pull from her arsenal of persuasion tactics and settled on conspiratorial girlfriends. "Listen. I get it. You don't want someone hanging around getting in the way. But I'm used to staying on the sidelines. I assure you, I will stay out of your way. And I won't print anything you don't want." She found it disconcerting the way Elle's dark green eyes scrutinized her, like she was waiting for her to commit an offense.

"You didn't answer my question," Elle said, still standing.

She shrugged. "Why wouldn't someone want to write a story about Turlough? Or you, for that matter? Female sheriff in a small town. With everything that's going on in the world right now, people will eat this shit up."

Elle's eyebrows rose.

Robin internally chastised herself. *Dial it back a bit.* "Sorry. The company I usually keep isn't all flowers and sunshine. What I mean is, women in power positions is a story. America needs to see more of this."

"I'm sorry, but I was under the impression you were doing a profile piece on Turlough for the Beer and Berry Festival."

"No. I'm doing a profile on you."

Elle blinked. She was unsure how to react. She took refuge in the most comforting: fury. "You told Brady this, didn't you? Did it ever occur to any of you that I might not want to be written about?" Her usually pale skin began to color as she built momentum.

"Phone, boss," Neil yelled from the outer office.

Elle grabbed at the receiver, glad for the reprieve. "Sheriff Ashley," she said.

Robin scanned the room again, each item taking on new meaning now that she'd gotten a glimpse of the owner. She walked to a small bookshelf stuffed behind the opening of the door and the love seat. It, like everything in the office, was very old and falling apart. Books were shoved into every space, like a life-size game of *Tetris*. Mostly criminology books. Several of John Douglas's profiling books stood out. She picked up a book draped across the arm of the love seat. The title read *Corpse: Nature, Forensics, and the Struggle to Pinpoint Time of Death*. She opened a page at random and began to read. Robin stopped reading and looked again at the title. Interesting. She'd have to pick up a copy.

"Wait—you're mad I didn't press charges? He's eighteen, they would—" There was a pause as she listened to the speaker on the other end.

Robin watched with growing intrigue as Elle stood with her fists balled, eyes closed, trying to rein in her temper. Her uniform was rumpled like she'd slept in it and much of her hair had escaped her bun, but there was no doubt in Robin's mind, beneath that sleepy exterior was a woman of passion. In fact, the image was breathtaking. If she hadn't been there on business she might consider getting to know Sheriff Ashley a little better. But she had a hard and fast rule of never shitting where she ate. It had served her well.

"I appreciate that you're trying to find the best way to discipline your son. But trespassing and underage drinking are not good reasons to give your son a permanent criminal record," she said.

Robin had once read it was difficult for people to imagine the other side of a phone conversation. Robin's imagination was better than most. She loved eavesdropping on these phone calls, trying to piece together all the possibilities.

"Hold on," Elle said, a little too loud. "My brother being there had nothing to do with why I didn't file charges. I have never compromised my position as sheriff for EJ."

Robin turned to see if the volcano would erupt. Still standing, Elle had closed her left fist around a stress ball. Her lips were a thin line. She breathed. Her hand squeezed tighter.

"I know you're relatively new to the area, Mr. Baker, but things work a little different here. Turlough has a way of ebbing the reactionary instinct out of people over time." She tried to smile, restoring color to her lips. Her eyes opened. She caught Robin watching her and turned her back.

Robin replaced the book on the shelf, convinced more than ever that Sheriff Elle Ashley was going to be a wicked temptation during this assignment.

Chapter Three

Mr. Rutherford took his time. Each step was a snake pit. Sharp pains struck at his legs, starting with his weedy ankles and working their way up his thighs. People watched as he progressed toward the sheriff's office, each wondering if it would be his last trek from the old Victorian tucked into the woods behind Turlough.

He sucked in a sharp breath as he pulled open the station door. Neil rushed to help.

"Off!" Mr. Rutherford slapped at Neil's hand. "Off! I can manage a silly door." The way he used it for leverage, he appeared to be heaving himself onto a ledge. "Where's the sheriff? I'm tired of waiting for her to return my calls." He puffed himself up. "Elizabeth!"

"The sheriff's in a meeting right now. You can wait if you like." Neil waved toward Elle's office and the row of chairs outside her door.

"I do like." Mr. Rutherford hobbled over to the chairs, peering inside to see who Elle was speaking with. If his hearing was any better he would have liked to eavesdrop. But even up close, you needed to shout to be heard.

"Can I get you something while you wait?"

Mr. Rutherford waved him off with a furious hand gesture.

Inside her office, Elle held up a hand for Robin to stop talking, distracted by the sight of Mr. Rutherford wobbling past her door.

She rounded her desk toward Mr. Rutherford and sat down beside him. "I'm sorry I haven't had a chance to return your calls, Mr. Rutherford."

He squeezed her arm. "Gives me a chance to get some much-needed exercise." He smiled for what was probably the first time all day. His teeth hadn't fared better than the rest of him. Many of the back molars were missing, and a few bicuspids. The ones he did have were the color of old ivory. "And this gives me a chance to flirt with you."

"What was it you needed?" Her face relaxed and some of the tension she'd felt earlier eased out of her shoulders.

"I wanted to tell you about Mrs. Collard and her hedges. I checked the bylaw. She has an obligation to cut them if they're too high. She says they're not too high." He took a big gulp of air. "I had my nephew measure them last time he was here and that was several weeks ago. They're too high." He nudged her arm. "You remember him? He's single again, you know."

Robin watched from the door, a small smile curving her lips.

"Mr. Rutherford, you know I'm far too busy to worry about dating." She tried to brush his comment off with a smile, but the color creeping from her ears gave her away.

"It's nice to see you smile." Mr. Rutherford patted her cheek. "You're far too serious these days, Elizabeth." He began the long process of standing. "And far too pretty to let yourself go to waste." Elle helped him to his feet. She hooked his elbow with a strong grip.

"I promise to talk with Mrs. Collard about her hedges, as long as you promise me to stay put. I'm sure your family doesn't want you using up all your strength for bylaw complaints."

He turned grave eyes on her. "And what else do I have to occupy my time with? I don't have much of it left. I would think my prize for making it this long would be a free pass on unlimited complaining."

Elle sighed, but smiled despite herself. This argument was old. "I'll come by when I have a free moment and you can beat me at cribbage. How's that?" She let go of his arm in increments, allowing him to take possession of his own gravity.

"Okay. As long as you bring your own money. I'm not spotting you this time."

Elle waited until he was through the door before she turned back to Robin.

"Who's that?" Robin asked, following Elle into her office.

"That would be Mr. Rutherford. Turlough's oldest resident. He's about ninety-eight." She sat, nodding for Robin to do the same. "Everyone's just waiting for him to die. It's sad." Her anger, so recently on firm ground, had slipped away. Mr. Rutherford, with all his fruitless flirting, had a way of doing that. He was more than just the oldest resident of Turlough. He was an institution, and as far back as Elle could remember, always had an easy smile for her.

"Is the whole town like that?" Robin asked, easing herself into the scarred wingback across from Elle. She had this idea about small towns being retirement communities.

Elle gave a lopsided shrug and studied the blonde sitting across from her with new scrutiny. She was what Elle would call a cool blonde. There was something remote and hidden about her. But she was stunning. Thin, delicate eyebrows framed her pale blue eyes. She wore just the right amount of mascara to make them pop. Her skirt suit was pale gray with a matching silk blouse. A beautiful gold chain with some symbol Elle couldn't make out hung around her neck. Everything about her screamed expensive.

"Listen, I'm not exactly sure what you're expecting to dig up here. There's no crime because most of the offenses aren't worth reporting. I'm not going to write someone up for a bylaw violation. So if you're here for something juicier than that, you're wasting your time."

"Why do you assume I'm here to get the dirt on you? Sometimes people just want a feel-good story."

Elle squinted in disbelief. Her focus shifted to Robin's legs as she crossed one over the other. Her skirt hiked up a few inches, giving Elle an excellent view of firm, long legs. "What exactly did you tell Brady? He presented a very different story idea to me."

Robin shrugged. "He didn't seem the type that would be interested in hearing about empowered women and how that's beneficial for the economy in general."

Elle almost snorted. "True. He'd rather one of the good ole boys held this seat. I guess I don't scratch his back enough." Elle gave a mental shudder at that thought. She picked up a pen, twirling it around her finger. "To be completely truthful, I'd like you gone as soon as possible. I mean, who would want to write about some Podunk town in the middle of nowhere. And this," she indicated Robin, her suit, shoes, hair, "doesn't exactly scream 'feel good' story to me." From Elle's experience, which wasn't a whole lot, reporters were opportunists. She didn't trust Robin Oakes to put the best interests of the town above getting a great story.

Robin leaned forward, offering a spectacular view of her cleavage, and nodded toward the phone. "Looks to me like you do more than deal with bylaw complaints. Underage drinking, trespassing? Sheriff helps younger brother escape the charges of youth. Could be a story." She was goading her.

"Really? That's the best you can do?" Elle leaned away, twirling the mug of coffee on the blotter. The inscription read: World's Greatest Mayor.

"All right. I'm not here to make enemies or write up the dirt on your family. But it is a free country and I'm paid up for the week at the B and B down the road, so I plan on sticking around."

Elle stood. "It is a lovely B&B. Probably one of the best in the state." She brushed at her pants, considering, weighing her stubbornness against her common sense, both of which were losing to the beautiful reporter sitting across from her. Part of her wanted to leave it at that. Let her write what she wanted. But another part, the less intrusive, more rational side knew, if she helped, she could control the information instead of letting the town gossips dictate the truth. "Look, I'm not promising anything. But if I can't convince you that Turlough is the most boring place on Earth in words, maybe I can show you." Not only was this idea bad, it was dangerous. She could feel her coveted control breaking. There were plenty of stories from her youth she'd rather not have this woman hear. No matter how many years separated her from that version of herself, there were parts of Elle's past she didn't want dredged up.

Robin clapped her hands together. "Perfect. I'll need full access to the town. I'd also like to follow you around for a couple days, get a feel for your day-to-day—"

"Whoa." Elle held her hand up. "I said I'd be cooperative. I'm not looking for a tail."

The phone rang. Elle picked it up before Neil could grab it. "Flynn County Sheriff's Office." She frowned after a moment. "How long has she been like that?" As she listened, she grabbed her jacket from the back of her chair. "I'll be there shortly. Thanks."

"Can I come?"

"No."

❖

Elle's hat lay in the back seat, usurped by Robin riding shotgun. Triumph carpeted her face as the wind blew at her hair. They had already passed out of the downtown and were riding the back roads, trees and ravines enveloping the cruiser. Robin breathed in the scented spring air. It reminded her of the yearly camping trip when her parents and little brother would drive out into the middle of nowhere. They'd load up everything in her dad's ancient minivan and drive until the mosquitos outnumbered people. Then they'd set up two tents, one for her parents and one for her and her brother. They'd swim and hike during the day and make fires at night. On the Fourth of July they would light sparklers and write letters in the air, usually dirty words they weren't allowed to say out loud. She hated it as a kid. It was weird, but being out here made her kind of miss it. She couldn't remember the last time she'd sucked in fresh air.

"Where are we headed?" Robin asked.

Elle kept her eyes ahead, navigating the roads like a familiar room in the dark. "The Maverty house."

"Ah." Robin's arm hung out the window, both sleeves rolled up, creasing the smooth silk. "That explains it, then."

"It's what everyone calls this abandoned house out in the woods." She pushed at her hair, curling some wind-whipped tendrils behind her ear. "All the kids hang out there. Hell, I used to hang out there when I was in school." She glanced at Robin, who was absorbed in the thickness of the forest. When she'd threatened to follow in her rental car Elle relented in bringing her along. It was only a simple noise complaint. This was the perfect opportunity to show how boring Turlough was.

"The council has been trying to get it demolished, but a couple of months ago it was named a historical landmark."

"So what do kids do at this Maverty house?"

"The usual. Drink, do drugs…have sex."

"How many times a month do you bust this place up?"

Elle sighed. "I don't bust it up. I have patrols come by on weekends, make sure no one's doing anything too stupid."

"Makes you sound like a babysitter."

Elle laughed. It echoed throughout the cruiser, joining the wind. Her shield dropped for a moment. "I guess that's a really good description of what I do."

Robin watched the dying embers of her laugh fade. She liked it. It made her more alive somehow. She'd have to remember to be funny more often.

Elle turned the cruiser into a drive obscured by trees on both sides. Only someone familiar with the road would know it was there. Branches scraped at the sides of the car and dug into the paint as if hoping for a souvenir. The car rocked from side to side, a jarring, rough effect on the passengers inside. Robin's head almost hit the ceiling of the cab as they came to the bottom of a steep hill. When they rounded the last bend in the drive, a tall dilapidated Victorian in a small clearing was visible. Its original color had eroded over time. The porch leaned into the earth and forest around it, bucking where a large tree root had pushed through. A shiny silver BMW coupe parked in the drive made an incongruous scene next to the decay.

A young woman sat on the steps, hugging her knees to her chest. Mascara trails ran down her cheeks. Her stringy blond hair was tucked behind her ears. She appeared tiny next to the forest and house as she rocked back and forth, staring into the distance.

"Stay. You can observe from here." Elle exited the cruiser.

Robin raised her hands in surrender. "You're the boss."

Elle snorted, mentally girding herself against the battles she was sure would be fought with Robin Oakes in the coming days.

Elle approached the girl as one would a spooked horse. She'd taken her jacket off in the car, throwing it over her discarded hat. Her hands were loose at her sides. "Tanya?" Her voice was calm, sure. She knelt down and placed her hands on Tanya's knees. Tanya jerked away from her. As if noticing Elle for the first time, Tanya looked down at her. Elle kept her hands still, reassuring.

"I got a call about screaming. Were you in an argument with someone?" Elle peered around Tanya toward the front door. "Are they still here?" She turned to look at the BMW behind her. "Was the car here before you arrived?" Seeing the Beemer worried her most of all.

Tanya broke into a sob, her shoulders rolling forward as she crumpled into Elle. Tanya shook her head. "I waited." She gulped in a lungful of air. "I don't like to go in by myself." Another sob as she burrowed into Elle's shoulder, leaving black smudges on her epaulette. "But they didn't come. So I went in to see if maybe they were already inside." She muffled the last bit.

Elle stroked Tanya's hair, making soothing noises, letting her cry it out. Several minutes passed. Cicadas chirped in the trees surrounding the house. That and the low mewling from Tanya were the only noises. Elle moved to sit beside Tanya on the steps, enclosing her in her arms. She rocked her back and forth, like her mother used to when she was young.

Tanya raised her head. "Why didn't they come?"

"Who, honey?"

Tanya shook her head. "I shouldn't have gone in." She hugged her knees in tighter. Her breath was shaky, but she had stopped crying.

"Feel up to moving?" Elle asked.

Tanya nodded.

"Okay." Elle helped Tanya to her feet. "Let's get you home." She guided Tanya to the cruiser and set her in the back seat.

Robin had turned in her seat to get a better view. Her remark about babysitting, having taken root in her mind, now sprouted branches.

"I'm going to take a quick look around," Elle said to Robin.

"I'll go with you." She was undeterred by the look Elle gave her. "Come on, I'm as curious as you."

Elle shook her head. "I want you to stay with Tanya. If it's nothing serious, maybe I'll let you look around when I come back out."

Robin eyed Tanya. What she thought of this idea and of Tanya was not lost on Elle.

Elle unclipped a small Maglite from her belt. The underbrush crunched beneath her feet as she approached the front door. She turned before she entered. "I mean it. Stay." If she'd had the guts, she would have handcuffed her to the cruiser. She didn't trust Robin Oakes to stay put. She looked like the sort that felt rules didn't apply to them.

She would never forget the smell of it. The odor was engrained into her senses the way blueberry pie reminded her of summer and hot chocolate of winter. The scent of the Maverty house would always remind her of him. Decades of abandonment had imparted the house with its own distinct aroma. A mixture of decay, mold, stale beer, marijuana, and a hint of nature reclaiming its territory. As Elle entered, there was something else, something new she couldn't place.

She panned the flashlight across the foyer. The downstairs was dark even in the day. The little light that did filter in came from scattered cracks in the boarded-up windows. Upstairs was a different story. A storm had ripped part of the roof off, leaving several of the rooms full of light and open to the elements. Mounds of dirt huddled in corners, composted from fallen foliage. The battered furniture lay in a funk, preparing to return to base elements as if in purgatory.

Elle stepped over a few strewn beer cans toward the kitchen. She searched the ground for anything out of the ordinary, which was made harder by the nature of the place. She moved with purpose, scanning each surface, then continuing to the next room.

Not much had changed since high school. The same furniture, a little worse off than she'd last seen. She recognized the wingback chair he always sat in. Its position had changed and there were a few more holes and burn marks, but it still stood like a throne. It was occupied by a different quarterback. Different name, same attitude. There had been a time when Elle had spent most weekends and evenings here with Jessie and their crew, wrapped in teenage fantasies. Before the accident.

Her light passed over something in the far corner of what had once been the living room. Like the light through the slats in the window, Elle's stomach flickered. The new smell was finally identified. She stepped over a fallen rafter to get a clearer view. The distinct shape of a man lay face up near the far wall.

The beam from Elle's flashlight worked its way up the torso, then stopped, wavering at the head. Elle choked back a sob. Her flashlight dropped to the floor with a clank, rolling under some refuse. Her hand flew to her mouth to hold in the bile.

She'd seen his face, that face. His mouth was twisted in its final expression. Her eyes snapped shut. But like a bright light, the image was fused to the back of her lids. His soft gray eyes, unblinking. Their last image was of the wilted ceiling above.

"I heard you scre— Holy shit!" Robin stumbled, her heels, sinking into the soft floor of the Maverty house.

"Out! Get out," Elle said, her voice faltering. She pointed at the door behind Robin. As she followed Robin outside she removed a pair of handcuffs from her belt. She placed one around Robin's wrist and clicked the other end to the crumbling porch railing. Elle tripped down the stairs, running for the edge of the glade. She only made it to the side of the porch before she bent forward and threw up on a patch of dandelions. She straightened, wiped her mouth with the back of her hand, and swallowed a steady gulp of air. Tears escaped her tightly shut eyes. Some from panic, others anger. Acutely aware that she had an audience, Elle rubbed at her eyes, as if to erase her embarrassment. "Don't touch anything," she said. She stomped away, leaving Robin cuffed to the rail.

Chapter Four

A myriad of cleaning bottles—mostly empty—huddled together, clogging what little space was left under the sink. Stan fumbled with the wrench and pliers, unscrewing a slip nut connecting the trap to the adapter. His uniform shirt was draped over the back of a kitchen chair. A pair of baby blue slippers padded back and forth at Stan's feet.

"Did you find it yet?" asked the soft, feminine voice.

"Not yet, Ma. Hand me the bowl on the counter?"

An old wrinkled hand appeared under the sink. It shook from the weight of the glass bowl and old age. Stan placed the bowl on his stomach and removed the trap. A few inches of discolored water landed in the bowl. He upended the trap into his hand, catching the modest diamond engagement ring that fell out. It sparkled as the light refracted through the prism. There were days when he wished she'd lose it some place he couldn't get to. Maybe then she would move on.

His father had died over seventeen years ago when Stan was only seven. There wasn't much he could remember about his father. Sometimes he would wake with the fading sounds of yelling and stomping, the smell of cigarettes and stale beer in his nostrils.

He knew from friends and family that his dad was a drunk. The kind who got meaner the more he drank. He'd seen that kind of mean firsthand. Early on he'd accompanied Elle on a call. This was before Sheriff Bailey had died. He was all excited to be part of something that made a difference. They'd shown up to a noise complaint at a residence a little outside of town. It was in one of the newer complexes. The trees in front of the brick houses hadn't matured beyond the two trainers holding them in place.

Before going in Elle had turned to him and said, "Remember, whatever happens, whatever the husband says, stay calm. He'll bark a lot, but that's about it. I've been on a lot of these types of calls. You want to deescalate the situation. Watch what I do. Knowing procedure is one thing, but actually being on a call and seeing it in real life is another thing entirely."

Stan nodded, not exactly sure what she meant but eager to show he could follow instructions.

When the door opened to a small woman, eyes red, cheeks blotchy, he wasn't sure what he was supposed to do. Then the door whipped open wider and a tall, slim man in his late forties swayed into view. When he registered that there were two deputies standing on his front porch he turned to his wife. "Great, you called the cops. Real smooth, Diane. Now all the neighbors will have an after-dinner show." He stepped forward and yelled out into the front yard, "Come on, guys! Pull out some chairs, bring some drinks!"

"I didn't call anyone." His wife took a step back as she spoke.

"Sir, we got a call that there was a crash followed by shouting. We came to make sure everything was okay." Elle kept her hands loose by her side, her legs apart, sturdy, cautious.

The husband leaned forward, his eyes dropping to breast height. "I remember you. You've been here before." He smiled then. "Want to come in for a drink?" His eyes hadn't left her chest.

Elle ignored this and instead motioned behind the husband. "May I come in?" The husband bowed and swept his hand forward in a mocking formality.

Stan nodded at Elle and led Diane down the steps from the front porch to the driveway. He made sure to keep within sight of Elle.

"Is everything all right?" Stan asked.

Diane folded her arms across her chest. She too hadn't taken her eyes off Elle and her husband. "Everything's fine. He gets like this sometimes." She looked down at her feet. They were bare and contrasted against the dark asphalt of the drive. "He doesn't mean anything by it."

"Can you tell me what happened?"

Diane pushed a few rocks toward the grass with her toes. She didn't look up at Stan when she spoke. "We were watching the game, having a few drinks."

Stan didn't hear what Elle asked but the response was loud

enough to pull his attention. "We were just having a little bit of fun. It's Saturday." He shouted this last bit into the yard.

Stan stepped around the corner.

Elle raised her hands, placating. "Sir, we're not here to stop any fun. We're only here out of concern. There was a crash. People were worried someone may be hurt,"

"Of course we're okay. It was just the TV."

"If it was the TV, I would suggest you lower the volume."

The husband rolled his eyes toward the ceiling, then gazed back at Elle, his eyes glassy. "The TV fell over. It crashed because," he pointed at Diane, "some people are a little bit clumsy. Aren't they?"

Stan stood there watching the entire exchange waiting for a clue as to what he was supposed to be doing. He hoped that standing there feeling stupid and lost would qualify as calm.

"I didn't touch the TV. The bracket must have come loose," Diane said to Stan.

The husband stepped out onto the porch and looked to Stan. "Do you believe this? She thinks a bracket came loose on its own. Don't ever get married, kid. It's not worth it." He leaned forward. "They beg you to marry them and you think it's going to be all fucking and lingerie, but trust me, kid, it's more like bitching and granny panties." He laughed and hiccupped.

"I'd ask, sir, that you keep a civil tongue when speaking to us." Elle edged forward enough to block Stan off, so the husband would know he should be dealing with her. Stan's blood was pounding through his body like a high-speed train. He pulled Diane farther down the driveway from the scene. Elle had been right. This wasn't anything like when he'd been at the academy.

The husband looked confused for a second, wondering what he'd said that was so offensive. Then his face brightened. "Oh, you mean the word 'fucking'?" He laughed, a raucous sound that echoed into the night. "Is 'bitch' okay to use? I bet you hear that word a lot." Stan's whole mouth had gone dry. He found it was hard to swallow. Elle stood still as stone, her hands still loose, the pink in her cheeks the only sign that she'd registered what he said.

She was about to say something when the husband cut her off, leaning in and whispering, "I bet you like hearing that word. Am I right? You like a man who can take control." Stan stepped away from

Diane and began walking toward the front porch, but Elle put a hand up to stop him.

"Sir, I'm going to repeat to you what I said last time. There are only two ways this can go. You can choose to be polite, calm down, and you'll be able to end your Saturday night at home. Or you can be combative and disrespectful and end your Saturday night in the basement cell at the sheriff's office. Your choice."

"My choice? No, sweetheart. I never had a choice." He stepped closer to Elle, his eyelids starting to droop. The smile on his face was meant to be enticing, but instead he appeared menacing.

Elle took a step back, now out on the porch, just as Stan moved forward. He didn't like the look in the man's eyes. "Elle?"

"Oh, I get it now. You're getting a little pump action in the back of the cruiser, huh, kid? She pulls over and tells you how she likes it down there, huh? That it? A little fish snack during your shift?"

Before he'd even realized he'd done it, Stan's baton was out of his belt. He had it halfway toward the husband's foul mouth when Elle's hand blocked it. He could hear the sickening crack as the hard plastic hit her ulna. With her other hand, she grabbed his baton and stepped in front of him, a wall between him and the husband.

"Which way is this going to go?" she asked the husband. Her stare was hard, her jaw clenched against the pain in her arm.

After a bit more chest puffing, the husband backed down. Stan followed Elle back to the cruiser. He hadn't known her very long, but he could tell she was furious with him. As they drove away, both silent, Stan wondered how many times deputies had come to his parents' house and relived that scene.

A couple blocks from the house, Elle pulled over and turned to Stan. "Carrick, I'm going to give you some good advice right now, so I want you to listen. You are going to come across hundreds of encounters like that. Their number one goal is to goad you into getting angry. They want a reaction. Guys like that are plain mean. They need to tear you down so they don't feel so small anymore. It's why he treats his wife like crap. Because if she's crap, he must be a saint for putting up with her. And unless she presses charges, we can't do anything about verbal abuse except make it worse for her. It's her word against his. If he were the hitting kind that would be different, but there are no marks. I've stopped her at the market a couple times and asked, but she won't leave him. So when you come up against guys like that, you need to pretend you're watching a TV show. You need to pretend it's not happening to you. Whatever it takes to make it impersonal. If they get a reaction out of you and you do something stupid like tonight, they can press charges against you. Then you're fired and facing a civil suit."

Stan looked out at the night, at all the houses along the street with lights glowing behind curtains. "How do you do it? Make it not personal?" For the first time, Stan realized how much people hid from each other. He'd wanted to hit that guy. He'd wanted to see what happened when a baton connected with a skull. Not because what the guy said was true but because he couldn't understand how someone could be that vile.

Elle shrugged. "I pretend I know the next part of the story. That he's going to get what's coming to him. Everyone's different. You have to figure out what works for you."

"Are there records? I mean of domestic abuse calls?"

Elle nodded. "Yep, there's always dispatch records. But if we pull in either of the parties, there's a record at the station."

"How far back do they go?"

Elle sighed. "I'm not exactly sure why you're asking, Carrick, but I can guess and I think you should just let it go."

He nodded, sucking in air. He was trying so hard not to cry in front of her, worried she would think him weak, worried she might tell Neil or Bailey.

What hurt the most whenever he thought about that night was that Diane stayed with him. He couldn't help but wonder if that was what his mom's life had been like. It made him glad his dad had died. He just wished she'd move on.

The ring from his cell phone made him jump, sloshing water onto his pants and white undershirt.

"Want me to answer that?"

"No, Ma. I got it."

The ringing stopped.

"Hello?" she asked in a cautious voice. "This is Stanley's phone."

Stan clambered from under the sink, knocking the bowl of water to the kitchen floor. He grabbed the phone.

"This is Deputy Carrick." He dabbed at the water on his pants with a dish cloth. A quick smile grew across his face, his hollowed cheeks becoming more pronounced. "Great. I'll be there in under thirty." He paused. "Okay, I'll stop by the station on my way over."

His mother watched from the corner. Her milky blue eyes matched her oversized dressing gown and slippers. Disease had eaten away at a once beautiful face and left behind the bones and gristle of a satisfying meal.

Stan took her hand and placed the ring in the palm. "Remember to take it off before doing dishes. I make a lousy plumber."

She nodded, returning the ring to its place of prominence on her left ring finger, eyes downcast.

"I'll try to be home later to feed Missy. Do you need anything from the store?" he asked as he scrambled into his uniform shirt.

"We need milk." She stooped to pick up the fallen bowl.

"Okay." He kissed her on the cheek and ran to the front door, not even bothering to button his shirt.

A large golden retriever lay blocking his way. Her head rested on her paws, and an oversized diaper was secured around her backside. Stan grabbed hold of her front legs and pulled her out of the way. Her back legs were prone. A surgery on her hips when she was still a pup had taken its toll. Her bones had become arthritic as she aged, making it impossible for her now to do much more than lie about. As a result, she gained weight. Stan knew she wouldn't be around much longer. He didn't want to be the one to make the decision to put her down.

"C'mon, Missy." She let him pull her into the living room without even a whimper. "God, you're getting heavy." He dashed out the front door.

❖

Elle sifted through the objects in her trunk. It overflowed with assorted tools and equipment, some pertaining to her job as sheriff, others not. There was a box labeled Goodwill from three Christmases ago. A pair of garden shears. A squashed box of blue latex gloves. There was a windbreaker with the word Sheriff printed on the back, and several other things that had nothing to do with processing a crime scene.

Her hands shook as she shifted everything to one side, then back again. Her throat hurt, constricted by the effort of maintaining her composure. She placed her palms on the lip of the trunk. Her fingers felt numb. Her head was bobbing on her shoulders, light and surreal, making the forest surrounding her appear far off and close up at the same time.

Elle wasn't sure if she was going to faint. She rested her forehead against the cold metal of the trunk lid. It felt better. It would get better. This bubble inside her chest would pop and she'd be able to breathe without having to hold herself together. After.

She turned at the sound of a vehicle ricocheting down the drive. It was several moments before a rusted Chevy Malibu pulled through the brush, a silver-haired man behind the wheel. By then, she'd managed to locate a long black toolbox.

He nodded at Elle as he stepped out of the silver sedan, carrying a nylon bag, and tromped toward her with the gait of an old man.

His eyes scanned the scene, missing nothing.

"Is that a suspect?" Jack Case pointed to Robin still chained to the rail.

"No. She has trouble following instructions." Elle tried to smile, but it crumpled on her lips, becoming a tremble.

"You don't look so good." He rubbed her shoulder, peering into her ashen face. "It can't be that bad. Remember that kid on the train tracks? Jesus that was some mess, took days just to find all the parts."

Elle nodded remembering the day they'd been called out to the train bridge that spanned the Potawatomi. He said kid because he couldn't say Crystal Cipriani. A few years ago Crystal and her boyfriend had decided to use a shortcut over the train bridge. Halfway across, they heard a train coming up from behind. Her boyfriend made it across, Crystal hadn't. She tripped a third of the way. Three days later they were still finding pieces of her in the shallow waters under the bridge. After fifty years on the job, forgetting Crystal's name was one of many coping mechanisms Jack had come up with. For Elle, the name Crystal Cipriani screamed neon in her mind.

They say every new memory created pushes an old one out, but some things are unforgettable. The four months spent as Case's assistant gripped onto Elle's memory with claws. The day she applied to the sheriff's department at twenty-three, she'd already experienced more death than most did in a lifetime.

There wasn't a lot of work for a coroner in Flynn County, mostly identifying the remains of careless drunks and old people. Occasionally, there was an accident.

Elle lowered her voice. "It's Jessie. The victim. It's Jessie Forrester."

"Oh, Jesus, Elle, I'm sorry." His hand moved to her back, strong, comforting. He studied her with his dark brown eyes.

"Don't look at me like that."

"Like what?"

"This is going to be tough enough as it is. I don't need your pity."

"This look?" He pointed to his face. "It's concern, not pity." He let his hand drop. "Are you going to be able to manage this?"

"Of course. I haven't seen Jessie in years. It's just the shock of seeing him like that." Elle felt the absence of Case's hand, like a cold hole had opened up on her back creating an escape hatch for her anxiety. But it refused to budge. She set her toolbox on the leafy ground and began searching through it, taking inventory. It appeared brand new, fully stocked. Each item fit perfectly into a slot, nestled tightly to the next. No gaps, nothing missing. Elle snapped it shut, prepared.

"I've already questioned Tanya. She doesn't know anything. She was supposed to meet someone here, but she won't say who."

"Strange."

Elle shrugged. "Probably a boy she doesn't want anyone to know she's seeing."

"And the blonde?" Case picked his way through the fallen branches toward the front porch of the house.

Robin leaned against the railing, defiant, relaxed, observing them.

Elle let out a long, breathy sigh. "She's a reporter for some magazine up in Chicago."

"You brought a reporter to a crime scene?"

Elle's stomach lurched. "I didn't know it was a crime scene. Brady set it up. He's been on my ass about it all morning. I thought if I played along, showed her how boring this place actually is, she'd go home and forget about the story."

"That plan backfired."

Elle snorted. "And then some."

❖

EJ stood guard, his arms crossed, eyes swinging back and forth across the high school parking lot, sucking on a Marlboro Light. The air was thick with gnats, large balls of them hovered like dark moons. EJ swatted them with little effect.

J.P. Flynn High School cozied into the woods behind him, the tall pines acting as sentinels. It wasn't a large building, unchanged since the late seventies when it had replaced its predecessor, but it was large enough to fit all the high school students in Turlough and surrounding areas.

"Hurry up. Lunch bell's about to ring." EJ flicked his cigarette into a pool of green radiator fluid.

"One sec." Dan's voice was muffled, his head and upper body jammed into the trunk of a beat-up '82 Mustang GT.

Just then, the bell sounded. Within seconds, students streamed out of the building. The quiet of the early afternoon shattered like the glass guarding a fire alarm.

"Hurry up."

"It's got to be here."

EJ leaned over, peering into the junk filled trunk. "Maybe Randy didn't take your pump." His eyes darted back to the school entrance. "Shit. Here he comes."

Dan stood up, shutting the lid with his elbow, one fluid motion. A hulking senior rambled toward them. Randy Pritchard. The team's linebacker. Beefier than beefcake. He stomped down the entrance path, a Chicago Bears jersey stretching where his muscles bulged, his jeans straining against his thighs.

"You think he saw us?" asked Dan.

Randy's and EJ's eyes locked.

"Oh, yeah, he saw us." EJ grabbed at Dan's shirt sleeve, pulling him away from Randy's trunk. But Dan stood firm, itching for a fight.

Dan yanked his arm back. "I can handle little ole Pritchy."

"Get the fuck away from my car." Randy's voice sounded like someone had slowed down a tape recorder. His words rumbled in his drum of a chest before driving toward his throat and out the gaping hole that was his mouth.

"Oh hi, guys." Dan beamed at the football team forming a barricade around him and EJ.

Randy popped his trunk and dug through several weeks' worth of soiled workout gear, searching for anything missing. He slammed it shut when nothing appeared to have been taken. "What were you looking for?"

"Your sister. I heard you kept her in there for quickies between classes," said Dan. The playful tone of his voice matched his eyes. "That is why you rushed out here, wasn't it?"

A smattering of laughs.

"Heard you two had a little cuddle on the cot in the drunk tank last night." Randy turned to check for an audience. A large crowd had formed around the threesome. Half the school was closing in for front-row seats to what promised to be an interesting diversion. "Fair game, boys. Even baby Ashley's sister knows he's a flamer." At the word flamer, he let his right hand go limp.

"Screw you, Randy," EJ said. He was coming around to the idea that they wouldn't be getting out of here without a little blood splatter. The more from Randy, the better.

"Oh, I bet you'd like to, wouldn't you?" Randy said.

In a flash, the pack surged forward, anticipation palpable. Dan stepped back, fist balled, preparing to strike when a voice shouted above the din.

"What is going on here?" The crowd scattered, washed away like dirt off the concrete. Principal Withers thrust himself into the center of the group. He found three faces and one thought: oh, shit.

❖

Flies buzzed above Jessie's corpse. The spare sunlight creeping through the wood slats caught their wings like diamonds falling through the air.

The flash from a camera sent them scattering. Elle cupped the lens and refocused on a burn mark near his left shoulder.

"Are you planning on fingerprinting the place?" Case crouched next to the body, a clipboard balanced on his knee.

To the side, vials and evidence bags lined the wall, ready to be taken to the state lab. Elle and Case had been at it for hours, systematically scraping and peeling. Any thought of lunch had been swept away by the fetor and imminent decay of the body between them.

Elle dropped the camera to her side. "I had planned on getting Stan to do it." She waved toward the front door with her free hand.

"Want me to go check on the kid?" Case nodded toward the front porch where Stan sat, hat in hands, trying not to retch all over his polished shoes. On arrival, Stan hadn't managed to make it all the way outside before ridding himself of breakfast. His mound of puke in the foyer now mingled with the odor of putrefaction.

"He'll be okay. When I'm finished here, I'll start fingerprinting. I honestly don't think it's going to be much help. Half of J.P. Flynn's been through here." She wiped the sweat pooling at her hairline with the back of her arm. Elle's sleeves were rolled to her elbow. Several strands of hair had escaped her bun, the humidity teasing them into a frenzy. Piled next to the evidence collection were several sets of spent blue latex gloves. Elle ripped her current pair off and added it to the heap. "I didn't exactly create the most professional impression myself."

Case's lips formed a straight line, barely opening as he spoke. "Stan didn't know the man, Elle. Give yourself a little credit."

She had seen worse. There would always be worse. She hadn't thought about it in years. For some reason today, the image of her parents lying in the morgue crawled out of the place she'd thought she'd buried it.

Over the years, dealing with the dead had gotten easier. But the corpses she worked on with Case didn't come with memories. When she looked at them, she didn't see their smiles or scowls. Their arms raised in victory when she came in first during varsity track meets, the disappointment in their eyes when she skipped school, the anger when she missed curfew. They were just bodies.

Elle kept Jessie's body divided in her mind. A muddied shoe. Blood on the fisted fingers. Matted hair. It made it easier to think of him as parts to a larger puzzle, the pieces of which were now scattered in a bloody mess throughout an abandoned house in the middle of the woods.

"High school was a long time ago. I'd rather we keep the personal aspects out of it."

Case harrumphed. "That's about as likely as Brady showing up to work in flip-flops and a leisure suit."

Case was right. There was no way she could keep the town gossips from rehashing her and Jessie's past. Her mind skipped to some of the less brilliant aspects of her youth. She cringed. More so because there were worse things that could happen. She needed to stop thinking about herself and focus.

"So are we going to talk about this or not?" Case stood, his knees cracking.

"About what?"

"About who the hell would want to kill Jessie? What in the Christ was he even doing in town?"

Elle rested the camera on her shoulder. She waited three seconds before making a choice. A choice she would later regret. "I don't know. But that's where I'm going to focus the start of my investigation. As soon as I'm done consulting with the SPI."

"You know what they're going to say."

She nodded. "Yeah, but maybe this'll be my lucky day and they tell me they magically found some extra resources and can send someone our way." Case gave her a look. "A girl can dream."

"Yeah, well"—he pointed to the dead body between them—"dreaming isn't going to make this go any faster."

Elle capped the camera lens and placed it back in the bag Stan had brought from the station.

"As far as places to kill someone goes, this is a pretty good choice," Case said.

"Tell me about it." It was so isolated a door-to-door was out. On top of that, the place was so full of trash it was impossible to know what was important and what had been there since she'd gone to high school. Elle scribbled a few ideas of where to start the investigation below her reminder. Top of the list was a visit to Jessie's parents. This she dreaded. All things considered, she'd rather have a root canal and a pap smear done at the same time. Without the nitrous oxide.

"What am I going to say to them?"

Jack didn't need to ask who them was. "You tell them what you'd tell anyone in this situation. Don't let yourself get pulled in. Don't make it personal." He reached over and squeezed her arm.

"I've never had to tell anyone their son was murdered. This isn't like an accident. There's going to be an investigation." Elle folded her notepad and placed it in her pocket. "Shit."

"I was thinking the same thing."

"What?"

"Why couldn't he be murdered in Chicago and be their problem?"

"That's not what I was thinking." Elle tramped out of the house.

CHAPTER FIVE

"Did you know the victim? What was his name? Jessie Forrester?" Robin asked. Three and a half hours of standing in the sun hadn't deflated her appearance. She still looked like she had when she'd walked into Elle's office earlier that morning: crisp and professional.

Elle shrugged. "Turlough's a small place." Shadows from the hanging canopy danced up the hood of the cruiser and over the windshield as she meandered, slow and deliberate, through the back roads.

"Is that a yes?" While Robin's appearance might have looked neat on the outside, her insides were anything but. She'd spent her morning fantasizing about chaining Elle to a tree. In the middle of the desert. In another, she'd dragged her out to a set of tracks surrounded by scrub grass and tumbleweeds and tied her to the rail. Only once had she let it get out of hand. She wasn't sure why she was forming her revenge in western motif, but it was working for her.

Every time she'd managed to get Elle's attention she'd wave her off as if she were dismissing an annoying fly buzzing around her head. Robin hated to admit how much that had gotten under her skin. She wasn't used to being ignored.

"We went to the same high school. He was a year ahead."

Robin shifted in her seat to face Elle straight on. "Are you being vague on purpose?" The seat belt strained against her breasts. "I've spent the better part of my day chained like a punished dog. I'm exhausted, pissed off, and sweaty." She brushed her bangs off her face, but it did nothing to make her look more disheveled. "I don't appreciate vague."

"Can you stop talking for one minute, please?" Most of Elle's hair had escaped its bun in the last few hours, choosing instead to blow free in the wind like flames licking at her face. "I need to think what to say to Jessie's parents." Her hands tightened on the wheel as she said his name.

Robin turned back around, arms folded, lip jutting out. She felt like a pouting child, but she couldn't help it. Elle was turning out to be nothing like she'd expected. When she arrived, she expected to be in and out. Complete the assignment and leave almost as soon as she'd arrived.

Robin hadn't spent much of her life outside of the city and she preferred it that way. She could navigate in the city. She knew what people expected of her and she of them. Things were simpler. Here, nothing made sense. She'd expected the local law to be a pushover, to give her what she wanted so she could get the hell out of there. She'd also expected the local law to be the equivalent of Kathy Bates in *Fried Green Tomatoes*. But Sheriff Ashley was proving a different beast.

She turned her attention to the passing sights, hoping to calm down before she lost her temper and ruined any chance of completing this job. They passed a shack squeezed between two giant trees. A child ran out. The screen door smacked the frame with a loud crack. She couldn't believe people actually lived there. The yard housed several cars in various forms of decay. From the mirror, Robin watched the child chase the cruiser down the road, a big grin on his face and part of his lunch smeared along one cheek.

In big cities, urban poverty looked different than rural. What was it about giving humans space that allowed them to fill it with junk? Was this a North American thing or a universally human trait? If she traveled to Germany, would she find the transportation history of a family displayed on their front lawn the same way the rich hung expensive pieces of art around their homes?

Was everyone in Turlough this poor or just the unlucky few? Did Elle have vehicle carcasses ornamenting her front yard? Or did she live in a small apartment above the sheriff's office? Then Robin remembered Elle's brother and wondered if she still lived at home.

She didn't ask any of these questions. Instead, she sank lower in her seat trying to get a feel for this town and its people. If she was going to make any progress, she would need to.

Elle pulled to a stop in a front circular drive, reluctant to turn off the engine. She willed her brain to come up with a script for how this should go.

Ten years had passed since Elle had spoken with Jessie's parents. Janice and Chuck Forrester faded into the backdrop like white noise. They rarely ventured into town, choosing instead to inhabit a world of two.

Robin whistled. "Nice place."

Their quaint colonial was tucked into the forest, masked from the main road by large oaks and maples. The diligence of upkeep was plain, even from a distance.

There was a woman in her early sixties working in a flower bed. At the sound of the engine, she stood. A floral scarf hid her hair from view; dirt-encrusted gloves did the same for her hands. She removed the gloves and tossed them onto a pile of gardening tools.

At first she was curious, but upon seeing Elle, her face transformed into pleasure.

"Oh, God." It was only a whisper, but Robin heard it and turned to Elle. She was clutching the worn steering wheel, her face as pale as the white cruiser. Seeing Robin watching her, she straightened. Before getting out she said, "Do I need to pull the handcuffs out again?"

"No. I'll sit here, like a good little doggy." Robin gave her a lopsided grin to show there were no hard feelings. She didn't envy Elle this task. She'd wondered, on occasion, what it would be like to receive news that a loved one had died. Both her parents were still alive, living comfortably in a two story in Evanston. But she'd encountered enough death in her job to see the toll it took on someone.

"This shouldn't take very long." Elle corralled her hair back into its bun.

As Elle approached the woman, her frame was stiff like her baton, which was currently propping up her kitchen window. And like that window, she was stuck halfway between her past and present, unsure if she should be the warm teenager who had dated their son or the stoic sheriff of Flynn County.

"Elle, what a pleasure to see you. What brings you out this way?" There was a genuine smile of affection on the woman's face as she took Elle into a warm embrace. "It's been too long." She paused to consider. "It must be well over ten years since you've been here."

"Around that, Mrs. Forrester." Elle took a measured step back, distancing herself from the older woman.

"How many times have I told you to call me Janice?" She eyed Elle's sheriff uniform, which was now in its second day of wear. As much as she'd tried to fortify the creases in her trousers, the constant bending, sleeping, sitting, and humidity had deflated them.

"About a million. Is Mr. Forrester around? I'd like to speak with you both."

"Of course. He's in back fiddling with the pool heater. It's been on the fritz lately." Janice motioned toward Robin. "What about your friend? Would she like to come in?"

Robin perked up at this. The promise of a front-row seat was more than enough to make up for her less than stellar morning. But she too was deflated when Elle shook her head.

"No," Elle said. Her abrupt tone put Janice on alert. She softened her voice. "This isn't a social call, Mrs. Forrester."

"What is it?"

"Let's go inside." Elle guided Janice into the house with a soft hand to the back of the older woman's arm. She wasn't exactly gripping it, just nudging her in the right direction. A good excuse to escape the heat, and Robin's eavesdropping.

"Would you care for something to drink?" Janice asked as she led Elle into the living room. Fans buzzed overhead, dispersing the unexpected late spring heat.

"No, thank you." Elle cringed at the procedural tone her voice had taken on.

The interior matched the outside's meticulousness. It was neat, but lived in. The furniture was well maintained, but with the hint of favorite spots that had worn grooves into the cushions over the years.

"I'll grab Chuck, then. Make yourself comfortable."

Elle skirted the overstuffed couch, choosing instead to stand. Comfortable was out of the question. The room was dotted with pictures. They covered every surface, not just the walls. A timeline of their family. At one time, Elle was a prominent feature in many of them, as if already part of the family. The room had since been wiped of Elle. She'd been replaced by Jessie's wife and the past seven years of their life together. She had been reduced to a single picture. In it, she and Jessie mugged for the camera. She had taken the blue sash from her dress and wrapped it around his neck as if to strangle him. A prom corsage dangled from her bodice. Their faces were suspended mid-laugh.

Elle replaced the picture on a side table as Mrs. Forrester entered carrying a tray with a pitcher of sweet tea and three glasses.

"That was such a great picture of you two. I hated to get rid of the rest, but…well, you know. I guess it wouldn't have been appropriate with Cindy here and everything." She set the tray on the coffee table.

"You didn't have to go to all this trouble, Mrs. Forrester."

She waved Elle off. "I know, but it's such a hot day out and you look like you could use a little pick-me-up."

Self-conscious, Elle surveyed her appearance, deciding she should have showered. At the very least, she should have changed before coming. But with Robin in the cruiser, the last thing she wanted was to pull up in her driveway. The idea of her invading so much of her personal life was mortifying.

"Ah, there she is. The impressive sheriff of Flynn County," Chuck Forrester said as he burst into the room. His old khaki shorts were covered in grime, his graying hair tucked under a Cubs hat. "We voted for you, you know." He grabbed her in a bear hug, forgetting the filth on his shorts.

"I got your bouquet. It was very thoughtful. Thank you." She was relieved his booming laugh had masked the tremble in her voice. She had almost forgotten how easy it was to be around Jessie's parents.

Elle spent more time here during high school than at her own house. At the time, she was oblivious to how few years she had left with her parents. It was a safe haven. Free from judgment and punishment. Now, she felt guilt.

"So polite now. Where's the rowdy girl we remember cannonballing into our pool?"

Janice handed Elle a glass of sweet tea. "Leave the girl alone. She's here on official business. She has to be professional." Her smile was that of a proud parent.

Chuck and Janice Forrester inhabited their surroundings like uncut gems. The dirt from their earlier activities was only surface deep. Beneath their faded and worn clothing was the same understated elegance of the house.

Elle sank into the couch, feeling the cushions envelop her, clinging to her thighs, cool against the fabric of her uniform. She took a sip of sweet tea. Her face puckered.

"Not sweet enough?" asked Janice. "I forgot, you like lots of sugar."

"It's fine." And she took another sip before placing it on the coffee table. Her hands regretted it immediately. Now they had nothing to do but twist themselves into knots on her lap. "The reason I'm here—" And she stopped. Gazing into the serene and curious faces of Jessie's parents, like glossy eight-by-tens come to life, she lost her nerve. This was the last time they would ever be happy. Sitting here together on their couch. The clear glee at seeing their son's ex. Refreshed from an afternoon of being productive. And she would be the one to shatter it.

"What is it? Has something happened to EJ?"

Being back in this house a million thoughts came to mind. Had Buck, the evil cat that stalked Elle her entire junior year, finally died? And if so, had they buried him in the backyard next to the tulip garden? She still had a scar on the back of her thigh from his claws. What happened to the blue couch, velvet to the touch, the one she'd given her first hand job on? Did they know that while they'd been at a PTA meeting she and Jessie had been here siphoning from their liquor cabinet? Was the screen on Jessie's window still loose? Could it still be popped from the outside with a well-placed key? Did any of that matter now that she was the only person left to remember?

She decided to treat it like any accident. "This morning I was called out to the old Maverty house for a noise complaint."

Chuck actually laughed at the mention of the house. "Are kids still using it as a clubhouse? I remember you and Jessie used to get into a fair amount of trouble in that place." Elle hoped to God he wasn't aware of even half the trouble they'd gotten up to in that house.

Janice shook her head, the knot in her scarf coming loose. Almost as an afterthought, she slipped it off and folded it, smoothing the fabric onto her lap. "I don't know why they haven't torn that place down yet."

"The historical society declared it a landmark building last year."

Janice turned to her husband, shocked, almost like it had been his choice and not the society's. "I don't know why. That place is a fire hazard if anything." She shook her head, harder this time. "What a silly, sentimental thing to do. Some child is going to hurt themselves there and then they'll be sorry." She looked to Elle. "Isn't there anything you can do? Can't you barricade the place?"

Elle shrugged helplessly. "They would just tear them down." She remembered the lengths to which the sheriff's department had gone to back in her day to keep Jessie's crew out, even going so far as to board up every window and door. It didn't matter, though. They always found a way back in. Eventually, Sheriff Bailey realized the futility of it. When Elle took over she did little more than keep an eye on the place, just to make sure the kids didn't go too far.

Chuck patted his wife's knee. "Elle came to tell us something. Let her tell us."

Elle smiled weakly. With her heart pounding against her sternum, she proceeded to tell the Forresters that their only child had been found murdered in the old Maverty house. Instead of that happy, carefree girl who used to date their son, the Forresters would always remember Elle in this moment. She would forever be the one who shattered their ideal existence. It was this that paralyzed Elle. Scared her more than anything. She'd spent the ten years since she'd come back constructing this professional exterior, giving the people of Turlough someone they could rely on and respect. In order to do that, she'd wrapped her past up like a package and left it where it belonged, in the past. Now it was like she was taking the package out and leaving it to tarnish in the sun.

And when she finished, her heart in her throat, she didn't get the reaction she expected. There was no crying. No screaming. In fact, there was no sound coming from the Forresters at all. They stared in polite silence at Elle as she clung to her knees.

Then Janice laughed. "That's impossible. It can't be Jessie. He called me from Chicago two days ago. We wanted to know if he would be down for the festival, but he said Cindy and he couldn't make it. They never do, but I always ask. Just in case." She looked at her husband to confirm this.

"I wish it weren't true. But it is. I found his body this morning."

"No. You're mistaken," Janice said, shaking her head from side to side. But each sway left a small chink in her composure. Elle moved to kneel beside her, taking her hands. Cupping them.

Janice recoiled at her touch. "Get out!"

Her yell was so unexpected, so charged with hatred, Elle fell backward onto the carpet. Janice reared, towering over Elle.

"How dare you? How dare you tell such lies? Get out of here." Her face contorted in anguish. A sob bubbled out.

Chuck enfolded Janice in his arms. "You better leave, Elle."

She was being pulled in. Again. Case had warned her about this. Elle dragged herself up to full height with support from the coffee table. She blinked a few times, hoping to erase the sight of the Forresters huddled together for support. "I'll be back tomorrow to ask you some questions. In the meantime, you know where to reach me if you need anything."

"Don't come back. You're not welcome here," Janice said, her tears falling freely. "Not anymore."

"If you like, you can come into the station, Mrs. Forrester. But I will need to ask you questions about Jessie." Elle moved closer to the door, stepping past the line of the carpet dividing the living room and front hall. "I'll give you time now." Her voice was subdued but firm.

"What about? About identification?" asked Mr. Forrester.

Elle shook her head. "I knew him well enough to—You won't need to come in for that."

He nodded. But Elle didn't notice. She had turned and walked out of the cool house into the heat of the afternoon.

CHAPTER SIX

A wall of grease belted Robin in the face as she entered Dell's. The smell stormed her nostrils. As they passed to take a booth, Robin heard one of the younger men cough "Ice Queen" into his napkin. She was sure Elle had heard it too, because the muscles in her back tensed.

Elle wanted to put as much distance between her and the Forresters as possible. But small towns only offered so much.

Before she had even climbed into the cruiser, Robin said, "I don't mean to be insensitive, but is there anywhere to eat around here?"

Elle started the car but didn't say anything. If Robin hadn't been there she would have liked to rest her head on the steering wheel. Just for a moment.

The change was palpable. From when she entered the house until now. There was a scoured look to her. Robin figured she could use some food. "What about that diner across from your office? I imagine it has a bit of local flavor to it," she said.

"I'm not all that hungry."

"Really?" She took in her pale face and general dishevelment. "When was the last time you ate?"

She thought about it. "Last night, I guess."

"No breakfast?"

"Coffee." Then she said, "Look, if you'd been doing what I was doing all morning, you wouldn't be hungry either."

Robin held up both hands in supplication. "It wasn't an accusation. The way your deputy reacted, I suspect it was more gruesome than the glance I caught."

Elle noted Robin hadn't mentioned her reaction and was grateful. "It's not exactly the outcome I was expecting when I took you out on that call. I hope you didn't see too much."

Before she had a chance to answer, Elle pulled into her spot at the sheriff's office. Parking spaces weren't assigned, but it was generally understood that the sheriff got the closest one to the door. Not that the other two were far. Still, it was the tradition of the thing.

Even as Elle entered the diner, followed by Robin, she knew it was a mistake. The place was only half full, but everyone stopped to stare. Most were curious, some indifferent, a few hostile. Of course they'd heard. This town was as good at keeping secrets as a torn pocket was at storing change. Elle stood staring at the curtain of faces waiting for a show. She shored her face and chose a side booth near the back.

"What was that all about?" Robin cocked her head toward the grubby, bearded man in the greasy overalls near the front. Elle had deliberately sat with her back to Frankie Cheever.

"Let's say he's the type of guy who doesn't take rejection well." Frankie was the type of guy whose misogynist attitude amplified with rejection. Assuming that if Elle wanted nothing to do with him, there must be something wrong with her. "Ice Queen" was one of many terms he'd come up with to let her know it.

"How you feeling, honey?" Tully asked. She set two cups of coffee on the table without asking. "You must be a wreck, and to think you're going to have to investigate and all." Her tone was sympathetic, but her face resembled a child who'd discovered Christmas was coming twice this year. She scanned the counter behind her. "And isn't it a shame? I've only got blueberry pie left."

Tully Dell ran Dell's Diner with a robust efficiency like an all-in-one espresso maker. With very little outward effort, she managed to do a variety of tasks in a short amount of time. Like her husband Neil, she had an ample figure. Only her breasts were bigger. They spilled over her apron, giving the appearance that you could rope them in to stop them from flopping about. Her face was open and pleasant, but like a charity plate, you tended to give more than you meant to.

"It's okay, Tully. I'm not hungry." Even key lime pie couldn't dissolve the dead lump in her stomach.

"Don't give me that nonsense. You weren't in for breakfast and I know you didn't have any at home 'cause Neil said you slept in your office again."

Elle flushed. She wanted to crawl under the table and hide. She became self-conscious again of her appearance, sitting across from this woman who, despite her morning, still looked immaculate. And that was typical Tully. If you wanted to know who was behind on their mortgage or what someone paid for their new truck, ask Tully. In fact, you rarely had to ask.

An uncomfortable feeling settled into Elle's stomach. This was the moment she'd been dreading since she was elected sheriff a little over a year ago. Up until now her job had been perfunctory. In fact, on any given day, she didn't feel any different than when she had been one of Bailey's deputies. The main difference being a love seat she slept on more nights than not, and her signature on everything that passed through Flynn County. She had taken charge in a quiet sort of way. Almost like one sneaks in after curfew, quick and silent like you'd been there the whole time. But now the town expected her to solve a murder. This was more than petty infighting and bylaw violations. Solving Jessie's murder would require more than babysitting. And she was doubting whether she could handle it as she'd told Case earlier that day. And Robin's presence wasn't helping matters. She felt like at any second someone would flick the lights on and catch her out of bed.

Elle sighed. "Bring me some soup, then." She handed Tully back the menu. Truth was, she didn't even need it. Elle was there most days for lunch and dinner, never having learned to cook herself. She'd rather admit defeat and have someone else do it. EJ was rarely home. Most nights he ate at a friend's house. She often wondered what their parents must think of her.

Tully planted a hand on her hip, a well-known stance that indicated she was about to lay in about something. "Don't be mad, honey. Neil's worried you're spending too much time at the station. He says lately you've been there most nights. I'm amazed you don't have back problems." She turned to Robin, her voice like a spider coaxing its prey. "It's such a tiny couch." She smiled at Robin then, bringing her into her web. "Sandy says you're a writer, says you're writing a book about Turlough."

"That's almost right." Robin handed Tully the menu, her smile wide and humorless. "I'll have the Reuben, unless that's deep fried as well, in which case I'll have the soup."

"We don't deep fry our sandwiches." She snatched up her menu. "We fry 'em on the grill like normal." She huffed away.

"It's not a good idea to piss in her pool. Tully chooses what people know about you and she tends to go for the throat if you end up on her bad side." Elle stared into the black abyss of her steaming coffee before seizing the sugar. Around them, the diner had swung back into motion. More interested, for the time being, in their lunch. The sounds of the diner were familiar and comfortable. Outside, the slow traffic of the main drag rambled by, barely adding to the clatter inside.

"I'm sorry I suggested eating here," said Robin.

Elle shrugged and dumped a gallon of sugar into her coffee.

"It must be hard having everyone know your business like that. Who's Neil?" Robin took a sip of her coffee, choosing to drink it black. She grimaced and pushed it to the middle of the table.

"You saw him earlier. He was manning the desk this morning. They're married, Tully and him." She took a sip of her coffee, scowled, and added more sugar. "Which means, like it or not, the biggest gossip in town has a direct line to pretty much everyone's dirty laundry." She wrapped her hands around her coffee. The heat barely penetrated her skin. She looked up at Robin. "Can I ask you to consider the impact your prying would have on the people of this town? Couldn't you walk away, just this once, and leave us to mourn in peace?" She took a sip of coffee, hoping Robin hadn't noticed she'd said "us."

Robin leaned back in her seat. She pushed her bangs aside, then folded her arms across her chest. The act lifted her breasts, enhancing her cleavage. Elle too would mourn Jessie Forrester, she'd noticed that.

"These are people's lives. Real people who can get hurt by what you write. The Forresters don't deserve this. Neither does Jessie."

"Why are you so sure that what I write will be unflattering? I've been here less than a day, I haven't even formed an opinion yet."

Elle let out a loud bark of a laugh. "Right. You formed an opinion the second you stepped out of your rental car. I've seen the way you've been watching us. You may not realize it but you're pretty easy to read."

"Really? Okay, go. Tell me what I'm thinking."

Elle took another sip of coffee, trying to get the mash of thoughts to coalesce into actual sentences. "You see us as a bunch of redneck inbred hicks, most of us barely having graduated high school, let alone going off to graduate from some fancy college. None of us has been outside of the county lines so we assume this is the best it's going to get for us. We're skirting the poverty line so fiercely we can't even afford to move the trash off our lawns. Everyone gets married right out of school because the girls don't know any better and the guys think they'll get laid more often. How am I doing so far?"

"Is that why you're not married? First of all, I don't think you're all inbred, I know the difference between Illinois and Kentucky. Second, anyone worried about what level of education I think they've had has definitely had more than high school."

And then, almost from thin air, Tully was at their table, setting food down. She whipped out two sets of utensils from her apron and placed them on the edge of the table.

Robin hadn't noticed. She was gauging Elle to see whether she'd pissed her off or impressed her.

"Is there anything else I can get for you?"

Robin smiled up at her. "Tell me, Tully, did you know Jessie Forrester?"

Tully smiled at her, their past difference forgotten. "Know him? Of course I knew him, everyone did. But you shouldn't be asking me. Elle knew him best."

"Really?" She turned to Elle, a look close to regret on her face. "She hadn't mentioned it."

"Aw, poor thing." Tully placed her plump hand on Elle's shoulder. "I can't imagine what you must be going through right now."

"It was a long time ago."

"But you two were engaged."

"We were never engaged."

Tully waved her off as if she knew better than Elle about her own personal life. She was still smiling that same sympathetic smile when she left to give refills to several regulars at the end of the counter.

"We weren't engaged. We only dated in high school. It was a long time ago and, no, I don't want to talk about it."

"God. I'm sorry. I had no idea you knew him so well." Robin opened the napkin surrounding her utensils and slid them out. "I'm not here for that kind of story. I was being honest when I told you I wouldn't publish anything without your say-so."

Elle nodded. But she didn't look convinced. Robin took a bite of the Reuben, noting that even though they grilled it, the bread was soggy. She placed it back on the plate and wiped the grease off her fingers. "Let's pretend for a second that I'm not here for a story. That we're just two people having lunch together."

Elle took a minute, her eyes on her soup. Finally, she dipped her spoon and nodded.

"Can I ask you a question? Totally off topic," Robin asked.

"You can ask anything you want. Doesn't mean I'll answer it."

"How do you stay so damn skinny eating here all the time? It's giving me a heart attack just being in here. They don't have anything close to a salad on that menu."

Despite herself, Elle smiled. "I eat a lot of soup."

Robin laughed and took a sip of her coffee. She'd have to find another place to eat if she wanted to make it out of Turlough alive.

The rest of the meal they ate in silence, Elle absorbed in her soup and Robin absorbed in Elle. She'd formed an impression that first meeting and now it wasn't adding up. Robin was aware of how she looked. She took great lengths to look the way she did. Good genes and a healthy attitude about food and exercise went a long way. She was used to the attention she got—in fact, she welcomed it, especially from women.

There were two types of looks she got. The one, usually from men, that said they'd like very much to do dirty things to her. The other, usually from women, that said they wished they could look half as good as her. Elle had given her the first look. When she'd bent forward, Elle's eyes had dipped to her cleavage and lingered. She'd also noticed Elle appreciating her legs when she'd been talking to the old man. So this new information about a past fiancé or boyfriend or whichever, was something of a shock.

It was possible Elle was so far in the closet she wasn't even aware of her lust-filled glances. Or, more likely, the sheriff of a small town. And Turlough didn't feel like the kind of place that would elect a gay sheriff. One thing she was sure about, she was intrigued more than she should be. This would be a line of enquiry that she would have to drop. It wasn't worth her job to risk compromising her principles now.

After Tully had cleared their plates and they'd settled the bill, Robin asked, "So what's next?"

Before Elle had a chance to answer, her phone rang. She pulled it from her pocket. "Sheriff Ashley." She listened. The longer she listened, the tighter her grip on her mug became. "I don't understand, Mr. Withers, what's he being accused of stealing?"

❖

A long stream of soapy water trickled down the cement steps leading to a low brick building behind the school. EJ and Dan stood on either end of a pitted wall attempting to wash the graffiti off. A line of sweat drooled down EJ's back, showing darker where it seeped through the light cotton.

"As if she recommended this over a three-day suspension." EJ plunged his hand into a bucket of lukewarm water and pulled up a rough sponge soaked with suds. He slapped it against the wall. He worked it in large circles over the word *cocksucker*, which dissolved at a pace equal to drying paint.

The fading sun stained them a harsh orange and hardened the lines and shadows of everything around. The campus was empty. A few stray cars dotted the parking lot. The quiet dinner hour settled around them.

Dan stopped to light a Winston from a smooshed pack in his back pocket. "And of course little ole Pritchy walks away with an apology instead of detention." Gripping the cigarette in his teeth, he took his scrub brush up again. "And how come your sister gets to call the punishment?"

EJ kicked at his bucket, sending a wave over the side. "I know, right? It's like lately she's been on my case about every little thing." He punctuated the last three words each with their own period. "It's one thing for her to do her job, but she has no right making us serve detention."

Dan nodded. EJ's temper seldom erupted, but when it did, it was a great show. More often he would let it stew, burying it deep. He gave Dan the fights. Dan was good at fighting. Dan was more like a tiger, he would bide his time waiting for the right moment to pounce.

"Fuck this!" EJ smacked his sponge into his bucket, creating an explosion of water. A large part of it landed on a pair of leather shoes that had snuck up without either EJ or Dan noticing.

Edgar Withers had a way of sneering without speaking, which

intensified when dealing with any of the Ashleys. "I agree that a suspension would have been more satisfactory. Your sister, however, believes your time will be better served in detention. Perhaps hard labor is what's needed to set you on the right path. Her words, not mine." His voice made his pinched face seem even more so. "I personally think you're both destined for the penal system."

Principal Withers gave the impression of trying to appear taller than everyone. He stood a good foot shorter than both Dan and EJ. But he strained his neck and puffed out his stomach, giving himself a few more inches. Elle had once joked in front of an auditorium of students that he probably wore lifts in his shoes. He did, but it wasn't Elle Ashley's place to broadcast this to the entire school. He hadn't suspended her. Instead he set her to the humiliating task of serving her peers in the cafeteria for a week. He would come each day, stand in the back and wait for her to break. He told himself it would do her good, learning humility. But he'd not broken her. She'd turned it into a game, laughing and joking as she slopped coleslaw or dried clumps of meatloaf onto passing trays.

"If you don't agree with her, then why'd you call her in the first place? You could've suspended us," EJ said.

Withers gripped his briefcase, clenching his hand like his jaw. "As your guardian she asked to be informed if you should ever end up in my office. Believe me, Mr. Ashley, if it were solely up to me, you wouldn't be here right now."

Dan edged closer to the little man. "What do you have against the sheriff?" He let his cigarette fall to the ground. It rolled along the cement, still lit, catching in the wedge between sidewalk slabs.

Withers followed the progress of the cigarette. "Ms. Ashley somehow managed to land on the correct side of the law. Of course, this was only after spending a much greater time on the other side of it." Withers stretched his neck out a little farther, resembling an indignant crane. "And I'll remind you only once, Mr. Baker, there is no smoking on school property, even after school hours."

"Are we free to go?" EJ asked, uncomfortable with the topic change.

"Ms. Ashley was a hellion, her and that Forrester boy." The next thought that sprang to mind he didn't voice. But not because he didn't believe it, more because Dan and EJ looked the sort who would carry a concealed weapon. Withers stepped back. "You may go for today."

EJ whooped and dumped his bucket into the grass as celebration.

A slow smile crept onto Wither's face. "Of course, we will see you tomorrow after school, and the day after that and so on. Until all the graffiti has been washed clean."

EJ kicked the bucket across the sidewalk. "That'll take forever."

But Dan wasn't surprised, he'd been expecting this. "There's only a week left of school, what happens after?" He waited, knowing the answer already.

Withers had turned to leave, but swiveled back now and said, "You and Mr. Ashley both have incompletes, which means we'll have the pleasure of seeing you here throughout the summer." He hefted his briefcase and walked down the steps. But his gait was lighter as he strode across the parking lot to his shit-brown Corolla.

CHAPTER SEVEN

The Collards' bed-and-breakfast backed onto the boreal forest that encircled Turlough. From her third story window, Robin could see the tops of trees farther down the hill.

The room was small and served only one purpose: sleep. They'd wedged a single wrought iron bed between the window and far wall. It looked like it could strangle you in your sleep. It certainly wasn't the Peninsula, or the Holiday Inn, for that matter. But it had a view.

Less than half a mile away she noticed a small clearing and the remnants of a stately roof. The old Maverty house, she guessed. She hadn't realized it was that close. The winding ribbon of road leading to and from Turlough was misleading. It must have been Mrs. Collard who'd reported hearing screams. She'd wondered about that.

Sandy Collard fell all over her when she'd checked in earlier that morning, like a golden retriever welcoming her master home, pawing at her leather satchel and Lotuff duffel. "Ken said you'd be coming by." Her jowls swayed as she spoke. It wasn't just Sandy's personality that resembled the fair-haired dog; her complexion and blond shaggy mane gave the impression that she shook herself dry after showering. The rest of her was robust yet still young for her fifty plus years.

Before Robin could change her mind and look elsewhere for a room, Sandy had pushed her toward the slim stairs. They passed several landings with bright hallways and colonial furniture, but Sandy didn't stop until she reached the top, panting softly from the effort.

Robin's intake of breath put Sandy on the defensive. "Your timing's unfortunate. It so happens I'm renovating the other two rooms. They promised me they'd be done before the festival." Her hand fluttered as if to say, "that's life." "They're a little bigger."

Robin's closet was bigger.

Sandy brushed past her and swept open the curtains. "But it has a real nice view of the ravine." As if this would make up for the postage stamp of a room she was leaving her in. Robin hadn't slept in a single bed since her first year of college.

Robin hadn't put any forward thought into accommodations when she'd planned this trip. But the closest she could come was a Motel 6 in Mason, twenty-five miles west of Turlough. And now here she was having to use a guest shower located two floors down. The one upshot to being the only guest was she didn't have to share amenities.

Before jumping in the shower she made a quick call to her boss to give him an update. She had no doubt he'd be happy when she was done. She just had to find a way to bond with Elle, get her trust. Elle held her cards close. Robin didn't blame her—in fact, it made her respect Elle more. These days people were too quick to share every little thing about their lives like it made them special.

It had taken her years, but she'd honed her skills as a conversationalist. Sometimes, that's what she needed to be. She needed to know what to say, when to say it, and when to shut the hell up. For the next week or so she was going to have to work harder than a politician a month before elections. She needed to charm the locals, get them to trust her and spill all Turlough's well-known secrets.

As she stepped out of the shower, her cell phone rang. She checked the screen. A goofy grin and shaved head stared back at her. She groaned.

"Hey, dipshit." Her little brother rarely called her unless he needed something. "What do you need?" She switched the phone to speaker and placed it on the side of the sink.

"Why do you think I need something?" A loud crunch, then mumbling. "Can't a guy call his sister to shoot the shit?"

"How much?" She removed her towel and bent over to towel-dry her hair.

"What?" He tried to laugh, but it fell flat.

Robin snapped up, her hair hitting her back with a loud slap. "Cut the shit, Jason. How much do you owe this time?"

"I don't owe anything, I swear." More crunching, then silence as he slurped something from a straw. "I just need a wee favor from the bestest big sister in the world."

She sighed, but didn't answer. This was classic Jason. Every couple of months he would come crawling to her for something. Money, a place to stay, a job. Anything he could mooch off her. He was a sweet kid and she loved him. In fact, he was probably the only person she'd ever loved. But he came with a large price tag, and one of these days she knew she wasn't going to be able to afford it.

"I need you to put in a good word for me with Jamie's crew."

She closed her eyes. This would not end well. She could already see it. Her job sometimes led her to run in circles with the less savory denizens of Chicago. She had a reputation for being honest but ruthless, which led people to give her a certain amount of respect.

She grabbed her moisturizer and unscrewed the cap. "Why should I do that?" She scooped up a few fingers' worth of cream and began applying it on her face, making sure to always stroke upward.

"I heard they have the inside—"

"I don't want to hear it. I'm not going to help you get in with them. They're dangerous. If you fuck up, they will kill you."

"Who says I'm going to fuck up?"

"Jason, I'm serious."

"So am I. I'm sick of being treated like the fuckup in this family. Why can't you for once trust me? Huh? Why do you always got to assume I'm going to mess up?"

Because you always do. But she didn't voice that thought. She sighed. What she was sick of the most was how easily she capitulated. She always gave in because it was easier than arguing.

"Okay. Fine. I'll talk to Brian and see if Jamie is looking to add to his crew. But this is it. This is the last favor I ever do for you. Got it? And I want you to be care—"

"Thanks, sis." He hung up before she could finish.

"Goddamnit." He'd reeled her in again. She'd like to think of it as the one skill her brother had. But in truth, he got his way because she was a pushover.

❖

The house was still as Elle entered. It had a stuffy feeling, like breathing air trapped in a box all day. The fridge kicked on, humming a low monotonous tone. She grabbed a beer on her way through the kitchen, slid the screen door open, and stepped out onto the back porch. She went to the edge, which overhung the ravine, and leaned over.

Years ago, when her parents had first built the deck, the trees hadn't been so high and you could see all the way to Nelly's ravine. Now you could barely see the edge of their property.

She popped the lid and threw the cap into a long-dead fern behind her. The first half was gone before she'd even had a chance to loosen her tie.

"Worst. Day. Ever." She made a silent promise to herself to keep it together until the funeral. There were too many things to deal with before she could take the time to mourn a dead ex-boyfriend. She leaned her head back. The first star of the night blinked in the spreading indigo sky.

Back when she and Jessie were in high school, they used to sit out here all night watching the stars. If there's one thing Turlough was good for, it was stargazing.

She could see him now, lying on one of the lounge chairs, tanned from a summer of playing shirtless football, one foot looped over the side, the other resting on Elle's lounge.

"Will you still love me when I go off to college in the fall?" he'd asked.

He asked that a lot so she gave her standard response whenever she didn't want to think about her answer. "Of course. Why would you even ask that?"

He shrugged. "Shit, I don't know. Maybe some other guy will come along and one thing leads to another, you're lonely, he's hot."

"You going off to college isn't going to change anything. We'll still talk on the phone. It's not like you're leaving for the whole year."

He rolled over on his stomach and grabbed her hand, entwining his fingers with hers. "But what if I get lonely? Is it okay if I hook up with a hot football player?"

She laughed and leaned over to kiss him on the forehead. Also a standard response.

He'd been a lot of firsts for her. The first boy she'd ever dated. The first boy she'd ever kissed. The first boy she'd ever slept with and a million other firsts that were important in those early years of discovery.

They'd met in detention Elle's first day of high school. She'd shown up fifteen minutes early, thinking it would buy her points. She'd sat by herself in the empty classroom for the first thirteen minutes, worried she'd mixed up the classrooms. Then he strutted in, all swagger, dropped his backpack on the ground, and took the seat next to her. She'd gotten a whiff of outside and cigarettes and the fruity fragrance from the Jolly Rancher he was sucking on. She'd noticed him earlier in the hallway arguing with one of the science teachers. He didn't think it fair that he'd been kicked out of class for showing up ten minutes late.

"What're you in for?" he asked Elle, his stare intent like he was trying to memorize every part of her face, skin, and hair.

She shrugged, blushing. His smile got even brighter, which just made her blush deeper.

He leaned back, cupping his head in his hands, propping his feet on the desk, his eyes never leaving Elle's face. "Well, if you're wondering what I'm doing here, I told Withers he'd probably get more chicks if he kept his head up his ass instead of leaving it on his neck."

Elle laughed. "The guy's a serious dick."

If possible, his smile got bigger at the sound of her laugh. "No kidding."

Jessie stuck his hand out. "I'm Jessie."

Elle paused, looking at it, surprised at how formal he was. But she took his hand and said, "I'm Elle." It was warm and smooth. He had long, strong fingers that curled around her hand as if they'd taken possession of it.

"No talking. And get your feet off the desk." They both turned to see the science teacher Jessie had been fighting with earlier march up the aisle to the front of the classroom.

"What're you doing later? Want to come to the Maverty house? A bunch of us are meeting up later," Jessie whispered. Elle nodded, feeling a warmth of acceptance spread from the pit of her stomach to her fingertips. And that was it. That was all it had taken for Jessie Forrester to woo Elle Ashley. The truth was, she'd liked him because he liked her. He was the first boy to ever notice her, and at fourteen, that was everything.

Elle downed the last of her beer, thoughts of a shower pushing everything else out. When she stepped back into the house, EJ was standing in the kitchen, rooting through one of the cupboards. He glanced at her as if she were a potted plant. He began arranging a large bowl and jug of milk on the counter. Elle had almost passed him when he spoke.

"So thanks to you, I'm not graduating." He shook a giant box of Cap'n Crunch over the bowl.

Elle sighed. "I'm going to have a shower first, then we can have a go."

EJ slammed the milk jug down. Silky liquid arched through the spout and splashed onto the counter. "You had no right to butt in!"

"I'm sick of cleaning up your crap, EJ. I was told you wouldn't graduate if you missed any more school. You had no choice but to take detention." She yanked her tie over her head, threw it onto the nearest chair, and strode into the cramped kitchen, matching EJ's defiant stare.

"But I'm not graduating." He shoved the jug back in the fridge. "I'm stuck in summer school."

"And that's my fault?" Elle pushed a cloth from the sink into EJ's hand. "Put your big girl panties on and take some goddamned responsibility for your actions. Why were you even breaking into Randy Pritchard's trunk in the first place? Stealing? You're better than that."

"We weren't stealing. We were just getting back what was ours. Dan's. Randy stole Dan's pump from the party. We were just looking for it. That's all. Like I'd want to steal moldy jock straps."

"Did you find it?"

The heat and effort of scrubbing graffiti off the walls had melded EJ's shirt to his torso. His mop of hair hung limp, framing the scowl on his face in a red wreath. Nearly a half foot shorter, Elle glared up at him, the flush in her face matching his.

"Well?"

He shook his head. "Must have stashed it somewhere else."

"And that justifies breaking into someone's vehicle?"

"Mr. Withers totally overreacted. He hates me. And that's your fault. Why'd you have to be such a bitch in high school?" He threw the cloth back at her and stomped off to his room. The dishes sitting in the dish rack smacked together as he slammed his door shut. Within seconds, the heavy metal sounds of Slayer were screaming through the house.

Elle didn't even debate it. She ripped his door open and slammed her foot down on the power bar connected to his computer. The silence was absolute. A voluminous void. They stared at each other, panting like two bellows trying to stoke the same fire from different angles.

When Elle's breathing settled she said, "Where is all this anger coming from? You need to sit down and seriously think about why you're not graduating. And it has nothing to do with how Mr. Withers feels about me." She sank onto EJ's rumpled bed. EJ's room, with its curtains drawn and dank smells, resembled a cramped cave. The dust on the hardwood floor had recruited hair and formed armies. "He's a bitter, bitter man and his dislike of you has nothing to do with me. He hates us because of Dad." There was a mug on EJ's nightstand with mold so old the spoors had elected their first mayor. From the walls, the demented masks of Slipknot stared back.

"Dad? What did Dad do?"

Elle grabbed hold of EJ's arm and pulled him onto the bed beside her. Sitting, she still had to look up at him. He waited, skeptical.

"My first day of high school he walked up to me and said, 'So you're the oldest Ashley spawn.' And gave me detention."

"What for?"

"He said I was dressed like a 'loose woman.'"

"Were you?"

She shrugged. "Probably not on my very first day. It doesn't matter, though. He had it out for us the moment we entered that school. I was valedictorian, but the guy treated me like I cheated on every exam."

EJ kicked a discarded shirt across the floor to lie within the boundaries of his hamper. "But why? What did Dad do that made him hate us so bad?"

"Dad beat Withers out of the school superintendent job. What can I say? The guy can hold a grudge." The corner of her mouth curled into a smirk.

"Then how come he didn't get the job when Dad died?"

"Because there was a better candidate. And I'm sure he was rotten to Mr. Buchannon's kids too."

EJ glared at Elle. His eyes darkened. "Well, you sure didn't help matters." He shot off the bed and opened the door wider. "Get out."

Elle stood and moved to the door. Before leaving, she turned to EJ. "You sure as shit aren't helping by hanging around with Dan. It's like he came along and you sank to his level, which I can tell you isn't very high."

"Whatever." He slammed the door. It hit Elle in the shoulder and bounced back. He pushed with all his strength until he heard the latch catch. He flopped back onto his bed. He clasped his hands behind his head, glaring at the stains on his ceiling. Ten minutes later he heard the shower in the hall spring to life.

Neither one had wanted to take over their parents' room. It sat like a museum, untouched, leaving EJ and Elle to share the only other bathroom in the house.

As he dozed, EJ heard two loud raps at his window. He sat up, confused, just as Dan pulled himself up and through the window.

"Doesn't your sister ever complain about your room?" Dan eased himself off the ledge.

EJ shrugged. "How can she? Hers is almost as bad. What was wrong with the front door?"

Dan plopped himself down on EJ's desk chair, the only surface not overflowing with clothes. "I'm surprised she doesn't make you sanitize your hands before entering." The other night wasn't the first time Dan had ridden in the back of the sheriff's cruiser.

EJ fell back onto his bed, pushing the twisted sheets aside. "That's just for show. Can we talk about something besides my sister?"

Dan swiveled in the chair, his excitement practically gushing from him. "Did you hear what happened today?"

EJ shook his head. He wasn't in the mood to talk. But Dan couldn't contain himself. He was practically bouncing on the chair. As Dan told him about the body the sheriff's office had found earlier that day, EJ passed from excitement to dread. His eyes instinctively went to the bathroom where they could still hear the shower going. That explained the beer. He propped himself up on his bed.

"Who was it?"

Dan shrugged. "I don't know. Heard my parents talking about it. Said it was some football stud from back in the day. Won a scholarship to Georgia Tech."

And like that, EJ's mood shifted from dread to guilt. "They didn't say a name or anything?"

"No. Come on, let's go check it out. They probably still have the tape up."

"Was he a local? Did they say if he lived near here?"

Dan deflated a little at the lack of enthusiasm his news had spurred. "Fuck, man, what's your problem? He wasn't a local, they said he lived in Chicago." He nudged EJ in the arm, but EJ wasn't paying attention anymore. All his focus was on the sound of the shower running in the next room.

He hadn't been very old when they broke up, but they'd been dating for as long as EJ could remember. It was Jessie who'd always stuck up for him, against bullies, his parents, Elle. It was like having an older caring brother for a while. Jessie had even come back for the funeral. He tried reconciling with Elle after the accident, but she shut him out. Her anger and grief were absolute. He sometimes wondered what had happened to make Elle hate Jessie so much. But he knew better than to ask. If she'd wanted anyone to know she would've said.

He wanted Dan to leave. To stop talking and laughing like this was some great thing. All he wanted right now was to shut the world out and curl up into his memories. The world was better and safer in the abstract of his own thoughts. But a tiny part of him wanted to crawl into Elle's arms and have her tell him everything was going to be okay, even though he knew she didn't believe that anymore. He didn't either, really, but it would ease his guilt.

Chapter Eight

E lle heard the clinking of metal against metal as she approached the morgue located in the basement of the sheriff's office. She dragged her feet, prolonging her progress. She willed the autopsy to be over and a sheet to be covering Jessie's open body before she arrived.

A little after ten now, Elle's day had started with the soft click of EJ leaving the house before seven. The stealth was more disruptive than if he'd slammed the door. A quick run hadn't cleared her mind, nor had the scalding shower after.

Her first stop at the Collards' B&B to square off against Sandy had brought a bubble of pressure to her chest, the unmistakable sign of her heartburn returning for another bout.

Elle pulled the cruiser up behind a blue Jetta. She spied Sandy, bent over her azaleas, or what was left of them, wiping perspiration from her brow. There were pink petals strewn across the dark mulch surrounding her hedges. Someone had ripped the plants out of the ground and left them to die. New plants in black plastic containers sat along the edge.

Elle sighed as she stepped out of her cruiser. She could hear the indignant huff all the way up the drive as Sandy, covered in earth from her garden, strode toward her, her trowel grasped like a knife.

"I hope you've come to do something about this." She pointed to the mess behind her. "I came out yesterday morning to find my garden murdered." To Sandy, her garden was her life. She mothered and pampered it the way some people did their children. Lacking kids of their own, Sandy and Travis Collard put all their energies into their bed-and-breakfast.

"I've actually come about your hedges. Mr. Rutherford was up to see me yesterday." Elle shut the car door. She meant to keep the impatience out of her voice, but her sleepless night was losing the battle for her.

"That man's nerve. My hedges are fine. I had them trimmed last week." She ripped off her gloves, revealing pink nails to match her azaleas. "That man will find anything to complain about."

"It gives him pleasure." Elle nudged the cuff of her shirt to check the time without being obvious. Case began his autopsy at eight. She planned to catch him as he finished.

"Pleasure?" Sandy scowled. "What could possibly be pleasurable about complaining?" Behind her, towering above her three-story bed-and-breakfast, was the forest. The trees dappled the roof and parts of the yard with shade, and shook in the morning breeze.

Elle suppressed a smile. "It makes him feel useful." She walked over to the garden and bent to inspect the destruction. There were a few footprints in the dirt, but they were small and thin, likely Sandy's. Someone had definitely ripped the plants up on purpose. Most likely teenagers out for a night of what passed for fun in Turlough. She picked up one of the gnarled plants. It smelled of earthworms and deep soil, an ancient bouquet that reminded Elle of home and safety.

She threw the plant onto a pile and wiped her hands together, dislodging any dirt. "Stop by the office if you'd like to file an official complaint. I can't promise we'll be able to do much." She stood, brushing her pants straight, glad to be wearing a fresh uniform. "I'll put Stan on it. He can ask around. See if anyone saw something."

Sandy tramped toward the house on her left and pointed an enraged finger at Mr. Rutherford's front stoop. "I can tell you plain as day it was John Rutherford who ripped up my garden."

Elle turned toward Mr. Rutherford's house. The front stairs were equipped with an extra metal handrail. An old Chrysler sat in the driveway, one of its tires deflated from lack of use. "Sandy, the man is, like, a hundred years old. He barely has the energy to make it to the station to file his complaints. How do you expect him to rip out an entire garden without you seeing it?" She was glad of Sandy's outrage. It kept her mind from thinking of Jessie's open body a little over a mile away.

Sandy stiffened. "He had all night to do it."

Elle's patience, bored from lack of use, got up and walked out. It was at this moment Robin chose to enter the scene. She stepped onto the porch where she had an overview of the two women squaring off, Sheriff Elle Ashley towering over the sturdy Sandy Collard.

"For Christ's sake, Sandy. You can't actually expect me to believe that a ninety-eight-year-old man with arthritic knees made it into your garden in the middle of the night to tear out your plants?" She put her hands on her hips. "And why the fuck would he want to?"

Sandy stepped back and huffed. She'd never heard Elle swear before. Silence permeated the air, broken only by the morning stirrings of nesting birds. Sandy was used to getting her way. Her husband was on the city council while she served on the festival committee. They both belonged to Turlough's Business Association and went to church every Sunday. If Sandy wanted something done it was usually a matter of deciding which person to talk to. Elle had never played the same kind of politics as Bailey. She never did favors for anyone. This didn't bother most since she tended to be fair. Sandy didn't work that way. She owned the most successful B&B in three counties. Since she took over the decoration committee for the festival, everyone said it was the prettiest they'd ever seen it. Sandy Collard deserved special treatment. Without her, Turlough would be just another third-rate Podunk town. The fact that Elle wouldn't stop everything and personally investigate the matter herself was tantamount to spitting on the baby Jesus statue outside the alcove at Holy Name.

"Feel free to file a complaint. Stan will look into it." Elle turned and stomped toward her cruiser. Once inside, she sat for a moment, waiting for her hands to stop shaking and her breath to find a much more comfortable rhythm. She hated swearing in front of people. It was unprofessional. But it was so ridiculous to think Mr. Rutherford had anything to do with Sandy Collard's azaleas.

Elle's body jerked at the soft knock by her head. She turned and saw Robin watching. Her embarrassment was complete. She rolled down the window.

Robin jerked a thumb behind her at the garden. "If you want a witness, I was here the whole night. Whoever it was, they were very stealthy. Like ninjas." Her grin spread across her face, revealing two dimples. "Mind if I grab a lift into town?"

Before Elle could argue, Robin had buckled herself in and

arranged her skirt so it didn't ride up. Elle caught the hint of a garter belt. Her cruiser suddenly felt a lot more crowded as the smell of Robin's perfume invaded the car.

It took her a second to focus. "Um, Sandy said they were torn out two nights ago. Were you in town then?"

"Huh, I guess I didn't notice it when I checked in yesterday. I got in Monday morning."

If possible, Robin was even more decked out today. Her charcoal skirt and matching blouse were crisp and so clean Elle could smell the detergent from the driver's seat. It was as if she'd gone out of her way to show Elle how a professional was supposed to dress. She glanced down at her uniform, glad she'd showered and changed.

"I'm sorry," Robin said. She turned toward Elle wearing her most earnest expression. "I wasn't the most sensitive person yesterday and I can't imagine how hard this must be for you." When Elle didn't respond, she continued, "I would still love to interview you, but I understand if you need to take some time. I'll try to keep my distance."

Not sure how to take this, Elle remained silent. She pushed the speed limit as much as she dared, in hopes of dropping Robin off as soon as possible. This woman was dangerous with her dimpled smile and easy charm. If Elle wasn't careful, all her years of guarding secrets would end with a few questions from the charismatic reporter.

"Busy day?" Elle asked.

Robin nodded. "Yep, I've got an interview with your illustrious Mayor Brady this morning. Any tips?"

"Bring salt."

"Pardon?"

"I'd take everything he says with a grain of salt. That man loves to hear himself speak, and about half is bull."

"I take it you two don't get along?"

Elle took a moment to think of a response. Already she'd said too much. She didn't want Robin to think all they did was fight. "We get along fine. It's only that he's very much a politician."

"I'll keep that in mind."

As Elle opened the door to the morgue, the smell of formaldehyde wafted out, mingling in an unpleasant way with the mug of coffee she carried. She breathed an audible sigh at the white sheet covering

Jessie's body. Small pockets of red were beginning to form in strategic places like a morbid game of connect the dots.

"This isn't TV, Ken. The answers don't magically appear after half an hour." Case wiped the blood off his Stryker saw and placed it on a cart between his skull chisel and toothed forceps.

"We don't have the budget for that." Elle closed the door behind her.

Brady stood off to the side, putting distance between himself and the corpse. He held a white handkerchief over his mouth and nose. His ideas of what a morgue looked like were threatened every second he stood there.

The room was the size of a galley kitchen. Along the far left wall were two stainless steel sinks, and to the left of those, two morgue drawers. The examination table stood in the middle with a white sheet draped over the corpse. What distinguished Case's morgue from others was his collection of jars. Opposite the morgue drawers stood a floor-to-ceiling shelf covered with various-sized jars containing things found in nightmares.

To keep himself occupied, Case collected and anatomized roadkill. He displayed some of the more interesting organs on these shelves. Elle found it soothing. Case had organized the specimens by size and color, and when she stood back, there was almost an artful pattern to the arrangement.

"When will you know what killed him?" Brady asked, his voice muffled by the handkerchief.

"I can tell you right now he died from a bullet wound in his chest. Anything more than that will have to wait until we get the results back from the state lab," Case said.

Forgetting the smell, Ken dropped the handkerchief, his irritation escaping. "And when will that be?"

"They're coming by this morning. But it'll take several weeks until we get the results, if we're lucky, months if we're not." Elle finished the last of her coffee.

The closest lab, in Jackson County, was sixty-two miles from Turlough. All the evidence they had collected yesterday had been sealed and placed in the safe in Elle's office awaiting pickup by the state police. It was a rarity for the Flynn County Sheriff's Department to have dealings with the Illinois State Police. The lack of a serious crime rate and interstate highway kept the county autonomous. The staties usually didn't pick up evidence, but they'd done Elle a favor because they knew how tight her budget was.

"A couple of weeks? That's ridiculous. Can't you get them to push it through?"

Elle sighed. Keeping her voice flat she said, "And how am I supposed to do that, Ken? That kind of rush costs money." She motioned toward the door with her empty mug, her other hand on her hip. "We'll let you know when we find anything out."

As if a restraint had been lifted as soon as Brady left, Case threw back the white sheet, revealing the grotesque scene of a body half dissected. Jessie's chest cavity was spread open, exposing a pliant pink crater. Elle immediately wrenched her gaze away, finding herself eye to eye with a jar filled with the stomach pouch of a small rodent.

"I'd like to walk you through what I've found." Case pointed to some unseen place on Jessie's body.

"I'd rather it wasn't a visual presentation, if that's okay." What if this was how she pictured Jessie for the rest of her life? Like some splayed animal on a dissection tray. The only thing missing were the metal pins to hold the skin in place. Elle had seen her share of accident-mutilated bodies over the past eight years. This wasn't even comparable. It reminded her of the day she had viewed her parents' bodies. Only her parents hadn't had their chests opened like the hood of a car waiting to be inspected.

"Elle, you can't afford to be squeamish on this one." Case picked up a white hand towel from a stack near the sink and placed it over Jessie's head. "Is that better?"

Elle turned to see what he'd done. Somehow it did make it easier. She could pretend it was someone else on the table. She circled around to stand next to him.

"You told Ken he died from a bullet wound. Why would someone shoot him, then stab him a dozen times?"

"Well, that's one of the things I wanted to talk with you about. He died from a single bullet to the heart. A nine millimeter, if my guess is correct. This would indicate a clean kill. However, there was a fair amount of mutilation. His abdomen had been sliced open, revealing his lower intestines." He pointed to a small circular burn on his left shoulder.

"A cigarette burn?"

"That was my guess too. The...excavation and burn mark are much messier."

"And why mutilate someone you already shot?"

Case shrugged. "Your guess is as good a mine."

Elle took a step back. None of this made sense. "How long?"

"Did it take for him to die?"

Elle nodded.

Case covered Jessie's body. "It was very quick. I promise. Jessie didn't suffer. In fact, he had very little time to figure out what was happening to him."

"Thanks. I keep picturing him lying there all alone, staring up at that stained ceiling."

Case wrapped a hand around Elle's arm. "He was likely unconscious before he even hit the ground. And he was definitely dead before anyone used a knife on him."

"I'll find who did this. There would have been blood on their clothing, hands. There'll be evidence. We just have to find it."

Case nodded and pointed to a bag of vials and scraping samples. "Can you give these to the staties when they come? Tox screen, fingernail scrapings. I also found some blood on his hands. I swabbed to see if it matches. Might be we get lucky and it's from the attacker. Everything's labeled."

Elle nodded, grabbing the bag as she left. At the door she turned to ask, "It looks a little too personal to be random, doesn't it?"

"That's your department, Elle. I just dissect."

A patrol officer from the state police arrived at ten thirty to take possession of the evidence. Elle ushered the tall, well-built uniformed officer into her office. He whistled when he saw the safe. Elle began the arduous task of unlocking the behemoth. The two doors met in the middle with a bronze combination dial on the right door. The first set of massive doors revealed a miniature version of the outer doors. When Elle had those open she pulled at a thin silver chain around her neck holding a set of keys and unlocked one of the boxes lining the left side of the safe.

"I'd like to see someone try to break into that thing." He grinned.

"I usually leave the doors open. We don't have much worth stealing." She pulled a large Ziploc bag with evidence tape sealing the top edge. "I use it for payroll." She handed the bag over to the officer. "The safe's probably worth more than anything we keep in it. We'd be better off selling it to afford something we could actually use like new tires for our cruisers."

There was a knock on her door. Neil stuck his head in. "Cindy Forrester is here to see you."

"Thanks, Neil. Show her in." She turned to the officer. "Can you have someone call and let me know how long they figure it'll take to process all that?"

"You bet." He left, passing a petite blonde coming into the room. Neil shut her office door, giving them privacy.

Elle reached out and shook Cindy's hand. "Thank you for coming down. I can't express how sorry I am for your loss," she said. It was rote, she couldn't help herself, but she meant it more than Cindy could know.

Cindy nodded as she took a seat opposite Elle. She reminded Elle of all those sorority girls she went to college with, self-possessed and assured well beyond her age. She had a grace and sophistication Elle associated with having rich parents. As soon as she sat, her hands found each other and wrapped themselves in her lap. Her cool blue eyes stared out at Elle from beneath her rigid bangs.

Elle pulled a notepad toward her and clicked the tip of her pen. Any nervousness she felt she plunged deep into the pit of her stomach, leaving her voice strong and fluid as she began asking questions. "Do you know why Jessie was in Turlough? Or where he was staying?"

Cindy pursed her lips, coming to some conclusion in her own head. She spread her hands out. Her fingers were long and elegant. "I would have assumed if he was here he would be staying with his parents. As for why he was here, I have no idea. He didn't exactly share his travel plans with me." When she spoke, it was very soft with a slight Southern drawl.

"When was the last time you saw Jessie, Mrs. Forrester?"

Cindy inspected her hands. "A couple of days, I suppose."

"Two days?"

Cindy shook her head. "Probably three? He was very busy the last couple of months, traveling a lot, and I've been working so much. I'm putting together a new project with the Flechmann Group. I'm in charge of two different teams so it's been—" She stopped at the sound of the growing excitement in her voice. "We didn't see much of each other."

There was a tentative knock at the door. Stan poked his head in, carrying a cup of coffee in each hand. Elle waved him in. He set one on the desk in front of Cindy. "Here you go, Mrs. Forrester. Two sugars, no milk." He placed the other one in front of Elle. "Here you go, boss. Lots of milk and lots of sugar." He arranged some papers in front of her so the coffee wouldn't sit on anything important. He was like a hen, fussing over his chicks.

As soon as Stan left, Elle resumed her questions. "You said Jessie had been traveling. Do you know where? Can you be more specific?"

Cindy took a sip of her coffee. "Did you know my husband?"

Elle had been waiting for this, so she wasn't surprised. She probably should have informed the woman before beginning. She nodded. "Yes, we dated in high school."

Cindy smiled. It was abrupt but warm. "Of course. I grew up in Atlanta. I forget that everyone knows each other in these places."

Elle opened her mouth to say more, but stopped. The less information she volunteered, the better.

As Cindy sat, her hands curled around her cup of coffee, recognition suddenly spread across her face. "Elle. Elle Ashley. I didn't connect the name at first. Jessie spoke of you. Not very often, but he's mentioned you."

"It was a long time ago."

Cindy nodded but didn't say anything more. Elle decided to continue, to get this over with as soon as possible.

"Do you know of anyone who had a grudge against your husband? Anyone who would want to cause him harm?"

Cindy paused, considering the question. Her ankles were crossed right over left and tucked under her chair. Her posture was as straight as was possible in the worn wingbacks opposite Elle's desk. She gave every impression of being a woman who would have full control over her husband, yet she hadn't known where he was. "Besides the occasional client after seeing their check sans my husband's sizable commission, I can't say there would be anyone who'd want to harm him. Not seriously anyway."

"Were you two having any problems in your marriage?"

Again, she considered the question. Wondering how little or how much to tell Elle or how much relevance this had to the investigation? "I had suspected for a while that he was seeing other women. When I confronted him, he denied it. Of course. They all do. But I overheard him on the phone, a few days ago." She looked up at Elle. "Three, I guess. He was making plans to meet up with someone at a motel."

Elle stopped taking notes, her full attention on Cindy. "Did you hear which motel it was?"

Cindy shook her head. "He just said the motel."

Elle frowned and scribbled a note on a Post-it. "You're sure it was three days ago?" Cindy nodded. "And you're sure it was a woman he was speaking with?"

Cindy laughed despite the question. "I think I know my own husband's seduction voice, Sheriff Ashley. He used to use it with me." She eyed Elle as she made notes, observing the woman who had dated her husband for most of high school, wondering if he'd perfected that voice on her.

Jessie's parents had been reluctant to let her go alone to the station. Cindy insisted. But there had been something they weren't mentioning. She now realized that it was the sheriff's relationship with Jessie.

Cindy's relationship with the Forresters had always been a little strained. Early on in their marriage, Cindy made it very clear that she had been the one to make all the sacrifices. She was the one who'd moved away from her beloved Atlanta. She was the one who had to make a lateral career change. And as the marriage wore on, it was obvious these sacrifices had not been worth it.

They'd met their sophomore year in college. Jessie was on a football scholarship to Georgia Tech. Word had gotten around that he was a bit of a dog. Cindy always liked a challenge and knew it wouldn't take much to wrap Jessie around her pinkie. It had taken less than a year to get him to propose. She'd graduated with a degree in art history, but even more importantly, a husband.

"What about money? Were either of you having money problems?"

"The recession hit our savings harder than we liked. And about a year ago I switched jobs, so I'm not making as much as I used to." She smiled as if to say it wasn't her fault but the economy's. "But I think, because Jessie was in real estate, it was worse on him. He didn't want me to know, but he'd cashed in some bonds recently."

Elle made a note. For the first time in the interview, Cindy appeared upset. Elle got the impression that she was more worried about money than her husband being dead. "Do you know why Jessie wouldn't want to stay with his parents if he was visiting Turlough?"

Cindy shook her head as she eyed her hands, watching as they twisted into a puzzle.

Chapter Nine

The large overhead fan did little to drown out the voice of Ken Brady, who was reciting his campaign promises with the eloquence of an evangelist. Across from Brady's expansive desk sat Robin, a notepad on her lap. She glanced at the wall clock behind Brady's head: five after twelve. Robin's stomach gurgled.

There were no windows in the room. The air was stifling. An electric fan sat on the credenza behind Brady, blowing so hard it was flipping his golden hair into a frenzy.

Robin raised her pen to interrupt and waved it back and forth like a surrender flag. "Actually, Ken, I'm going to stop you there. I'm more interested in getting a little background information on Sheriff Ashley."

Brady stopped mid-sentence, lips pursed. People didn't usually interrupt him. With his face scrunched up, he said, "Well, what do you want to know?" He had been aware of the connection between the reporter's attention span and the length of his tirades on the voting practices of the city council.

"What was she like growing up? What kind of impact did she have in the community? Are there any interesting anecdotes that you can share? That sort of thing." As an afterthought, she asked, "Has she always been this stubborn?"

Brady started nodding his head slowly, sitting forward. "Yes, she's always been this stubborn. As for the other questions, I didn't grow up in Turlough, so I'm not the best person to talk to about when she was younger." He smoothed out his tie, trying to visualize a younger Elle with difficulty.

"What about her now? Can you shed some light on that?" Robin flipped to a spare page of her notebook. She'd been in Brady's office for over an hour and had yet to glean anything useful from the man.

"What's she like now? You mean besides stubborn?" He pulled his gray patterned tie through his fingers, feeling the soft fabric caress his skin while he thought of an answer. Brady's dealings with Elle had been an odd mixture of public professionalism and private exasperation. In public, they presented what they thought was a solid front with shared opinions and policies, but privately they couldn't be further apart.

"I don't know what you want me to tell you." Brady shrugged. "Professionally, she's competent. A bit of a hothead, but she gets things done."

"She's kind of young to be sheriff." From the moment Robin had spotted Neil she wondered why Elle was sitting in her own office and this man was answering the phones. She didn't care if it was sexist or ageist. This was a small town, and from her experience, they took longer to catch up with the rest of the world.

"Before Sheriff Bailey died, he let it be known he wanted Elle to succeed him, even though Neil had seniority. She's young, sure, but Neil's got a bit of a Barney Fife thing going on. Then there's the whole Chuck Dell fiasco."

"Chuck Dell?"

Brady paused for effect, back in his element. "First off, Chuck Dell was an asshole. When he was alive, he ran this town. He owned the brickworks before it got shut down, which put an end to any economic value this city had. He ran the diner and a bunch of other small businesses. Almost everyone owed him something." Brady reached back and poured himself a glass of water. Robin waved off Brady's offer to pour her one too. She didn't want this to take any longer than it had to. Brady took a restoring sip, cleared his throat, and began again.

"When his wife died without giving him a son, he started shopping it around that he was looking for someone to marry his Tully. But they had to be willing to take her name. It was all very hush-hush." Which of course meant everyone in Turlough had heard about it from several different people. "And, of course, this was long before women started keeping their own names and all that hyphenation bullshit." He waved his hand around like the thought of a woman keeping her name was infecting the air around them. Brady leaned his chair back, relaxing into the story.

"Then Neil steps forward, but not without conditions. He wanted a cash settlement. A large one. Well, as you can imagine, Dell didn't like it. He may have been the tightest millionaire in the Midwest. I swear to God, you had a better chance of getting a horse to climb a tree than getting five bucks out of Chuck Dell. I remember this one time, I don't know how much of the city you've seen, but behind the main strip there's a whole other street with a bunch of two-story houses."

Robin looked up at the clock behind Brady. She debated whether any of this was worth her time.

"Back in the day, Dell owned all that, he'd rent them out to brickwork families—"

"I'm going to stop you right there." She waved her pen in front of him like a matador getting a bull's attention. "Does this story have any relevance to what we were talking about?"

Ken blinked. "Relevance?"

Robin smiled. It was a dangerous smile. She only used it when she was sick of someone's bullshit and was about to put them in their place. She wondered if anyone in this town ever stood up to the man. Or told him to shut up. "Relevance, as in, is this story you're about to tell have anything to do with the sheriff?" Or more likely, is it going to have some spin that paints you in the best possible light?

"Well, not specifically. It was more an offshoot of the story about Neil and how much money he suckered out of Dell."

"So how much money did Neil get?"

"Who knows. But in the end, Dell paid. I guess he figured it was a sound investment because Neil Tomey became Neil Dell." He laughed next, slapping his knee. "And to make the whole thing hilarious, Tully found out she can't have kids. So, in the end, that bastard wasted all that money and never ended up with an heir after all." Brady smacked his lips as if this piece of gossip had been a delicious meal. Robin didn't find it all that funny. She was about to get up and leave. This had been a huge waste of her time. And then a thought occurred to her. Maybe it wouldn't be a waste of time after all.

"Neil had set himself up as a man with a price. That kind of thing runs sour with people. They don't want a sheriff that can be bought. Not to mention a man willing to take a woman's name, now that's a whole other thing."

"So what can you tell me about Jessie Forrester?"

Brady leaned forward. "Who's that?"

"The man they found murdered in that abandoned house outside of town."

Brady frowned. The gesture created very few lines. "Was that his name? Why would you want to know about him?"

Robin imagined Brady was the sort who would rather lie than admit there was a problem. He was that guy on the *Titanic* who told everyone to go back to their rooms. "I heard he used to date Sheriff Ashley. I just thought it would add a poignant element to the story." Robin wasn't above a little lying.

Brady began shaking his finger at Robin before she'd even finished. "No, this isn't going to be that type of story. You're writing a tourism piece."

Robin flipped her notebook shut and placed it in her bag. She stood and smiled gamely. Now it would be worth it. "I came down here to get a story and I found a great one. I don't really care that it's not the one you want me to write."

A few seconds passed before Brady could speak. He braced his hands against the armrests of his chair. "Well, we'll just see what your editor has to say about this."

"Go ahead. I've already spoken to him. He loves the new angle." She wasn't worried he'd ever get in touch with her editor.

"Angle?" Brady's face went pale. "You can't write about the murder. People will get the wrong idea."

Robin strode to the door and placed her hand on the handle. "Thanks for your time."

"Turlough is not a dangerous place."

Robin opened the door while still facing Brady. "It's been a pleasure." And left. The look of horror on his face as she did was worth the hour of her life he'd wasted.

❖

A smoky haze hugged the main strip of Turlough in a late afternoon embrace, choking the life out of the peach blossoms hanging limp along the boulevard. The thickness of it deadened any sound within arm's length.

The midday sun beat down on Dan as he ran the rubber tip of

his Chucks through the dirt. His gaze drifted down the main strip. He cleared his throat and horked into the dirt.

"Gross," Tanya said. She was sitting next to him on the curb, trying to replicate the same aloofness as Dan and EJ.

"It's just a little snot. You probably swallow a jug of it every day." Dan leaned toward her, letting a glob of mucus dangle from his lips. The sheen of the sun gave it a glazed appearance. Before it could fall, he sucked it back up into his mouth.

Tanya pushed Dan away. "That's disgusting."

"Yum." Dan grinned to show the picket fence of teeth in his mouth.

EJ leaned back, turning his face skyward. He let the afternoon bathe him in its warm glow. Even with his eyes closed, the sun painted his lids red. Like this, he could imagine he was somewhere else, anywhere but here in Turlough. Every spare thought he focused on one thing: getting the hell out of this shit-ass town. The second he drove past the boundaries of Flynn County, freedom would course through him. It would well up inside him like a geyser preparing to erupt. In his mind, he could see the towering skyscrapers of Chicago, feel their looming shade. He would get a job as an apprentice in a mechanic's shop. And once he was out, there would be no putting him back. He wouldn't return for anything, not like Elle.

A piercing squeal shattered the peace, followed by an exuberant "Dan!"

EJ opened his eyes to see Lisa, Dan's little sister, making her way up the sidewalk toward them. She did a half skip and sped up as soon as she saw the threesome sitting on the curb.

Dan's grin moved to a softer position as he spotted her skipping toward them. He waved and got up to meet her halfway.

Lisa was only a year younger than Dan. When she approached, Dan slouched to give her a big, affectionate hug. She was wearing a simple dark blue checkered dress that stopped above her knees. She twirled for Dan to admire.

"That's a pretty dress you're wearing. What are you doing all the way downtown?"

Lisa grinned. She had the same wide-mouthed smile as Dan, only hers created two dimples in her cheeks above the corner of her lips. "Mom said I could have an ice cream. She said I was big enough to come all by myself." At seventeen she had the appearance and demeanor of a ten-year-old. It was unlikely she would mature beyond her early teens. Lisa pulled out a bright pink velvet wallet from a purse hanging on her shoulder by a thin blue strap. She opened it to show three crisp dollar bills. Dan took the wallet from her and placed it back in her purse.

"Your ice cream is on EJ and me today. Wait here with Tanya and we'll go get everyone something slurpy." He didn't have to ask which was her favorite. Her loyalty to mint chocolate chip hadn't wavered since the age of five.

"Tanya? What flavor do you want?" EJ asked, but she shook her head no.

Tanya waved at Lisa and patted a spot on the curb next to her. Lisa flipped her braid behind her shoulder. Her hair was the same butterscotch color as Dan's. Fine strands poked out of her braid in spots. Her dark brown eyes followed Dan as he strolled away.

It was cool inside the pink-walled shop. The fans lining the ceiling rotated at full. They sucked and blew at the napkins anchored with a large scoop to the sprinkles counter. Along the far corner, a glass-lined counter displayed a plethora of choices. They varied from simple chocolate all the way to delectable caramel-veined moose tracks.

Dan strolled up to the counter and ordered a single scoop of mint chocolate chip and a sugar cone with strawberry for himself. EJ peered through the glass at the rows of ice cream tubs. He hated this part. He always worried he'd make the wrong choice. What if he ordered chocolate but then Dan's enjoyment made him want strawberry? Or Lisa's mint chocolate chip? He sighed as he looked over the flavors. He could try something completely new, but if he hated it, that would be an entire waste.

Dan stood off to the side, waiting, secretly enjoying his friend's discomfort. Dan's philosophy was simple. If he always chose strawberry, then he never knew what he was missing in other flavors. EJ started biting his thumbnail, sweating over which one to choose. The shop only allowed two taste tests to stop teenagers from gorging on samples.

Finally, he pointed at butterscotch ripple. "I'll get one scoop in a regular cone," he said, then immediately his face contorted and he shouted, "Wait. No. Rocky road in a sugar cone."

The attendant paused, well familiar with EJ Ashley and his second thoughts. "You sure? You don't want to try them both?"

EJ shook his head. "I feel good about rocky road."

When they exited the shop, a group of boys stood surrounding Lisa and Tanya, jeering and laughing. Dan recognized Randy Pritchard's expansive back. The number fifty-one, stretched across the orange Bears jersey, bookmarked by his jutting shoulder blades. Three of his teammates flanked the girls. The shortest, with a Marine haircut, yanked Lisa's purse from her shoulder. This started a new ripple of laughter that echoed down the street toward Dan and EJ.

In less time than it took to think it through, Dan crossed the gap between them and tapped Randy on the shoulder. He had to reach up to account for Randy's height. When Randy turned around, Dan shoved his strawberry ice cream cone into the middle of the lazy smile on Randy's face.

❖

Elle leafed through the autopsy report spread open on her desk, making notes every now and then on a pad. It was quickly filling with black strokes and small diagrams.

She rubbed her eyes, working in circular motions to dislodge the image of Jessie's blank eyes staring at the ceiling. She leaned back in her chair and pulled her hair elastic out, sliding her hands through her hair, trying to smooth a headache that gripped her roots. The stains on the ceiling stared back, benign and ordinary. They didn't belong in this world. Just like Jessie didn't belong in a world of guns and violence. He belonged to her past where even her worst memories had become nostalgic over the years.

The first time she'd ever sat in this office, seated across from a silent Sheriff Bailey, was with Jessie. He'd caught them smoking pot at the Maverty house.

"Are you going to call my dad?" asked Elle, sitting on the edge of her chair. She'd been dating Jessie for three weeks but hadn't told her parents yet, afraid they'd think she was too young and ban her from seeing him.

Bailey tucked his lips in, forcing his cheeks to puff out. It was a look she'd grow to know well. His brooding face she used to call it. He sat like that for several minutes, eyeing the two of them. Elle fidgeted with the buttons in the armrest while Jessie sat stone-faced, staring at the ceiling.

"Hey, Mac," Bailey called to the outer offices. "Take the Forrester kid down to the basement, will you?"

"What?" Elle jumped up from her chair and turned to see as Mac sauntered into the office. The basement. That's where the cells were. "What are you going to do to him? Are you arresting us?" Her voice was near panic. The effects of the joint they'd smoked earlier had dissipated but left a lingering paranoia.

Bailey waved her down. "Relax, will you? I'm not arresting anyone just now." He pointed a finger at her. A warning. Elle sat back down, cowed. Her eyes never left Jessie, whose arm was forced into Mac's iron grip and hauled out of Bailey's office. She didn't turn around again until the door to the basement shut with a loud clunk. They stared across his desk at each other for several minutes. Bailey sucked his lips in and frowned, pinching his face together. Elle's heart pumped so hard she thought it would burst through her sternum.

Finally, Elle asked, "What's going to happen to us?"

Bailey pushed himself forward on his chair and leaned his elbows on his desk. "Your dad's going to be here any second."

"What?" Elle turned back to the door, all the heat in her body drained out. He'd kill her if he knew she'd been pulled into the station. She'd been doing drugs. With a boy. An older boy. In a deserted house her parents had specifically told her to stay out of.

"Calm down, will you?" Bailey couldn't stand hysterics. "I called him to come take you home. He doesn't have to know about the Forrester kid, but he knows about the other stuff." He pointed a beefy finger at her. A sure sign a but was coming. "But this is your only get-out-of-jail-free card. Your dad's a good guy. I don't want to see him worry about what his daughter's up to. And you. You're a smart girl. Don't let that boy take you places you don't want to go." He leaned back, the chair squeaking under his bulk. The way he kept her gaze she knew he wasn't talking geography.

Elle almost vomited when her dad stomped through the door, livid.

"Dad, I—"

"Get in the car."

"But I—"

"Now!"

The drive home that night was the worst of Elle's life. Her dad had always been a boisterous guy, but when he got mad the volume went up by the power of ten. By the time they pulled in the driveway she was sure everyone in Turlough had heard at least a part of his tirade.

Her parents had grounded her for two weeks.

That night was a catalyst. It set in motion a trend that would continue for the next four years. She'd snuck out every night during those two weeks, proving to herself or her parents—she wasn't sure which—that they couldn't contain her. Would things have been different if they hadn't gotten caught? If they'd left with everyone else that night? Instead of lingering? Would she have traveled down the destructive path that led here?

The more she thought about it, the more everything seemed interconnected. It stemmed from that one moment. That fight was the first of many. The tighter the leash, the harder she struggled against it. By her sophomore year, Bailey'd pulled her into his office a dozen more times. Each time they'd stare across at each other, waiting for her father to show up. And each time it was the same thing, only by then Elle had found her voice and learned to scream back.

She'd chosen criminology to piss her dad off. She knew it would cause the most arguments. Why couldn't she do something productive, what would a degree in criminology do? Make her a better criminal?

While most of the kids from her graduating class were finding jobs at gas stations and grocery stores, she had a partial scholarship to college. But nothing was ever good enough, everything was cause for an argument.

Even now, she felt the connection to that night. If they hadn't gotten caught would she still be sitting behind this desk?

And if she hadn't helped Jessie, would he still be dead?

Neil burst into her office, his chest heaving against the buttons of his uniform. Sweat had pooled at the edge of his thinning hairline, ready for the slalom down his face. "Fight. Down the street," he called as he raced back out. Elle was close behind. "Six boys, from the high school most likely. It's getting dirty." He punctuated each line by an intake of breath.

Neil was out the door first, but Elle, fit from a daily routine of morning runs, outpaced him, reaching the fray first.

A few stores up from the sheriff's office, a crowd had gathered. Some cheering, others quietly enjoying the entertainment. Elle knew by the size of the crowd how much time had passed. She pushed through the throng, pulled short as she spotted EJ discarded on the asphalt. His ball cap was knocked to the side, revealing his red curly hair. A gash along the side of his face was caked in dirt. The soft rise of his chest told her he was still breathing. She pushed through toward the fight, leaving him until later.

Robin, having stepped out of the mayor's office, saw a streak of red dart into the middle of the clash. She joined a couple of late stragglers.

"Enough," Elle yelled. It came out muffled as she pressed herself between Randy and Dan. She thrust both arms against their chests, trying to act as a crowbar and pry them apart. Before Elle could separate them, someone knocked her from behind. She stumbled face-first toward one of Randy's powerhouse fists. The mob seemed to pause, waiting for the crack of bone on bone, but she managed to duck out of the way and miss the full force. It struck the edge of her jaw, sending her back. Robin squeezed herself between two spectators to get a front-row seat when Elle slammed backward into the crowd. She caught Elle under her shoulders. Elle felt warm beneath the thin cotton of her uniform. When she turned back, her eyes caught hold of Robin's, then her muscles flexed and she pulled away. It had only been an instant, but Robin could still feel the heat on her hands.

Robin watched from the edge of the ring as Elle dove back in, reckless, oblivious. She kicked the back of Dan's left knee, forcing him down. Reaching around, she put him into a choke hold and shoved him face first into the ground. As she did this, Neil came up behind Randy with the same move, only he used his baton to add some height to his reach around Randy's thick neck.

As the brawl came to an end, the crowd surged forth like a wave trying to mount a levee. As she was jostled, Elle felt something sharp bite into her lower back near her right side. But she kept her hands and attention firmly on Dan's arms as she subdued him.

After the calm of the hazy afternoon returned, and as Neil escorted the boys toward the station, Elle knelt to examine EJ. She brushed the mop of hair away from his face. He was still out cold. His lip was cut and he had the beginnings of a bruise on his jawbone. The blood from the cut on his cheek was beginning to congeal. She rolled him onto his back and lifted his shirt to check for any stab marks. As she ran her hands along his ribs to see if any were broken, he jerked awake.

They stared at each other for a long moment, their fight momentarily forgotten as the concern in Elle's eyes registered the fear in EJ's.

There was a soft whimper behind Elle. Lisa had tucked herself into the crowd like a rabbit in a cave. As the crowd dispersed, she was left out in the open.

CHAPTER TEN

Elle paced the row of chairs opposite the reception desk where Randy, Dan, and EJ sat. A mar of browning blood, dried spit, and seeping sweat covered each.

A scuffed Randy shot out of his chair toward Dan. Elle wedged herself between the two, shoving Randy back into his seat.

"Enough. Dan, in my office. Now." She nodded to Neil sitting behind Heather's desk to keep watch on Randy and EJ.

Once she shut the door and sat behind her desk, she switched tactics. "I think it's sweet, Dan, the way you stick up for Lisa. But you can't use that as an excuse to pick a fight on a past grudge." Elle uprooted scattered pages and folders, searching for a hair elastic.

The smirk on Dan's face had spread to include his eyes as he watched Elle try to tame her hair behind her head. "Family's important." The way he was staring at her made Elle feel exposed like she had taken off more than an elastic band. She shifted. That spot in her shoulders tightened into a knot that would only get worse by the end of the day.

"This is something that, unfortunately, Lisa will have to deal with for the rest of her life. On some level. And when you react the way you do, it scares her." Elle leaned forward. "It also doesn't help her deal with her issues herself."

"Issues? She has Down syndrome. That's not issues. That's life. Sometimes it sucks, sometimes I got to stick up for her." Dan leaned back in the stiff wingback. "Sometimes the things we do aren't so pretty. But over time, when you approach it from a different angle, you can see it's the right thing."

"That's not how it works." Elle shook her head. "We don't always get to choose how others see our actions."

"Like you, for instance." Dan picked at the webbing on his torn jeans. "The benevolent Sheriff Ashley. Acting for our benefit when you bust up a party. Or pull someone over for a busted taillight."

Elle sighed. She struggled with this every time she came upon mischief and EJ in the middle of it. The first time she showed up to a noise complaint after becoming sheriff, she knocked on the door and there was EJ. He had a beer in one hand, a cigarette in the other, and a party full of underage drinkers behind him. It meant she had to pick a side. Too tough or too lenient, just to prove she wasn't playing favorites. She resented him for it.

"I can't be EJ's sister when I sit here. I have a larger responsibility than to myself." She stood, trying to dislodge the knot forming in her back. Her fingers found the key to the safe around her neck. She began sliding it along the tough chain in a practiced motion. "A sheriff doesn't have a family. Or friends. Not on the job."

Dan leaned back, a laugh in the back of his throat. "You know, if it becomes too much for you, no one would judge you for stepping down. It's hard being put in the middle like this." Dan had this way of making people feel small as if it were a game to see how tight a package he could wrap you in.

Underage drinking, the occasional brawl after the Beer and Berry festival, that was what she dealt with. Sometimes she'd bring in a good ole boy who'd had a few too many at Finnegan's. She'd spend a couple of minutes swatting away wandering hands before sliding them into the back of her cruiser. More time the next morning fielding sheepish apologies. There was never any paperwork. There was no need to keep records. But ever since finding Jessie, things felt different. This felt different. Dangerous. As if Turlough had been covered in his blood and everything had become tainted.

"I, for one, have always thought you were more of a big-city girl." His smirk shifted to a leer as his eyes met hers.

Elle rubbed the back of her neck, exhausted and dejected. She was sure Bailey never had to deal with this shit. There was something about Bailey that had demanded instant respect. Perhaps it was because he'd spent so long playing the game people knew what they were getting.

Elle was still an unknown. When it came down to it would she side with the good ole boys and maintain the status quo? Or would she become a liability? One of those liberals with too much education and not enough of the right kind of perspective.

When she opened her eyes, her stare hardened. "Dan, I want you to stay away from Randy Pritchard. I know my words won't even make a dent in that thick fucking head of yours, but if you don't, I swear to God I'll make sure you regret that decision."

The laugh in the back of Dan's throat escaped, loud and dangerous. He leaned forward, gripping the edge of her desk and smiled. "Hard-ass suits you, Sheriff Ashley."

❖

After the dust had cleared and calm was restored to the sheriff's office, Elle shut herself in the only bathroom. At first, she thought she'd come to have a good meltdown. But the anger and defiance in her reflection put it on hold. The last two days had carved frescos on her face, etching the corner of her mouth into hard lines and allowing shadowing to crop up under her eyes. The pall of her skin left the motif unfinished, almost like the painter had forgotten to color in the details.

And now at the corner of her mind, something flickered. A forgotten moment. Something she'd meant to come back to. She reached around and untucked her uniform shirt, feeling underneath. There was a sharp pain. When she pulled her hand around it was covered in blood. She unbuttoned her shirt and turned around to examine her back in the mirror. Along the lower edge was a deep gash. The neatness of the cut made her think knife. Which meant at some point near the end of the fight someone had taken a swipe into the foray. Had it hit its mark or missed? Was this the same knife that had cut up Jessie's torso? A million more questions rushed into her head as she stared at her reflection in the cracked, moldy mirror.

Without warning, the door opened. Neil paused, his hand already on his fly. Elle froze, too shocked to be mad. It had finally hit her. For the first time, Elle realized that someone among them might have murdered Jessie. As much as she wanted to believe that it had something to do with his life in Chicago, what if it didn't? She looked up at Neil more for comfort than denial, but he didn't seem to understand what the worry in her eyes meant.

Instead, he said, "You need to go to the hospital."

The closest hospital was in Rosiclare, about a twenty-five-minute drive from Turlough. Flat and unimaginative, Hardin County General Hospital had been set down in the middle of Shawnee National Forest like a flagstone dropped onto a lawn. To the right of the drive, some battered tarmac with a faded red cross indicated the helipad. Weeds had pressed through the cracks, announcing their determination to exist. Outside the emergency room, an old man with thick-framed glasses sat on his walker, coughing through a smoke. On any given day there would be five or six battered pickup trucks, in various stages of life, parked outside, the owners inside nursing wounds ranging in severity. Robin pulled up beside Elle's cruiser and hoped out.

She'd been passing the sheriff's office when she'd seen Neil wrestling Elle into her cruiser. Curious, she'd followed.

What Robin had seen was only the end of the bout. There had been a row back at the sheriff's office with Elle taking on both Neil and Stan. There was no way she needed to visit emergency. In the end, her own policy defeated her. Policy required all injured officers to seek medical attention no matter how small. Establish policy was one of the first things Elle had done when she took over as sheriff. Policy was a foreign word to Flynn County under the supervision of Sheriff Bailey. As much as she loved the man, he had been somewhat lax when it came to rules. Elle had discovered early on what sorts of things could handle policy and the types of things that couldn't. Keeping track of how many sweat it off in the basement cell, for instance, could be left to the imagination. Her deputies and those under her supervision, however, would take on policy. The very first policy Elle put in place was to ensure there was a deputy on call in the county at all times.

Robin entered the emergency waiting room and plopped down next to Elle. "Why is it that police officers always hate hospitals?"

"What're you doing here?"

"I thought you could use a little company." Robin looked around the waiting room. The room itself was the size of a large cubicle, the admitting nurse behind a desk at one end and a clump of chairs at the other. Elle sat beside her in a hard and uncomfortable chair.

"There are a million other things I'd rather be doing with my time," she said. She shifted the gauze the admitting nurse had given her to stanch the bleeding. She folded it one size smaller. The air smelled septic, ominous, as if the bleach was holding something at bay, stopping whatever would seep out of the walls from consuming her. Incongruous with the smell was a poster of Mickey Mouse with a message reminding hospital staff to always wash their hands after using the bathroom. "Filing taxes, having an appendectomy done by a first-year med student, awaiting trial, being interviewed by you..." Elle trailed off, too bored to continue. "Don't you have anywhere else to be right now?"

"Nope."

The fan above drowned out the cicadas from outside, licking at the crisped magazines piled on a side table next to Elle. She flipped through the top magazine, then tossed it back onto the vintage pile.

There were two other people in the waiting room ahead of them. One was a farmer who had accidentally severed his middle finger above the knuckle. He sat calmly, his eyes examining the cracked floor tiles at his feet, his detached digit neatly wrapped in a handkerchief with the corners folded over in his lap. It looked as if his wife had packed him a lunch. The other was an old man with a walker, who looked as if he was suffering from chronic gout. He'd rolled his left trouser leg up above his swollen ankle.

"So who's your favorite front-runner for this murder?" Robin switched the position of her legs. Her charcoal skirt was still as crisp as it had been that morning.

Elle gave her a scathing look.

"I'm getting this vibe that you don't want to talk to me right now."

"Come up with that on your own, did you?"

Behind the front desk, the admitting nurse hooked a stack of folders under her arm and carried them to a giant filing cabinet in the corner. Each one had a name in bold black Sharpie across the flap. She flipped through them, expertly shuffling them into alphabetical order. Beyond her, the door to the main hospital wing stood closed, no sound, no sign of life.

"Why aren't the state police involved in the investigation?"

Elle wondered if she was trying to goad her into becoming defensive, a dig at her small-town experience, or more likely she was trying to get her to reveal more than she wanted. She shrugged. "Haven't you ever worked the crime beat?"

"I did. But this small-town stuff is a whole new beast."

They sat for a few more moments listening to the hum of the lights above.

"Why won't you just tell me? It's not like I can't google it later. Besides, I'm not asking anything specific about the investigation." She searched around the room until her gaze landed on the poster of Mickey. "Okay, let's say for instance that you went out to the Maverty house and found Mickey Mouse murdered. How would that investigation go?"

Elle shifted the gauze, folding it and replacing it on her back. She was stalling, trying to find a way to phrase it without revealing too much. "Well, if Mickey were murdered out at the Maverty house, if Turlough had a police force, they would investigate."

"But they don't have a police force."

Elle shook her head. "I should have phrased that as, if Turlough could afford a police force. The county's so small the sheriff's office acts as the city's force. However, even if it did have a force, as sheriff I would have been called in to consult. Technically speaking, sheriff has jurisdictional control within the county."

"So it's just you?"

"Mostly, yes. But we don't get a lot of murders in Flynn County. In this case—the case of Mickey being found murdered," she added, almost forgetting not to talk about the case, "I would consult with the SPI for forensics and database help."

"SPI?"

"Each state has its own bureau of investigation. They're like the state version of the FBI. Back in the seventies, Illinois merged the bureau with the state police to form the State Police Operations Division, SPI. Am I boring you yet?"

"Not yet." She smiled. "So you'd consult with them to see why someone would want to murder Mickey?"

"We don't have the kind of resources they have, so I would send any forensic evidence as well as blood work, fingerprints, that sort of thing to get help with processing. The only problem is, we're not much of a priority to them, so it takes a long time to get anything back. If this were a series of murders, then that would be a different story."

"And if it does become a series, say someone killed Pluto too?"

"Mickey's dog?" Elle almost laughed. "As bad as animal cruelty is, the most you'll get in Illinois is a thirty-day jail sentence and a twenty-five-hundred-dollar fine."

"We're talking about a mouse and now you're picky about a dog being considered human enough to be murdered?"

"Mickey could talk."

"Fine. What if Goofy were murdered too?"

"Isn't Goofy a dog too?"

Robin pointed a finger at her. "Ah, but he talks." Winning by her logic.

Elle shrugged one shoulder, too tired to debate the semantics of cartoon animals. "Then the state police would send in a detective to first determine if they were required. If they were, then they would open a joint investigation. We don't have a lot of experience with this sort of thing, to begin with."

"When was the last time you investigated a murder?"

"Me?" Elle shook her head. "I've never investigated a murder. Come to think of it, I think the last murder we had in the county, Bailey had just become a deputy." She thought back. Her father must have told her the story a million times. "Thomas Rakely. Shot to death by his wife with his own shotgun while their son watched from under his bedroom door. A god-awful mess, according to Bailey."

"That's the previous sheriff?"

Elle nodded. "The whole town was in an uproar because Rakely was superintendent. That's like a mayor in an unincorporated town. He apparently had been breaking rule number one: Don't sleep with your secretary."

"Ah, I've heard that's an important rule."

"That's why it's number one."

"What happened then?"

Elle turned to her. "She got off on an inventive use of the Second Amendment."

"The right to bare arms?"

"Her lawyer claimed she thought it was a burglar she was shooting.

My dad was always really interested in trial law. He used to sit in on all the civil cases. He was too young, he said, to remember much. But what he did remember was how it polarized the town. Everyone took sides. People practically walked around with buttons saying 'him' or 'her.'"

"You don't believe in the Second Amendment?"

"Not when it's an excuse for murder." Elle shook her head, trying to picture what it would have been like to live here in 1967. "I can't imagine how anyone could side with a murderer. It amazes me how quick people are to jump to violence to solve something and justify it, like they deserve it because they screwed up. We make mistakes. People make mistakes. It's what makes us human. Unlike every other animal, we don't run simply on instinct."

"But isn't murder a mistake?"

Elle's head whipped around fast. She stared at Robin, gauging whether she was serious or not. "Murder isn't a mistake. It's a crime."

"But still, it's a mistake. You can be sorry after."

"It doesn't change the fact that you killed someone. It's not something you can erase with a simple apology. It's forever. Adultery doesn't justify murder."

"But isn't adultery the number one rule you don't break? I'm confused now, Sheriff Ashley." She was half smiling, an uneven grin tugging at the corner of her eyes. "Can adultery be erased with a simple apology? When you think about it, it is the ultimate betrayal."

Elle exhaled between tight lips. She shifted in her seat, trying to find a comfortable angle without leaning back. "I would think murder the ultimate betrayal. But that's just me." Her mouth was dry. Her tongue felt like it had swelled, sticking to every surface of her mouth at once. She wanted out of this chair, out of this hospital, but mostly out of this conversation.

"I don't know." Robin leaned back. "Haven't you ever been cheated on?" She caught Elle's eye and something there made Robin ask, "Or been the one to do the cheating?"

The cicadas outside quieted as if to hear her response. On the outside, the mood was like a corpse, an eternal pause, but inside the room buzzed. Elle could feel the heat of her blood as it reached the surface of her skin. The follicles of her arm hair sizzled with electricity, reaching out, dying to escape. Her breath felt bottled up. She wanted to push it out in one long gasp, but she tightened up. "I'm not sure which is worse, that you asked the question, or that you're expecting an answer."

Robin shrugged. In her mind, Elle had already answered the question.

The admitting nurse snatched another pile of file folders off the desk and started toward the filing cabinet. Halfway there a single piece of paper slid out of a folder. She stopped to look, then, like a dam with a crack, a cascade of white fell from beneath her arm. Each one struck the floor and curled up, caught by the circling fan above. The contents of her folders scattered, carpeting the floor in white and pink and yellow. A rainbow of triplicates. The farmer, a proper gentleman with more manners than common sense, stooped to help pick up the mess, forgetting both the handkerchief holding his middle finger and the blood-soaked rag wrapped around the other half still attached to his hand. As he reached to collect a pink form that had landed at his steel toes, the package on his lap slipped off.

The door to the main hospital wing opened and a young nurse in light green scrubs stepped out with a clipboard. "Jackson Culpepper?" she said, then looked up. The room had become a tableau: the farmer stopped mid-grab, trying to decide which to go for, the form or his finger; Elle reaching down to help, her right hand still holding the gauze tightly to her back; the admitting nurse on hands and knees, scooping up folders.

"Pamela, is everything okay?"

The admitting nurse waved her off. "Just a filing mishap. Nothing I can't sort out." She then turned to the farmer. "Mr. Culpepper, please retrieve your finger and follow Nurse Parks."

Jackson Culpepper had always done very well with instructions. He reached past the form, picked up his bundled finger, and straightened up to follow the nurse into the hospital with one swift movement. Nurse Parks let him past, then turned back to the room. "Actually, Sheriff Ashley, why don't you come too. I'm sure Dr. Crawford will want to see you."

Robin stood to join her, but Nurse Parks shook her head with practiced pity. "Just patients beyond here. You can have a seat." She nodded to the row of chairs and was gone.

CHAPTER ELEVEN

It was dark before Elle made it back to the sheriff's office. As she hung up the phone with the motel in Mason, Elle realized she hadn't eaten all day. She felt light-headed. And what had started out as a sharp itch on her lower back had now blossomed into a full explosion of pain. The numbing agent the doctor had used was wearing off. Instead of concentrating on the case, the pain in her right side was all she'd been able to think about for the past hour. The only thing she wanted to do was down two or three of those painkillers Dr. Crawford had prescribed and curl up in oblivion for the next ten hours.

Neil shoved his head in the door and rapped on the doorjamb. "You ready for us?"

Elle waved him in. A few seconds later Stan followed with three mugs of coffee balanced on his clipboard, which he handed out before sitting down.

Elle pulled out a folder and opened it to reveal a stack of photos. A series of thin white lines ran along the bottom of each indicating they'd come from the basement printer. It was an ancient clunker shoved into a small storage room in the back next to the morgue, which also served as Case's office. "I won't keep you guys long. I just want to catch everyone up on what we have so far." She didn't add that it wasn't much or that she felt it was more likely they'd find Jimmy Hoffa's body than get an arrest for this. She thought it best to deal with the facts.

"According to Jack's autopsy report, the victim was killed by a single bullet wound to the heart. The body was mutilated and there was a single stab wound just above the opening of the abdomen. Jack was able to get the outline of the hilt of the knife." She sighed, took a sip of her coffee, and continued. "Of course, that's useless if we can't find the weapon to compare it to." She flipped through a couple of the pictures and passed two of them around. "We found two cigarette butts and a boot print on the victim's chest. Again, useless without anything to compare it to."

Twice now, she'd replaced Jessie's name with "the victim." She could almost believe it wasn't him lying dead in those photos. "The staties came and picked all that up today, so I'm expecting it back in about two years.

"Jack estimates time of death between eight p.m. Sunday and three a.m. Monday morning. We can narrow that down a little more because when I did my patrol at nine Sunday night, there wasn't any dead body."

She opened her notebook to see what else she wanted to cover. "I talked to his wife today. His parents are still refusing to come in to answer questions, so I'm going to get you to go over there tomorrow, Neil." She flipped a page and took another long gulp of coffee. "His wife didn't have much except that they were having money problems. I don't think she has any idea how serious. I've asked her to contact their accountant and get him to send over their financials." She looked up at Neil. "You deal with the diner's books, right? Can you have a look at them?"

Neil bulked up slightly, raising off the wingback as he nodded. "Of course. You know what kinds of things they're sending over?"

"Filed taxes, income statements, their mortgage payments, that sort of thing, I'd imagine. We didn't go into detail. She said she'd send over what they had. Which means we may not get what we're looking for if Jessie was hiding anything."

"What makes you think he was hiding anything?" Stan asked. He'd grown up in Mason and hadn't known Jessie. But as word spread, he felt he knew more about Jessie Forrester and Elle then he should. Some of it made him blush. He'd made a conscious decision to avoid Dell's for the next week or so. There are some things you shouldn't know about your boss.

Elle rubbed her eyes and yawned. "Sorry, guys." She waved over her yawn. "He's dead, Stan. That's why I think he was hiding something."

Stan nodded, feeling stupid for having asked something so obvious.

"We rule out the wife yet?" asked Neil.

"Yeah, I don't think it was his wife. I confirmed she was at her monthly book club until ten forty-five Sunday night. She didn't have any flights booked and it's at least a four-and-a-half hour drive from Chicago. And that's if you're speeding the whole way. That puts her in Turlough after three a.m. It's cutting it close, but then there's the boot print we found on the victim's chest. It was far too large to be a woman's."

"What about other woman problems?" Stan could only imagine a life where you could incur the wrath of one woman, let alone plural. He'd read books and fantasized that one day he'd fulfill at least a quarter of the qualifications it took to have women problems.

"What do you mean?"

Stan swallowed. "Um, what if he was seeing someone around here and her husband found out?"

"So he drags Forrester out to the Maverty house and kills him?" Neil leaned back in his seat, staring at the ceiling thinking about it, then nodded. "Could work."

"It's a nice thought, but it doesn't add up. He was killed by a single shot. And then cut open. If you found out your wife was cheating on you and were mad enough to kill, would you make sure the guy didn't feel a thing before you mutilated him?" Elle winced. They'd started talking about Jessie as if he was an object and not a human being. "His wife said she thought he was seeing someone, but I doubt they were from around here. He hadn't been back in years."

"What if the husband followed him out here?"

"Yeah, but it still doesn't explain what he was doing here in the first place. I want to look into their money situation and we'll work from there."

Jack walked past Elle's office door. She had to call out to him twice before he heard, stopping just outside her doorway.

"Did you want to sit in on this, Jack?" she asked.

His scruffy brows fused. He looked confused. "What are you guys going over?"

"The autopsy report for Jessie. I'm filling them in on what you found." She took in his appearance. His shirt was untucked and his trousers were wrinkled like he'd been sleeping on the cot in the basement. "Are you okay?"

He nodded. "Just tired. I'll pass if that's okay. You've got my notes. There's not much else to add." He gave a salute. "Night, folks."

"Night, Jack." Elle took a moment to process that. She'd never seen Jack act like that. Not even after his wife passed away a couple of years back. She shook it off, promising to follow up later.

"What have you guys come up with?"

Neil cleared his throat. "I talked to Mrs. Collard this afternoon." The way he said it made it clear he felt he deserved hazard pay for that.

Elle waved him off. "Don't worry about her, I'll smooth it over. She's got her panties in a bunch over those stupid flowers."

Neil made a huffing sound as if that were just the beginning of what he'd had to deal with.

"Did she hear anything or see anything suspicious on Sunday night?" Elle asked.

"Nada. She said her and Travis went to bed around ten, watched some TV in bed, and fell asleep around ten thirty. I tried to talk to Mr. Rutherford, but his hearing aid was out of batteries, and you know what that's like." He sighed as if he'd had the longest day ever. "So instead of yelling at a brick wall, we thought you could go over and talk to him. He actually likes you." Neil cleared his throat and flipped a page. "Also, I talked to all his old high school teammates, those we could get ahold of. Only four of them were still in Turlough. The rest kind of scattered. I'll follow up with the ones I got voice mails for tomorrow, but no luck so far. He hadn't been in touch with any of them since the reunion a couple of years ago."

"Okay, thanks. Stan, you have any luck with Jessie's phone?"

He shook his head. "No. If we want to get past the lockout code we're going to have to take it to a specialist." But he perked up as he pulled a small Ziploc bag from his clipboard. Inside was a folded piece of paper. "But I did go through his wallet and found this." He handed it to Elle. "It's a phone number on Motel 6 stationery, the one in Mason."

Elle recognized her handwriting immediately. She should recognize it. It was the cell phone number she'd jotted down for Jessie just three days ago. Her cell phone number.

"It's a local number." Stan grinned like he'd solved a big chunk of the puzzle. "Not listed, though, so it's probably someone's cell."

Elle couldn't believe he hadn't recognized it, having used it at least once a day, every day for the past two years. But then she realized she probably wouldn't recognize his cell. On her phone, it showed up as "Stan—work."

"Great work. I want you to go over to the motel tomorrow and bring a photo of Jessie to show the clerk. I just got off the phone with them. They said nobody by his name had checked in, but there was a guy who paid cash and fit his description." She motioned to Neil. "Go with Neil when he questions his parents and get one from them. I'll pull his phone records and see if he ever called this number." She felt like the biggest asshole in the world knowing it would show up on his phone records at 7:45 Sunday night.

"Any luck with his keys?" Elle asked. She'd sent Stan to search the Maverty house for a set of BMW keys earlier that day. It was the one thing they'd not found on Jessie. And yet, the passenger's window of his car had been smashed in. She hadn't figured out why yet.

Stan shook his head. "Sorry, boss. I scoured that place. Inside, outside, even parts of the woods, but they weren't anywhere."

"Okay, thanks, Stan."

"You think the killer took his keys?"

"Possibly. But then why is the window smashed?"

"Could be kids came along, saw the Beemer, decided to see what's inside, and smashed the window. We didn't find anything of value in it. It was a rental," Neil said.

"Why didn't the alarm sound, then?" Elle finished off her coffee. "Have McGrath take a look at the wiring, see if the alarm's still intact when he goes over the car." She leaned back in her chair, indicating she was finished. "That's all I've got. You guys have any questions for me? Anything else you think we should be doing?"

"So what's our working theory right now?" asked Neil.

Elle sighed. "I think we work on figuring out what he was doing here, then go from there. Anything else?"

Stan raised his hand, "Um? If I'm going with Neil tomorrow, does that mean I'm off night shift?" He smiled, hopeful.

Elle nodded. "I'll put Toby on the night shift the next day or so. He's been asking for hours."

Neil snorted. "Brady's not going to be happy about that."

"This is why we have reserve deputies. Don't worry, I'll handle

Brady. Okay, see you guys tomorrow." She flipped her notebook to a new page and began making notes.

Neil stood, but instead of heading for the door, he walked around Elle's desk and lifted her to her feet by her elbows.

"What are you doing?" she asked.

"Go home. Eat something healthy and sleep. And when I say healthy, I mean I want it to have at least four of the five food groups." She began collecting her notes and folders, but Neil pushed her away. "Shoo. Forget this for one night."

She raised her hands in surrender. "Yes, Mother." But as soon as his back was turned she grabbed the case folder before heading out.

EJ's knee scraped along the hardwood as he lifted himself on top of her. Through the thinning denim of his jeans he could feel the dirt and debris surrounding them in the mess of the master bedroom of the old Maverty house. He fumbled with her bra, quickly abandoning his suave one-handed maneuver for the relative safety of two. Despite her eagerness, she let an impatient sigh escape. It drifted in the air above them unspoken, but deafening in the silence. With a triumphant breath, he released the clasp of her bra and began removing it. She grabbed his wrist.

"It's kind of gross in here. I'd rather leave it on," she said.

He let go of it and leaned back, watching as she redid in two seconds what had taken him minutes. He cupped one of her breasts and squeezed in what he hoped was a provocative way.

"Ouch." She slapped his hand away. "They're not udders. You don't have to milk them." The testiness creeping into her voice was all too familiar. This was as far as he ever got. A tantalizing peek of what lay beneath tight T-shirts and jeans. A quick, furtive reach beneath her panties before his hand was wrenched out and placed somewhere safer. He had once made it to the folds between her legs. They were wet, enticingly so. He still remembered the way the coarse hair rubbed against his wrist, the way her breath suddenly caught. He'd managed to sweep past the first guard, finger poised to take the plunge when she pulled his hand back from the brink.

"You two lovebirds done yet?" Dan asked. He was leaning against the wall, watching them. One leg hooked over the other, arms folded, a bemused look on his face. "I need EJ for something."

Jessica Reid grabbed for her tank top and pulled it on, her generous C-cup closing up shop for the night. "Whatever." She shrugged. "I'm done with him."

❖

Elle sat crossed-legged on a lounge chair on the back deck, open beer next to the open autopsy report, working her way through a bowl of Cap'n Crunch. All the windows were thrown open in an attempt to coax a breeze through the house. The night air was thick with mosquitoes and gnats. The humidity hung in the air like some long-winged creature hovering over the town. Silent. Waiting. Everyone agreed, it felt hotter now than when the sun was up. The back deck light was hosting a moth party. Their buzzing added to the crush of crickets coming from the forest beyond.

She chugged the last of her Coors, washing down the sugary cereal. She rose to replenish it and as she did the bell rang. She trudged back into the house. The suffocating heat enveloped her. She flicked the curtain back to see Brady standing there, still in a suit and tie, staring at her front door. It was too late to pretend she wasn't home. All the lights were on. She slid back the security bolt and opened the door.

Before Elle could even ask why he was there past ten o'clock on a weeknight, Brady barged past. "Why in heaven's name did you bring that woman to investigate a dead body?" Brady paused to take in her cutoffs and tank top, her tousled hair and empty beer. Elle put a hand on her hip and stared back. "Did you even think about what this could do to our city? People are going to think it's unsafe," Brady yelled.

"What people?" she asked. "The nonexistent tourists knocking each other over trying to get here to discover—what? That there's nothing to do here except work, drink, and screw?" Brady could piss her off faster than a Taser on a bull's ass. "Or the people who actually live here and know better?"

"It still doesn't excuse the fact that you brought a reporter to a crime scene. You know what she's planning on writing, don't you? She's planning an exposé. She's going to weed out all the seedy goings-on and plant in people's mind that Turlough is bad news." He rapped his knuckles against Elle's kitchen counter as another idea popped into mind. "We'll be famous for this. You wait. When people come by, they're going to ask where that murder victim was found. They'll organize tours." He scrubbed hard at his chin, worrying away the stubble. "What if she killed this Forrester guy? We don't know her. Nobody knows her. What if she knew him from Chicago and followed him down here? And then—" Brady mimed taking aim with a gun and shooting.

"Gee, thanks, Brady. With you in office we don't even need a sheriff's department."

"How do you know she didn't? She's as likely as anyone else."

Elle leaned back against her kitchen counter and folded her arms, wondering how much to tell Brady, whether he would be more of a pain in the ass or less.

"Robin was in Chicago at the time of the murder. Her flight didn't arrive in Barkley until eight Monday morning."

They stared at each other for a few seconds, then Brady pulled his tie away from his throat. "Christ, it's hot in here. Don't you have air?"

"You invited her. This is your mess." Elle shrugged. Childish as it was to say, Brady needed to hear it. Too often he jumped into ideas before they were fully formed and the consequences properly thought through. She yanked open her fridge and fished out another beer, popped the cap, and took a long swig. She didn't offer Brady one. Didn't want him to get the impression this was a social call. "You're being paranoid."

"Oh, really? I didn't invite her. She called me."

"And you jumped at the chance to show off the town. What's the matter? Aren't so happy now that we're proving to be less of the ideal tourist attraction than you hoped?"

"You know who she's been talking to, don't you?" He paused, waiting for her full attention, knowing he would get it in a second. "Sid Derry." His hands were on his hips, his neck outstretched.

Elle's blood cooled at the mention of that name. She even shivered in the heat. "Why is she talking to him?"

"Why do you think? Now, Elle, we might not always agree." Elle snorted but kept quiet. "But one thing we can both agree on is that Sid Derry is a useless turd. How he ever got on the city council is—"

"Don't give me that crap. You couldn't care less who's on the council as long as they're voting your way, and more often than not, Sid Derry votes your way." Elle grabbed the bottle of pills sitting on her counter, poured two into her palm, and swallowed them with a mouthful of beer. At Brady's gaping look she said, "Not that I give a crap what you think, Ken Brady, but they were prescribed to me earlier. I hurt my back today."

"What'd you do to your back?"

She shrugged it off. "Threw it out stopping that fight. No big deal." They stared at each other for several seconds. "So is there a reason you've come to my house? Besides pointing out the obvious?" She put extra emphasis on "my house" in hopes he would get the hint and leave.

"Ah, I wanted to make sure you hadn't done any sort of interview with that reporter."

"I told you I wouldn't the first time you asked. What makes you think I changed my mind?" She refrained from mentioning that she had, in fact, changed her mind, even if it was only for an hour or two. "Despite what you think, she was never here to write some puff piece on the town."

"Okay, I had this crazy idea that you two were working together." When he laughed, it came out smarmy. Elle fake laughed with him.

"Are you done now?" She waved her beer toward the door. "I have work to do and I'm probably going to pass out from these pills in about ten minutes." She could already feel them taking hold. It was like a warm hand spreading out from her center and smoothing out all her aches and pains. She was already anticipating her first full night's sleep in two days.

Brady brushed his hands together, wiping sweat on his suit pants. "I just wanted to make sure we saw eye to eye on this Robin Oakes issue."

"Great." Elle opened her front door. "And, Brady? Don't come to my house again." She didn't see him nod. She'd already shut the door.

CHAPTER TWELVE

obin awoke to the incessant, pervasive scent of frying bacon. It
Rcurled into her nostrils, pulling her from her pillow. Every day she
vowed to pack her duffel and move to the motel in Mason. Yet every day
some new culinary marvel greeted her from Mrs. Collard's kitchen. She
berated herself at the ease with which she'd been wooed. Several slabs
of melted butter and she was willing to put up with cramped quarters,
a lumpy mattress, and a washroom two flights down a steep staircase.

The quickest way to Robin's heart was her stomach. Well, maybe
not her heart, but close enough. It was a rare treat to have someone cook
for her. As a rule, she didn't date much. There wasn't the time with her
job. But when she did, she chose women who could cook.

There was something about being pampered with a hot meal. As
if each second of preparation was a little bit of foreplay. An amuse-
bouche, if you will.

Robin lived alone. She was happy with that fact. There was
nothing on Earth that would make her willing to share space with
another human being. She hadn't lived with someone since she left for
college. After fifteen years of that, you get set in your ways. Dealing
with towels on the floor or dishes in the sink was not her idea of a well-
spent morning.

The only roommate she'd had on and off was her brother Jason.
But that would only last about a week before he found some woman to
shack up with, which suited her fine. There was only so much of Jason
she could take. She'd been ignoring his texts for the past day. She still
hadn't talked to Brian about getting him in Jamie's crew. And she had
no plans to. She'd thought about it and decided his hate was worth the

alternative. Jamie didn't mess around. If you fucked up once, he'd kill you. And she knew her brother too well.

Robin yawned and grabbed her bag of toiletries before heading downstairs to the washroom.

Elle found Robin, a forkful of waffle and berries poised halfway to her mouth, a coffee and plate of bacon on the table next to her. Sandy followed Elle into the makeshift dining room she had set up for guests. It was a table shoved into the alcove of a bay window in the living room. It afforded the diner a view of her magnificent garden out back but was a little awkward if either of the Collards were in the living room at the time.

"Can I get you some coffee, Sheriff?" Sandy's hospitality outweighed her previous grudge over her murdered azaleas.

"That would be amazing. Thank you, Sandy." Elle pulled out one of the wrought iron chairs around the small table. It scraped across the hardwood floor, echoing through the lower half of the house. She smoothed her hand down her tie as she sat. It was a practiced movement, elegant in its unconscious simplicity.

Robin's fork resumed its path toward her mouth. She placed the fork on her plate as she chewed, observing Elle as she fiddled with a miniature pitcher of cream. Elle didn't say anything. She chose to stare out the bay window at the trees that bordered the Collards' backyard and beyond those, Mr. Rutherford's chicken coop. Despite Sandy's best efforts, she hadn't yet managed to create a barrier high enough to obscure Rutherford's brood.

Her interest piqued, Robin waited. In her experience, the less she said, the more they talked. She continued to savor the crisp texture of the bacon and studied Elle, who managed to fill the room as if she were the only object. Elle finally stopped playing with the cream. Her long fingers curled around the porcelain container, obscuring it. Elle's nails were trimmed short. A clear nail polish coated each one, most of it chipped away. Easy to miss from far away. It spoke of a need to maintain a certain aesthetic while being practical at the same time.

Sandy waltzed back in with a mug of coffee and set it in front of Elle. "Would you like breakfast? Robin here's not managed to eat me out of house and home yet." She pushed the sugar bowl closer to Elle and grinned at Robin the way a proud mother would a chubby child's healthy appetite.

Robin smiled. "I'm surprised at that myself. Everything's so good." This made Sandy preen.

"No thanks, Sandy." Elle began adding heaps of sugar and cream to her coffee.

"What about some nice pie? I'm experimenting with a new blend. Hoping to win the blue ribbon with something special this year." She rung her hands together, undecided. "Although, messing with tradition. What if Tully wins with one of her key limes?"

Elle rolled her eyes for Robin. "Don't believe her. She's won every year since I can remember." Elle took a tentative sip of her coffee to test it was to her liking. It was. She took a deeper gulp.

"Well, that's not true. I only started winning seven years ago."

Elle froze, her coffee halfway from her lips to the table.

"What changed seven years ago?" asked Robin.

"My mother stopped entering her blueberry pie." Elle placed the coffee back on the table and pushed it away as if the cream had curdled.

"Oh, Elle. I'm sorry. I didn't think." Sandy placed a hand on Elle's shoulder. Her mouth opened to say something more, but she closed it again.

"It's okay, Sandy." Elle grabbed for her mug, wrapping her hands around it. It was a conscious movement to dislodge Sandy's hand from her shoulder. The heat of it felt like it was burning a hole through her uniform. She hated the words even as she said them. It was never okay. But she said them anyway. To make people feel at ease. To let them off the hook. To stop the looks of pity. She wished, in moments like this, that she could be EJ. That she could just get in her truck and drive off somewhere to hurl stones into the river.

"Okay." Sandy pursed her lips together and nodded. "I'll leave you two alone to talk."

Robin couldn't help herself. "Why'd your mom stop making her blueberry pie?" As far back as Robin could remember she'd had a knack for asking the wrong question at the right time. This didn't always work in her favor as a human being, but in her line of work, it was like owning a chicken that laid golden eggs.

"I think you already know the answer to that."

Robin frowned. "I don't follow you."

Elle began fiddling with the sugar jar. "I heard you'd been talking to a few of our residents, Sid Derry in particular. And if Brady's paranoia has actually paid off and you're now writing some article about Jessie's murder, then there would be no reason for you to talk to someone like Sid Derry. But if I'm right and you're still trying to do some ridiculous story about me, then talking to Sid Derry would make a lot of sense if you wanted to get a differing opinion about Sheriff Ashley. You follow now?" She kept her eyes on the sugar, not able to look up at Robin.

"Who told you I was out to talk to Sid Derry?"

"Doesn't matter."

"Look, I've never been anything but up front with you. I'm not going to write anything you don't want me to. It's an interesting story even without the murdered ex-boyfriend angle. I'm not here to exploit you or lay bare any deep dark secrets. This is stuff people are interested in, strong females in roles of leadership. It'll resonate well with our readers.

"As for Sid Derry, I did go out to talk with him yesterday, but if your informant had stuck around long enough, they would know he refused to speak with me."

Elle almost laughed out loud at the idea of Brady being her informant. She didn't even need two guesses as to who had told her to go visit Derry, she'd practically made a roadmap for her. "You've been talking to Tully."

Robin shrugged. "She did have a couple of very cute anecdotes, but nothing of substance. I've still got my fingers crossed that I land that big fish interview." She exaggerated crossing her fingers. "What do you say?"

Before Elle could answer, the radio at her hip crackled. Neil's voice came through the speaker, garbled. Elle unclipped it. "Repeat, Neil?" She adjusted the channel knob at the top.

The static lessened. "Are you on your way in?" Neil asked.

"I'll be there in about ten, why?" She stood, forgetting Robin and her half-finished coffee on the table.

"Just get here as soon as possible." With that, the radio went silent.

"So you're not going to tell me about Sid Derry?" Robin called to Elle's fleeing back. But she was gone. The door slammed behind her.

❖

Elle noticed the throng of spectators clustered around the town square the moment she pulled onto the main strip. They were grouped in twos and threes, pointing and laughing at something hidden behind the bulk of their bodies. A warning shot through the pit of Elle's stomach. Whatever Neil had called her in for was going to test the strongest heartburn medicine she could find. With the weather like this, Elle was surprised so many people were out; she would've thought they'd be holed up in front of their window units.

As she stepped out of her cruiser to push her way through, she heard snippets of conversation.

"How'd they get it up there like that, d'you wonder?"

"I got a pretty good idea who did it."

"I remember back in eighty-three when the Parker boys managed to balance Old Bailey's truck on that bridge over the Red there. He had to use his mother's cane to push the clutch in 'cause he was afraid to sit in it." Laughter rolled through the crowd like a wave finding shore.

"Has Randy seen it yet?"

By the time Elle shoved herself to the front she had a pretty good idea of what she'd find, but her breath caught anyway. There was no doubt in her mind who had done it. Her hair prickled with rage. Every eye turned from Randy Pritchard's car—which teetered atop the town's historic stone well—to watch the sheriff's reaction. It promised to be almost as entertaining as the prank itself.

Without her noticing how or where he came from, Case was by her side. He gently wrapped his hand around her arm, lending the still considerable strength from his bent frame just by being close. Elle took a calming breath and counted to ten in her head before walking out toward the engineering marvel making a new home in the town's informal square. She bent down to see if there was a way to get it dislodged without destroying the well. She stood and scanned the crowd. When she spotted Cabe McGrath standing off to the side, chewing his tobacco like cud, she waved him over. The mechanic wandered up. The top half of his coveralls hung off his waist, revealing grease-stained muscles and a tattered wifebeater.

He whistled as he got a closer look. "That's a real sweet piece of work."

"I'm glad you approve. Can you remove the car from the well without damaging either?"

He bent to examine the undercarriage. Finally, he got on hands and knees to inspect where the base of Randy's car met with the top of the stones forming the rim of the well. He grunted as he squirmed farther beneath the vehicle. After a few minutes of silence, the crowd quiet around them, McGrath spoke. "Well, here's your problem," he said, his voice muffled. "They've propped the car on blocks on either side of the whatcha call it." He wormed his way back out. "The side of the well. Means you try and move it off the front or back, it'll collapse the props."

Elle nodded, stoic, aware of being onstage, her performance judged by the entire town. "How many people would it take to do something like that?"

McGrath shrugged and moved his tobacco from one cheek to the other. He spat a wad onto the ground. "Depends."

"Depends on what?"

"On how they got the car onto the well. There's lifting, then there's coaxing. Lifting takes more manpower for sure. Coaxing could take less."

Elle shook her head. "I'm not sure what you mean."

"Well," he let the word draw out for several seconds, thinking of the best way to explain. "See. A car's heavy."

Elle rolled her eyes. "Yes. Thank you, McGrath. I realize a car is heavy."

"But people can lift 'em. You seen those strongman competitions where they lift the back end of a car? Those fuckers are strong. But I doubt we got anyone in town who can do that. Not by themselves anyway." He spat again, missing Elle's black boots by less than an inch. "Now if you got a bunch of men to do it, that's possible. The frame on a Mustang is steel. Steel's heavy. If this were a Saturn, I'd say maybe two really strong men. But with a Mustang you're looking at around three thousand pounds or thereabouts. That's a lot of weight to lift by yourself. Adrenaline could help."

"McGrath."

"Yep?"

"How many guys?"

He squinted up into the sky. A vulture circled in the distance, somewhere above the back roads leading out to the Old Bailey farm.

"A lot a guys make a lot a noise. So I'd say you're looking for a lot less than a lot."

"Jesus, McGrath, go find something useful to do."

"Sure thing, Sheriff." McGrath sauntered away, disappearing as the crowd swallowed him.

The main strip had gone quiet. It was the sound of fifty odd people gathered close, straining to hear. In the distance, a radio guttered to life. Static washed through the streets, mingling with the oppressive heat rising from the ground. It was claustrophobic, impossible to escape.

Elle turned from the sea of eyes, hoping the car could stall the inevitable, a decision. A sparrow landed on the hood, hopped a couple feet, pecked at a spot of mud, left a calling card, and fluttered off.

The quiet shattered. "What the fuck is this?"

"Jesus." Elle spoke so quietly, it was almost mouthed. She didn't turn from the car. Instead, she watched in the driver's window as the mayor forced his way through the wall of people and up the few steps to the well to stand next to her. Still, she didn't turn. She tried to focus on the car and ignore the heavy breathing happening beside her.

"What the fuck is this?" Brady kicked the back tire. The air inside absorbed the sound and gave back a dull thump. It floated into the air with Brady's question, echoing in the stillness. "I told you months ago you should've sent him to military school. Get some goddamn discipline through those thick red Ashley curls." He smacked his hand down on the trunk of the car. It teetered for a moment. The audience gasped. More than a few hoped it would slide off its perch and add to the telling later.

Elle jumped at the sound, then turned, her movements molasses. A million things rushed through her mind at once, most of which focused on how to put Brady in his place. But blind rage was blocking all rational thought. How dare he treat her like some child? Like a subordinate who had disobeyed an order? Her face and ears had gone red. Her fists unfurled and she planted them on her hips.

Through it all, she was aware of Robin, who had sidled up to Case a few minutes ago. Robin's focus was so intently on her it made her all the more self-conscious of her reaction.

Elle could hear the smack of satisfaction on the crowd's lips as if they were consuming this face-off like a meal they enjoyed. She wouldn't allow them to be sated. Without answering Brady, she turned and descended the worn stone steps of the well and stalked off toward her office. She passed Randy stomping toward the inevitable.

In the distance, she heard him scream, "What the hell happened to my car?"

Unable to stop herself, she smiled.

When Elle entered the station, a young woman was sitting behind the reception desk. "Morning, Heather. Feeling better?" But Elle didn't wait to hear the answer. She rushed into her office and slammed the door.

Heather nodded, even though there was no one to see it. After a moment, she went back to the files on her desk, clicking away on each file, some of them ancient. She was trying to digitize Turlough. Her hair fell in strips over her face; a combination of frizz and grease kept it from becoming one cohesive mess.

Elle stuck her head out of her office. "Can you get Stan to come in?"

Heather's whole face brightened. She tucked a lock of hair behind her ear as she dialed. Elle watched her, seeing the anticipation on Heather's lips as she said Stan's name. The smile went all the way to her eyes. She was pretty when she smiled.

When she hung up the phone, she caught Elle watching and blushed. "He's on his way. Is this about the car?"

Elle nodded. "Where's Neil?"

Heather shrugged. "Probably at Tully's getting some coffee."

"That's a great idea." Elle sighed. Anything to avoid Ken Brady and Randy Pritchard's car. Before she could take two steps, Brady barged through the door, followed by Case.

"So, what? You're just going to leave the car out there to become a permanent tourist attraction?" He pointed behind him, emphasizing that there was a car sitting on top of a well outside. As if she'd forgotten.

"Why not? It'll make a better pull than some stupid pie and beer festival. We could advertise on the interstate. 'Come look at Randy Pritchard's car!' Rent out a billboard. The born-agains are doing it, why not us? We could put your face on it. People would come from miles away."

"Elle." Case's stern look stopped her from continuing with what she was about to say.

"What?" She let out a long breath. "I've got Stan coming in. He'll investigate. I'll call Kate to get Randy's car off the stupid well and everything will go back to normal."

"That dyke?" If possible, Brady's face pinched in even farther as he said it. Elle cringed at the name he used for the only female mechanic in the county. "Get Cabe to do it."

"I'm not having that man anywhere near that vehicle." In truth, she had a good feeling he'd helped put it there. "He's got too much work as it is. I need this investigation—"

"Investigation?" Brady said it like an insult. "Like there's going to be witnesses? Who the fuck are you kidding? We know who did this."

Before he had finished, Elle was nodding her head. "Yes, investigate. I can't arrest people without evidence, Brady."

"Evidence. Jesus, fuck, Elle. How can you be so blind? This isn't skipping school or smoking pot at the Maverty house. This is theft and destruction of property. The Baker kid and Randy were punching the shit out of each other yesterday. And you're going to tell me that he didn't get your brother to help him? Come on. That's ridiculous and you know it."

"According to McGrath, it would have taken a few guys to pull it off. Who's to say Randy and his friends didn't do it themselves to get EJ and Dan in trouble?" It was one of the stupidest things she'd ever said. She knew it. But she wasn't going to let Ken Brady bully her.

"You're an idiot. Evidence my ass. Look up the word 'bias' and come give me a call when you've got that figured out."

"Get the hell out of my station. Go do something mayoral."

"Jesse Flynn built that well with his own hands. If she scratches even one stone on that wall, so help me…" He let the threat fill the air as he glared at Elle, her eyes flaming, arms akimbo, seething. They faced off for several more seconds before Brady stomped out of the station.

When the door slammed and the sound of Brady's shoes faded, Case turned to Elle. "Well, that was lovely. I'm sorry the rest of town didn't get to witness such a display of professionalism."

"He's being a prick and you know it. I'm sick of everyone assuming

EJ is involved whenever anything goes wrong in this town. God." She pushed her hand through her hair, dislodging most of it from her bun.

Case took her arm and turned her toward him. "In all seriousness, this is not the time to get Ken Brady's back up. Keep your head down. And for Christ's sake, don't let him rile you up." He left Elle to wonder what that meant.

Chapter Thirteen

The sound of a motorcycle reverberated down the main strip. Elle closed her eyes as the rumble filled the air.

There was something about motorcycles. She wasn't sure if it was the smell of fuel or the sound they made as they sped past, but she'd always had a thing for them. She'd never actually owned one. She couldn't justify it when she still had a perfectly good working truck.

She'd ridden dirt bikes when she was younger. Their neighbor had created a track in an old abandoned cornfield not far out of town. She'd gotten decent at the jumps before her father had found out and forbidden her to ride.

The rumble grew louder until it drowned out all other sound. And then it was gone. Elle opened her eyes, turning from the sight of Randy's car to the owner of the Harley stopped at the base of the monument.

Kate Wells shut the engine off and removed her helmet, revealing short-cropped black hair. Kate exuded a certain aesthetic with her hair and leather. Despite Ken's derogatory moniker, Elle didn't think Kate was your quintessential lesbian. She looked more like a cute pixie and had a graceful nature to her that belied the clunky biker boots and leather.

Kate mounted the stairs, her full attention on the car behind Elle. She whistled loudly. "Well, shit. When you called me out here, I thought McGrath was busy and you needed a flat fixed on one of the cruisers or something. This"—she waved her arm at the red Mustang—"this has made my day." When she smiled, she did so with her whole face. Her eyes crinkled, her cheekbones rose, and her mouth and teeth took over the lower half of her face. "The kids are so much more inventive than when we were kids, huh? Back then, they just beat the shit out of each other. This is a whole new level of deviousness."

Despite the situation, Elle couldn't help but laugh. "Unfortunately, this bit of inventiveness is going to cost the town a lot of money if we can't get the car off without destroying the well underneath."

Kate bent down to examine the underside of the car, much like McGrath had earlier, only the view now was better.

Elle crouched down as well. "Can you get it off?"

Kate pulled out her phone and turned on her flashlight. She poked around for a few more minutes before coming out. "Yeah. I've got a friend who owns a great big winch. Owes me a favor. I'll get him to come out this afternoon and we'll just lift the thing off."

Elle's shoulders relaxed. She hadn't gotten a morning jog in and the tension around her shoulders had worsened.

Kate squirmed back out and looked over at Elle. Her deep blue eyes were wide and serious. Elle knew what was coming. "I was sorry to hear about Jessie. It's horrible what happened."

Elle stood, hoping to get the unpleasant conversation over with as soon as possible. "It was." She looked at her hands, not able to meet Kate's eyes.

"How are you holding up?" Kate reached out to touch her arm in comfort, but Elle moved out of the way, looking around to see who was watching. Then she cringed at her own cowardice and prejudice. Kate was only trying to be nice. But Kate just shrugged it off.

"I'm fine. We hadn't seen each other in years. We lost touch a long time ago."

Kate nodded at the unspoken need to end the conversation and walked down the steps toward her bike.

"I know we don't run in the same circles, not that we ever did, really. But if you ever need anyone to talk to, you can call me." Kate straddled her bike and lifted her helmet, moving the straps aside. "Although, from what I hear, you don't really run in anyone's circle." She winked and placed the helmet on her head.

She revved the engine and took off down the strip, raising her hand as she left.

Caught up in the sound and rush, Elle stood for a few more moments wondering if she'd ever take Kate up on her offer.

❖

Neil gulped the last of his pint in three heavy swallows. He belched proudly, slamming the glass on the counter when finished. He grabbed a handful of unshelled peanuts from a bowl beside him. Husks littered the counter and floor three feet in each direction of his stool. Shucking the outer hull, he caught the nut between his teeth before crunching down.

Finnegan's was quickly building momentum as Saturday afternoon transformed into Saturday evening. Toby always marveled at the change in mood and how fast it could shift from a mewling kitten into a ferocious panther. It was as if time slowed; one slip, one nudge, and it was enough to bring the claws out. Toby watched Neil shove his empty glass toward the front of the counter, indicating he wanted another. His eyes were half focused on the highlights from the Cubs game earlier in the day. They'd lost three to four.

Toby eased himself off the back counter, took a fresh pint glass from below, and began pouring Neil a Schlitz from the tap. He nodded toward the television. "You get a chance to see the game?"

Neil snorted, shaking his head. "Nah. Spent most of my afternoon babysitting Kate as she hoisted the Pritchard kid's Mustang off that damn well."

Toby smiled. His eyes puckered under great bushy eyebrows. "Heard about that. Didn't get to see it, though. They'd already finished the thing before I came in to open." He finished his pour, tipping the excess head into the tray before passing it to Neil. "Heard Brady had a good brawl with the sheriff. She get her knickers in a knot over that?"

Neil shuffled peanut shells into a pile with cupped hands. Behind him, someone roared as the eight ball sailed into the corner pocket on the only operational pool table in the establishment. He shrugged. "Brady's an asshole, he'd get anybody to spit fire."

"You could fry bacon on that temper of hers, though." Toby nodded to an older couple who walked in and took a seat by the large bay window in the front. "Wouldn't want to come toe to toe with that."

His crow's-feet deepened. "Unless of course, they were horizontal at the time." He chuckled and slapped the bar with an old rag.

Neil grabbed his pint glass and took a large swig. He wiped his mouth clean and swiveled on his stool to watch as another game of pool was racked. A cloud shifted outside, spilling light through the grimy windows of the pub. A streak hit Neil's glass, sending golden shards onto the ground next to him. He sighed.

People didn't get it. This was what he wanted. The chance to drink his dinner every Saturday night when Tully was out getting liquored up with the girls from the beauty parlor in Mason. He liked set hours. In every morning by nine, done by five and a day off every six. His entire life he'd been told what to do. First by his mother, then by Sheriff Bailey, and now Tully. He didn't mind. In fact, it felt comfortable, like pulling on his wool sweater when he went fishing in the mornings and the sun hadn't yet dried the dew.

Everyone thought he had this big grudge against Elle for winning. He'd only run because Tully made him.

The day of the election he'd been so nervous he'd almost hit the fence pulling out of his own drive. Everyone mistook it for jittery anticipation, but the truth was he was so goddamned worried he'd win. Jesus, the last thing he wanted was Elle's life: an endless pile of paperwork and bullshit from every direction. Hell, she spent more nights than not at the station curled up on that cramped couch of hers. Elle had won that election because she deserved it. She was the right person for the job. He just hoped she didn't end up like old Bailey, cranky and alone.

Neil swiveled back to the bar for a refill of nuts. As he did, he noticed Robin Oakes watching him from two barstools down. She had a plate with a half-eaten corned beef on rye sitting in front of her and a fresh glass of wine in her hand. A notepad pushed off to the side was half-filled with black scribble. She looked more at home in jeans and a men's shirt tucked in the front than she had earlier in her suit.

"Buy you another?" Robin nodded toward Neil's pint glass, still gripped in his hand.

"Got one, thanks." But when Neil put the glass to his lips, he realized he'd drained it. He placed it on the bar and pushed it to the edge.

Leaving her soggy corned beef behind, Robin and her wine

slid closer by one stool. Neil ignored the journalist's overt attempt to ingratiate herself, choosing to focus on Toby as he poured another Schlitz.

They sat in silence, absorbing the atmosphere of Finnegan's. Years of spilled beer, cigarette ash, and dropped food had turned the carpet a dull charcoal. The smell itself was a combination of stale beer, grease, and cigarettes. Even though it had been years since you could smoke in Finnegan's, the memory lingered in the furnishings, seeping out of the wood and cushions.

"Care for a game?" Robin pointed to the now empty pool table across the bar. "I haven't played since college, but I'm willing to bet I'd still kick your ass."

Surprised, Neil twirled to face Robin. "You want to play a game of pool?"

"I have to find some way to work off the bucket of grease I just ate." Robin patted her trim stomach and cast a meaningful look at the plate of food sitting next to her notepad.

Neil snorted. As if that were answer enough. He hopped off his stool and ambled to the pool table to begin racking the balls.

The first two games Neil won easily, sinking the eight ball before Robin even had a chance to clear half her balls off the table. Robin kept the conversation light. They talked about the food at the diner, Sandy Collard's obsession with her garden, the horrible state of the pool table and cues. On the third game, Neil peered up from the length of the cue as he poised to sink the eleven in the side pocket and grinned. "Maybe I should go to Chicago sometime, if you were considered good, that is. I'd make myself a killing."

Robin laughed. "Have you ever been to Chicago?"

Neil shook his head as the clink of the eleven landing on the nine drifted out of the side pocket. "Landed in the airport once." Neil circled the table, on the prowl for his next kill.

"I guess a lot of the people in town have been here their whole lives. Pretty thick bonds."

Neil nodded, spotting the fifteen hovering on the edge of the corner pocket. He bent down to line up the shot and help nudge it toward its final plummet. In life, Neil personified patience. He applied that patience to everything he did, fishing, work, his marriage, and most definitely pool. There was no point to rushing a shot or any such thing as a sure thing. He took his time, lining up the cue perfectly, readying his shot.

"It must be strange, having to investigate a murder. If it was me, I'd be worried I might screw up somehow." Robin waited for a reaction.

Neil missed the cue ball, smearing the lip of the table with red chalk. When his eyes raised to Robin, they expressed exactly what he thought of her.

Robin's hands raised in surrender. "I didn't mean that you couldn't handle it." Robin grabbed her wine and took a thoughtful sip. "I'm just curious how you'd go about it if you'd never done it before. Getting stabbed to death is pretty gruesome."

"Who said he was stabbed to death?"

"I got a peek." She sighed and looked away as if it had been too traumatic for words.

"That's not what killed him." Too late, Neil realized his error. "I mean…Ah, shit." He pointed his pool cue at Robin. "And that's off the record." Remembering the phrase he'd heard in a million TV dramas.

"So who's Sid Derry to Elle?" Robin leaned in to line up an easy shot she'd miss on purpose.

"You ask Elle about that?"

Robin nodded.

"And she didn't tell you nothing? Well, neither am I." He threw his cue on the table, indicating he was done with pool and Robin.

From the vantage point of her front steps, Elle felt swathed in a cocoon of leaves. It was as if the world beyond their yard didn't exist. Very little traffic came along Dunne's Hollow road, especially at three in the morning. It gave the crickets the entire stage. The house and lawn cut out an oval shape from the surrounding forest, framing the sky with black silhouettes of pine and oak. The stars seemed so close, a blanket of diamonds on black velvet hiding the world from sight. Elle wanted to crawl beneath, wrap herself in the familiar constellations, and pretend the last six days hadn't happened. If she could wipe them from existence, maybe she would sleep.

When she closed her eyes to dream, she didn't imagine arresting the killer. Instead she saw Jessie as he would be: alive with bacteria, teeming with blowflies and beetles feasting on a buffet of flesh and intestines, buried under six feet of dirt in a suit that would fray and crumble with the elements. His facial structure would contort as it decayed and disappeared from memories as if the beetles could chew at her thoughts and history.

She wanted that history to rearrange itself. To become, just briefly, the one she had imagined for herself in high school when hard meant a calculus exam. What she wouldn't give to go back, to live in a world where that girl still existed.

She shot off the stairs, unable to sit still any longer. She needed to do something, anything to stop the jumble in her mind. She was itching for a run. But she would be lying if she said insomnia was the only reason she'd staked out the front steps. She was waiting for EJ. She hadn't seen him since the brawl Friday afternoon, and she'd be damned if she let him sneak into his cave in the dead of night.

That had been Elle's trick. Stay out all night after getting into trouble for something and sneak back in when she was sure Mom and Dad were asleep, hoping a night's rest would ease their anger. It usually worked. It was hard to bring back the anger seeing Elle, covers tucked under her chin, a heavy layer of red coating her pillow, mouth slack. In the quiet of the morning, it was easier to forget the hellion that rampaged the cafeteria with water balloons or the sixteen-year-old caught skinny-dipping in Karber's Lake.

Farther down Dunne's Hollow, a truck grumbled, breaking through the cocoon of pine and oak. Elle was caught by how unfair it was that she had to deal with her brother's rebellion. This shouldn't be her fight. All because of a moment. A decision. When Sid Derry turned the key in the ignition of his Ford Fusion, his blood alcohol level was well over the legal limit. When his car collided with her parents' Buick along County Road 12, her role as the rebellious older Ashley child died along with her parents.

Instead of passing the entrance to their drive, the truck slowed and turned up toward the house. It got about halfway, the headlights ricocheting off the trunks lining the lane, and stopped. Elle stepped back onto the porch, hidden in the shadows, and waited. She folded her arms across her chest, despite the humidity, she felt a chill roll down her spine. She almost choked from anticipation when she saw EJ break free from the headlights, heading toward the front porch. The twin beams eased away, back down the lane, leaving EJ in silhouette against the yard.

She waited until he was mounting the steps before she said, "Kind of late, aren't you?" She stepped from the shadows, blocking the front door.

EJ jumped back, startled. "Creep much? Since when do I have a curfew?" He shoved his curls out of his face.

"Since you and Dan defiled Randy Pritchard's car. I didn't think Dan would listen when I told him to stay away from Randy, but I thought you had enough sense." She shoved her finger into EJ's chest. "If Stan finds enough evidence, Randy can charge you with grand theft, which is a felony." Like most arguments with her brother, she could never decide if it was her anger or frustration that left her exhausted. It was like she was swimming against the current. Every time she felt she'd made progress, she'd pick EJ up doing something stupid and find herself back where she started. Was this what her dad felt every time he picked her up from Bailey's office?

EJ crossed his arms and stared. She could tell by the slight sway of his stance that he was drunk.

"It doesn't bother you that you could go to juvie, and over what? Pride? Some stupid prank Dan put you up to?"

He wasn't even looking at her now. Just staring straight ahead like a POW being interrogated. A breeze shuddered through the yard, lifting and shaking branches as it passed.

"And you're an ass if you think Dan gives a shit about you, because he won't be there to hold your hand in juvie. He's eighteen. He'll be in jail."

He swatted her hand away. "What the fuck do you know about it? Dan and I were at Tanya's all night hanging out. Besides, how the hell would we get it onto the well in the first place?"

Elle folded her arms, a vise against her heart. "McGrath didn't help you out any?"

"McGrath? What the hell did he say about it?"

"He didn't have to say anything. The guy's a moron." McGrath hadn't said anything with his mouth, but his body language had given a full confession. "But I do know that Dan bought his truck off McGrath a couple weeks ago. It doesn't take much to put the two together."

"Why are you even bugging me about this when you have Deputy Do-Right on it?" Stan had come by earlier in the day, questioning both him and Dan about the incident. EJ had watched Dan maneuver around Stan's questions the way he drove his car around the back curves of Turlough. But mostly Dan had teased Stan about his crush on Sheriff Ashley, calling him a lapdog and panting to add to the effect.

"You think I'm waiting up at three in the morning because I'm working an incident? Jesus, EJ. I'm worried you're giving your life away to a detention junkie. Why can't you see that Dan isn't your friend?"

"Really? Dan listens to what I have to say. He cares about what I think." He punched his chest with each sentence, as if the harder he pounded the more true it would be. "Unlike you. All you care about is your stupid job. Well, here's the thing, you're a joke. They're all laughing at you. Everybody's waiting for you to fall flat on your ass and fail." As soon as he said it, he wanted to take it back. He needed to wound her. If she were limping, maybe she would back off and leave him alone. But the moment he'd said it, the look on her face made him feel worse than if he'd actually taken a knife to her heart.

Elle turned away, tightening her arms. Whenever she brought up an image of EJ in her mind, he was ten years old, standing on the Cases' porch, his face molded in pain. This moment had forever overwritten it. Now she would see his face contorted in hate and rage. It wasn't the words, or even the intent behind them. He'd taken her greatest fear and force-fed it to her. A bitter meal of rejection and inadequacy. But worst of all was that she'd been so transparent, like a film of plastic wrap stretched across her diffidence for all of Turlough to see.

EJ waited for her to meet his gaze. If he could see her eyes, he could gauge the damage. But she turned toward the front door, wiping a stray tear as she did. Instead of wounding, he'd maimed. Only after the door had banged shut did he see that he'd managed to rip his own heart out in the process.

EJ plopped down on the porch swing. It creaked from lack of use. Threadbare as it was, they hadn't thrown it out, out of either loyalty or laziness.

The night air had thickened with humidity and the sound of crickets. EJ leaned back, wrapping himself in the isolation of the night.

For the second time in a week, the only thing he wanted to do was cry himself to sleep. He felt like everyone was trying to grab hold and take a piece of him, but he didn't have enough to give. With every decision, with every act, he dug himself in deeper. Pretty soon he would be so entrenched no one would be able to pull him out.

CHAPTER FOURTEEN

EJ stared out Dan's windshield. In the distance, a pile of dirt sat waiting to fill the coffin-sized hole next to it. The group of mourners gathered around the mound, waiting until they could leave. The Forresters stood out by themselves, like an island. Janice Forrester clung to her husband's arm. Her fingers were wrapped around his in such a tight bundle they had turned white. Blotch marks flecked her face, standing in contrast to her pale skin. Cindy stood inches behind Mr. Forrester, her expression unreadable.

Elle stood at the edge of the crowd. Her black dress clung to the sweat forming below her breasts. White as paper, her expression dragged at her features. It was the effort of mourning. It etched along the creases of her mouth and eyes as if the bitterness of being made to stay had converted to gravity instead of tears. The weight of life. Not for the first time, EJ wondered if this was who Elle would have become had their parents lived.

A day had passed since their argument, leaving a thin layer of frost over every interaction since. He'd found her this morning staring at her bed where she'd laid out her sheriff's uniform and a simple black dress. He'd almost passed her by on his way out to meet Dan, but something stopped him. It was as if she had completely wrapped herself up in this shell, determined not to let people see how much she was affected. Almost as if she were embarrassed by how much she still cared. He took a bite of the Cortland in his hand as a way of announcing his presence. It echoed around the room like a gunshot.

Elle jumped and turned toward the sound. He pointed his apple at the clothes on the comforter. "You planning on interrogating people at the funeral or you going to mourn Jessie?"

In a daze, she picked up her uniform shirt. It held the promise of a shield. If she were wrapped in the comforting black and khaki, she'd survive the day. But the black dress promised anonymity. With it, she could blend in among the mourners, no longer separate, but a small piece of a larger machine.

"Can't be both," he said.

"We're leaving in ten." It was a whisper. "You ready?" But when she turned, EJ was already at the front door.

"Getting a ride with Dan." He slammed the door behind him.

Now, as he stared out at the group of mourners, he was having second thoughts about asking Dan to come with him. There was something too loud about his presence.

"Hey, listen," EJ looked over at Dan, who was drumming his fingers against the steering wheel. "This thing's going to be pretty boring." He fingered the ripped seam of his only dress shirt. His wardrobe consisted mostly of rips and holes, but he had managed to find a pair of dark dress pants and this shirt. If he tucked it into the pants, no one could see the rip along the seam. "I mean, you don't have to come. It's not like you knew him."

There was a brief pause as Dan surveyed the group in black up on the hill. A couple of men had removed suit jackets and draped them over their arms. Some had rolled their sleeves up as well. Then he shrugged. "Whatever. I got things to do anyway. Need me to come back around, give you a ride?"

"Nah." EJ shook his head. "I'll find a ride with someone."

"With her?"

EJ gave a lopsided shrug. "Not sure." He reached for the door handle. The air in the cab was dry. He felt himself almost choking on his words. "She's taking this kind of hard. Maybe I should have gone with her."

"She's old enough to babysit herself." Dan pushed in the car lighter and fished out a smoke from his pack.

The texture on the door handle had worn away with use, leaving it smooth under EJ's hand. He suddenly didn't even want to be at this funeral. He would have given his left nut at that moment to be down by the Red, where it curves around before the ravine. It was deep there.

Great for swimming. Hell, he'd take getting rejected by Jessica as an option, or even detention.

He pushed open the door. A wall of humidity slammed into his face. Already his armpits were beginning to seep. He turned to say good-bye to Dan, but he was busy lighting his cigarette, sucking rapidly to make it catch. Already onto the next thing.

EJ took the long way up through the back and around the hill so he could approach unnoticed. For some reason, he wanted to stay hidden. He felt his chest would burst. He was afraid if he locked eyes with someone he might actually start to cry. The last time he'd cried was at his parents' funeral. They'd held the viewing at Porter's Funeral Home just off the main street. It had been called something different back then, but EJ couldn't remember the exact name. Only that it started with an "H." He'd spent most of the evening hiding under the refreshment table, watching people two step along the edge as they helped themselves to coffee and biscuits.

After everyone had left, he'd crawled out. Silence—the kind that made you want to hide under your covers—filled the room. The table was strewn with biscuit crumbs and stir sticks. A deep brown stain under the coffee urn slowly inched toward the sugar bowl, which had been knocked over. Two sugar cubes stood in its path, about to be absorbed into the dark sludge.

Mrs. Case came into the room carrying a pot of chrysanthemums. "There you are. Elle's been searching everywhere for you." Mrs. Case had always been a towering, stout presence. Taller than a lot of the men in town. Before the chemo. Before the ravages of disease.

EJ didn't move. Instead he kept staring at the sugar cubes and their impending doom. The edge of the stain closing in.

Mrs. Case came up beside him and put her arm around him. "Come on, honey. We'll get you something to eat at home." Her hand cupped his shoulder. She pulled him close. She smelled like Tic Tacs and lavender. "Let's get out of this drafty old building and go curl up by the fire."

EJ's head barely reached her armpits. Before Mrs. Case pulled him away from the table, he grabbed the two sugar cubes and stuffed them into his pocket.

EJ leaned against an old craggy oak on the ring surrounding the service. He still had those two sugar cubes. He'd placed them in a shoe box and hid it in the crawl space behind his closet with the rest of the stuff he didn't want Elle to find.

The reverend stepped forward with a tattered blue Bible clutched in his hands and his head bowed. Wisps of hair sprung out lightly, grazing the edge of his bald spot. When he looked up, his eyes cut through the crowd, blazing with an intensity close to the color of EJ's curls. When he spoke, it was with the hard edge of a knife, chopping his words into splinters.

"Jessie's death, as untimely as it may seem, has a place under God's plan." He thrust his Bible forward as testament to the truth he spoke. Always an alarmist, Reverend Hansen took every opportunity to warn of the coming downfall of the human race. By technology, globalization, and video games, but not necessarily in that order. EJ had been subject to more than a few lectures, accosted at every opportunity. He'd even shown up at one of EJ's many after-school detentions, asking if EJ had discovered God's plan for him yet.

The only plan EJ had ever come up with was to get the hell out of Turlough as soon as he graduated. He'd go to Chicago and find a job, a place to live. He knew who he wanted to be and the only surety was that he'd never become it out here, suffocating under Elle's unrealistic expectations.

A hazy heat blanketed the cemetery, undulating the horizon as if the tombstones swam in the collective tears of a town. Sweat pooled in crevices, darkening the already dark.

The reverend's voice rose. "We are already blessed with the knowledge that Jessie is with God. And we must take this knowledge as our reward for those who have sinned against us." He snapped the Bible shut. "Let us pray." He bowed his head.

After the hill had cleared, Elle lingered. Bunches of white carnations blanketed the lid. EJ held back, watching from his oak tree as she pulled something from her purse and placed it on the coffin.

❖

The noise from dozens of voices tumbled out the door. They'd removed most of the furniture from the Forresters' living room. The rest backed against the wall, creating space for the crowd milling about with cups of beer or wine. Mr. Forrester had erected a projector screen at the far end. He fiddled with one of the cords, lost in a world of distraction, flitting from task to task. It kept his mind off the one thing that would drive him down.

Robin went unnoticed as she swam through the crowd, nudging her way to the periphery. The appropriate viewing box of the observer. Mrs. Forrester had invited her the other day when she spoke with her. Midway between sitting and standing, she said, "You should come to the wake." The words were strung together as one. Not for the first time, Robin felt like a leech attaching herself to the pain of others.

Everyone had broken into smaller groups, munching on snacks from tiny paper plates held in one hand, a drink in the other. A circus act in the making as they balanced their drinks in various positions to shovel crab cakes and deviled eggs into their mouths.

The entire affair made Robin's skin crawl. It was the inevitable awkwardness of missing your mouth and dropping the food either on the floor or, worse, on yourself. Then would come the required cleaning. First, finding somewhere to set your plate and drink. Then dabbing at the spot on your shirt until it blended enough that some might wonder if that dark smudge was, in fact, part of the pattern. The ceremony was such an ordeal. Like anyone cared if your neighbor's carpet had one more stain on it. This was why Robin never ate at these types of functions. She also rarely drank, in case she had too much and said something stupid or insulting. A wallflower under duress because, truth be known, her natural instinct was to butt in and argue her opinion with every gigantic ass who mistook superiority for ignorance.

If she wasn't here on assignment, she would have grabbed a gin and tonic in the kitchen. If she wasn't here on assignment, she would have pushed her way into the conversation happening over by the palm in the corner. She would have demanded the obese woman in the stretchy black dress explain why gay conversion camps weren't a form of child abuse. If she wasn't here on assignment she would have walked over to Sheriff Elle Ashley as she stepped into the room and offered Elle her gin and tonic. She wanted to see the effect it would have on her lips as she took a sip. But also because she looked like she could use it. Her hair was loose around her shoulders, one side pulled back and tucked behind her ear. The red framed her pale skin to perfection. The dress she wore was all cling and plunge and scoop. Robin gulped.

Robin wasn't the only one to notice Sheriff Ashley's arrival. As she made her way to Janice Forrester standing in the corner, eyes broke free from conversations and followed her progress. Not only male eyes either. Something in the room had changed. A current had charged the atmosphere. The entertainment had arrived.

But before the first act could begin, Chuck Forrester stood up, slapping the projector as he went. This got a few people's attention. He cleared his throat. A few more turned as he faced the group. Elle stopped moving through the crowd. Intermission. The rest of the assemblage forced their attention on Chuck.

"I want to thank you all for coming." He sighed and rubbed his forehead at the banality of that statement. He started again. "Jessie would've been very grateful...if he could be here." He turned back to the fast-fold screen. A faint blue logo grew darker as the projector warmed up. "I wanted to do something to remember Jessie by so I put together this compilation from over the years. It's still kind of rough, but I wanted something to show everyone." His eyes met Elle's as he said this last bit. She smiled. It was a comforting smile. As if to say that everything was going to be all right. He stepped out of the way and pressed a button on the remote tucked into his hand.

The room became quiet, waiting for the black screen to become something. The unaffected grin of a toothless baby popped onto the screen, Jessie, Robin assumed. This was replaced with a few more school pictures of Jessie as he aged. They gradually morphed to look like the adult he would become. The white curls shortened and darkened. The giant teeth grew less so as his face developed to match. The pictures faded into a video of a preteen Jessie throwing a football at his dad. A strong arm, even at that age. His dad laughed as it sailed over his head. There were more videos now, of Jessie climbing a tall oak tree, running up to the camera, grinning. Jessie tanning on a pool lounge chair, his chest dark from a summer of doing that. From out of frame an avalanche of water soaked Jessie and he jumped out of the chair. Loud feminine laughter echoed off-screen. The camera jerked to include a figure in a green bikini running toward the pool. Long red hair flowed behind her. Robin's face and chest went red hot as the woman turned toward the camera, running back away from Jessie. It was Elle as a teenager. The recognition burned a hole through the pit of her stomach. Carefree laughter as Jessie scooped her up in one arm and jumped into the pool with her. It was only a flash, almost over before it had begun. The images moved onto more football, graduations, birthdays.

Robin turned to gauge Elle's reaction, but she was gone. She started inching toward the kitchen as images from Jessie and Cindy's wedding flickered on screen.

Chapter Fifteen

The grass felt cool scrunched between Elle's folded toes, despite the heat. Her shoes lay discarded halfway between the Forresters' back door and the homemade swing she had plopped on. She pillowed her forehead on the rope. It snaked up into the foliage canopying the backyard. The roughened barbs dug into her skin. It felt good to feel something, even if it wasn't pleasant. The first physical release she'd had all day.

The funeral hadn't been so bad. Not until the end. When the other mourners escaped to their air-conditioned cars, leaving Elle standing at the head of the casket alone. Green Astroturf covered the surrounding ground to hide the mess of digging a grave. It dug into her bare knees as she knelt.

"I'm sorry." She leaned her head against the polished edge. The smell of fresh earth clung to the insides of her nostrils. She wrapped the scent up to be opened and remembered later.

She pulled open her purse and removed a CD case. Written along the top in purple gel pen were the words *For Jessie*. Liquid Paper hearts and stars covered the surface of the case front to back. It was the CD she'd made to give him as soon as he got home from college. The last CD she'd made for him. It had spent the last decade keeping her socks company. Elle placed it on the coffin and pushed herself to her feet. There she stopped, unable to move beyond the green Astroturf carpet. Lying next to the white flowers on the coffin, the image of the CD took on a frivolity her mother would have called inappropriate for the occasion. Somewhere behind her were two stones, side by side, waiting to be joined by two more. She didn't remember their funeral. Only the white sheets thrown back over their dead bodies. That's what she'd taken away from it all. Two white sheets in place of tombstones she'd never visited.

People weren't their final resting places. They were memories and gifts and forgotten items. An old bottle of cologne lost among expired prescriptions, favorite song associations. Even now, whenever she heard "Lady in Red," she couldn't help but picture her mother humming at the sink, cutting flowers. Her feet bare, covered in fallen leaves. A decade from now, what would she remember about this funeral? She hoped it would be the CD case among beautiful white flowers, but the string of nightmares she'd had the last few nights told her it would be something else. An image she couldn't even wipe from her waking hours.

The sun at its apex beat down, the heat oppressive. But Elle couldn't leave. She wanted more than a silent good-bye. She wanted answers. More than anything, she wanted to find who had put him here and wash the memory of a life not lived from her mind.

In the end, it had taken Janice Forrester coming up behind her to jerk her back to reality.

"Reverend Hansen never misses an opportunity, does he?" Janice asked, stopping next to Elle.

A polite smile from Elle.

"Will you join us at the wake?" Janice touched Elle's arm, then jerked it back. Elle turned toward warm eyes. They were sad but held only concern. The anger and betrayal from the past week were gone. Buried like her son under polish and sorrow. A hawk cried out above and swooped down toward the low hills of the cemetery. It was carrying something in its mouth. Janice waited for Elle's response, but when she didn't get one, she said, "You know where we are. It would be nice to have you there." She squeezed Elle's arm.

Now, as she sat under the shade of the Forresters' giant oak, she wondered if she'd made a mistake coming back here. Like a lion's cage, some things weren't meant to be opened. Just being here, Elle had freed the lion. It rampaged her thoughts, ripped through memories, attacked her senses. This backyard and every inch of it had imprinted itself on her.

The slap of the screen door made her look up. It was Robin. Her black suit jacket hung over one arm, curtaining the pair of beers clasped in her hand. She stopped at the rail of the deck, taking in the enormity of the oak before her. It had that effect on people. That tree had been there long before Private Jesse Flynn settled his family into farm life. It would outlive the Forresters. Its branches spread out across the backyard, offering its shade as easily as a child offers a smile. In fall, Chuck trimmed the branches closest to the house so that winter storms wouldn't bring them crashing onto the roof. But by summer the foliage had grown back to touch the edge of the eaves.

Robin stepped off the deck and headed toward Elle near the center of the shade. She paused at Elle's discarded heels. Lying in the grass, they were almost obscured by the unmown lawn.

Robin toed her own heels off and walked the rest of the way in bare feet. She thrust a beer at Elle. It perspired, like everything else in Flynn County that day. "Here, I thought you could use this." She took a seat on the other swing, arranging her skirt so it didn't ride up.

Elle took the beer but, instead of taking a sip, placed it on the ground next to her feet.

"What are you doing here?" Elle asked.

"Janice invited me."

"Why?"

"Why did she invite me? Or why would she invite someone like me?"

Elle shrugged as if it didn't matter which one she answered.

"I honestly couldn't tell you why she invited me. I almost didn't come but then thought it would be rude if I didn't," Robin said.

The only sound for several minutes was the creak of rope on the giant bough above them. The afternoon sun glazed the tips of the trees. The shivering leaves made a sound like waves rolling up a sandy bank.

Robin swept her hair off the back of her neck. "Is it always this hot?"

"Did you come all the way out here to ask me about the weather?" Without meaning to, she'd thrust all her hostility, all her frustration into that one question.

"My mother always says, 'if you're talking about the weather, then it's time to go.' I find it's usually a better opener than 'how are you holding up?'"

"Maybe next time you should just say nothing."

"If you were aiming for the biggest bitch award, I think you've cinched it." Robin softened it with a wink.

"Huh." Elle picked up the beer at her feet and brought it to her lips. "I've never won an award for anything." She sipped. Robin watched her mouth form around the rim. "My mother used to win awards for her pies. I'm horrible at baking."

"I suppose that's because you're better at other things."

Elle laughed, "Sure, like breaking up illegal keg parties." She took another sip. "I'm great at that." With the sweaty beer clutched in her hand she began pumping her legs. "I've had the oddest memory going around and around in my head all day." She pumped a few times more, reaching greater heights, before continuing. "One night when I was seventeen, Jessie and I decided to sneak out and meet up on the edge of Old Bailey's spread. There's this great pond tucked away in the forest about a mile into his property on the north side. We decided it would be a great idea to hijack one of his hogs and see if it could swim. Hilarious, right? We had this grand idea that it would just float around like a dog using its tiny legs to paddle across the pond. Well." She turned to make sure she had Robin's full attention. She did. "I don't know if you've ever tried to get a hog to go where you want it, but I suspect you'd have an easier time getting your virginity back. So there's Jessie, in the pen crouched down like a football's about to be hiked to him, big grin on his face, waiting for me to open the gate. Which I do. And this hog barrels out like I'd lit its ass on fire." Elle slowed her swinging so she could use her hands to demonstrate.

"It runs straight at Jessie, knocks into him like a linebacker, then comes rounding back for me. It broke two of Jessie's fingers. He was on the sideline for six weeks, which of course everyone blamed me for. The next morning my father told me the only thing I'd ever be good at was getting into trouble. I spent the next year and a half proving him right."

"I thought this story was going to have a completely different plot when you first mentioned the middle of the night and a pond," Robin said.

"That was a different pond." Through the hint of powder on her face, Robin could make out the faint markings of a bruise from where Elle'd caught Randy Pritchard's punch. "My father thought it was a joke when I told him I wanted to study criminology at the University of Chicago." She pumped her legs harder, soaring into the sky as she did. "I wonder if he'd be laughing if he could see me now?"

"If he could see you now, would you be in this situation? I mean would you be sheriff of Flynn County? Would you be investigating Jessie's murder?"

Elle slowed, dragging her feet along the grass until she came to a stop. She turned to look at Robin, wondering if she was trying to be cruel or just curious. "No. I wouldn't have come home after school."

"Are you sorry you did?"

"Sometimes." She surprised even herself. Most days Elle could trick herself into pretending she was happy here. She liked her job and she enjoyed working with Stan and Neil. But it was too easy. She missed the challenge. She'd spent her whole life proving she was smarter than everyone, either by not getting caught or by excelling in tasks others failed. Now her biggest challenge was keeping EJ out of trouble, which wasn't so much rewarding as it was frustrating. She sighed. "I never wanted to be EJ's jailer. But he's so hardheaded I don't know what else to do." She leaned back on the swing and closed her eyes. "He's too much like me."

"But you turned out okay."

She shook her head, silent for a few moments before she said, "I was kind of forced to grow up."

Before Robin could voice her next question there was a loud crash from inside the house. Elle took off from the swing at a run.

❖

Elle entered the Forresters' living room to see Cindy squared off against one of the stubbiest men she'd ever seen. There was no other way to describe him. His girth almost exceeded his height. He stared up at Cindy, his bulk more intimidating than if he'd been seven feet tall.

The remnants of potato salad and tuna casserole blanketed the floor around them. The presentation had finished, and Chuck had stopped packing up to watch, along with the rest of the crowd. Janice gripped Cindy's arm, for support or encouragement, Elle wasn't sure.

Seam Holt raised his hands in peace. "I'm not here to ruin your get-together." He swayed a bit. Drunk. That was just like Holt. The last time Elle had seen him, he'd been drunk too. But that was over a decade ago. He'd followed Jessie to Georgia Tech on a football scholarship but had ruined his knee first term. He'd come back the last term demanding a job on the Cavalier coaching staff. He'd made a big scene their last game. Coach Saunders told him to get lost and Holt had thrown a bucket of Gatorade at the man's head. Sheriff Bailey put him in lockup for the night and that was the last time she'd seen him. She heard he'd gotten a job in Evansville with UPS.

"Your husband was a good man, I just want to acknowledge that and pay my respects." He placed his hand over his heart at this last bit. His fingers were like sausages tied tight at the joints. Then he pointed to the ground. "Sorry for the mess," he grumbled in a voice full of phlegm. He turned to leave.

As soon as the screen door slapped shut, Elle crossed the living room to follow him.

She found him standing next to a rented Taurus, fumbling in his pockets for his keys.

"Holt?"

He let his gaze run the length of her. "And you are?"

"It's me, Elle."

He blinked a few times, clearing the fog. Then his face came alive in a broad grin. "Elle the belle!"

He grabbed her in a bear hug, lifting her off the ground. He smelled like BO and whiskey. He bounced her a few times, then let her fall back to the ground.

The screen door slapped against the frame and Elle turned to see Neil coming out of the house. He leaned against the wall, watching, munching on a plate of crab cakes. He knew Elle could take care of herself. He'd seen her take down drunks twice her size with little more than the will to do it. But he wanted her to know he was there. Just in case. He even gave a little wave.

Elle turned back to Seam. "How are you?" She tilted her head as she asked.

He nodded toward the house. "You and Cindy get along okay, do you?" He found the key and twirled it around his thick finger. "Jess said he was coming down to visit you. He get in touch?"

Elle shook her head. "Nope. I haven't seen him in years. When was the last time you saw him?" Like Cindy, Elle towered over the man. Even without her heels, which she'd forgotten in the grass out back.

"Couple weeks ago. He came down to see me. Asked to borrow

some money. Wasn't the first time. I wish like hell now I had it to give. Is it true someone killed him?"

Elle nodded. Her throat had closed up, making it hard to speak. It was hard seeing Holt like this and not getting sentimental. He represented an earlier time. An easier time. She wished like hell she could go back and leave all this behind.

"How long are you in town for?" she asked.

His giant shoulders heaved. "Couple days, I guess. You?"

"I live here."

"Well, shit. I heard you'd left for Chicago."

It was Elle's turn to shrug. "Shit happens."

"We should get together before I leave. Catch up and stuff." He swayed toward his car.

"You weren't planning on driving yourself, were you?"

He put a finger to his lips. "I bet I make it to the motel in Mason without seeing a single cop."

Elle smiled, but it was a sad smile. "Too late." She raised her arms and let them drop.

"Too late for what?"

She sighed. Holt had never been too bright. "You've already run into the sheriff and a deputy."

"Where?" He looked around, spooked.

She jerked a thumb toward Neil. "Deputy." Then pointed to herself. "Sheriff."

His eyes bugged out. "No fucking way." He laughed followed by a small hiccup. "You're shitting me."

Neil stepped down the stairs. "I'll drive him, Elle. I was about to leave anyway. Tully can follow us in our car. I'll go grab her."

"Thanks, Neil."

"You're not kidding, are you?" Holt still hadn't grasped this concept. "Who the hell was stupid enough to vote for you?"

"It's a long story." She guided him to the passenger seat and helped him in. "Maybe when we catch up, I'll fill you in."

Neil came back outside, followed by Tully. He grabbed Holt's keys and opened the driver's door.

"You know, Neil, I can take care of myself." She grabbed the driver's door as he arranged himself, moving the seat back a couple feet.

"Oh, I don't doubt that for a second, boss. But it's been a long day and an even longer week."

"Tell me about it." Elle waved as they pulled out of the drive.

By the time she reentered, the mess had been cleared. Guests were back in their clumps. The men huddled in the kitchen swapping football stories from high school, swigging bottles of beer. Elle recognized most of them from the team. At the time they'd been like brothers. She wondered how many had kept in touch with each other. Or why none had gone out to see Holt off.

The women tucked themselves around the refreshment table, stuffing handfuls of baked goods into their mouths. As if filling their stomachs with food would hold their grief down, buried beneath snickerdoodles and low-fat blueberry muffins.

Elle found Cindy mixing herself a drink in the dining room. She was helping herself to the stiffer collection tucked away in the back of Janice's curio cupboard. When she saw Elle approach she waggled her glass, clinking the ice together, as if to say, you want? Elle nodded.

They slipped out the back door onto the deck. The sun had dipped below the tree line, offering shade and a bit of respite for the first time all day. They stood in bare feet, leaning against the rail, sipping their bourbons in silence. Neither woman seemed to want to be the one to start the conversation off.

Cindy had chosen a dark blue pantsuit—she'd since discarded the jacket. Her loose camisole blew in the breeze. It made her look like she'd been attending a business meeting instead of a funeral.

"Can I ask you something?" Cindy jiggled her glass and swallowed the last of the liquor in one gulp. She paused, the question on her lips. "When you were dating Jessie, did you ever get the feeling you were just another one of his trophies? Like if he could, he would've placed you on his shelf and left you there?" She pointed her now-empty drink at Elle. "And I don't mean any offense. I'm sure you're quite intelligent, but you look like you would've made a great trophy." Cindy's slight drawl elongated the end of "trophy."

"That wasn't the question you were going to ask, was it?"

"The real question wasn't any of my business. I was curious because Jessie had a way of reworking his past so it painted him in the best light. When I was younger, I ate it up. But now..." She shrugged. "Now, I'm more cautious. Hold that thought." Cindy grabbed Elle's glass and scooted back into the house, leaving Elle alone with her thoughts.

These days, when people mentioned Elle and Jessie, they always talked about the engagement, but she'd never said yes. He'd asked her the night of the Beer and Berry festival that last summer he spent in Turlough before moving away to college. He'd given her a ring and everything. It was black onyx—all he could afford—with a thin sterling silver band. She knew he'd only asked because he'd wanted to claim his territory when he left. He wanted to let all the other guys know that she belonged to him.

But she handed it back to him and told him to keep it until they were both ready.

Elle often wondered what would have happened had she married Jessie. What kind of life would she have? Like Cindy, would she have a big house and fancy cars? Would she be facing financial ruin or would she have had enough sense to keep an eye on Jessie's spending? She certainly wouldn't have ended up at the University of Chicago studying criminology. Or sheriff. As much as she loved her job, this road had been paved in tragedy and heartache. And she certainly wouldn't have been happy. She'd known that even at that early age. Eventually she would've left him because as much as she loved him, she would never have been in love with him. She loved what he brought to her life, comfort and acceptance. But in the end it wouldn't have been enough.

Cindy stepped back out onto the deck carrying the entire bottle of bourbon with her. "It'll save us time in the long run." She set a full glass down in front of Elle.

And that's where Robin found them, an hour later and half a bottle emptier.

CHAPTER SIXTEEN

Elle popped two Advil and washed them down with a bottle of V8 in the parking lot of Earl's Gas and Gulp on her way out of town. After that first glass of bourbon, the rest of the night was a blur, but she clearly remembered Robin tucking her into bed.

Dressed in civvies, she climbed into her Ram pickup, pressed the clutch, and turned the key, and it sputtered to life.

She grabbed her radio. "Hey, Neil. You copy?" She pulled at her skirt, trying to hide the expanse of thigh. Perhaps she'd tarted it up too much.

"Yeah, boss, what's your ETA?" More static than voice came over the radio.

"I'm heading over to Mason to check out a lead. I shouldn't be more than two hours."

There was a long pause before Neil came back. "You think that's a good idea, going up there by yourself?" Another pause. "You packing?"

She had her service pistol in the lockbox of her truck. But that wasn't going to do her much good. Looking down at her barely there skirt and the extent of boob showing from her tight shirt, she wasn't sure where she could put her gun. "I'll be fine. Just hold down the fort while I'm gone."

"Will do, boss. Be careful."

"Will do."

Dressed like this, she could handle men. It was the reason she'd chosen this outfit over her uniform. Holt had always been sweet on her and she was hoping this outfit would help loosen his tongue a little. Plus, people had a way of clamming up when they saw the uniform.

While the feminist in her cringed, the cop in her was okay with anything that got results.

She was only going on a hunch. Something Holt had said piqued her curiosity: This wasn't the first time Jessie had asked him for money.

The Motel 6, with its whitewashed walls, rose stark against the green of the grass. The second-floor corridor wrapped around the outside of the building. Leaves floated on the surface of the pool out back, and geese poop lay at the bottom. A giant sign out front advertised $69.99 per night.

She parked the pickup near the stairs leading up to the second floor. The last time she'd been here, a little over a week ago, she'd felt just as nervous. She'd been in civvies then too. Jessie had been waiting for her, leaning over the balcony, smoking a cigarette.

"You smoke now?" she asked, stopping a few feet away from him. He'd aged since she'd last seen him eight years ago, but in a good way. From the tightness of his shirt she could tell he still worked out. His skin was smooth and tanned. He looked good.

He shrugged. "Only when I'm nervous." He flicked his cigarette over the side. It bounced once, then rolled to a stop, a lone glow of red against the dark parking lot.

"What do you have to be nervous about?"

"I've been standing out here for the last hour wondering if you'd show."

She almost hadn't. When he'd called her earlier at the station and asked her to come meet him here she'd gone home, changed into pajamas and crawled into bed, determined to ignore her curiosity. But thirty minutes later, she'd been dressed and out the door again.

"Why did you call?"

"Let's talk in here." He guided her into his room. The bed was unmade. The garbage overflowed with fast food wrappers and a six-pack of empties lined the wall next to the TV, which was bolted to the dresser. He'd been there more than a day.

"You want a beer?"

She shook her head and leaned against the dresser, the only other place to sit besides the bed. "So what are you doing here? And why aren't you staying at your parents'?"

He opened a small fridge disguised as one of the cupboards in the dresser and grabbed two beers. He handed her one and opened the other for himself. Elle placed the beer next to her, unopened.

He took a long pull from his. "My parents brag about you all the time, you know."

"I haven't seen your parents in years. How are they?"

"They're good. Over the moon about you, though." He laughed. "Who'd have thought you'd replace old Bailey as sheriff. I bet Withers is beside himself."

Elle laughed at that. "Yeah. That man's a prick, though."

"How's EJ?"

Elle sighed. "You asking because you care or because you want to make it look like you care?"

"That's not fair."

Elle shrugged. She twisted the cap off the beer sitting next to her and took a sip. "Neither's calling me out of the blue and asking me to meet you at a motel."

"Look. I'm sorry about that. It's just I can't go to my parents with this. Even coming to you with this..." He stood and walked over to her. He placed his beer on the dresser next to hers. He smelled like cigarettes and beer. She wondered if maybe he hadn't been here more than a day. What if those beers were from earlier?

"Back up." She placed a hand on his chest, keeping them arm's length apart. Her mind screamed in warning. "If you had it in your mind that you were going to call me over here and charm me into sleeping with you, then you need to replan your seduction model."

Jessie didn't say anything, just watched her, like he was examining her for the first time.

"Tell me why you're here," she said.

"No bullshit, all right? Things haven't been going so well for me." His chest heaved suddenly, gulping in a big lungful of air. "I did something stupid a couple of weeks ago and I need your help. I know I don't have any right coming here after all these years asking you for this, but I don't trust anyone else."

"What do you need?"

"I need to borrow some money, just for a little while, to get back on top of things."

"How much?"

"Twenty-five thousand."

"Jesus!" Elle scoffed. "What makes you think I have that kind of money?"

He just stared at her, not wanting to say it.

"What makes you think I still have that kind of money?"

"I called your house before I called the station, so I know you still live in your parents' old home. And I just saw the piece of shit you pulled up in. Unless you developed a really expensive drug or gambling problem, I'm guessing you set a chunk aside for EJ's education and the rest has just been sitting there."

"What could you possibly need twenty-five grand for?" She'd won over five hundred thousand dollars in a civil suit against Sid Derry. A small consolation after the prosecution had failed to win their vehicular manslaughter case. Jessie had been right. Apart from paying off her student loans and setting up a fund for EJ, which looked like he'd never use, she hadn't done a thing with the money. It had been sitting there for the last five years, tainted.

"It's not like I wouldn't pay you back."

"That's not what I'm worried about."

He took a lock of her hair and twirled it around his finger. "It's not what you think. I promise." He leaned down and kissed her lightly on the lips.

She pulled back. "Don't."

"You know, it makes sense, you becoming sheriff. You always did want to protect people from themselves."

She'd just never been any good at protecting herself. Elle crossed her arms and retreated to the other side of the room.

"So nothing's changed, huh?"

"Yeah, a lot's changed. You're married, for one."

"And you're still into chicks."

Elle didn't say anything. Her stomach knotted itself in the silence. It dragged on. The only sound was the soft sips of beer from Jessie's side of the room.

"You could've told me. Before I bought a ring and proposed."

"How the hell was I supposed to know you were going to propose? We were kids. You were going off to college. I figured it would take care of itself."

"So you are, then."

"Why do you need an answer? Because then the rejection won't be because of anything you did? Is that why? How about this, I don't sleep with married men."

He plopped down on the bed. "Hell, I'm not asking to be judgmental. I just want to know is all. Are you seeing anyone? Are you happy? Am I not allowed to want to know these things?" He lay back on the bed, resting the beer on his stomach. "You know the first time I came home with Cindy, all they could do was talk about you. Wanted to know what I'd done to fuck everything up." He laughed. "I wanted so bad to tell them. And I almost did. So many times. But Cindy told me not to."

Elle closed her eyes, mortified.

"She's a good person. I don't really deserve her. Didn't really deserve you either, did I?"

"Did you call me over for a pity party? Stop being such a boob." She dropped down onto the bed next to him. "What do you need the money for?"

"I made some bad investments and I need to replace some bonds I borrowed against before Cindy finds out."

"Twenty-five grand worth?"

"I'm sorry. Everything's just gotten so out of hand."

He passed out soon after. On her way out she wrote her cell number on a notepad. Two days later she would find him lying dead in the Maverty house.

As she climbed the stairs to the second floor, she wondered if this was a good idea after all. Sometimes Elle couldn't tell if her ideas were brilliant or stupid.

She knocked on Holt's door. He opened it after several seconds with the same giant smile he'd had the night before. "Didn't think you'd show. You know how people are always saying 'we should get together.'" His eyes roved up and down. Elle cringed. It's what she'd wanted. If she was being honest with herself, it was to dispel anything Jessie might have told him.

He waved her in. "It's a shit hole, but then I guess you already know that."

Like Jessie's, this room also had nowhere to sit except the bed. She settled for leaning against the dresser. "So how are you?"

Seam took a seat on the bed. It sagged into the box spring. He picked up a pack of Marlboro Lights and waved it at Elle. "Do you mind?" he asked. Elle shook her head. He waited until he'd lit one and inhaled before answering. "I've been worse." He laughed suddenly. "Which is saying a lot." Sitting on the bed, his feet didn't even touch the ground, they wiggled as he laughed.

"About two months ago I bumped into Jessie at a friend's party. We started talking about real estate. Did you know Jessie was in real estate?" He didn't wait for Elle to respond. "He said they were eating up those tiny houses all over the country. It's a novelty, but they're not that bad. My brother and I make 'em. Not sure if you knew that. Jessie said he knew a guy who would help us expand." Ash from his cigarette dropped onto his light blue polo shirt. When he brushed it off, it left a faint trace of dark gray. "So that's how I joined up with Jessie again." He stubbed out his cigarette. "I'm sorry about the wake. I didn't mean to cause any drama. Not too many people were happy to see me." He turned away, peering out the window at the parking lot. "That's the other reason I was surprised to see you."

Elle heaved a huge sigh and sat down on the bed next to Holt. "What'd you do this time?" Holt was always getting in trouble back in school. It was never anything he meant to do, but it had a way of happening anyway. Jessie and Elle had gotten him out of a few jams. They usually had to do with too much drinking and his big mouth. Holt had no filter. He also had no social etiquette.

He spread his hands. "Who knows. All I know is that no one was talking to me after Rob and his wife's tenth anniversary party. So I probably said some stuff I shouldn't have."

She wanted to give him a big hug, but decided it might give him the wrong impression dressed the way she was.

"I'm sorry, Elle. I don't know who would've killed him. If that's what you wanted to know." He might not have been too bright about social situations, but sometimes Holt was perceptive beyond reason. "That's a nice top, though."

"You said it wasn't the first time he'd asked to borrow money. When was the first time?"

"A couple months ago. But I didn't have it to give then."

"How much was he looking for?"

"Fifty grand. I mean, if I had that kind of money lying around I wouldn't be living in my brother's basement, right?" He pulled out another cigarette, rolled it between his fingers, then put it back in the pack. "Oh, don't look at me like that. My life isn't that bad. Brad's wife's a good cook. I get a nice cool basement with my own entrance and get to see my niece and nephew any time I want. I have a pretty decent life considering. Honest. Things have been going better lately."

"How much did he want this time?"

"He wanted a hundred grand. I told him I could maybe find him five, but then he said he'd found someone who could lend him the money."

"Did he say who?"

"Nah, but he didn't have to. I was pretty sure he got it from that chick…" Holt trailed off, looking at his socks. There was a hole in the left and his big toe stuck out. "He found it somewhere."

"You know who he was sleeping with?"

Holt looked over at her and heaved a giant sigh of relief. "You knew about that?"

She nodded.

"Thank God. I didn't want to rat him out. Even if he is dead. I don't mean to, Elle. These things just pop out."

She patted his hand. "It's okay. Who was he seeing?"

"Her name's Kitty."

"That's it? Just her first name?"

"That's all I know. I swear." But he couldn't meet her eyes. He pulled out another cigarette and lit it, blowing smoke up into the air.

"Holt. If you know her last name, tell me."

He turned to her, his eyes puppy like. It was hard to believe he'd spent most of high school pummeling kids. "I don't know her last name for sure. I'm just guessing."

"I still need to know."

"I'm pretty sure it was Sedona's wife. Kitty Sedona."

"Last question. Do you know what he needed the money for?"

"He said it was for bad investments, but I knew better. Guys talk." Holt shrugged. "He had a gambling problem. Poker mostly."

Elle squeezed his hand. "Thanks for answering my questions."

"I bet you look just as good in your uniform."

Elle laughed, but inside she was seething. She should've guessed the money wasn't for bad investments. But he'd pulled her in again.

Chapter Seventeen

She found Neil in her office sorting through some papers on her desk. He looked up as she strolled in, still in her previous getup. His eyebrows shot up. "We start a vice squad I don't know about?" he asked.

"Yep. I ordered you a similar outfit but it doesn't come until Monday."

"Hardy har." But he didn't say it with his usual humor; instead he held up the Ziploc with the note from Jessie's wallet. "You want to explain, or are you just going to give me some bullshit story?" He dropped it on the desk between them.

"Neil." The longer his name hung in the air, the harder it was for her to speak up, to come clean like she knew she should. But what could she say now? Was there anything that would make it right?

"I checked the phone records they sent over. He called this number, your cell, the night he was murdered." His face hardened. His jaw flexed. "And there you are, not saying a word. Just letting Stan and me think we're actually investigating." He kept his eyes on the desk unable to look up at her, his hands melded to his midsection, like a pouting child.

"What's that supposed to mean?"

"Forget it. I've got things I got to be doing. Heather'll fill you in." He tried to stomp past Elle, but she blocked the door and grabbed his arm. He peered down at her tiny hand wrapped around his beefy arm. If he wanted to he could get by.

"Hold on. Wait. I didn't…" He was staring at her so intently she knew nothing she said would help remove the hurt behind his eyes.

She knew why Jessie had been staying at the motel instead of his parents'—he didn't want to worry them. And she knew also why he'd paid cash—he didn't want his wife to see it on their credit card statement. And yet she'd wasted Stan and Neil's time chasing down these blind leads. Her gaze shifted to her shoes.

"I'm sorry."

"Right." He yanked his arm back and stormed past her, boots slapping on the tile, past Robin standing in the doorway. He didn't even wave good-bye to Heather as he left.

"Is this come as you aren't day? Should I have worn my overalls?" asked Robin, she pulled at her immaculate gray shirt.

Elle thought it best to ignore her. She turned to Heather. "I'm going to run home and change real quick. If you need me, I'll be on channel two."

"Sure thing, boss."

Robin caught up to her at her truck. "Hey, you okay?"

"Yeah, why shouldn't I be?" She jammed her key in the lock and yanked the door open. The hinges groaned.

"You did manage to suck back a bottle of bourbon last night."

"Thanks for driving me home. I'm fine."

"So you do remember."

With her hand on the wheel, ready to pull herself up, she turned to face her. "What is it exactly I'm supposed to remember?"

"That I'm a good sport."

Elle rolled her eyes and got in the truck. It rumbled to life after a few tries. She rolled down the window. "How did you get home?"

"Mr. Forrester followed us in his car and gave me a lift back to Sandy's." Robin rested her arm on the window ledge, saw the dirt, and thought better of it. "You pretty much passed out the second you got in the truck. Mr. Forrester had to carry you into the house."

Elle shut her eyes and leaned her head back. She was never going to live that down. "Great."

"You're pretty cute when you're drunk. Argumentative, but cute."

"Oh, God. What did I say?"

Robin pursed her lips and looked to the sky. A smile spread across her face. "You were adamant you could undress yourself. I had to help a little with the zipper."

Elle's face flamed red. She'd woken up in the nude and hoped she'd done that herself. The temperature in the cab rose ten degrees.

Robin leaned in closer. "Not to worry, Sheriff Ashley. You were still in your underwear when I left. Not that I wouldn't have helped if you'd asked."

It had been years since Elle had experienced this, but she wasn't so lost that she couldn't recognize it when she saw it. "Are you flirting with me?" Looking back on their exchanges, she couldn't say that she hadn't sensed an interest. But never in a million years would she have guessed Robin was into women.

"Sheriff Ashley, I've been flirting with you since the moment I met you. Don't tell me you're just noticing now." Robin grinned at her as she backed up.

Elle ripped her gaze away before the heat in her chest engulfed the rest of her face. She was so out of her depth. This should have lifted her mood. Instead she felt like she'd boarded a train and there was only one stop. Once she got on, there was no changing her mind. For the first time in years, she was attracted to someone. There had been a few women in college, but not since she'd moved back to Turlough to look after EJ. She'd shut that part of her life off.

As she passed the houses leading out of town, Mr. Weatherby waved from his front garden. She waved back. But then a sudden panic overtook her. Had anyone seen her and Robin. Would they have known what they were talking about? She'd done so well to keep that part of herself hidden all these years. The last thing she needed was for Robin to come in and ruin it all.

Her mood turned foul the second she got home and found Dan and EJ out on the back deck trying to cover up the smell of pot wafting through the air.

"Po po's home. That's my cue." Dan gathered his cigarettes and lighter. When he brushed past Elle in the door, his eyes spent an extra long time on her breasts. He waved to EJ and was gone.

Elle glared at EJ for all of two seconds before trailing Dan out the front door. "Dan, I need to speak with you."

He had one foot up in the cab, ready to hoist himself up. His eyes roved over her Mr. T. T-shirt and its low-cut neckline. "Giving up the law, Ms. Ashley?"

Elle crossed her arms over the shirt. The words "shut up, fool" were still visible below her arms. She wished for the hundredth time that day she'd worn something a little more professional.

"From now on, I want you to stay away from EJ." She knew it sounded desperate, but the anger that had been building for days was about to boil over.

His eyebrows shot up. He hopped down from his cab to face her, but there was amusement behind his eyes. "Your brother's a big boy. He can hang out with whoever he wants."

"There's a lot of things EJ can do once he graduates. But that's not going to happen if he keeps getting mixed up in your idiotic revenge schemes." This was not going well.

Dan nodded. "So you think I'm the problem? Your brother had nothing to do with that fight or breaking into Randy's car?"

"I think he wouldn't if you weren't around."

Dan leaned his hip up against his truck and crossed his arms. A smirk on his lips. "You want me gone, Elle?"

The use of her first name, the familiarity of it on his lips, knotted her insides on a visceral level. "I want you to stay away from my brother."

"Is this the same empty threat you used before?" He pushed off, stepping closer. He was taller by several inches. "The one where you said I would regret it if I messed with Randy?"

Elle refused to give him any ground. As much as she wanted to step back and distance herself. Instead she looked up at him in what she hoped was her hardest, meanest stare. "That threat now includes my brother. And if you think it's empty, just fucking test me. Just test me." She turned and stomped off toward the house, hoping it looked badass instead of a good imitation of a petulant child.

A used pile of Lysol wipes lay on the pavement next to the open door of Elle's cruiser. Inside, Elle scrubbed the upholstered seats, attacking the interior with long methodical strokes. As soon as she'd disposed of one wipe, she yanked a new one out of the dispenser and continued the assault.

Normally a daily ritual, Elle hadn't cleaned the cruiser in days. Not since they'd found Jessie. The back and forth monotony of the act helped clear her mind. Helped soothe the ache in her heart every time she thought of Neil. It helped calm her fears about EJ and where his life was heading and helped quell thoughts of Robin and what her smile had done to her insides.

So now she cleaned. Each swipe erased the dirt, subduing the threat of her mind, which only worsened the moment Brady strolled up and kicked the back tire.

"Hear anything back from the staties yet?"

She sat back on her haunches, throwing the soiled wipe into the pile. "Pass me the Windex." She grabbed a handful of paper towels, circling them around her hand, cocoon like, and tore them off the roll.

Brady stooped to pick up the bottle but paused, dangling it on his index finger out of reach. "The results?"

"Ken, don't worry. I guarantee you will be the," she stopped, counting a tally in her mind, "fifth person I give the results to. So keep your panties on. They'll get here when they get here."

She reached out and snatched the Windex, beginning her assault on the rear windshield. She could tell him that even if they did get the results, it wouldn't make a difference. They didn't have anything to compare it to. But she didn't, knowing he wouldn't hear a word she said. He'd be back tomorrow with the same questions.

She could feel him standing there watching her. The longer he stood there, the tighter the knot in her back twisted. She could almost feel him breathing down her neck. Was he expecting a different answer if he waited five more minutes? She wanted to turn around and shout at him to go back to his office, but it would only cause a scene.

Finally, she stopped cleaning and turned to face Brady. "Was there something else you wanted?" Her voice had a hard edge to it.

He rocked back on his heels, contemplating.

"You know if you really want those results, why don't you call up the lab in Jackson yourself," she said. "I'm sure they'd be happy to oblige. Might cost you next year's road repairs, but, hey, at least you'll know. I'm sure the council will understand. Or better yet, why don't you cut some of our salaries. We don't need them." She had to drop the Windex bottle before the urge to squirt him in the face became too great.

He let out a long, slow breath, stuffing his hands in his suit pockets. "You're not the only one who's had that thought, you know."

"Ken, I was joking." She unfolded herself from the back seat. If he tried to cut her payroll she might actually hit him. He was the only person she'd ever seriously thought about slapping in the face.

"We're thinking of combining the sheriff and coroner position within the county."

"What did you say?"

Behind Brady, a young girl with impossibly blond pigtails passed by. The training wheels making her bike tilt to the side, back and forth, creating a staccato effect.

"The council's voting on it next Monday, the day after the festival. If it goes through, there'll only be the one position."

"What does that mean?" Her heart rate accelerated, drawing all her blood to its center. She felt light-headed.

"It means, for now, you would take over Jack's duties. Most of what he does is paperwork anyway."

"That's not fair. It'll kill Jack. Can't they wait until he retires?"

"Elle, that man is never going to retire. We can't afford to wait another week, let alone another decade." He exhaled loudly through his nose. "Lots of towns are doing it." He made that sound like justification enough.

"You're trying to get rid of him is what you're doing. It's wrong," she said. "Was it you who suggested this?" The girl in pigtails made a second round past Brady, digging her heels into the peddles and leaning back to get as much speed out of the little pink and white bike as she could.

"No, it wasn't me. But I agree with the principle. There's not much to his job. And if we needed something more than the sheriff could provide, we'd call in a state medical examiner."

With a clarity Elle hadn't felt in weeks, she saw how this had played out behind her back. They wanted to get rid of an aging, doddering old man, not because he was incompetent but because someone had sold the council on a way to save money. She wanted to be furious, but she didn't have the energy. What if it was a way to get rid of her too? There were several members on the council she was sure hadn't wanted her in office. Could this give the city an excuse to have another vote if they chose?

"This is why he's been in such a stoop lately, isn't it?" she said. "He already knows about the vote."

Brady nodded. "And if you'll take some good advice, I'd stay out of it. Just keep your head down."

"Or what? I'll be on the chopping block too? That's not how this is supposed to work."

"No, Elle, it's not. But it's politics." Another excuse. Brady was overloaded with them. It was like he'd packed a suitcase full of them to absolve him when he entered politics over two decades ago and just kept unloading them whenever he needed until he was as light and unburdened as air.

Elle squinted up at him, the sun having moved above the tree line, and said, "If it's just politics then it can still go the other way."

"I've talked to most of the council members already. Most of them are for it."

"Who haven't you talked to yet?"

"You can't go around bending people's ears. The voting is just a formality now." An impatience had crept into his voice, like dealing with small children when they've found a hole in your logic but you're too proud to admit it.

"Why not? Isn't that what you're doing?" She had a way of turning a menacing question into the most innocent by tilting her head.

Brady hooked his thumbs into his belt, a clear sign he was about to give up ground, and looked down at her pile of wipes. He sighed. "I'll give you the names, but you're not going to like them."

"Quit screwing around and tell me."

"Judge Keeler and Sid Derry."

Elle recoiled at the sound of their names. He was right, she didn't like those names one bit.

Chapter Eighteen

Elle spent the rest of the day with her head in paperwork, checking statements. Neil had left copies of the Forresters' financials with his notes on her desk. It only proved what she'd already suspected. They were overextended and living well beyond their means.

When she'd finished inputting all the new information they'd gathered, she went back to the beginning, starting with his wallet and phone. By midnight, Elle had finished sifting through the contents of Jessie's trunk again. It was all pretty standard stuff—clothes, toiletries—nothing unusual jumped out at her.

No matter how many times she sorted through everything, she just couldn't make it work in her head. If the money wasn't in the car or hotel, what had happened to it? It hadn't been on Jessie, nor in the house, as far as she could tell. Which meant the killer had taken it, which was a thought that would keep her awake for most of the night. If she hadn't given Jessie the money, would he be dead?

Elle wasn't sure what she should be feeling at this moment. She covered her eyes. Her headache from this morning had come back worse than before. The fans above cranked away, sweeping the office with tepid air. What she needed was to go home, get some sleep, and tackle this problem with a fresh mind in the morning.

She turned off all the lights and locked up even though Stan was still out making patrols. He wouldn't be back for hours.

The night air was humid. Laughter drifted down from Finnegan's, making her wish she had somewhere else to go besides home. But as she climbed into her truck, a new wave of exhaustion washed over her and all she could think about was crawling between her sheets and passing out for the next six to seven hours.

Where the ravine curved was a bend in the road, just before the bridge that crossed over the Red. The trees to the left were painted in a blue and red hue. First red, then blue, like two partners dancing in circles. When she rounded the corner, it was Stan's cruiser parked on the shoulder creating the light show. Elle pulled up behind him, scanning the forest on both sides of the road for any signs of movement before stepping out of her vehicle. The gravel's press beneath her boots echoed through the trees as she crunched toward the driver's side door. She pulled a small flashlight from her belt and raised it toward the window of the cruiser. She flashed the back seat. It was empty.

The next few moments happened in a blur. When Elle tried to piece it together later, she couldn't remember if pulling her gun had caused her to drop her flashlight, or if she had purposely thrown it to the ground to unholster her gun. All she would remember was the spinning action the flashlight made as it disappeared under Stan's cruiser.

Elle glanced around before ducking her head into the front seat. Stan slumped back, his eyes closed, mouth gaped open. His blood ran over his shirt where someone had shot him. Elle placed two fingers on his neck to check for a pulse. As she did, he jerked awake. His eyes went wide with confusion and panic. Inches apart, they stared at each other. He gulped back air, but didn't say anything.

Still keeping eye contact, she unclipped the radio and switched it to the emergency channel. "This is Sheriff Ashley, I'm reporting a ten-thirty-three. I need assistance. Send an ambulance to County Road Six," she glanced around, "between mile marker sixty-five and sixty-six." Her voice wasn't more than a croak by the time she added, "Please hurry."

Elle reached for Stan's hand, sticky with blood. She held tight. For some reason, this reminded her of Bailey finding her father sitting in the driver's seat of their Buick. Only Bailey hadn't known her father was dying. To Elle, it was obvious Stan wouldn't be alive by the time the ambulance arrived. His breathing was forced and loud. Much too loud for the confined space of the cruiser. She had this inexplicable urge to call a time-out as if she could yell toward the forest and put the game on hold. She felt helpless. There was nothing she could do to calm the fear in Stan's eyes. They were so clear, it struck Elle how young he was. He didn't deserve this.

And that's how Stan Carrick spent the last moments of his twenty-four years, gazing into the emerald green eyes of Elle Ashley.

He wanted to let her know he'd be okay because he knew she would blame herself, but he would be fine now. He wished he could tell her that. But every thought took forever to pull from his brain. Like slipping underwater, the deeper he went, the darker everything became. He would be fine. It was only a short swim to the top. There was something he wanted to say. Something about a face, but as he sunk deeper the less it mattered, the less he cared. He was fine now.

Elle removed her fingers from Stan's throat. She staggered back, away from the car. The dancing red and blue was the only movement for miles. Blood from the puncture in Stan's chest covered her fingers. He had bled to death in a few minutes. She froze, opening her ears to the movement in the surrounding woods. Instead of the silence she had expected, the forest came alive. And she had definitely heard a crunch farther down to her right. Every noise amplified, every rustle heightened, until she imagined the killer stalking her from every tree.

Slow as the grass grows, Elle unhitched her radio, keeping an eye along the edge of the trees.

"Come in, Neil."

Several moments of static passed before a voice come back. Groggy. "Yup?"

"I need you to come out to County Six. Out by the ravine, just before the bridge."

"Now?"

"Yeah, now. Bring Case." She switched her radio off. Neil could bitch to Case. She wasn't interested in hearing it.

Elle heard the snap of a twig, only a few feet into the trees. Without wasting too much thought on it, Elle walked toward the edge, her gun at her side, her boots crunching on the gravel, and entered the forest. Immediately, the dark enveloped her. The sliver of moon couldn't penetrate the canopy, even at the edge. It made for difficult navigation. Her footing was slow at first, as her eyes adjusted, then gained momentum. A lot of the boys in town were hunters and knew these woods better than Elle knew the layout of the sheriff's office.

They were experienced trackers who could stalk and kill just about anything. Elle was not one of them. She knew she was making too much noise. Her footfalls should be silent, not a stampede.

When she was around ten or eleven, her grandfather took her out hunting once. He'd woken her up before the sun had come over the hills. He put his index finger to his lips, not wanting to wake her folks. She remembered the way the air smelled that early in the morning, fresh, as if nothing had yet marred the new day. There was something so pure about being in the woods before the day had begun, like you were experiencing something only the animals got to see. At first, she thought of it as a magical forest. A place where humans didn't exist yet. She could see why the natives had settled in the hills thousands of years ago. This world was beautiful. But as the morning wore on, and their purpose for being out there grew near, the forest began to turn on Elle. Halfway up a hill they came upon a rabbit, its foot maimed and bloody, limping through the brush. Elle rushed toward it to help. Her grandfather grabbed her arm. Even at seventy-eight his grip was like handcuffs, rooting her in place.

"You don't know where it's been." His Irish brogue lilted on the word "been."

"It's just a rabbit, Granda." She could see the panic in the animal, like it was seeping out its pores and wafting into the air. "Who would do something like this?" To Elle, bunnies were cute pets, harmless and playful. She thought everyone must see them like that and couldn't understand anyone who would hurt such a defenseless creature.

"Not who. What," her grandfather said. "Something has attacked this animal. A coyote or possibly a bobcat. I've seen them in these woods." He knelt next to the rabbit, covered its eyes with one large wrinkled hand. This seemed to calm the rabbit. He turned its injured leg to examine the damage. "Sadly, for whatever reason, it didn't finish the kill."

"Sadly? But she's alive."

Her grandfather sighed, it was a large sigh. It moved his shoulders like he was lifting a pack to readjust his burden. He shook his head. "No, it's suffering now. We can't leave it like this. It needs to be put out of its misery."

"What do you mean?" Her voice went up two octaves.

He took her hand and pushed her toward the top of the hill. "I want you to go up to the top and wait for me there."

"What are you going to do?" She knew exactly what he was going to do, but she wanted to hear him say it. To hear him say it was okay.

"It's a good thing we're doing. She's in pain now, we're going to help her out of that." The more he said "we," the less she wanted to leave. If she stayed he wouldn't be able to go through with it. But she did leave.

Her grandfather never took her hunting again. When she thought of it, she always felt like she'd failed some test, like she'd let him down. A few years later, her grandfather passed away. But she always wondered, if EJ had been born first, would he be a hunter now?

About twenty yards into the forest Elle stopped. She heard a faint rustling up ahead. Whoever was moving through the forest wasn't a hunter, nor were they taking particular pains to be quiet. The crunch of twigs and branches echoed through the quiet of the night forest.

They must have assumed she'd stay with Stan and wait for backup. They weren't that far in, which also meant they had watched her with Stan, waited for discovery and watched her. It could have been a sadistic impulse or they had simply wanted to make sure Stan was dead. Was this the same person who'd killed Jessie? The thought of two killers walking around free in Turlough gave Elle the shivers. She had acted on impulse, running into the forest without backup or any idea of who she was chasing. If Bailey were here, he'd tell her she'd left her senses back at the cruiser with Stan. What she should have been doing, instead of going off half-cocked, was securing the scene, searching for evidence to link the two murders, waiting for backup. Then after that lecture he would have suspended her.

Would she have had the same reaction if it had been Stan out here running after a suspect in the middle of the night with no backup and no sense of direction? Probably. She would have reamed him out, just to prove they had rules that had to be followed.

Maybe that's why Bailey had always come down so hard on her, then turned around and supported her succeeding him. He was laying the foundation. Not that she'd listened.

The gap between Elle and her prey was closing. Every so often she could see a black shadow bob up, then disappear behind a tree. If she could maintain this pace for another mile she might catch a glimpse of who she was chasing. That's when they'd reach the pasture at the back of Old Bailey's property. That is, if she recognized them.

Moving deeper into the woods, the terrain became treacherous. Heavier underbrush meant deeper thickets to pass through, and ditches and roots to maneuver around. It was impossible to see more than a few inches ahead. She had to feel her way through, grabbing onto trees, onto stumps, anything she could use to steady herself. She was so focused on keeping the suspect in view that she didn't notice the fallen tree blocking her path. Her shins slammed into it, knocking her to the ground. As she fell, her gun scattered into the underbrush and she smacked her head hard. It disoriented her. The soft cry she let out as she fell was enough. Whoever she was chasing took off at a faster pace through the forest.

She gave herself an instant to catch her bearings. When her instant was up so was she, running through the forest, fast. Her breath thumped against her chest, straining her lungs. She pulled out her backup flashlight, sweeping the beam across the foliage.

As Elle thudded through the forest, she used her sleeve to wipe the blood from her face, which was streaming like she'd tipped a jug of it out of her nose.

If she could make it to the clearing up ahead, she'd be able to see who it was. She could get a description even if she didn't recognize the person. It was the break she'd been hoping for. The strongest chance of actually catching the killer.

Her blood rushed through her body so fast the sound was deafening, drowning out the noise of the forest. The adrenaline she was producing was enough to cause a heart attack.

She kept her flashlight dancing in front of her, scanning the trees for any sign of movement. Elle's instincts told her the suspect was male. The baseball cap hid a lot, but the motion was masculine.

It had been several minutes since she'd seen him, but that could mean he'd made it to the field. She pushed harder, scrambling over branches and forest debris. The light made it easier to see, but it also made her easier to avoid. If she didn't make it to the clearing fast enough, she would lose this opportunity. There were a million places for him to disappear. She had to close the gap.

Coming over the last gully, a branch slammed into Elle's ribs. She bent forward, winded, clutching her abdomen. As she did, the branch smashed down on the back of her head. The wood splintered in a spray around her. She wanted to vomit but didn't. Her face smacked into the ground. She inhaled a deep breath and choked on the dirt.

The last thing Elle remembered before passing out was a hand reaching out toward her.

CHAPTER NINETEEN

The worst part was still to come, which was a testament to how bad the last few days had been for Elle. First, waking up at the edge of the forest with a fuzzy recollection of how she ended up crumpled in the dirt and her own dried blood. The morning haze obscured the grass in a pink fog. The humidity had already settled in for the day. As she stumbled back through the forest, the daze lifted. Slow at first, then rushing at her like the tree branch that had whacked her in the stomach.

The worst hadn't been finding the bloodstained T-shirt stuffed in the roots of the tree next to her head. Or that she recognized it as EJ's.

The worst hadn't been the worry and concern on everyone's face as she crossed the road toward a throng of cars and two EMTs loading Stan's body into an ambulance. When she stood alone later in her bathroom, stripping off her uniform, she saw what they had seen. Micro scratches with beads of blood covered most of her body. Blood was caked around her nostrils. A bruise was forming on her left cheekbone, the side she'd used as a battering ram against the ground.

But nothing could compare to what was underneath her clothing. Dr. Crawford had called her lucky. She hadn't broken anything, but she didn't feel lucky as she stared at the deep purple crawling up the side of her body. It hurt to move, to breathe, to cry. It took forever to get undressed.

EJ found her curled up asleep in the shower, still mostly in uniform. He wanted to take her back to the hospital, but she refused to face Dr. Crawford for a third time. Instead he made her a cup of tea and helped her into bed. That had almost been the worst. Two days' bed rest. Doctor's orders.

Jack Case had come to visit her. He'd brought her coffee and lunch from the diner, as if she were an invalid in some nineteenth-century novel.

"It's a chicken club on rye." He handed her the paper bag. The bottom half was shiny with grease. "I assumed you weren't up to cooking for yourself."

"You're assuming I ever cook for myself."

He smiled, pulled up a chair and opened his own bag. Jack had brought himself a sandwich so Elle wouldn't have to eat alone. They munched in silence for a while. Elle took large bites. She hadn't eaten much that day. A bowl of Cap'n Crunch. It was the only thing to eat in the house.

EJ made a better adversary than nursemaid. Elle had always been the one to buy groceries, clean the house, and repair anything that needed fixing. EJ barely mowed the lawn or shoveled the driveway. It was only after Elle threatened to cut his driving privileges that he did anything.

Elle inhaled her coffee before taking a sip. They'd been out of coffee for two days. Just the smell sent shivers of pleasure down her spine. "Thanks for this."

Jack grunted. "Have you looked at yourself in the mirror?"

"Jack, please. I don't need the lecture."

"You look like you lost a fight with a barbed wire fence."

"I've had plenty of time to think over what I did. I had a chance. To end this, to catch the man who killed Jessie and Stan. That's worth some scrapes and bruises." She crumpled up her sandwich bag. "It's worth the bed rest and boredom. All of it."

"Is it worth alienating the only deputy you got left? I found Neil practically shitting himself on the side of the road, wondering what had happened to you. Did you think about that when you took off into the woods?"

Shit. She hadn't. And the shame of that made the bruises and cuts feel ten times worse. All she could do was shake her head.

"I didn't think so. Okay, I'm not going to say anything more. You're a grown woman. Just be careful is all I ask. And think things through—all the way through—next time you go chasing a murder suspect into the woods in the middle of the night. Alone. Without backup," Jack said.

There was a dull, all-too-familiar ache in the pit of her stomach. She hadn't felt like this since high school. The shame and disappointment, the collection of bad decisions accumulating. The only time she'd ever felt more humiliated was the time Bailey had caught her and Jessie in the back of his truck. She'd been mortified as she scrambled for clothes to cover herself. Even now, picturing Bailey, his eyes averted as she squeezed back into her jeans, made her skin flush.

The only noise for the next while was the whirring fan above and the sound of Jack chewing. The one thought Elle had refused to think about all day was Stan's body lying on Jack's autopsy table. She knew he would have performed one, but she hated the idea of Stan's last days above ground spent having his insides excavated.

She kept thinking about the first time she'd taken him out on patrol. They'd gone out to the Cheevers'. It happened a lot when the Cubs lost.

There'd been a noise complaint. And Frank liked to yell at his wife. She wasn't sure what they'd get when they knocked on his door, but what happened was so much worse than she was expecting. Listening to Frank talk about her that way and not being able to do anything about it hurt.

She'd wanted to tell Stan then that the worst part of the job was how useless you felt most of the time. But she didn't want to ruin it for him. She could tell how excited he was to be out on patrol. It would've only been a half truth anyway. When they got back to the station, she'd locked herself in the washroom and cried great, big sobs. She'd shoved her face in her jacket, afraid Stan would hear. She'd felt like such a fake.

"How long do you think? Before Stan…"

Jack took her hand. "It would've been fast, he didn't suffer much."

"When I found him, he was still alive. He looked so scared." She took in a huge gulp of air. "All I could think about was my dad and what he must have been thinking when Bailey found him." She began crying then for the first time since all this had started. And once she started, she found she couldn't stop. Within seconds she was hiccupping, trying to pull air into her lungs.

Jack moved next to her on the bed, taking her in his arms, and let her release her pain and guilt. "There was nothing you could have done." He stroked her hair.

"I should've been thinking about Stan. I could've helped him." She buried her face in Jack's shoulder, letting him rock her. She gave in to all the raw emotions rising from her mind. All the guilt. All the frustration. All the second guesses. She'd wished then that she'd told Stan the whole truth, that the worst part of this job was how exposed it made you feel.

After several minutes, she pulled back and wiped the tears away with the palm of her hand. "This isn't the Turlough I remember growing up in. Deputies don't have to worry about getting shot pulling someone over. We're not a dangerous place."

"You think that's what he was doing?"

"Of course, why else would he have been on the side of the road? I'll get Neil to contact dispatch and find Stan's last call in."

"Could've been someone passing through."

Elle snorted. "You know as well as I do, there's nothing worth passing through. No, I'm going on the hunch that these two murders are connected."

They sat in silence for a few minutes as they both contemplated what this meant for Turlough.

"Why didn't you tell me about the vote?"

Jack leaned back to look at her. "Why do you think I didn't tell you?" He handed her a napkin from his takeout bag. "I didn't want you to worry when you had so many more important things to deal with."

She took the napkin and blew her nose. "It is important, Jack." She didn't know how to put it into words. Doing this job without him would make it less important, like he was helping carry on a tradition. Without him, part of the history of it would die, like it had when Bailey died. "If they vote yes you'll be out of a job."

"That might not be so bad." He gave her shoulder a squeeze. "I'm not as young as I used to be. Maybe it's time I give someone else a chance."

"I don't want your job."

"But who better to have it?"

He got up from the bed and fished out a manila folder from his case. He handed it to Elle. "This is the other reason I came. Neil wanted you to see them."

Elle opened the folder. Inside were several pictures of a knife sitting in gravel. She flipped through each one, stopping at the last.

"It was found next to Stan's cruiser."

The last picture had a close up of the knife with the initials FA carved into the handle. She recognized it immediately. She looked up at Jack. Apparently he had recognized it as well.

No, the worst was still to come.

❖

Neil cast his line and watched it dance along the surface of the calm river before sinking beneath the ripple. The air had congealed into one sticky, humid mass. It hung low like the sun, flecking the water and grass in an orange haze.

Neil popped the tab on a can of Schlitz and gulped down half. He belched and began reeling in his line for another go.

Peace and quiet. From the moment he'd woken that morning, he'd had one goal. Get his line in before the sun set. Out here on his dock, with the sun low, a cold beer at his feet, he could forget the dread he felt. Forget the hopelessness he felt every time Elle left him in charge. But most importantly, forget the betrayal and anger he felt toward her.

She'd known Jessie was in town and why and she'd kept it from him. He could understand her embarrassment. Nobody liked getting caught sleeping around. But what if she'd been keeping other things from coming to light?

Elle was the most honest person he knew. Time and again he'd seen her come up against EJ, never playing sides, always keeping it fair. Yet this guy, Jessie Forrester, had her acting like a silly schoolgirl. If she'd been afraid to tell them about being in Jessie's motel with him, what else was she hiding?

When he'd found Elle's truck parked behind Stan's cruiser, Stan dead and Elle missing, it scared him shitless. He'd thought the worst. That she'd come across some maniac shooting Stan and he'd pulled her into the woods to rape and kill her.

He was angry she'd lied to him and he was angry she'd been reckless with her own life. And those two thoughts kept butting heads in his mind. How could he be angry with her for keeping him in the dark and angry that he'd almost lost her at the same time?

Out here with only the lapping at the dock and the sounds of insects doing flybys, he could forget the rest of the world even existed. It was his equivalent to Elle's runs or Tully's candlelit baths.

On his third throw, he got a tug back, but the line had only snared on some reeds.

Fishing was Neil's sport as much as you could call it one. In his younger years, he'd fantasized about football and baseball, joining the school teams. But he wasn't built for those kinds of activities.

In his senior year, he'd joined a tree planting expedition up north in Manitoba, mostly to impress the girl he was dating. But he also wanted to prove to his mother that he could achieve something on his own, something active.

Halfway through the week, Mark Walden, one of the other planters, went missing. Neil volunteered to help with the search. Six hours in they still hadn't found anything. Neil came to a large ravine. With no heed to his trousers, he charged down the hillside, vaulting over fallen trunks, crashing through brush, thumping past evergreens. He felt brave and courageous like all those adventurers he'd read about as a kid. He was James Bruce sailing into the unknown, discovering great things that needed discovering. About halfway down, he had to pause, resting his large pulpy hand against the needle-sharp bark of an oak. The air thickened. Black flies surged in unison. He'd forgotten exploring took an effort he lacked.

He could hear his mother's cracked voice telling him to slow down, to take it easy. Always wary of overexertion, his mother the cautious, the protector. "Don't go too far. Don't go so fast." Her eyes cast to the sky, looking for confirmation as if lightning would rip through the clouds and strike down anyone moving too fast over her lawn. That's not to say he didn't appreciate his mother. They had a very supportive relationship. She'd baked, he'd eaten. And eaten. Until he resembled the portly dough boy prominent on his mother's favorite baking supplements. It was no wonder he'd been so quick to marry Tully. Wasn't food just another word for love? A way to look after those you cared for?

When he reached the bottom, his efforts were rewarded. He found Mark sprawled on the ground, his left leg at an odd angle, blood and scrapes covering his face and hands. Instead of being revolted, Neil felt exhilarated. Because of his actions, his initiative, he'd been the one to find Mark. He knelt and felt for a pulse. It thumped against his finger. Not only had he found him, he'd found him alive.

After the ambulance pulled away, after the accolades and celebrations, Neil gazed up at the sky. The stars were framed by a silhouetted break in the canopy. A feeling of contentment washed over him. He knew then that he wanted to help people. As soon as he was eligible, he applied to the Flynn County Sheriff's Department.

He hadn't regretted that decision. Not even when his mother threatened to disown him. Not even on days like today, investigating the murder of a fellow officer. He knew this was where he belonged. Just like he knew the moment he'd shook Stan's hand that he belonged on the force.

After a few more casts and one more beer, he got another tug on his line.

That's how Elle found him, gutting a trout on his picnic table. Entrails dripped through the slats.

"Just what you needed, more blood and guts."

He stopped mid-chop to see Elle picking her way across his lawn. "Shouldn't you be in bed? Resting?" He brought his knife down with a loud thwap, slicing the trout's head off.

"Did you really think I'd lie around after seeing these?" She waved the pictures he'd sent of the knife.

He held up his hand, the one covered in scales. "I just wanted you to be aware, that's all." He set down his knife, wiped his hands on a cloth and folded his arms. "So what's the game plan?"

"What do you think?"

Neil didn't say anything, just stared across the picnic table at her, then shrugged.

"Jesus, Neil." She smacked the folder on the table. "I didn't mean to hold out on you. I was...I don't know. But I'd never hide evidence, and I haven't."

"So you lied to us."

"I needed time to figure things out—"

"Elle, what were you even doing in his motel room?" The way he said it sounded the same as when she asked herself that very question the morning after. It sounded like disappointment. "It's none of my business." He turned and walked toward the edge of the dock. Elle had no idea how to make this right. It would take a lot more than coming clean to get Neil to trust her again. She'd broken a code they'd developed early on. No bullshit.

He leaned down and grabbed two beers from his cooler. "You look like you could use this." He handed her one of the cans. It was Neil's version of a lifeline.

She figured the best way to start would be to apologize. She opened her beer, took a long drink, then began the story from the first time Jessie called her to come meet him.

The sun was long down by the time she began telling Neil about her rendezvous with Jessie the night he was murdered. He had the look of someone watching a fatal bus crash without being able to do anything about it.

"I mean, what else is there to say? I screwed up. I should never have met him that night. I was on duty, but I figured I had to swing by the Maverty house on patrol anyway." She stared out at the river, which was now a black strip. Moonlight glinted off the few ripples carving out the rocks. She looked back at Neil. "How was I supposed to know when I walked out of the house that was the last time anyone would see him alive?"

"So he calls you up after twelve years and asks you for twenty-five grand and you run right over and give it to him?"

"Neil, it's not like that."

"Well, then tell me, because I can't understand why you would give anyone that kind of money. You know it's not for anything good, no matter what they say. And an ex to boot. Jesus, Elle. This doesn't even sound like you."

Elle couldn't explain it to Neil. She couldn't explain it to herself. There was something about Jessie that had always made her do things she didn't think she could and, more often, things she shouldn't. It had been that way since the day they met. And the worst part was he knew it.

Back in high school, he'd started a tradition as captain of the football team. On the last day of summer, he would bring the new football team out to the cliff overlooking the Red. If you had the guts, the cliff made a great place to jump. The river swooped around the bend like a roller coaster ride. The last rookie to jump spent the next season washing the team's jock straps. The last year Jessie was captain, he brought Elle with him. At the time she hadn't known why. Was it to show off that he could make a bunch of dumb jocks do even dumber things? Or did he want to impress her with the daringness of his team? He'd lined them up along the edge to explain the exercise. More than a few balked. Not only was it high, but it was midnight, which made the river below impossible to see. The full moon illuminated the surrounding grass in direct contrast to the dark chasm below. If you gauged it wrong, you would end up on the shallow bank along the edge of the cliff instead of the middle where it dipped. In some places it was more than three meters deep.

"Come on. You're a bunch of pussies," he shouted. He turned the full power of his grin on Elle. His teeth were so white they shone in the moonlight. "Even my girlfriend has bigger cojones than you pussies."

And with that, Elle knew why he'd brought her. Without thinking, she took a step back and leaped. The night air sucked at her as she fell, enveloping her in its velvet embrace. She didn't have time to think about the consequences. The only thing that flashed through her mind was that grin of Jessie's, no doubt laughing from the safety of the clearing. She had become invisible as she jumped, only an echoing splash somewhere at the base of the cliff.

When she hit, she hit hard. Her head bounced off the surface of the water as she went under. Unprepared, her breath whooshed out, left behind as the current carried her around the bend. She fought the momentum but couldn't see the obstacles in front of her. They ripped at her clothes, which weighted her, pulling her to the bottom. She wrestled her jean jacket off, letting it sink as she swam to shore. A rock caught her elbow. Branches scratched at her bare legs. By the time she crawled onto the rocky beach and lay panting beneath the stars, she had a broken eardrum and scratches over most of her body. "Well, that was dumb," she said, then vomited up a lake of beer onto the rocks next to her.

That was the last time she ever jumped into the Red from the cliff. It had scared her more than a little. Not only at what could have happened, but what she was willing to do for Jessie.

If she was being honest with herself, the real reason she met Jessie at the Maverty house that night was because she felt guilty. This guilt had consumed most of her adult life. She felt like a fraud for most of high school. Pretending to be something she wasn't. Even now, she only dealt with it by keeping part of herself so far hidden that it was more like a memory. She thought if she could make it up to Jessie somehow, maybe she wouldn't be so damned scared of herself all the time.

"It doesn't matter why. Not now. The simple fact is, I met him at the Maverty house to give him money, and after I left, someone killed him for it."

Neil sat back digesting that thought. He didn't know if he should be happy Elle was giving him all the facts or pissed off that she'd withheld the most important one. "So you think that after you left, someone came by, saw Jessie with a bag of money, shot him, mutilated him, and ran off with the money?"

"We didn't find the money, so what other conclusion is there?" Elle asked.

"But who would be hanging around the Maverty house except a bunch of teenagers?"

"I don't know. There was no one there when I arrived except Jessie. Everyone was at that keg party. Maybe someone followed him there?"

"Christ. Who in town's been spending a lot of money in the last week or two?" Neil asked.

Elle's cell phone chirped. She pulled it out of her back pocket but didn't recognize the number. It had a Chicago area code. She answered it assuming it had something to do with the case. "Sheriff Ashley." She waited. "Hello?" No answer. She hung up and checked the number again. "Ask your wife, she'd know."

He nodded. If there was anyone on a spending spree, Tully would know. "The other possibility is a drifter got him. He sees the drive, follows it looking for a place to spend the night. Sees your cruiser so he hides out waiting for you to leave and sees the exchange. Then, stabs Forrester after you leave and takes the money."

"But then who shot him? That's what's not sitting right with me. If you've got a gun and can kill with it, you're not going to take the time to pull out a knife and create a big mess. It's almost like two people tried to kill him."

"Shit. You think we got two people working together?"

Elle dropped her head into her hands, rubbing her eyes. "It's too early to speculate. All we know is that Jessie had twenty-five thousand dollars on him when I left. And when we found him a day later, he didn't. Until we know more, I don't want to play guessing games."

She raised her head and looked toward the river. "The truth is, I'm too involved in this. I hate to do this to you, Neil, but I'm going to have to put you in charge."

Neil was already shaking his head by the time she finished. The last thing he wanted to do was relive the last two days without Elle in charge. "You are the best person here to get this solved. If you step down that only leaves me and two part-time deputies."

"I was the last person to see him alive. I created the motive to kill him. Those are two good reasons to step down."

"You weren't the last one to see him alive. The killer was. Think about this: If you step down, that's going to create a whole lot of questions you don't need right now. Not with everything that's happening with Case and the coroner's job. How is it going to look to the city council if you step down from this investigation? They're going to think you're not up to the job, or worse, that you can't be trusted with the job."

"A second ago, you were pissed at me for withholding information from you. Now you want me to lie to the city council? I can't do it."

"That's different. They're on a need-to-know basis. I'm not. If you step down now, you can pretty much kiss this job good-bye. They'll force you out. The same way they're forcing Case out." And that would leave Neil in charge.

He reached out and patted the table in front of her. Neither of them were the touching type. They'd set their relationship ground rules years ago. And it didn't involve touching. Or hugging. In fact, Neil couldn't remember Elle ever hugging anyone. She was a very guarded and solitary person. Maybe that's why she'd met Jessie in his hotel room that night. She was starved for companionship. God knows she didn't get it from that brother of hers.

"Please, Elle. Give it a few more days. We have no idea why Jessie was killed. And now Stan."

Elle nodded but didn't say anything, too afraid the tears would come out with her voice.

"Did you find anything else besides the knife?"

"Not yet. Like Jessie, he was shot. Missed his heart by an inch. Case thinks it's a different gun too."

Elle groaned. "That doesn't make sense. There's no way I'm going to believe we have two, possibly three killers running around Turlough. Stan's murder has to be connected to Jessie's somehow."

"And we'll find it."

They sat in silence, sipping their beers, watching the river pass by. After some time, Neil pushed at the folder Elle had dropped on the table. "What about the other thing?"

Elle rubbed at her eyes, just thinking about the other thing exhausted her. "We pull him in for questioning. God, Brady's going to love this."

"You and I both know he had nothing to do with it."

She almost laughed at how absurd it was, but there was no mistaking it. The knife they'd found on the ground next to Stan's cruiser, with the initials FA carved in to the handle, was her grandfather's. The last time she'd seen it was in her underwear drawer after confiscating it from EJ. There was no doubt in her mind he'd taken it again.

"Can you do it?" Elle asked. "He'll probably be less of a drama queen if I'm not there."

Neil nodded. "I'll do it as low key as possible."

She reached across the table and squeezed Neil's hand. She needed to feel the solid presence of him, needed to know he would still be there for her, even if it would take a while to build that trust again.

Chapter Twenty

Elle lay in the back of her pickup, stargazing. She was out in one of the fields near the Old Bailey place. It was her favorite spot to come think, and boy, did she need a good think right now.

Neil was right about one thing. If she stepped down from this investigation she could kiss her job good-bye. She should feel honored to work with someone with so much loyalty, but instead she felt gutted. She wished she'd trusted him earlier. Now the whole thing felt sour in her mouth.

In the distance, she heard a car crunching up the gravel path. It was probably Harper coming to tell her to get the hell off his property. She usually came out later to avoid him since, as a farmer, he went to bed early.

But when a blue Jetta pulled up behind her, she became suspicious.

The door opened and long legs unfolded from the vehicle. Robin slammed the door. It echoed in the night.

She was wearing tight jeans and a black tank top with her ash blond hair piled haphazardly onto her head.

Elle's mouth went dry.

"Sorry if I startled you. I saw you pull up the lane and was curious." Robin stopped at the back of Elle's truck. "Holy shit." Her mouth dropped when she looked up at the sky. There were so many stars out there was barely any black. The milky way arched through the sky. "Is this what you guys get to see every night? This is amazing. We don't have this in Chicago. I'm lucky if I can see the North Star or the Big Dipper."

"It's the only good thing about living this far out. Best place to think on the planet."

There was a moment of silence as Robin stared up at the stars and Elle unconsciously stared down her top. Seeing her like this was so out of context. Since the wake, every time Elle thought of Robin and what she might have seen when putting her to bed, a tiny tremor rippled through her stomach. She wasn't sure if it was from fear or desire. Judging by her current reaction, she'd say the latter.

"Do you come here a lot?" Robin laughed. It echoed through the field. She had a great laugh, deep and throaty. "That sounded like a line, but I didn't mean it that way. Do you come here to think a lot?"

"I used to when I was younger. Now I don't have much time." A dark wool blanket layered the bed of her truck. She'd folded it over several times, making a soft cushion. Perfect for stargazing.

"Do you mind if I join you?"

Elle hesitated, but only for a moment. She moved aside and indicated the spot next to her on the blanket. She was careful to keep her arms tucked in. Her ribs still ached, but she didn't want to let on.

Robin lay down and tucked her hands behind her head. After a moment, Elle joined her.

"I'm sorry about your deputy. What was his name?"

Elle stayed silent, unsure of Robin's motive for asking.

Robin turned on her side and propped her head up. "What can I say to make you trust that I won't publish anything you don't approve of?"

Elle continued to stare at the sky, her hands clasped on her stomach. "I don't think there is anything. I don't share a lot."

"I've noticed. All work and no play makes Elle a dull girl."

That stung. "You think I'm dull?" She didn't know why it should matter, but it did.

"No, but it can't be easy, especially with EJ."

Elle groaned. That was the shitty part about small towns. Everyone knew your business. Robin had probably heard all about the accident and Sid Derry, the fact that she couldn't keep her own brother out of trouble. And who knew what she'd heard about her and Jessie.

Robin wrapped a hand around Elle's wrist. "I have a younger brother too. Jason. He's always making bad life decisions and I never know if I should bail him out or let him make his own dumb ass mistakes."

"Bail him out? Like, literally?"

"Sometimes. Mostly for dumb thug shit. My parents don't know what to do with him, so it falls to me." Robin released her grip and turned to lay on her back.

"EJ hasn't had to be bailed out, yet. But if he keeps hanging around Dan it'll get to that."

"Dan?"

"His family moved to town around Christmas. To be honest, that kid scares the shit out of me."

"How so?"

"He's just got a vibe, you know? And EJ's changed since he got here. And not for the better. Like, EJ never used to hang out at the Maverty house before Dan came along. Now, I've caught them smoking pot there most Saturdays. EJ said Dan likes the history of the place. Stan said he's seen Dan there by himself sometimes, just sitting on the roof smoking a joint. Do you know how dangerous that is? It terrifies me to think that that kind of idiot has an influence over my brother."

Robin was silent for a long while, then she said, "Listen, you can't freak out about it. When it comes down to it, he's his own person. And it's not up to you to decide what kind of human being he's going to turn into."

"Sounds like you've spent a bit of time thinking about it."

"Every time I see Jason's name pop up on my phone, I'm afraid to answer it. Because one of these days, I'm going to help him out and it's going to be the last time."

Robin's voice was low. It drifted up into the night. Elle liked the way she spoke. Clear and straightforward, like she understood. She could see why someone would trust her with their secrets. She wasn't sure she was ready to. Not yet.

"How much younger is he?"

"Three years. He's had enough time to grow out of this phase. I kept hoping he would call one day and tell me he'd gotten a job. Even if it was a shit job, like working in a warehouse or something." She shrugged.

Elle watched as the skin played over her muscles. She had amazing shoulders.

"Do you ever feel like you're part of the problem? As if the more you say yes, the more you're contributing to their problems?" Robin asked.

Elle sighed. Robin couldn't know how close she was to the truth, but that's exactly how it felt. Sometimes she pushed too hard. She set her expectations too high, which in EJ's case was setting him up to fail. She couldn't help it, though. She'd always set the bar high for herself. It was the only way to get ahead.

"But if you cut Jason off, would it solve any of his problems?"

Robin smirked. "No. He'd still get into trouble. And that's the rub. Do nothing, help him out, it's basically the same outcome."

Elle turned back to the stars. Out here, under this blanket of distant suns, she felt so tiny and inconsequential. It almost always put her problems into perspective. But tonight, it wasn't just the view that had helped. Knowing someone else shared her troubles was worth a million night skies.

Dell's was packed when Elle entered. Talk of the unbearable heat filled the air. She slid between two customers at the bar. One was chewing his steak like he was slaughtering the cow himself, the other was slopping up his egg yolk with a pancake.

"A coffee to go please, Tully," said Elle.

Earl Pepper called out to her, "Hey, Sheriff." A few bits of beef slipped onto the counter. "You know you're supposed to open the door before you walk in, right?" He picked the pieces up with black oiled fingers and popped them back into his mouth, then grinned, showing the gaps between his teeth.

"Oh, you're real clever, Earl." Tully poured coffee in a to go cup. "Don't worry, honey, you barely notice it." She handed Elle the cup and waved off her offer to pay, instead squeezing Elle's hand. "Neil told me about it. We're all reeling with what happened to Stan. But you got to be more careful."

"It was a real shame what happened to him. He wasn't much older than my nephew," one of the regulars at the end of the bar said.

"Yeah, happened right around the corner from our place," Will Pritchard said. He stuffed the last of his pancake into his mouth.

"You're out on the other side of the ravine, aren't you, Will? Neil and I looked out that way, but he likes his fishing, so we settled for our place on the river."

Will shook his head. "You're better off closer to town. That night poor Deputy Carrick died, we thought we had a prowler, but my boy chased it out. Turns out it was just a damn raccoon." He pointed his fork at Earl. "I swear to God, if I could, I'd line my property with nail mats so anytime they even thought of coming on my property they'd get nailed to the damn ground. Easy pickings then."

"Save that kind of talk for when I'm not around, Will," Elle said. She loaded her coffee with sugar.

"Oh, for Christ's sake. Don't tell me it's illegal to kill 'coons."

Elle took a sip of her coffee, testing the sweetness. She nodded. "It is if you don't have a permit to trap."

Will turned to Earl. "You believe this? I got to get permission from the government to rid my own damn property of pests."

Elle smiled sympathetically, choosing not to tell him that it was next to impossible to get those permits. Unless you could prove a health risk or excessive property damage, you were out of luck.

"Hey, speaking of your boy. He get that scholarship to, where was that again?" Earl asked.

"Kentucky State. Randy starts in the fall. His mom and me are real proud."

As soon as the talk turned to football, Elle picked up her coffee ready to leave. She motioned Tully over for one last question. "Has that reporter been in here asking questions?"

"That woman has been a busy little bee. She's been running her ass all over town. Been in here a few times too."

"What else did you let slip?"

Tully looked affronted. "Don't look at me. I think she hit the jackpot with Principal Withers."

"Speaking of asses. Thanks for the coffee."

Elle headed toward the station but slowed crossing the street when her cell rang. She groaned. She couldn't imagine who was calling her this early in the morning. Not many people had her number.

Elle had come in early that morning even though she was still on ordered bed rest. She wanted to get ahead of anything she'd missed—that was the lie she'd told herself. She wanted to be there when Neil brought EJ in. If she could lend moral support, she would. If he didn't want it, at least she'd tried. As his guardian, she'd still have to sit in on the interview. She would also have to call Bryce in; he'd need a lawyer regardless if she thought he did it or not.

It was the same number that had called her yesterday. "Hello?"

"Did I wake you?"

"Who is this?" She stopped in the middle of the street. At this hour she didn't have much traffic to compete with.

"Robin. I found—"

"How'd you get this number?"

"That doesn't matter right now." Her voice kept cutting in and out. "I found something at the Maverty house that you should come take a look at."

Elle continued across the street to avoid a pickup truck. "Why are you snooping around the Maverty house? That building is off-limits."

"You're right. I shouldn't have come out here. But I did." There was a long pause. "So are you coming?"

Elle set her coffee cup on the roof of her cruiser. The pickup truck had slowed trying to find a parking spot, probably to grab something from Dell's, but there wasn't anything available. It pulled up beside Heather's Buick, but when the driver saw Elle watching, he sped off.

Elle sighed deep. "Will it keep until this afternoon?" She didn't want to leave the station in case Neil got back with EJ, but she also didn't want to pass up a possible lead.

Robin's voice cut out again. When she came back she said, "About to lose battery, just come quick." Then the line went to static and died. She couldn't be positive but it had sounded like she said, "bring rope."

"Shit." Elle stood for a few more seconds watching the street, then radioed Neil to let him know she was checking out something at the Maverty house. She threw her phone onto the passenger seat, grabbed her coffee, and got in.

CHAPTER TWENTY-ONE

EJ perched on a train bridge, his feet dangling over the side, a smoke hanging from his mouth. Below, the Potawatomi ambled by, courting this season's bass. He heard a loud whistle off in the distance, the kind of whistle you had to use two fingers to achieve. It was a whistle you could envy. Long before he bothered to look, EJ heard Dan marching across the train bridge toward him. Dan had this knack of always finding EJ, even when he didn't want to be found. Especially when he didn't want to be found.

EJ was channeling the cat, as his mom used to say when he was in one of these moods. When there was some challenging task EJ wanted to postpone like studying for a school test, he would find a place and hide out from the world. Much like their cat used to do when avoiding a vet visit. A summer of laziness was all he wanted to think about right now. Summer school would be starting in the next couple of weeks and he would have to attend just to graduate. But what could a piece of paper tell him that he didn't already know? He was useless when it came to school.

Dan plopped down beside him and pulled a large Ziploc of pot from his backpack. "Saw your sister going into Dell's this morning. Looks like she ran head first into a wall."

"Of course you did."

"What's that supposed to mean?"

EJ shrugged, maybe now wasn't the time to get into it, but Dan tended to happen by his sister a lot. "Nothing. Forget it."

For the first time in EJ's life he was scared for Elle. He'd never seriously thought about what it would be like to live in a world without her. Sure, she was a pain in the ass to live with. She made it tough to get away with things. She nagged him to be better, do better, want better.

Seeing her in the shower, passed out, then fragile like she could be broken as he lifted her to bed, terrified him. It made him seriously think about what he would do if she was gone. He could tell her he would've been better off if she'd stayed in Chicago until even he believed it, but the consequence of her not being anywhere made him feel alone. It wasn't having to do things on your own, it was having to do them without anyone nagging you to do them.

He needed to think about this. To think about where he'd be if she wasn't stopping him from going one step too far. Sure, she picked him up for underage drinking, for skipping school. But it didn't mean anything. They both knew it.

Sitting on the train bridge, listening to Dan, all he wanted was to get up and keep going down the tracks. Escape and never come back. Would his heart harden the farther away he got? He hoped so. He wanted nothing more than to squash every last feeling deep inside. To be more like Dan. Nothing except anger touched him. And anger was a powerful tool.

Dan and EJ kicked their legs in unison, watching the clouds pass over them. Dan lay back and rested his head on the train rail, folding his hands on his stomach. He looked peaceful.

"You ever think about leaving this place?" Dan asked.

"All the time. As soon as summer school's done, I'm heading up to Chicago."

Dan laughed. "Summer school? You're not really going to go to that, are you?"

"I won't graduate if I don't."

"Get your GED in Chicago. You've learned everything school's going to teach you." Dan couldn't care less if he graduated high school or not. He wanted nothing more from Illinois in the way of education. They had taught him everything he needed to know about the system and how much it respected anyone who was different. Being different was like being a Jew in Germany during the Second World War to them. Time and again he'd seen how Lisa was marginalized because she didn't fit their cookie-cutter version of a student. When she was younger, they'd sent her to a private school specifically for special needs children. She improved under the one-on-one teaching, coming home each night full of hope and a growing confidence at her own growing independence. But he saw the toll it took on his parents. His mom worked two jobs while his dad sold his soul to a company he hated, working nights and weekends to afford a better future for their daughter.

But it wasn't enough. In the end, his mom had quit her two jobs and homeschooled Lisa. It was better than public school with their special education programs. But it was hard on his parents, especially his mom, who had taken on such a daunting task that it sometimes swamped her.

"Yeah, well. I'll think about it." EJ didn't want to admit that he couldn't pass his GED test if he had the answers tattooed all over his body. Learning from books left him dry. He'd rather learn from experience.

"You should, if a piece of paper is that important to you." Dan got up and walked toward where the bridge met land, turned, and waited for EJ.

EJ stood. He was starving. He doubted Elle would even be home. If Dan had seen her this morning it meant she hadn't lasted more than a day before going against doctor's orders. Typical. He kicked a rusted bolt sitting on one of the slats and watched it fall. It bounced off a rock and slipped into the water with a quiet plink. Why was she allowed to break the rules but he had to toe the line? It wasn't fair. His stomach gurgled. Maybe he would grab a pizza from Earl's. And with that, all other thoughts vanished. "I think I'm going to head home."

"Tell your sister I said hi."

"She's probably still at the station." He waved, even if Dan couldn't see, and headed back across the train bridge toward home.

When Elle arrived at the Maverty house, a sense of impending doom flip-flopped through her stomach. Robin had parked her car where Jessie's had been. She stepped onto the porch. It creaked beneath her boot.

She unhooked her Maglite before opening the door. At the entrance to the living room, she stopped. From her first cursory sweep, it didn't appear as if the scene had been disturbed, but she saw fresh cigarette butts littering the floor. If she had to guess, half of J.P. Flynn had passed through here in the last week. It was a high smoking and getting drunk in the same spot where murder took place. That they could see the evidence of it being a brutal murder made it all the more delicious.

She hated to admit it, but if this had happened in her day, she would've been right along with them. In fact, she would've been the instigator. Just for the thrill of something different, something that didn't involve football or someone's fist going through another's face.

That someone had actually lost their life wouldn't even factor into it. They were so far removed from the loss it could only be intoxicating. She didn't hate them for it because she understood it, but she didn't like them for it either.

"Robin." The downstairs was empty. Not for the first time did she feel she'd been brought out here chasing her own tail. Just as she was about to head upstairs she heard a muffled cry. "Robin?" She followed the voice to the far corner of the living room. Several slats covering the window had been pried loose, leaving a gap for the sun to stream through. It revealed a large hole in the floor.

"Watch your step," Robin yelled, but too late. As Elle got near the edge, the floorboard gave way and she fell through the floor.

Elle lay on her back for a full minute in absolute agony as the dust settled around her. When she opened her eyes, Robin leaned over her. "You okay?"

She didn't say anything. Her breath was still clogged along with her voice somewhere in her chest and wouldn't come out. Her ribs felt like someone had taken a crowbar and spread them apart. She tried to concentrate on why she was lying on a dusty cellar floor instead of the pain.

Why couldn't she for once have listened to the doctor and stayed in bed today? She'd much rather be staring at her ceiling fan than the jagged, rotted floorboards above her.

"Shit, you don't look so great." Robin examined her neck. "Did you get all those scrapes from the fall?"

Elle shook her head. Finding her voice she said, "I looked like this before I fell." She took another minute to brace herself to sit up, but in the end, she needed Robin's help. Elle was almost in tears by the time she was standing.

"What the fuck happened to you? You look like you tried to rescue the wrong cat out of a tree."

"You're hilarious. I bruised my ribs the other day."

"Doing what? Wrestling King Kong?" It had been too dark the night before for Robin to see how damaged Elle looked. In daylight, even the muted light of the basement, every scratch and cut stood stark against her pale skin.

"I'd rather not talk about it." The sun shone through the hole and the dancing dust to illuminate a very tiny, very old cellar. "Why the hell didn't you just tell me you'd fallen through the floor? Why all that cryptic shit about finding something that I needed to see?"

"First of all, I did find something and second, I didn't tell you I fell through the floor because…" She brushed at her now dusty and rumpled shirt, trying without success to bring it back from the dead. "Because, well, I felt like an idiot."

Elle wanted to point out that if she'd told her she'd fallen through a hole, she would've actually brought rope and backup and would've been more careful walking around up there. But she didn't. Given Robin's current state, the rumpled clothes, the cut on her forehead, she didn't feel like making things worse. Instead she started feeling around, looking for a way out.

There was a set of stairs leading to two large doors that would've opened into the backyard. Robin saw her looking. "Don't bother. I already tried. There's something heavy blocking them."

But Elle had to see for herself. She couldn't admit that she was stuck in this cellar, completely unknown to her before now, with this woman, the one person she didn't want to be confined in a small space with. Not when she looked like she'd been bathing with razor blades.

Elle braced her back against the doors and pushed. A new pain leapt out from her ribs. She took a deep breath, then tried again.

The word "stubborn" popped into Robin's head. Elle was worse than Jason. "Good idea. Injure yourself further."

"I left my cell phone and radio in the car. So if it helps us get out of here before we bake to death, I'll gladly break a rib."

"Okay, fine. Sit your ass down. Let me have another go." Robin slipped her heels off one at a time and sat them next to each other on the step. Elle watched the muscles in her legs flex as she struggled against the doors.

Elle nudged her to the side and they both tried. But after twenty minutes, even Elle gave up. "Whatever is blocking that door is there to stay."

Robin, sweating, breathing as if she'd just run the twenty meter dash, dropped onto the stairs and began rolling up her silk sleeves. She was back in a skirt suit, complete with killer black heels. She fluttered the front of her shirt, pushing air into the unforgiving silk.

Elle had been right. The temperature in there was unbearable. And rising.

"So what kind of time frame are we looking at here? Are we going to be rescued sometime today? Or should we start nesting?" Robin asked.

"My radio was digging into my ribs." Elle stood flat against the wall, folding herself into what was left of the shade. "That's why I took it off." Thinking of her radio laying on her passenger seat made her think of the half-drunk coffee sitting in her cruiser. It would still be hot.

"As much as I'm enjoying the company, I just want to know if we're going to get rescued before we die here."

"Relax. Neil knows where I am. When I don't radio in, he'll come find me." She didn't mention that he was currently out looking for her brother and wouldn't radio her before he found EJ. It could be several hours before anyone noticed she was gone.

After ten minutes of watching the sun creep farther across the floor, Elle gave up trying to stay out of the sun. She lowered herself onto a stair. "How did you get my number anyway?"

"A good magician never reveals her secrets." Robin's smile was all teeth.

"Are you at least going to tell me what you found?"

"Oh, yeah." In the excitement of Elle falling through the floor, Robin had forgotten all about it. "I came out here this morning to check out the place, get a better feel for it." Robin was tired of waiting for the investigation to get solved. She wanted answers now. She wasn't going to share that with Elle, of course. She needed Elle on her side if she was going to get anywhere on this assignment.

"I was here about ten minutes before I fell through the floor and that's when I found this." She pulled out a balled-up shirt and handed it to Elle. "It was tucked under the stairs."

Elle pulled the shirt apart. Dried blood stained the front, gluing parts of the fabric together, marring the Harley-Davidson logo on the front.

"You recognize it?"

Even if she had she wouldn't tell Robin. "I think more people worship Harley-Davidson than God around here." She laid the shirt next to her and checked under the stairs. It was empty except for some debris. "Didn't happen to find a gun, did you?"

Robin shook her head. Elle sat for a few minutes scanning the basement. Her eyes traveled along the floor where the brick wall met the stone floor. She stood after a minute and walked to the far edge.

Elle dropped to her hands and knees in the far corner. "Give me a hand with this," she said.

Robin joined her. "What do you need me to do?"

Elle pointed to a section of brick a few feet from her. "Get on that side. I'm going to need you to push from there."

Robin grasped at the brick with both hands. Elle rolled her eyes and demonstrated what she needed Robin to do, which was kneel like she had done and get a good hand grip. There was a pause as they both looked at Robin's attire, complete with stockings.

"Wouldn't it be better if we waited for the others to get here?"

"What else do you have to do? It beats waiting around doing nothing."

"Fine." Robin raised her hands in surrender. She walked to the stairs and sat. She pulled her skirt up slightly. All Elle's attention was on her as she unclipped first her left, then the right stocking from her garter. She rolled each one down to her ankle and pulled them off in one strip. It was done slow and deliberate. The effect it was having on Elle hadn't escaped her because she eased her legs apart ever so slightly as she unclipped each stocking.

Elle couldn't tear her eyes away if she'd tried. If possible, it had gotten hotter in the room in the last few seconds. When the act was done, Elle ripped her eyes back to the benign brick in front of her.

Robin knelt a few feet away from her. She inched up her skirt, revealing the dangling ends of her garter.

Something deep inside Elle clenched.

"Now that you have me here." Robin's voice was low and playful.

Elle cleared her throat before speaking. "Um." She looked up at the ceiling trying to gather her thoughts. "A lot of these houses were built during the Civil War. They all have hidey holes for storing valuables in case the Confederates came through." She pointed to the floor. "You can tell by this section. It's been moved because there's ruts in the dust on the floor."

They each gripped an end of the brick wall and pulled it out. It was heavy and slow, and scraped across the hard stone floor, but eventually a small section moved toward them. Inside was a room the size of a closet. Sitting in the middle of that space was a small canvas bag. Elle reached inside and lifted it. It was heavy and her heart beat a little faster at what it might contain.

Inside were twenty wrapped bundles of crisp one hundred dollar bills secured with bank seals. Elle stared, mouth agape, at the contents. She blinked a few times, then closed her mouth, holding tight. This was a lot more than the twenty-five grand she'd given Jessie. More like four times the amount.

"You weren't expecting to find that?" Robin asked, she appeared a little more cool about the whole thing.

"There must be like a hundred grand in here. Who would expect to find that in this?" She looked up at the ceiling again. Elle opened the bag once more and sorted through it, looking for a gun or anything that might shed light on how the cash had gotten there. Nothing. There was nothing else in the cubbyhole either. What the hell was going on?

She hugged the bag to her chest and looked up at Robin. "So you were just here getting a better feel for the place? At seven in the morning?"

Robin shrugged. "So you think it's possible someone killed Jessie for this money? Then stashed it here?"

"I'm asking the questions. What were you really doing here so early?"

"First of all, calm down. If you keep breathing like that you're going to hyperventilate."

Elle's breathing had picked up. She'd give anything for a glass of water.

"Second, I think you should take a seat."

"Oh, no." Elle shook her head, clutching the bag harder. "I don't like the sound of this."

"It's nothing too heinous, I swear." Robin guided Elle back to the steps. She let Elle keep her death grip on the money. "I wasn't completely honest about what I was doing in town. Yes, I'm here writing a story. No, it's not about you. Sorry." She smiled to lessen the blow.

Elle was way past caring. In fact, she was more relieved than anything. It hadn't been easy being in the spotlight in the first place, and she'd always known no one would want to write a story about her or the town. "What's the story you're working on?"

"A loan shark in Chicago. There's a story going around that he has an interesting way of getting his money back. Someone told me Jessie owed him a lot and I followed him out here." She spread her hands. "But when I couldn't find him, I called the mayor and asked to do a story about the town, and he gave me full access." She leaned forward, elbows on her knees. "Listen, I want to catch who ever did this as much, if not more, than you. This shit happens every day and nobody does a thing about it. I was here this morning looking for something, anything that might tie it all together."

Elle's nostrils flared. "I don't even know where to begin." She stood, dropping the bag of cash at her feet. What she had to say couldn't be said sitting down. This woman had come into her town and lied to her face. She had led her on and what's worse, Elle had fallen for it. "I could have you arrested for this."

Robin leaped to her feet. "For what? I didn't do anything wrong."

"Obstruction of justice. You had pertinent information regarding an ongoing murder investigation and you kept it to yourself. And then you go trespassing through a crime scene—in that getup." Elle's hand swept the length of Robin. "What the hell were you expecting to find? A tea party?"

Robin's hands latched onto her hips. "Hey, this is what I wear for work, okay? When I packed for this trip, I wasn't expecting to find the backwoods from *Deliverance*. And as for withholding information, all I knew was that Jessie might have owed some loan shark in Chicago money. Then when I went to his hotel, he wasn't there. What was I supposed to say? And if I did tell you this story, it would have biased you against other options."

"What other options? It's very obvious Jessie was killed because of this money."

"Really? Prove it."

That shut Elle up. She rubbed her forehead. This wasn't how she was expecting this to go. She collapsed back on the stairs. Robin joined her.

"Look, you're right. I probably should have shared what I knew. But it doesn't come naturally. In my profession, it's best to keep your head down and mouth shut when it comes to the cops. I try to have as few dealings with them as possible. I'm sorry."

Elle shook her head and laughed, but it was only to mask her frustration. She was on the verge of tears. Every step she took that brought her closer to solving this, also sent her three steps back.

Chapter Twenty-two

EJ opened the door to see Neil, standing on the front stoop. He had two large dark spots at his pits and sweat slicked hair. "You're a hard person to track down. Where you been all morning?"

EJ shrugged and took a bite of his pizza slice. "I was out. What's going on?" And then he had a moment of panic. "Is Elle okay?"

"Yeah, she's fine. She's probably back at the station right now. You worried about her?" Neil peered around EJ into the darkened living room.

"Aren't you?"

"You here alone?" Neil asked.

EJ stuffed the crust into his mouth, making his cheeks bulge and nodded. "What's going on?" A piece of crust fell from his mouth onto the ground.

"We found something the other night that we need your help with. Elle wanted me to bring you down to the station."

With his mouth still full so it sounded like he was talking underwater he said, "Why doesn't she come get me herself? Why's she sending you?"

Neil wiped his brow with the back of his arm. "It's not a big deal, we just have a couple questions. You think you can help us out? You can bring the rest of your pizza if you want."

"Nah, I'm done." He closed the door behind him without locking it. "What do you need help with? I didn't see anything the other night."

Neil led him to the passenger side of the cruiser and opened the door. "No, but you were at the keg party the night Jessie was killed.

There might be something you remember that could help us. Trust me, you're going to be a bigger help than you think."

EJ shrugged and slid onto the scorching pleather seat of the cruiser. "If I can help, you know I will."

Neil shut the door and walked around to the driver's side.

❖

"You wouldn't happen to have any gum, would you?" Elle asked. They had been stuffed into the far corner of the cellar for over two hours, the only place the sun hadn't invaded.

"Nope, sorry."

Elle had reached her pain threshold half an hour earlier. She had long ago discarded her utility belt. Just sitting was painful, but this, baking to death, was more than she could take. She needed something to take her mind off her body.

Scattered on the floor around them were several dust-laden shoe boxes. Elle flipped the lid off one at random and pulled out a pile of *Penthouse* magazines. "Wow, these are old." Absent of fake breasts and navel piercings, the models stared at the viewer through lowered eyelashes and feathered hair.

"And look at that." Robin picked up the top magazine and read one of the headings. "Who needs to see naked chicks when you can read the articles?"

Elle couldn't help herself, she laughed. It shot a spasm of pain through her ribs and up into her neck. "Shit." She took a deep breath. "I need to stand up."

Robin stood first, using the wall as support, and offered Elle her arm. Elle's skin looked even paler in the sunlight. The cuts on her face and neck jumped out in contrast along with escaped pieces of hair plastered to her neck with sweat. Elle pulled at her tie, loosening it until she could slip it over her head. She unbuttoned the top few buttons of her uniform and leaned back against the wall, trying to absorb the cool of the stone.

"I wish we had some water."

Robin nodded absently, flipping through the magazine. "I think I had this issue when I was a kid. I worry what kind of effect internet porn is having on this generation." Elle raised her eyebrows, momentarily surprised until Robin said, "They have it so easy. When I was a kid you either had to steal from your dad or sneak downstairs after midnight and hope you didn't get caught watching fuzzy porn on one of the pay channels. Where's the ingenuity in typing 'horny lesbians' into your web browser?" She caught Elle's stare. "I guess you had a different plight growing up, huh?"

"I have a younger brother. I'm all too familiar with internet porn." As much as she wished she weren't.

Elle tossed a magazine back into the box and toed open the one beside it. Inside was a black keg pump with a deep gouge along the top. She recognized the pump. The last time she'd seen it, she was steering EJ and Dan into the back of her cruiser. When she'd gone back for the keg later that night, the pump was missing. Somehow it had found its way into a shoe box in a hidden room underneath her murder scene.

"So why's this place called the Maverty house anyway?" Robin asked.

"I guess that depends on who you believe. Some say it was named after Joseph Maverty. He was a bootlegger who supposedly worked for Charles Birger during Prohibition. He used to receive shipments from Canada and store them before they could be delivered to Birger." She looked around the cellar with newfound interest. "And seeing this place, I can imagine it would've been easy to store and hide alcohol."

"But you don't believe the story?"

"Oh, I believe he was a bootlegger, but I think someone added the Birger part to up his status a little. I don't think he had anything to do with them. Turlough isn't a very easy place to get to. It would be more direct to go from Canada to Harrisburg than come here first. But Turlough would've been a perfect place to distribute to the surrounding counties like Hardin. Plus, we border Kentucky and Indiana, so it's more likely that he worked for someone set up in those states."

"And what's the other theory?"

"That it was already known as the Maverty house before that. A woman named Charlotte Maverty lived here in the 1800s when it was first built. Both her parents had died from typhoid fever, leaving Charlotte a very wealthy woman. According to legend, there were two young gentlemen who were trying to convince her to marry them. Instead of leaving it up to her to decide who she preferred, they had a duel to solve the dilemma the manly way." Elle's tone and expression made it clear what she thought of the manly way of doing things. "On the morning of the duel, Charlotte showed up to talk them out of it. One of them tripped and shot Charlotte in the shoulder. She died three days later."

"And what happened to Joseph Maverty?"

"He was shot by the local sheriff in nineteen twenty-eight. No one's lived in it since."

"Which story do you believe?"

Elle shrugged. She'd never seriously thought about it. One thing was for sure, it had an unfortunate history. "I think both stories are sort of true. People probably started calling it the Maverty house after Joseph died and it became abandoned."

For as long as Elle had been coming to the Maverty house, she'd never known about this room, but someone did. She wondered if Jessie had known about it. Would he have told her? She used to think he told her everything, but she'd learned the hard way there were things he'd kept even from her.

"So you used to come here a lot? Way back when?" Robin asked. She let her voice dip to a twang on the last line.

"We pretty much lived here. It was a clubhouse of sorts. If you hung out here, it meant you belonged." Elle rolled her sleeves up, but it was no use, the heat of the day had pervaded the basement.

"And that's important to you, isn't it? Belonging."

Elle shrugged. "It's a small town. There isn't much choice." Back then, belonging was everything. "You grew up in Chicago?"

"Evanston. But it's big enough and close enough to the city that no one gave a shit what you were." Robin inched closer, leaning her shoulder against the wall and facing Elle. "It's a shame, someone like you wasting away here in this godforsaken town."

"Someone like me?"

Robin smirked. "You've got that perfect mix of femme butch going."

"What's that supposed to mean?"

Robin leaned in even closer. "Listen. I could pretend I don't get that vibe off you—"

"What vibe?"

"Okay. We'll play it that way." She shrugged one of her exquisite shoulders. "We'll pretend your eyes haven't been glued to my cleavage for the past twenty minutes, or that—"

"My eyes have been exactly where they should be, which is nowhere near your cleavage."

Robin raised her arms in surrender and retreated to the stairs. She sat and leaned back on her elbows. The move pushed her breasts forward as if mocking Elle not to stare at them.

They eyed each other from across the room until Elle asked, "Did you always know?"

"What? That I was a prying bitch? Yes, from the very beginning." She offered a kind smile. "Will you bite my head off if I ask when you knew?"

Elle let out a very loud sigh and leaned her head against the brick. "Tenth grade. Kate Wells's pool party."

"Bikini or one-piece?"

"Blue bikini."

"Good color."

"Mmm."

The silence lengthened. Birdcall filtered through the hole in the floor, along with beams of light.

"And have you?" Robin asked.

"College."

"Please tell me you're talking about the first time, not the last."

"Oh, God, do you think I'd be sheriff if anyone knew?"

"Are you telling me you haven't had sex in ten years?"

"It hasn't been that long."

Robin shot her a give me a break look. "Ten years? You must go through vibrators the way Elizabeth Taylor went through husbands."

Despite herself, Elle laughed. "It's honestly not on my radar. I have too many more important obligations in my life."

"That's a shitty way to live. My dad's like that and he's miserable. He lives in a city he hates, commuting to a job he hates, and it's eaten away at him."

"I don't hate my life. It's not what I envisioned for myself when I was younger. But there are worse ways to live."

"Cut the shit. If you had a choice to live this life celibate or with someone, you'd choose to be celibate? If you answer yes, you're lying."

Of course Elle wouldn't live in celibacy if she had a choice. But she'd never thought much about it because it wasn't an option. Not in Turlough. As much as the world had changed in the last forty years, Turlough was perpetually two decades behind. Since Robin had arrived, she'd awakened something long dormant in Elle.

"You could leave, you know. Your brother graduates this year, right?"

"Why would I leave? I love my job."

"But if you didn't have it anymore."

Elle shook her head. It was a crazy idea. She'd never thought about leaving Turlough.

Robin stood and approached Elle. "Ten years? I'd have gone insane." She leaned her shoulder against the wall. When she spoke, her breath brushed the hair circling Elle's ear. It felt wonderful and dangerous at the same time.

Robin's thigh rested against Elle's and she could feel the heat seep through the cotton of her uniform. Robin reached over and slowly lifted the chain Elle kept around her neck. The keys caressed her skin as they glided up from between her breasts.

"The keys to your chastity belt?"

Elle laughed. "No. To the safe at the station."

Robin leaned in closer, pressing her breasts against Elle's arm. Her breath skimmed Elle's neck.

Elle swallowed.

Robin pressed forward, connecting their bodies at the hips, her lips inches away from Elle's. From this vantage point, she could see Elle's breasts rise and fall. She could see the edge of her bra peeking from her uniform. It was white and edged in lace.

Elle dropped her head. Robin was so close their chests were pressed together. She was breathing hard. Her mind went in a million different directions, but mostly it fastened on the image of Robin's garter straps trapped beneath her skirt.

Robin grabbed Elle's hip and leaned in farther. "You are by far the sexiest sheriff I've ever met." She smelled like apples and vanilla and her blue eyes were so clear as they watched for Elle's reaction.

Elle's cheeks flamed red, spreading down her neck.

"And it's adorable that I can make you blush like a schoolgirl."

When she grazed her lips against Elle's, they were soft. Robin's tongue darted in and licked the tip of Elle's. Elle's whole body lit on fire at that moment.

It took everything to pull away. "I'm in uniform."

Robin gripped her hip harder and yanked her closer. She kissed Elle again, deeper this time. And it was like a dam bursting. All those years of pent-up frustration exploded from Elle. Every emotion, every look, touch, thought, roared through her body, flooding her senses.

She slid her hand around Robin's waist, slipping her fingers down her skirt, pulling her, if possible, closer still.

Their embrace held, tight and furious, for minutes, hours, Elle wasn't sure. She skimmed her hand down Robin's leg, inching up her skirt, feeling for the loose strap of her garter. When Robin undid first one, then another of Elle's buttons, Elle gulped. It was too much. She pulled back. Her pulse was banging against her ears. She backed up, everything inside her head sounded so incriminating and loud. Including her breath.

"Elle?" Neil's voice came from up above.

"Thank God," she whispered to herself. "Down here," she shouted so Neil would hear. After buttoning her uniform and retrieving her tie from where she'd dropped it, Elle moved into the light so Neil could see her.

"Great, saved by the fat man," Robin said.

"Be careful where you step, Neil. The floorboards have rotted through."

Neil stopped a few feet from the opening and bent forward. "Holy fuck, Elle. You had me scared half to death there. When you didn't answer your radio or phone I thought something bad had happened to you." He noticed Robin then and his whole body stiffened. "You okay?"

"Yeah, nothing a few aspirin and a gallon of water can't solve. If you go around the back of the house, I think you'll be able to find the cellar doors. You might have to move some stuff. I think they've been hidden."

Sure enough, Neil found two fallen trees covering the doors as well as a layer of dead leaves. It only took him a couple of minutes to remove the debris and tug open the doors. When he finished, he was sweating just as much as Elle and Robin.

Elle emerged from the basement drenched and exhausted. She stood in the shade under one of the giant sycamores in the backyard enjoying what little breeze swept through the trees. Neil handed her a bottle of water. She drank half and used the other to douse the back of her neck with water. She caught Robin watching and her heartbeat picked up. There was something carnal in the way Robin eyed her. Elle looked away, wishing she hadn't started something she couldn't finish.

❖

Dan sat slumped in his chair. One arm dangled over the armrest in a lazy gesture. He was determined to remain insouciant, in an almost exact replica of EJ's posture in the same chair earlier. Only this time, Elle sat at her desk across from Dan instead of leaning in the back corner where Neil now stood.

"What happened the night of June eighteenth?"

Dan shrugged. He leaned back in his chair to stare at the ceiling. "If I could remember what happened on random dates I might have passed history with a better grade." He let this sentence escape his lips with one long, bored breath.

"I'll give you a hint, this date involves you and my brother sleeping it off on the cot in the basement cell."

He leaned forward to stare at Elle. A smile turned up his lips. "Well, that's a horse of a different color, then, isn't it?"

"Dan, cut the shit. What were you up to before you arrived at the party?" Unlike her interview with EJ, when she'd been relegated to the position of observer, unsuccessfully at times, she kept her voice low and calm. EJ had spent the entire interview evading. She could only assume that if EJ wasn't telling them where they were that night it had to be something incriminating. But what could be worse than murder? Unless he was protecting Dan, which just infuriated her more. She had called the state police to check into Dan's background. They hadn't told her much except that Dan had a sealed record. He'd spent three years in juvie because of what was in that file.

After the tenth time she'd interrupted Neil, he'd asked EJ to take a seat outside across from Heather in dispatch.

"I know, Neil, and I'm sorry. But I can't help it. He's my brother and he's protecting that ass out of stupid loyalty," she said.

"You know the old saying you can't pick your family, but you can pick your friends? Well, Dan is the furthest thing from you. Maybe EJ needs a little less structure in his life." If she were being objective here, Neil was right, but she knew there was more to it than that.

"The thing is, I think this is about a stolen keg. Only I don't think they stole it from Finnegan's. When I dropped it off to Toby, he seemed sure he wasn't missing a keg." She shrugged. "But no one reported a theft, so there wasn't any reason to pursue it further. I have this sinking feeling that when I check into it, I'll find where it really came from."

Neil sat back and watched her figure it out, knowing it was better if he just left her to it.

"He's protecting him. I know it. But what's worse than murder? Maybe it isn't worse than murder, just the simple fact that EJ is innocent and knows it. Maybe he thinks he can't get convicted so he'll just keep his mouth shut."

She looked over at Neil, who snorted.

Elle nodded. "I know. The only evidence we have puts EJ at the second crime scene. I have Case checking to see if the knife we found under Stan's cruiser is the same one used on Jessie."

"And if it is? What then? Jessie and Stan were shot to death."

Elle groaned and scrubbed at her face. "I know. None of it makes sense. I only have more questions since we started." She hadn't told anyone that the T-shirt she found was EJ's. She doubted very much the blood was Stan's. It was old blood, and besides, why would they place it somewhere she was sure to find it? Unless that was the point. And what about the Harley-Davidson T-shirt? How did that fit?

"If EJ's unwilling to give up his alibi, it looks worse for him. I'll get a DNA sample to see if it matches the cigarette butts we found at the Maverty house." The cigarettes they'd found were Marlboro Lights, which she knew were EJ's brand. But if she remembered right, they were also the brand Jessie had been smoking the night she went to see him. There was still so much she couldn't explain.

"So where were you before you got to the party that night?" Elle laced her fingers and rested her hands in front of her, waiting for Dan to answer.

"EJ and I went to pick up my keg pump before we showed up to the party."

"Really? That took three hours? And at what point did you steal the keg?"

"I don't know anything about where the keg came from."

"Everyone we've managed to talk to from the party said you and EJ split from the group around nine and didn't show up again until midnight with a keg."

"So what are you really asking?" Dan's gaze sank to her collar and the tight knot of her tie pressing against her throat. It lowered to where her breasts pressed against her uniform and stayed. She resisted the urge to check that a button hadn't come undone, exposing her bra. She also resisted the need to cross her arms over her chest. "Are you asking that I give your brother an alibi for that missing time?"

"Who suggested that time was missing? I know exactly what you two were doing between nine and twelve."

Dan smirked. "Really?"

"I'm sure if I looked hard enough I'd find an unlicensed convenience store along the outskirts of town missing a keg." In the distance, she could hear Heather answering the phone.

"If that were true, then why didn't he just confess to that? Me, personally? I'd rather be brought up on charges of theft than murder." He flicked an invisible piece of lint off his jeans. "Then again, maybe he doesn't know anything about a missing keg."

There was a knock, Heather stuck her head in. "Sorry to bother you, but the mayor's on the line."

Elle sighed visibly. This was the last thing she wanted to deal with right now. He was either calling to bug her about some last-minute festival detail or goad her into getting the staties to rush their evidence. Neil peeled himself off the wall behind her. He'd been so silent Elle had forgotten he was there.

"It's okay, Heather, I'll deal with him. Boss is busy." Elle smiled a thank-you at him.

She waited until Neil had closed the door behind him before saying, "Are you confessing to stealing the keg by yourself, Dan?"

He shook his head. "I told you we didn't steal any keg. We went to my house to grab my keg pump."

"And that took three whole hours?"

"Yep." He picked at his jeans some more. "Why? Where did your brother say we were?"

He hadn't said anything. He'd refused to even speak on the matter, never once asking for a lawyer or giving her a confession. But she didn't want to tell Dan that.

"Weird, huh? That he wouldn't just tell you that. When that's all we were doing?" He sat there, picking at a ripped thread, a small smirk at the corner of his mouth.

"I talked to your parents, Dan. They said you left the house around six that night and they didn't see you again until the next morning. So where'd you go?"

He shrugged. "They must not have heard us come in."

Elle stood and rounded her desk. "Listen to me, you little shit." She leaned in close, her voice very calm and very quiet, both hands gripping the armrests. "I've had enough of you. You can try to play this situation like you give a shit about my brother, but I see right through you. I can see exactly what you're trying to do."

He leaned forward, taking back his personal space, invading hers. "And what is it I'm trying to do?" His eyes wove down her shirt, stopping again at that midpoint where her breasts pushed against the fabric, straining the line of buttons keeping her shirt closed.

She couldn't help it, she looked.

He smiled like he'd won a prize.

Chapter Twenty-three

Elle stepped into the dark garage just before dusk. The smell of gasoline and grease assaulted her. It reminded Elle of her grandfather's workshop. He'd always loved tinkering with things, seeing how they worked. There was always one appliance or another in a state of disassembly.

"Hello?" she called.

Motorcycle parts littered the floor. Bikes from every decade lay in pieces around the edge of the room. To her right was a shiny black Yamaha in mint condition.

"Beaut, isn't she?" Kate stepped into the garage from out back, wiping greasy hands on a filthy cloth.

"Yeah. Where'd you get it?" Elle stepped closer, admiring the custom work.

"Found it." She pointed behind her. "It was tucked into this old field out near the Culpeppers'. Whoever hid it didn't want it found. It was camouflaged under some brush." Kate stopped next to Elle, smelling of grease and hard work. "I was going to call you tomorrow."

Elle raised her eyebrows.

"No, really. I was." Kate held her hand to her heart. "I swear. As much as this bike's beautiful, I could never cheat on my Harley." Her grin was mischievous.

"Is this what they call an honest mechanic? I wasn't aware any existed." Elle's heartbeat picked up. She was actually flirting. A few hours after kissing a woman in Turlough and now this. This was not good. "Uh." She cleared her throat. "Can you send the plate number to Neil? I wouldn't be surprised if it turned up stolen."

"Sure, I'll send him a pic first thing."

Elle sidestepped a pile of sawdust, darkened by the oil it had soaked up. "The reason I stopped by was to see if you had any more insight into how the Pritchards' car got onto the well."

Kate's smile faltered, but only for a moment. "Sure. Yeah." Kate crossed her arms over her chest and leaned back, staring at the ceiling. "I'd say they used boards to get it up. Line two up along the stairs and drive the car on up. Could've been done with two people."

Elle chewed on her bottom lip, staring off into space, unaware of how close Kate watched the action.

"You think EJ did it?"

Elle knew EJ did it. The whole prank smacked of Dan. And if Dan was involved, then EJ was as well. But she couldn't let on she thought like that. Even if she didn't find any evidence to charge them, the town would still know and treat them to their own brand of justice. "Could've been any number of people. So far we haven't found any witnesses."

Kate shrugged. "Just as well. Randy Pritchard's a sexist prick."

Outside, blue dusk swept through the streets, stirring the crickets. The heat hadn't let up and all Elle could think about was getting home and showering. She hadn't had a chance since her ordeal at the Maverty house and she was sure she stank.

They both spoke at the same time.

"I should go."

"How's the investigation going?"

Kate smiled first. "Of course. I didn't mean to keep you."

"The investigation is moving along. We're still waiting on results from the staties."

Kate nodded, as if she'd been expecting that answer.

Later that night, as Elle lay in bed waiting to fall asleep, she replayed the conversation over again.

It was always awkward with Kate. Ever since that last summer before college. Sometime between junior high and senior year they'd drifted toward different circles, Kate with the art club and Elle with the jocks. Occasionally, they would cross paths. Senior year, it happened a lot. They'd ended up working on the school play together. Kate was in charge of set design and Elle had taken an art elective that year and volunteered to help.

One night in April, they'd worked late at Elle's house. It was a warm night, so Elle suggested they work out on the back porch.

Looking back, Elle always had a crush on Kate. She'd never called it that because she was afraid of what it meant. But that last year, working together, there were moments when she thought Kate might feel the same. That thought solidified that night in April.

Kate had been wearing black jeans and a loose sweater that revealed a blue striped bra whenever she leaned forward. Elle couldn't help but look. She thought she'd been subtle about it until Kate asked if she should take her sweater off to give Elle a better view.

Elle turned beet red, making Kate grin. Then she pulled the hem up and over her head, dropping the sweater to the deck.

Elle hadn't even allowed herself to fantasize about this. When Kate reached back to unhook her bra, Elle held a hand up to stop her.

"You want me to stop?" Kate's voice wavered, unsure if she'd misread the situation.

"Believe me, there's nothing I want more." Elle bit her lip, trying to slow her breathing down. "But." She turned to look inside.

"Your parents are asleep. I saw them head to their room an hour ago."

"I don't know."

Kate moved closer to Elle on the lounge, draping her legs on either side. "How about this? I could take my bra off, but put my sweater back on?"

Elle's gaze dropped from Kate's eyes to her breasts. They looked perfect pressed against the fabric of her bra. She'd spent most of last summer watching those breasts parade around in a blue bikini. Instead of answering, Elle leaned forward and unhooked the clasp. She pushed the straps off Kate's shoulders and let the cups fall away, revealing two of the most beautiful breasts Elle had ever seen. Just sitting there with Kate topless was more exciting than anything Elle had ever done with Jessie.

Heat rose up through Elle's body. She ached to touch them but was afraid if she did they would evaporate like the dream this undoubtedly was. Elle sat with her hands in her lap, staring as the air thickened around them. Kate's breasts rose and fell; each second they seemed to get faster. Elle met Kate's eyes and they held there, for seconds, minutes, inches apart, both afraid to be the first to move.

It was Kate who finally did. She took Elle's hands and placed them on her breasts. At the feel of the soft skin, Elle closed her eyes. She ran her thumbs over the hard nipples. Her eyes snapped open at the moan that move elicited, surprised at her own wetness. She bit her lip and did it again, this time rolling them between her fingers. Another moan, more wetness.

Kate grabbed Elle's neck and pulled her in, mashing their lips together. Tongues entwined. Kate's fingers twisted in Elle's hair.

And that's how Jessie found them, locked together half naked on the lounge on Elle's back porch. He'd been shocked, then outraged, and finally hurt. She'd told him everything, even if he didn't believe it.

And that was it. She'd dropped out of working on the play and she'd avoided Kate until she left for college.

And now it was awkward.

She didn't want it to be, but ever since she came back to Turlough, their interactions were punctuated with long pauses and stilted dialogue. She wished they could go back to the way they'd been in high school. Back then everything was easier.

❖

Elle stood outside the front gate of a brown-sided house off the main strip. It was one of the houses Chuck Dell owned when he was still alive. Abandoned projects littered the front yard: a half-constructed bird feeder, three scraped porch pillars, one painted. The garden had several bushes planted; the rest lay skeletal and bare.

Elle had spent yesterday questioning every student at J.P. Flynn. Most were at the keg party, something they'd only admitted to once Elle assured them they weren't getting into trouble. It had all been for naught. No one had seen EJ or Dan between nine and midnight. She only had Dan's word that they were together at his house, and EJ still refused to say anything.

As she told EJ she'd be keeping him for the forty-eight hours, his face became a mask of panic and betrayal. When she placed him in the cell in the basement, it reminded her of that first week after their parents died. He'd had the same look anytime she'd tried to get him to do something. Asking him to do anything more than breathe was enough for his silent treatment. For weeks, he refused to even bathe. At first, she wasn't sure if she should let him be or scream and shout like she'd wanted to. Needed to. It wasn't fair that he got to fall apart and she had to be the strong one.

By the time Elle began her very thorough assault against her parents' rules EJ was only a baby. Having to compete with a helpless infant only made her transgressions appear all the more defiant. But after so many years she and EJ had gotten to know their roles so well it was effortless to play them. When her parents died they left more than holes in their lives. They'd left holes in the production, and Elle didn't know if she was capable of stepping into someone else's part.

Two and a half weeks after her parents' funeral, EJ still hadn't bathed. One night, after watching him push his dinner around on his plate for an hour, she grabbed him around the waist and carried him screaming and kicking into their shared bathroom. She plopped him into the tub fully clothed, turned on the water, and began scrubbing. The whole time she was bawling, worried helpless frustration was the only emotion she'd feel for the rest of her life. It was still a constant ache. She'd promised to look after him, keep him safe, but all she'd managed was to push him to be exactly like her.

She'd needed to get out of the station to distract herself.

And that's how she'd ended up standing at this gate belonging to the man who had made the worst day of their lives happen. The man who had gotten behind the wheel of his car with a bottle of whiskey tucked away in his belly. The man who had caused the death of both their parents.

She felt anger so acute it rose up in her throat like bile. If he'd never gotten in his car that night, would EJ be at home listening to music instead of shut up in a cell in the basement of the sheriff's office?

Elle took a deep breath. She wasn't here for herself. She was here to help Case keep his job. A job he'd held for over twenty years. They had no right to take it from him with a vote, despite the irony that he had kept it all these years because of a vote. Case ran uncontested for the past seven years. When Tom Hampstead passed away, the new funeral owner, who also doubled as the mortician, found the practice too much extra work for his taste. No one but Case wanted the job.

Stronger than anger and guilt, indignation pushed her through that front gate and up the porch steps. Elle pounded on the door. She heard wild barking on the other side. It got louder as it got closer to the door. Then shuffling and a man's voice telling the dog to shut up.

"Who is it?" There was no peephole. Most people in Turlough were pretty trusting, but Sid Derry had always been a bit paranoid.

"It's Sheriff Ashley."

A long pause, then, "What's this about?"

Elle shifted her weight to the other foot, annoyed at having to justify her presence, especially since she had no official reason for being there. Sid Derry had every right to order her off his property. "Open the door please, sir."

"Am I in some kind of trouble?"

"No, I'd like to speak to you about a personal matter." Elle hoped curiosity would win out over his paranoia.

But he didn't open the door. She felt like an idiot standing there, waiting. She could hear more shuffling on the other side of the closed door. A car passed on the street. Elle couldn't be sure, but it appeared to slow as it passed the house. She was about to turn and leave when she heard the dead bolt shift. A few more locks and a chain, then Sid Derry was standing in the doorway holding on to the collar of a very scruffy looking dog. It barked at the sight of Elle. Derry appeared to have aged decades, not years, since Elle had seen him last. He was slight and the way he held on to his dog made him look stooped. He peered at her through cloudy blue eyes.

"Sadie, down, girl," he said and yanked the collar. "Come in."

Elle stepped over the threshold into the gloom of the foyer. She felt like throwing up. Junk filled every inch of space. It had been decades since anyone but Derry had been in this house.

"Come on in. Have a seat," he said.

But when she entered the living room there wasn't anywhere to sit. Piles of newspapers and electronics covered every surface. Derry noticed this a second later and began to clear space on a dark green couch facing the kitchen. He took a seat opposite in a lounger, the only seat that looked like it was used for its intended purpose. Sadie circled three times, then settled next to Derry, keeping a wary eye on Elle.

Now that she'd sat down, Elle was at a loss for words. Somehow the regular pleasantries didn't fit. She could hardly care how he was doing or how he had been. She hadn't seen him since the civil suit, a year and a half after he'd walked away from a double count of vehicular manslaughter on a technicality. In the confusion after discovering her father's arterial leg bleed, they'd forgotten to do a sobriety test on Derry. Elle often wondered if they'd overlooked it on purpose because of his standing in the community. She considered, looking around, what the other city council members would think of Derry if they could see this place. Maybe they would see him for what he was, a barely functioning drunk with a hoarding problem.

"To what do I owe this honor?" He tried to make it sound like a sneer, but he couldn't keep the curiosity out of his voice.

"I came to speak with you about the upcoming vote."

Derry crossed his legs, casual like, as if they were at a country club about to order cocktails. His slipper had a hole worn through the sole. "What vote?" His eyes darted around the room, seeing it through the eyes of a visitor for the first time in years.

"Let's not pretend, Mr. Derry, that the whole town doesn't know about the upcoming amalgamation vote. You want to merge the coroner's job with county sheriff." He stared at her with watery eyes, dulled by hard years.

"So what's that got to do with you coming here?"

"I wanted to ask how you were planning on voting." She still had no idea how she was going to get him to change his mind if she didn't like the answer, but she knew she had to try.

Derry pulled himself up a little higher, which did nothing to improve his stature. He was already short to begin with, but years of drinking had reduced him. He looked in Elle's eyes like a vulture, hunched and leery.

"And what's that any business of yours?"

"It isn't, but it certainly affects me." If she could get him to agree to this she would have one less thing on her plate. One less worry so she could focus on finding evidence to prove EJ's innocence. "I came here to appeal to you to vote to keep the coroner's position." Having said it, the words tasted raw in her throat.

Derry leaned back, a smile growing on his face. "I see. And you thought you'd ask me for this because you felt I owed you something? Thought you could appeal to my guilty conscience?" Was that what she'd been trying to do? She wasn't even sure he had a conscience. The way he'd spoken at the trial made it sound like the accident had been her parents' fault.

"Jack's a good man. He doesn't deserve this."

"Why should I do anything that helps him?"

"Because it's the right thing to do."

Derry was enjoying this. For too long, he'd felt dismissed. He still held his position on the council. He was a pillar. One of the old guard. But a lot had changed since the accident. It happened so gradually it was hard to recognize it for what it was: a fall from grace. Elle wasn't as blind as the others. She'd watched as he metamorphosed into this recluse most people had forgotten. Before the accident, he'd run a successful law practice. After the civil suit, he'd declared bankruptcy and closed his firm. He'd stopped going into Finnegan's or even Dell's. Then he started getting his groceries delivered. Until one day, the only ones who ever saw him were the council members when there was a vote or mandatory meeting. For Elle, it wasn't even close to what he deserved. He should be serving time. Voluntary imprisonment wasn't the same thing.

"The right thing to do? And I guess you always do the right thing. I guess that's why your brother always finds himself free. Perhaps this time it'll stick."

Elle wasn't surprised that he'd already heard about her bringing EJ in for questioning. This town had a better communication system than AT&T. She remained silent. She could endure this. If it meant Case keeping his job, she could stand to have this man judge her.

"Let's face it," his eyes roved her body, making Elle feel as dirty as the room she was sitting in, "the only reason you got voted in was because Bailey bought it for you. He was respected in this community, he did a lot of favors for a lot of people over the years. And the second any of them thinks you're not holding up your end of the bargain, well, we'll see." He laughed, which was so short it sounded more like a hiccup. "After all, it's not like it's a hard job. I'm not sure what you and Bailey had going, but I do know he liked them young." The way he spoke it was like he was throwing each word at her like a dagger.

"And what is it you do exactly? Sit and pass judgment on a town that you have no involvement with and haven't for close to a decade?"

"And whose fault is that?" Derry shot out from his chair. His whole body was shaking, fists balled, ready to pound something. Sadie lifted her head, a low growl vibrated through her body.

"Excuse me?" Elle remained in her seat in case Sadie turned out to be deadlier than she looked. "You think that's my fault? I've been making your bad choices for the past decade?"

He glared at her. "You're the reason I'm in this situation. I had a thriving law practice before you came along. People respected my opinion. I lost everything because of you." He spread his hands to encompass the living room, as if it were a reflection of his retreat from society. "And now look what I have."

That this man would bemoan his lost privileges as if they were more important than her parents' lives spoke of his utter lack of perspective. There was no reasoning with a man like that, not in any logical way. She stood so fast, a pile of newspapers skidded to the floor. "I'll see myself out."

Before shutting the door, Elle stopped and turned. Derry was kneeling next to the couch scooping newspapers into a teetering pile with shaking hands. He looked pathetic, fussing over his junk like it was treasure. "Jack's a good man. He doesn't deserve this. I know you don't care, but think of it this way: If you vote yes, you'll be partially responsible for my pay increase."

Outside, she leaned against the door. Derry was easy to hate. It was almost enough to forgive herself for storming out. This is what happened when she wasn't able to run. Her anger got funneled toward less productive things, like people. There was a good chance he would vote against Case to spite them both. His bitterness had been palpable. It filled the room, leaving an aftertaste almost as bad as the rot throughout the place.

As she slid into her cruiser she noticed several missed calls, four of them from Robin. That was nothing new. She'd spent yesterday screening her calls. As much as she'd been putting off visiting the two swing votes on the board, this had been a welcome distraction from everything else, including Robin. She was hoping if she ignored her long enough she would go away, thereby removing herself from temptation altogether.

Chapter Twenty-four

Elle knocked loud. If she didn't, Mr. Rutherford would never hear it. Next door, Sandy had replaced her azaleas with gaudy pink flowers Elle couldn't identify. She glanced up, pretending to examine Mr. Rutherford's eaves. The light in Robin's room was on. She knocked again, louder this time. She'd spent far too much time standing outside front doors today. At least that's what she told herself.

"Coming. Coming. Good Lord, you'd think I was outfitted with roller skates. Give me a moment to get there before you break the door down," Mr. Rutherford hollered. All resentment vanished the moment he opened the door and saw Elle standing there.

"Hi, Mr. Rutherford. I thought I might coax you into losing a game of cribbage." Elle smiled for what felt like the first time all day.

"You're the one who's going to be doing the losing. Come on in."

Elle handed Mr. Rutherford the bag of peas she was carrying. He looked at it like she'd handed him a bag of poop.

"What am I supposed to do with this?"

"They're peas from Mrs. Keeler's garden." She'd visited Judge Keeler's before coming to see Mr. Rutherford. Elle stepped inside. The place smelled like dust and baked bread.

"Giving away your bribes, huh? Very generous of you." He shuffled down the hall much like a penguin on arctic ice. "You're in luck today. My goddaughter was by earlier and she baked bread." He said this as if it were the most wonderful thing in the world. "There's still some left."

Elle enjoyed two pieces of thick bread with elderflower honey. As she licked the last of the honey off her fingers, Mr. Rutherford dealt the cards.

Mr. Rutherford was a serious cribbage player, meaning you didn't play for fun, you played for money. Elle once made the mistake of asking why you couldn't have fun playing for money. Mr. Rutherford had turned those grave eyes on her and said nothing. She knew he'd grown up during the Depression and that his older brother helped keep the family afloat playing poker. He rarely mentioned his brother, but she guessed it had something to do with him going away to war and never coming back.

"So do you think he did it?" Mr. Rutherford asked an hour later.

"Do I think who did what?"

"Your brother. Do you think he killed Jessie Forrester?"

"Of course I don't think he did it." Elle picked up her hand and began sorting her cards into runs and pairs. She had an awful hand but continued to sort anyway, hoping Mr. Rutherford would think she had a better one.

"Then why'd you arrest him?"

"I didn't arrest him. I'm holding him for questioning."

"Mmm-hmm?"

"I had to."

Mr. Rutherford shook his head as he laid a three of hearts. "The only thing we have to do is die." He looked over, waiting for Elle to go. "I like you, Elizabeth. Always have. One of the reasons I voted for you is because you stand up to people, especially that excuse for a mayor, Brady. But you've got a blind spot when it comes to your brother."

"I know my brother's a bit of a troublemaker, but he's not capable of murder."

Mr. Rutherford chuckled, which erupted into a hacking cough. When it subsided he said, "A bit of a troublemaker? He wouldn't be an Ashley if he wasn't. No, I wasn't suggesting he murdered the Forrester boy. What I meant was you care too much about what people think when it comes to him."

Elle discarded a three and pegged two. She was ten holes away from passing the skunk line. "That's favoritism. I'm not going to treat EJ differently than any of the other people in this town."

"But you do treat him differently, don't you see that? If anyone else in this town was in the same spot as EJ, would you have held them? Even though you knew they couldn't have done it?"

Elle thought of all the evidence piled up against her brother, the knife, the T-shirt with blood, his lack of cooperation. It was staggering. Jack had linked the knife to a stab wound in Jessie's chest. It was all circumstantial since they hadn't found the murder weapons. But his evasiveness was suspicious and enough for her to hold him.

"Yes, I would."

"Okay, fine. That was a bad example. Would you lock up other underage drinkers for a night?"

If Elle were being honest with herself the answer was no, but she didn't want to concede this early, so she shrugged instead.

"Just because you're a public servant doesn't mean you have to serve them all the time. Sometimes it's nice to do what you think's best. I think it's a shame the way you hide yourself away. That's no way to live, Elizabeth. What happens down the road? After EJ leaves? When it's just you? Are you going to spend every night sleeping in your office, eating by yourself at Dell's? You can't hide your whole life."

For a moment, Elle wondered if that statement had a different meaning. But Mr. Rutherford had already moved on, discarding a three from his hand. He was only five holes away from winning. Even though you couldn't peg to win, it was his crib, which meant she counted first and might be able to score enough to get across the skunk line. You paid double when you were skunked.

"How do you know so much?" Elle discarded a four. Now she just needed him to discard a five and she'd score four, enough to peg close enough.

"My goddaughter brings me bread once a week. I hear all the gossip from her." He discarded an eight, pegging two.

Elle's heart sank. She laid her six down on the pile.

Mr. Rutherford discarded his king on top and pegged up to the final hole. He only needed one to win. "Your count." He grinned.

Elle picked up her hand in disgust. She had two points. Nowhere near enough to get her past that skunk line.

Mr. Rutherford picked up his crib and crowed. "Would you look at that kitty? A boatload of aces."

Elle perked up. "What did you say?"

"Did you see my kitty? Three aces and a two."

As Mr. Rutherford tallied his score—he was winning by a considerable amount—Elle glanced through the window into Mr. Rutherford's backyard. He had a chicken coop set up in the far corner of the yard with a wooden plank for the chickens to come and go. But from where Elle was sitting, it appeared empty. She got up to investigate. Only the coop and the feeder, which sat bare. The yard was deserted.

"What happened to your chickens?" When he didn't say anything, she turned to see him staring into the yard sadly.

"Dead. All of them. The last one died a few days ago." He shook his head. "Poor Betty. Just sat there all by herself refusing to eat or move. It broke my heart."

"I'm sorry to hear that. What did they die of?"

"Some disease I can't even say, let alone spell."

"Is it a common disease for chickens?"

"I'm not sure. I haven't heard of anyone having an outbreak around here. And the farmers are usually chatty about that sort of thing. I'll tell you what, I'd put money on it having to do with all that crud that woman next door sprays on those silly flowers of hers." He shook his head, unable to understand why anyone would put effort into growing something that couldn't be eaten or sold.

"Which reminds me. Do you remember anything unusual the night of the eighteenth?" Elle asked.

"You're going to have to give me something better than a date. My memory, like my teeth, has seen better days."

Elle thought back for a moment, trying to grab at some sort of marker. Then she remembered the azaleas. "It was the night someone ripped up Sandy's flowers."

"Huh, you sure?"

"Yes, I'm sure." She remembered because she'd given Robin a lift into town, and it was only the second time they'd met.

"Well, then it could be that I saw something unusual, as you put it."

"Could be?"

Mr. Rutherford shifted in his seat, eyeing the cards in his hands. When he looked back at Elle it was the look of a child who'd been caught sneaking cookies before dinner. "Now, Elizabeth, if I'm to tell you this you have to promise me client privilege. You can't tell anyone."

Elle sighed and took a seat across from him. "That's for lawyers or doctors or priests. I'm not any of those things. In fact, Mr. Rutherford, if you do know something and you don't tell me, you could get in trouble."

He frowned, debating his options.

"Please, Mr. Rutherford? If you know something that could help me I'll come by every night next week for gin."

He waved her off. "All right." He folded his arms in front of him and cleared his throat. "I was out that night in the yard when I noticed a young man run past me. I thought it especially odd because he wasn't wearing a shirt."

"What were you doing out in the yard so late? Did he see you?"

"No, he didn't see me. When I heard the rustling, I tucked myself up against the side of the house."

Elle's heart stilled, putting it all together. "Which house?"

Mr. Rutherford hitched a thumb toward Sandy's. He had the good grace to look embarrassed.

Elle rubbed her eyes. It had been a long day. "And I'm guessing you were doing a bit of complimentary gardening. That's why you were out that late?"

He stabbed the table with his finger. "That woman killed my chickens. All twelve of them. And I think she did it on purpose. She says the squawking bothers her guests."

"That doesn't give you permission to destroy her property. If you have a complaint you come to me or Neil."

Elle didn't have anything left emotionally to deal with this right now. Later, when she had time to think about it she would come back to it, so she focused on something more important. "So you saw someone run across your yard. Were they coming from the direction of the Maverty house?"

"Yes, they came around the back of my fence."

"Do you remember what time you saw him?"

Mr. Rutherford leaned back, eyes glazed toward the ceiling, fingers clutching the pack of cards. Finally, he nodded. "It would've been sometime after eleven but before midnight."

"How can you be that sure?" Elle was somewhat skeptical. Mr. Rutherford was sagacious, but that didn't mean his mind was infallible.

"*Dallas* was on that night at ten. I think that Sue Ellen's a hoot, but the rest of them are a bunch of morons. I went out during, what's that show with the mustached man? The one about the private detective in Hawaii?"

"*Hawaii Five-O?*"

"No, the other one, he's always wearing short shorts. The hairy-chested guy."

"*Magnum, P.I.?*" Elle was slightly disturbed that Mr. Rutherford even knew what short shorts were.

"Yes! That's the one. It was on when I came back in. And it starts at eleven, so that means he ran through my yard after eleven but before midnight because the show ends at midnight."

Elle nodded, impressed with his logic. "Do you remember what he looked like?"

"It was too dark to make out his face. But he was pasty white, if that helps."

It didn't. Ninety percent of Turlough was white. The sighting hadn't been helpful, but something he'd said earlier sparked her memory.

Neil stuffed the last piece of pizza into his mouth as Elle barged into the station. The empty box lay on Heather's desk. The crumbs, scattered in a two-inch radius, created grease rings.

"I thought I told you to go home," he said around a mouthful of crust.

Elle didn't even bother to point out that as sheriff, she gave the orders. "I went to visit Mr. Rutherford instead."

"Of course you did." He followed her to the computer in the corner.

She jabbed the space bar and the screen came alive. "Did we hear back from dispatch yet?"

"Yeah, Stan called in a ten-twenty-eight five minutes before you found him. I asked her to fax the transcript over to us. You want me to see if it came in yet?"

She nodded but didn't look up from the computer. Her hands shook from excitement. This could be it. The answer to who killed Jessie and Stan. She was sure Stan had pulled over the person who'd killed him. She was also convinced the murders were connected. Which meant, if her hunch was right, whoever owned the car Stan called into dispatch killed both.

She could hear Neil's heavy stomp coming up the basement stairs. He waved a sheet of paper in front of Elle, just out of reach. "You know, there are these places called homes, and how it works is, people go to them and do things like eat real food and sleep in normal-sized beds." He placed the paper in front of her. "Isn't that crazy?"

"Neil, don't cluck at me." But she wasn't really upset with the intrusion. It felt good to have Neil mother hen her. Just like old times. She fidgeted with the folders. "Did EJ eat yet?"

Neil gestured toward the empty pizza box on Heather's desk. "Who do you think ate most of that?" Then he pointed at Elle. "Go home and eat something. Get some rest. I mean it. EJ will be fine."

She picked up the sheet Neil had put in front of her and scanned it. "Damn."

"What? They didn't send the right stuff? You want me to get Jessica on the line again?"

She waved him off. "It's fine. I didn't find what I was hoping for. This says the car Stan pulled over was reported stolen."

"From here?"

Elle checked the readout. "No, from Chicago." She slumped in her chair. "It could be anyone. And now it looks like it might not even be related to Jessie's murder." She passed Neil the printout.

"So Stan calls in a ten-twenty-eight and finds the car stolen. Pulls it over and the driver gets out and shoots him while he's doing his paperwork."

"That's my guess. Looks like Case was right. It was someone passing through. God knows where they were going."

"Don't worry. We'll find out who killed them. Even if it was an army of people."

Elle groaned. The idea was so daunting. She'd gone from elation to desolation in a matter of minutes. "Put an APB out on a blue Jetta. Illinois license plate. Maybe the staties will find it for us." She opened a browser and typed Kitty Sedona in the search bar. A couple reviews came up for Bad Kitty Koffee in Sedona, Arizona. But at the bottom there was an article about Bobby Sedona's CFO. She clicked on that and scanned the page. It said that he'd gone missing five years ago and that they'd never found the body. Sedona had accused him of stealing from his company, but there was never any proof. At the very bottom of the page was a mention that he was rumored to have been sleeping with Sedona's wife, Kitty Sedona.

Elle sat back in her chair. "Huh. I did find something interesting. You remember Holt?"

"The drunk at the wake? Yeah, what about him?"

"He said he thought Jessie might have been screwing around with Bobby Sedona's wife. That she was probably the one who gave him the majority of the money he needed to pay off his gambling debts." She pointed to an article. "And the last guy who screwed around with Sedona's wife went missing."

"You think Bobby Sedona killed Jessie?"

She shook her head. "I think Sedona's the type who has someone to do that for him."

"Huh." Neil lifted her out of her chair. "I want you to go home and get at least eight hours of sleep. Eat food that doesn't start with a 'p' and end in an 'a.'" He pushed her toward the door.

"What if I want pasta? Or polenta? Or—"

"Hardy har. Get out of here."

CHAPTER TWENTY-FIVE

The sun hung at the edge of the horizon. But even as night set in, it did little for the heat clogging Elle's house. It was stifling. She had all the windows and back door thrown open, but the heat stuck around, like a sticky residue.

She returned from the kitchen with her second beer, rolling the perspiring bottle on the back of her neck. It helped for a few minutes.

She plopped down on her couch in time to see Jessica Fletcher sniff a small syringe and declare it smelled like cyanide.

"Pfft." Elle took a long swig.

She was wearing as little as possible, jean cutoffs and a tank top, and still it wasn't enough to cool her down. She was contemplating an ice bath when there was a knock at the door.

She waited a few minutes, hoping whoever it was would go away. If it was Brady, she was tempted to arrest him for trespassing. He'd called her no less than five times today. That was some kind of record, even for Brady. She couldn't wait for the Beer and Berry festival to be over and done with. It was easily the worst day of the year.

"If you're going to pretend you're not home, at least turn the TV down." Robin's voice came through the window.

Elle's stomach clenched, along with a few other places. She looked around her living room in a panic. It hadn't changed since the last time her mom had decorated. As a result, everything was too loud and colorful.

"Are you going to open up? I come with gifts."

Elle looked behind her at the patio door, wondering if she slipped out the back maybe Robin would go away.

She stood and placed her beer on the table a few inches to the right of the coaster. There was no time to clean. The place had gone to pot the last few days. The sink was full of cereal bowls and glasses. The counter had three days' worth of *Chicago Sun-Times* strewn across the top. Three days' worth of bras hung over the couch. She grabbed those and threw them toward her room. At least she'd made an effort.

She smoothed the front of her tank top. A large amount of cleavage peeked over the top and she wondered if she should change. Before Elle could decide, she heard another knock. A different-sounding knock. Like a knuckle on glass. She turned to the backyard. Robin was leaning against the patio frame door. She was in tight jeans and a peasant blouse. The neck was off-kilter, exposing gorgeous skin. Robin's mouth curved into a crooked grin. That grin alone was enough to make Elle's mouth go dry.

"Were you ever going to open up?" Robin held up a paper bag with Torrini's written in brown letters along the front and waved it back and forth. "I brought food." In the other hand she held up a bottle of red wine. "I thought you could use some booze after the week you've had. And from what I've heard from Tully, if you're going to eat at Torrini's, you should be sauced to enjoy it."

It took Elle a moment to refocus. "Um?"

"Don't worry, it's cold pasta salad."

"It's not that. I think you'll find better company at Finnegan's."

"Nah." Robin's eyes skimmed Elle's bare legs. She strode inside and placed the bag of food on the kitchen counter. "So. I heard."

"About EJ?"

"Sandy told me." She tilted her head back, thinking. "And, if I have this right, Sandy heard it from Tully who heard it from Neil, who was there when it happened."

Elle took a second to admire Robin's long neck and wondered how it would feel to press her lips to the exposed skin. Robin dropped her head and their eyes locked. If possible, the temperature in the place rose a few degrees as the moment held.

Elle broke first, turning to the cupboard. "That sounds about right." She pulled down a couple of plates. "You want a beer?"

Robin held up the bottle of red in answer.

"Okay, but you're on your own with that," Elle said.

"I can't stand beer and the only place around here that sells wine is Earl's Gas and Gulp. I'm guessing this is the Gulp part of the name. Do you have a corkscrew?"

Elle tapped the lid of the bottle playfully. It was a screw cap.

"Figures. That's what you get for trusting Earl when he recommends a," she read the front of the bottle, "2016 red wine."

"Good year."

"Mmm. Maybe it'll explode if I open it."

"I wouldn't risk it."

Robin grinned, showing beautiful white teeth and dimples. "I've always liked living on the wild side." She flicked her bangs to the side in a move that was both self-assured and mesmerizing.

Without taking her eyes off her, Elle reached up and grabbed a wineglass. Robin poured a purplish liquid into the glass. Glad she'd declined, Elle retrieved her beer off the coffee table. It was already piss warm.

They clinked glasses and took sips. Robin's whole body shuddered. She put her glass on the counter. "Maybe it just needs to breathe a little."

Elle laughed.

"I had no idea wine could taste this bad."

"I think I have some vodka or something somewhere." Elle went in search of something more palatable. "While I'm scouting your liquor options, why don't you unpack the food?"

Robin was happy to oblige. "So how is EJ anyway?"

Elle shrugged, her head half hidden in a bottom cupboard. "He's refusing to speak to me." She shifted through years of stored junk. This had been her parents' liquor cabinet, but Elle didn't drink anything other than beer, so it wasn't stocked. "Here we go." Elle stood, holding a bottle of mescal. It had a cartoon picture of a red worm carrying a jug in a cloth slung from its head. "The way he's acting you'd think I'd arrested him."

"He'll get over it. They always do. You're family." Robin eyed the bottle Elle placed on the counter next to her wineglass. "You're not going to make me drink this alone, are you?"

Elle made a disgusted face. "Yeah, you're on your own." She lifted her beer to her lips. "But if it makes you feel any better, I'm ahead of you by two drinks." She drank the last of her beer and dropped it into a box next to the fridge.

As Elle grabbed another beer from the fridge, Robin turned to the television in time to see the final reveal on *Murder, She Wrote*.

"I used to love this show as a kid." Robin wandered closer. "I haven't seen it in years." When it switched to a commercial, she picked up a picture from the mantel. In it, a young girl, tongue stuck out, sat on a man's shoulders. "You and your dad?" she asked.

Elle peered at the picture over Robin's shoulder. "Yeah."

Robin picked up another. Elle's parents were standing next to a barbecue, her dad wearing an apron and holding a spatula, her mom hugging him around the waist. Her mom's red hair spilled out of her ponytail, framing her face.

"How old were you when they died?"

Elle took the picture and replaced it on the mantel. "Let's eat."

"Sorry, I didn't mean to bring you down."

Elle sighed. She had to remember that Robin wasn't there to write a story about her. That should make talking to her easier and in some ways it did, but she'd never been good at talking about this.

"I was twenty-one. And that was it. The world collapsed. I came home from school to look after EJ. He was only ten and I had no idea what I was doing. One minute I was attending parties, finding out who I was away from this place, about to graduate, and the next..."

"I can't imagine having my world upend like that."

Elle straightened the picture of her parents, then shrugged and turned. "It was a long time ago." She took a sip of her beer. "Why don't we eat outside? It's cooler."

"With the bugs?"

"They won't steal your food."

Robin shuddered. "That's not what I'm worried about. Mosquitos love me."

"Don't scratch. It'll go down by morning."

"That easy, huh?"

Elle placed their plates on a small table outside and flicked her hand toward the trees. "I grew up in the middle of a forest. You're never more than a five-minute walk from being deep in the woods. You learn to get used to it."

"No bug spray? Citronella candles?"

Elle slapped Robin's knee. "I have something better." She disappeared for a few minutes and returned with a small clear container and handed it to a skeptical Robin. "One of the girls at the salon makes it."

"What is it?"

"Natural bug repellent. It works and doesn't smell like you'll burst into flames."

"The last time I was in the woods, I was fourteen and camping with my family." That wasn't entirely true. There had been that one assignment a couple of years ago. She'd almost forgotten about it. From the beginning, it had been nothing but trouble. She'd followed this guy to northern Michigan where her car had broken down. The nearest service station had been miles away. She'd gotten eaten alive. There was something about her blood. Mosquitos loved her blood.

Later, Elle asked, "So do you get home to see your family a lot? You said they live in Evanston, right?"

Robin slid her plate away. They'd made small talk through dinner. As easy as it had been, she couldn't keep her eyes off Elle. Her legs, one curled under her as she sat facing Robin, her arms, which moved constantly while she talked, and her eyes as they scanned every part of Robin. She could feel the pull deep in the pit of her stomach. It was delicious in its intensity. She had this need to touch every part of Elle. From the moment she'd met her, there was this string of desire pulling her in, but it had been manageable. Something she could deny herself in order to complete her assignment. Ever since that kiss in the basement of the Maverty house, the pull had grown stronger, and she found it impossible to stop herself.

Robin leaned close to Elle, never taking her eyes off those deep emeralds. Their lips were inches apart when Robin reared back and yelped. "Goddamnit." She scratched at her arm. Elle covered Robin's hand, stopping her.

"It'll just make it worse." She stood and pulled Robin to her feet. "Come inside."

As she followed close behind, Robin felt a little intoxicated. Even though she'd barely touched the mescal, there was a heaviness to her legs. Her desire had begun to spread through her whole body, reaching to the tips of her fingers and slowly melting down to her toes.

As soon as the screen door was shut, she grabbed Elle by the waist and spun her around. She slammed her against the wall. Elle let out a cry of surprise, which melded into a moan as their lips met. There was no taking it slow. This wasn't the sensual kiss from the Maverty house. This was possessive and rough.

Elle's hands found their way under Robin's top, her fingers gripping hot skin as they slid down the back of her jeans.

Robin pulled away, out of breath. "Jesus fucking Christ. We better move this somewhere more comfortable unless you want me to fuck you against this wall."

Elle grinned and circled her wrist. She led Robin through the hall into her bedroom, which wasn't much cooler than the rest of the house but had a ceiling fan, making it bearable. Robin stopped to pick up one of the discarded bras on their way. Her brow raised in question.

Elle shrugged. "I wasn't expecting company."

With a smirk, Robin said, "I can go if you'd like?"

Elle didn't answer. Instead she pulled Robin into her room, shoved her on the bed, and straddled her.

There was no slowing this down. Even if Elle wanted to, she couldn't stop herself. It was like she was possessed to touch, feel, taste. She yanked Robin's jeans open and slid her hand inside, running her fingers over the fabric of Robin's thong. Robin began to thrust her hips. Her head fell back onto the bed, exposing her neck. Elle ran her tongue from the base of Robin's shoulder to the edge of her jaw. She pulled aside the fabric of Robin's panties. They both groaned when Elle's fingers slid along Robin's wet folds. Elle kept the pace steady, enjoying the heat spreading through her own body but mostly the look in Robin's eyes, half-lidded as she watched Elle.

Before she went too far, Elle pulled back. She needed to see more. She pulled at the edge of Robin's top, hauling it over her head. Underneath, she was wearing a white lace strapless bra with light blue polka dots. Elle reached around and flicked it open with one hand.

Robin's brows rose. "Impressive."

Elle's laugh was muffled as she bent to pay more attention to Robin's long neck. She sucked at the soft skin, stopping at her collarbone before heading south again. The only other interruption was when Elle stopped to yank Robin's jeans down. They were inside out by the time they hit the bedroom floor.

Elle nestled herself between Robin's thighs, running her hands over the exposed skin of her inner thighs. Goose bumps rose in their wake. She started slow, taking Robin's left nipple into her mouth, sucking it, rolling it around her tongue. When Robin's hips started to lift in rhythm, Elle switched to the other nipple.

Robin's head rose off the bed. When their eyes met, she licked her lips. "Stop playing," she said.

Without breaking eye contact, Elle skimmed her fingers through Robin's folds before slipping inside. She couldn't remember the last time she'd felt so connected, so in the moment. There was something hypnotic about this dance of give and take. She'd forgotten how much she'd missed it.

Robin came alive the moment she entered her. Her body arched off the bed, her eyes met Elle's and stayed there as she rode each wave. She clutched the sheets, twisting the fabric as she rode the final crest.

After, she lay very still, hands still twisted in the sheets, catching her breath. "I'd say well done, but I don't think that covers it."

Elle collapsed beside her. She couldn't describe what she felt at that moment. It was more than content. She felt like she'd come home somehow.

Robin propped herself up on an elbow and leaned over Elle, watching her. She snaked her hand under Elle's tank top and lifted it. She stopped when she got halfway.

"What the fuck happened to your ribs?"

Elle looked down at the yellowing purple circling her midsection. She'd forgotten how bad it looked. It wasn't nearly as painful as it had been a couple days ago. "I ran into a tree."

"More like several." She skimmed the faint marks on Elle's neck with her fingertips. "Is this when you got the rest of these decorations?"

Elle shivered. "I'm fine."

"You sure?"

Elle leaned in pressing her lips to Robin's. "More than you know."

That was all the incentive Robin needed. She pulled Elle's cutoffs down her legs and dropped them onto the floor. Elle was wearing black bikinis. The dark contrasted against the creamy white of Elle's thighs. Robin ripped those off too, throwing them toward the headboard.

Robin didn't wait for an invitation or plea. She pushed Elle's thighs apart until Elle's knees rested on the bed and ran her tongue up the inside of her thighs.

Elle's fingers gripped the duvet in anticipation. It was going to be a long night.

Chapter Twenty-six

At six in the morning, Elle jerked awake. She was alone and naked in her bed, tangled in the sheets. She didn't remember Robin leaving, but she must have because there was a note on her pillow.

Elle opened the folded paper. *You make a great muse. Sorry I had to skip out early, but I got some much-needed inspiration.*

Elle tried not to feel too disappointed. She wasn't the type for one-night stands and she wasn't sure what Robin was, but this didn't feel like a one-night stand. She wished Robin had at least stayed the night. Waking up with a warm body snuggled up behind her was one of the better memories Elle had of college. Looking over at the empty pillow, it was like a deep chasm had opened in front of her and she could see every morning ahead of her just like this one, waking up alone.

Then she remembered what day it was. She stared at the ceiling fan. "Fuck." It was the day of the Beer and Berry Festival.

Her cell buzzed on the nightstand. It was Neil. She put him on speaker as she collected her things before heading to the shower.

"Hey, Neil. What's up?"

"I know it's early, but are you on your way in?"

"I'll be there in about half an hour. Is it urgent?"

"Yeah, I'd get here as soon as you can."

Damn. She'd bet Brady was already harassing her deputies. That was all she needed this morning. She showered as quickly as she could before throwing on her uniform and heading into the station.

When Elle walked in, she was surprised to see Neil sitting at the front desk by himself.

"Where's Brady?"

"Besides up my ass?" He pointed down the street. "He's called four times already. But that's not what I called you in for." He handed her a sheet of paper. "You remember that bike Kate found? She sent me the plates to run and it belongs to a Jennifer Trafford."

Elle looked at the picture on the driver's license. She looked back up at Neil.

"Look familiar?" he asked.

She looked down again, but couldn't believe it. Staring back at her from the Illinois driver's license was Robin Oakes's face. Her heart kicked into a steady beat against her chest as she tried to figure out what this meant. Robin had given them a fake name. Why? She rushed to her desk. She needed to verify what she thought she already had.

Neil was right behind her. "I already called. The magazine doesn't exist. The website's fake. A good fake, but according to Whois, the domain was created only a few days ago."

Elle crumpled the paper.

"What do you think this means? You think she's involved somehow?" Neil asked.

Elle put her hand to her neck. Her key. She'd looked this morning but figured it had gotten tangled in her clothes on the floor. And she'd been short on time. She figured she'd go back for it at lunch. Elle turned toward the giant Cary safe behind her. Inside was over a hundred grand.

"Shit." Was that why Robin was here? But how could she have known about the money before they found it? Unless she was the one there to collect it? "Shit."

"What's wrong?"

"Did you check to see if there were any hits on Jennifer Trafford?"

"So far nothing. It might not even be her real name."

"Goddamnit!" Elle threw the wad of paper against the wall. The sound it made was too unsatisfactory so she kicked the leg of her desk, which gave a good thud.

"What's going on, Elle?"

"Give me some time to think. Can you take charge of the festival today? Make sure everyone knows their assignments?"

"Of course. You want some coffee?"

Elle nodded, the phone already in her hand, ready to make the first call of many.

By the time Elle had finished her fourth cup of coffee, she'd phoned the Franklin lab, followed up with the staties at dispatch, and called in every favor she could. As far as she could tell, Robin Oakes was a ghost. She only existed on paper. So much of this still didn't make sense. It was possible Jennifer Trafford worked for Sedona and she'd been sent to kill Jessie. But then why was she still here?

The only thing she did know for sure was that Robin Oakes didn't exist and wasn't a reporter writing a story for some magazine.

Stan had called in a plate right before he'd been killed. The car he'd pulled over had belonged to a Scott Mitchell and had been reported missing several days ago. The car was a blue Jetta, the same car Robin had been driving. She didn't think it was a coincidence. In fact, Elle was pretty sure that Stan had pulled Robin over and she'd shot him before he could discover it.

Of course, she had no evidence to prove any of this. Just a hunch and circumstantial evidence.

She was about to head out for her fifth cup of the day when Brady strode in. "What are you doing in here? Why aren't you out there organizing everything? The festival's today and you're in here sitting on your ass?"

"Is that today? Shit." Elle searched through several piles of folders until she pulled one out and opened it.

Brady paused for a brief moment before exploding in apoplectic rage. "For Christ's sake, Elle. How could you have forgotten? We've only been preparing for it for the past six months."

Elle ignored him. She called Neil in with a loud yell to the outer offices.

Neil sauntered in, an apple fritter in one hand, a coffee in the other, and a lazy, almost somnolent way about him. "You rang, boss?" He leaned against the doorframe.

"Yeah, how's operation Drunk Hicks going?"

"Really?" asked Brady, an exasperated look on his face. "That's what you're calling it?"

"Well, we've got Gilford and his boys out making the rounds now. They all know the lowdown. No firearms, no open booze outside the beer tents, no brawling, and no tobacco spitting."

"Tobacco spitting?" asked Brady.

Neil took a bite of his fritter, ignoring Brady, and chewed for a moment before continuing. "We've got five off-duty state troopers out on loan showing up at three to help with security. I had Heather hand out that flyer you made up last year for businesses, warning them to lock up tight before heading out to the party. All in all, I'd say we're ready. Tully and Sandy are organizing the actual events going on and so I've kept my nose out of that."

"That's great, Neil. Thanks."

Neil patted his baton as he turned to leave. "No problemo, boss, I've got all the help I need right here."

Elle turned to Brady. "You were saying?" She flipped the file closed and placed it on one of the towering stacks.

"And what have you got in place if it rains? There's a forty percent chance we'll get that thunderstorm heading toward St. Louis." His face darkened as he thought of what sort of havoc rain would have on his festival. For Brady, it was just as disastrous as that spark that lit into Chicago or the asteroid that had killed all the dinosaurs.

"That's not my area, Brady. My guys are here to make sure nobody hurts themselves or others, that's it. Anything else, ask Tully or Sandy." She waved him away. "I do have more important things to handle. One being a double homicide investigation."

"That's the other thing I wanted to talk to you about. Now, I know you must feel like you've got a bit of egg on the face with this whole EJ thing, but I don't want you to worry. I completely understand how hard this has been for you." He tried to make his face appear understanding, but failed. "In fact, I called Ed over in Hardin and told him about the whole situation." He leaned back and folded his hands over his belly. "I think it would be best if you just gracefully let him deal with this."

"Yeah, about that." Elle got up from her desk, opened the top file cabinet and pulled out a large book. She threw it on the desk in front of Brady. The loud slap made him jump. "Why don't you have a read on page one fifty-five." She sat back down and leaned across her desk. Her first incoming call that morning had been from the sheriff of Hardin County. He had an amused, almost apologetic tone as he relayed his conversation with Brady. "You have absolutely no jurisdiction in this matter. None. So get your ass out of my office and let me do my job."

"Don't be so pigheaded. I've seen the evidence against him. Any jury in the country would convict him."

"The so-called evidence against him is why he's sitting in a cell downstairs. If I was as biased as everyone in this town makes me out to be, I wouldn't have detained my own brother."

"His fingerprints are on the murder weapon."

"His fingerprints are not on the murder weapon. Stop listening to town gossip and let me do my job."

"If you knew how to do your job we wouldn't be in this mess."

Elle stood. "Brady, I swear, if you weren't the mayor..." She let the rest of her sentence fall away. What she'd wanted to say was unprofessional, but just the thought of it made her feel better. "I have more important things to take care of right now."

Brady stood to follow her out of her office. "I'm not done. The other thing I wanted to talk to you about is the vote scheduled for three thirty tomorrow afternoon." He hiked up his pants as he said it and shoved his hands in his pockets. Elle was just at the door to the stairs leading to the basement, her hand on the knob, when she reared back at him.

"Brady, stay out of my way today. I mean it. Go enjoy yourself. Have some beer and pie." She waved toward the street, indicating that he should be anywhere but here, in front of her. "But just go."

Brady stood his ground, shifting his weight, jamming his thumbs deeper into his belt loops. Elle was stubborn, but Brady hadn't become mayor by giving up so easily. "Judge Keeler called. He said you were harassing him and Dell."

"Oh, please, I didn't even speak to Keeler, he let his wife give me some lie about being at work."

"This is going to happen whether you want it to or not. It's clear you've picked your side, but it's the wrong one, Elle."

She grabbed the knob to the basement door and yanked it open. "Get out of my station." She turned and descended the stairs at speed. Only when she reached the bottom did she realize she'd forgotten the keys to the cell.

She waited for Brady to leave before heading back upstairs.

EJ lay on his side facing the wall, his nose a few inches from the gray cement, his knees tucked next to his stomach. His mood was the color of the wall. This was the second time in weeks he'd spent the night on this cot. The weight of how much trouble he was in settled at the pit of his stomach, causing a storm of acid to swirl up and give him heartburn. He knew he deserved to be here, he just didn't have the guts to tell Elle why. It would forever damage their relationship, as much as she would deny it. He knew Elle better. They had a lot in common, but she had something he never would, which made her a better person: drive.

And here she was stuck in Turlough with him. Instead of leading the life she should've had with kids and a husband, a career up in Chicago, she worked late. Night after night, he'd come home to Elle asleep on the couch, paperwork scattered around her like petals sprinkled by a lover. This wasn't the life she would have picked for herself. Hell, it wasn't even the life he'd have wished on her. But she was here. For him.

At the sound of the door to the basement opening, EJ turned his back to the bars, feigning sleep. He didn't want to talk to Elle or Neil right now.

There was a soft chuckle. "Faker. You're not asleep." Dan kicked the bars. "Get up."

EJ turned to see Dan grinning at him from the other side of the bars. "What're you doing? You're not supposed to be down here."

Dan shrugged. "Who cares? Everyone's so busy with this stupid festival I could probably drive Deputy Do-Right's cruiser out of here and no one would notice." He gave two thumbs up. "Your sister sure did her due diligence there."

"What are you doing here?"

Dan's mouth curled into one of his shit-eating grins. "I came to say good-bye."

"Good-bye? You're leaving?" EJ got up and went to the bars.

"That's what good-bye means, doesn't it? I'm heading out of town. I need to get on with my life. I'd hate to end up stuck in this shit hole like your sister."

"Where're you going?"

He shrugged. "Don't know, someplace else."

"How're you going to live? You're just going to leave Lisa?"

Dan scowled and it transformed his face into something dark. He didn't like being told how to take care of his sister. "I'm going to come back for her. I just need to get settled first."

EJ didn't know why, but that thought gave him the chills. "I thought we were going to go together?"

Dan slapped his hand against one of the bars. "Well, I can't really wait around here for you to get out. Could be a while, you know, considering."

EJ stared. Dan seemed to shrink, as if announcing his departure made him smaller. EJ wanted to shout that he couldn't go, couldn't leave him behind like this. But in that moment, he realized it would be useless. Dan would go anyway and take pleasure in seeing EJ beg. In the end, any plea on EJ's part would make him lose more. So he shrugged and sat on the cot. He lay down, crossed one leg over the other, and laced his hands behind his head. "See you," he said.

Dan stood there for a second, waiting for something more. When he didn't get it, he turned toward the stairs. "Hey, at least I came to say good-bye." He mounted the steps.

At the click of the door latch, one painful thought passed through EJ's mind. Elle had been right, Dan was no friend of his.

Chapter Twenty-seven

Elle headed toward the station. After her blowup with Brady, she'd decided to head home to double-check her house for that key. She wanted to be sure she hadn't misplaced it. But she was sure she'd had it on last night because she remembered hearing it hit the floor with her tank. She'd spent twenty minutes shaking out every piece of clothing on her floor. Nothing. Jennifer Trafford had taken it. She was sure of it.

The main strip of Turlough had been transformed since she'd first arrived that morning. Tables and booths were erected parallel to the sidewalks. They'd set up barricades. Main Street was now a pedestrian-only area, forcing Elle to move her cruiser to a side street. A group of shirtless men hoisted a giant tent up in the square to the right of the sheriff's office. That would be the beer tent. Empty now, in several hours it would be overflowing with good ole boys becoming increasingly louder and drunker as the night wore on.

She heard a catcall coming from the vicinity of the tent. Then a loud "Morning, Sheriff!" She nodded, but kept her pace quick, entering the sheriff's office as another series of catcalls and whistles reached her.

"Jesus," she said when she was safe inside the office. Heather was at the front desk sorting through reports Elle knew would be complaints from the usual suspects.

"Morning, Sheriff." Heather looked up from her papers. "Mr. Case wanted me to let you know he's in his office downstairs."

"Thanks, Heather. Any calls you get about the festival, can you direct those to Neil?"

Heather nodded.

The safe behind Elle's desk stood closed. She tried the handle.

Locked, just as she'd left it. Although if that was because Jennifer hadn't been here or she'd already been and gone, Elle wasn't sure.

She closed the door to her office before picking up the phone and dialing.

"Travis here."

"Hey, it's Elle. Do you have time to come by the station today? I have kind of an urgent matter I need help with."

There was a long pause on the other end, which meant Sandy had him tethered to the festival today.

"I wouldn't ask if it wasn't incredibly important. If anyone gives you grief, tell them it's police business."

"Is it?"

"Yes, so bring your tools."

He sighed into the phone, but she knew he'd much rather duck out for work than set up tables and help his wife decorate. "All right. Give me ten minutes to grab my stuff. If I catch shit for this, I'm sending it your way."

"Fair enough."

When he'd finally arrived and she'd explained about the misplaced key, he looked less than happy at being pulled away from setting up tables.

"Elle, this is a safe. I'm a locksmith."

"And?"

"And you need a safe technician." He went to the double doors and spun the combination wheel that kept them locked. "Locks, yes. This is a whole other beast." He ran his hand through salt-and-pepper hair. "You don't know the combination?"

"I usually never lock it, so I don't need to remember it."

"And you don't have the combination written down anywhere?"

Elle bit her lip. "I do. It's etched into the key."

Travis scratched at the stubble on his chin. It made rasping noises. It was the warning sign that Travis was about to explode.

Elle spread her hands. "It wasn't me who did it. That's how it was when Bailey gave me the key. I'm not sure who the idiot was."

Travis stared at the ground in front of the safe, mumbling to himself before looking up at Elle. "Welp, I hope nobody finds it because you've just given them a neon sign to this monstrosity. Let me guess, the other side says 'key to the safe in the sheriff's office'?"

"I don't think that would fit."

"A keychain perhaps?"

Elle held her hand up stopping him from going any further. "Okay. I get it. Is there a safe technician nearby?"

Travis shrugged. "Even if there was, you got eight hundred bucks to give 'em?"

Elle ran her hand over the dial. Inside was one hundred grand. And twenty-five of that was actually her money, but it might as well have been Monopoly money for all the good it did. It was now evidence in a murder investigation. "Nope. Wish I did." She turned to Travis. "I have another question. You know that reporter who was staying at your place? Sandy said she left early this morning. You know what time she left?"

"Nah. It was pretty early though. I was up at six and her car was gone. She paid up, though, if that's what you're wondering."

"Cash?"

"It's king."

"No credit card on file?"

"No."

"You guys take license plate numbers of your guests?"

"No. Why?"

"It's nothing. Thanks for coming, Travis."

He gave her a weak salute and left, swinging his toolbox as he went.

She took a key out of her desk drawer and locked her office door before heading toward the basement. "Has anyone been in my office this morning?"

Heather shook her head, "Just you."

"Has the station been left unattended since I left?"

Heather checked her watch, centering it on her wrist, a nervous, twitchy habit. "Neil asked me to put a box of fliers in the trunk of his cruiser around ten thirty, but that only took a second, why?"

It was twenty past eleven now. "Was Neil here when you did that?"

A worried look planted itself on Heather's face, she glanced toward the front door, shaking her head. "He's been in and out all morning. He's been pretty busy getting everything ready for tonight," she said in case Elle thought Neil was slacking off.

"Is everything okay?" Her voice took on a plaintive, almost breathy whine as she said it.

Elle nodded but didn't answer as she disappeared into the basement.

Case was at his desk packing up a file box with various odds and ends, most of which were picture frames and leather-bound reference books. He was wearing a dark red golf shirt and khaki pants instead of his usual suit.

"What are you doing? The vote isn't until tomorrow."

Case waved her off. "I'm old, not an idiot. They want me gone, Elle."

"So what? You show up in a polo shirt and casual pants all ready to retire? You can't give up." Case continued to pack, ignoring the desperate look on Elle's face. "You have to fight."

Case harrumphed. "Fighting's for the young. By the time you're my age the only decent thing to do is roll over and play dead." He even managed to chuckle. "I had a good run, though. Made it longer than most."

"Stop." Elle grabbed a book on anatomy from Case. "You can't go yet, this case isn't finished."

He shook his head. "This is your case, Elle. I'm just the guy who roots around in the bodies."

"But I still need your help on this." Elle rushed through Neil's early morning discovery of Robin Oakes's real identity before Case could protest again.

Jack picked up a folder and handed it to Elle. "When I was getting samples of that first T-shirt you found, I tested the blood on it. Wasn't human. I don't know if that helps you at all. It was all circumstantial anyway."

"So the blood on EJ's T-shirt wasn't human?"

"Correct. I don't know what animal it came from. The other shirt you found in the Maverty house, that was human blood. It'll take the lab a couple weeks to test if it's Jessie Forrester's. But I'd bet good money it is." He set the book he was holding on his desk and folded his arms. "You've got a theory, don't you."

Elle shrugged. "A kind of theory."

"Care to share?"

She opened and closed the book she was holding a couple of times, collecting her thoughts. "Well, we know Jessie owed a lot of money. It's unlikely that he would be killed before repaying that money. So we can rule out the people he owed money to. We also know that he was cheating on his wife with a woman named Kitty. It's possible Kitty could be Kitty Sedona, the wife of Bobby Sedona, an entrepreneur, and I say entrepreneur lightly. Most of his business dealings are suspect. From what I learned, it usually doesn't end well for the guy who crosses Sedona. I'm guessing he didn't take kindly to the guy screwing his wife.

"We found a hundred grand at the Maverty house, twenty-five thousand of which was mine. Where'd he get the other seventy-five thousand? Holt suggested Kitty had given it to Jessie. Sedona hires someone to kill Jessie and get his money back." After coming clean with Neil, she'd paid a visit to Jack. She still wasn't sure which was worse, Neil's grumpy disapproval or Jack's grumpy disappointment.

"If that's the case, why'd we find it under the Maverty house? Wouldn't the killer have taken it back to Chicago with him?"

"Yeah, I thought about that. What if Sedona didn't know until later? It makes no sense to kill someone for money but forget to grab the money. I think Jessie was killed by a hit person hired by Sedona."

"Elle, you can't prove any of that."

"I know. But hear me out. The killer leaves, then finds out about the money and goes back. In the meantime, Jessie is found by someone who lives in town. Someone who uses the Maverty house a lot. Someone who wears Harley-Davidson shirts. He mutilates him, for whatever sick reason, and finds the money I'd just given Jessie."

Case nodded coming around the desk. "He's the one who took the Beemer keys."

"Right. And finds the rest of the money in the car and stashes it all in his hiding place in the Maverty house, along with his shirt. The killer comes back, can't find Jessie's keys, and smashes the window of the Beemer, only there's nothing there. Now, this person has to find this money or Sedona will be very angry. Who showed up the day after Jessie was killed?"

Case's eyebrows, which had been inching up his forehead the longer Elle spoke climbed, if possible, higher. "You think Robin Oakes is the hired killer?"

"No, I think Jennifer Trafford is the hired killer. Robin Oakes doesn't exist, remember? She insinuated herself into a position where looking for information and asking questions wouldn't make her suspect. All you have to do is talk to Brady on the phone for a second and you can read him like a book. She manipulated her way into this town and has been playing us all." Elle looked at the book, hoping Jack couldn't see her expression. Jennifer had played her most of all. And that hurt like hell.

"And she killed Stan?"

"She was driving a stolen car. It belonged to a Scott Mitchell who, after a bit of digging, turns out to work for a known bookie in Chicago. His wife reported him missing and the car stolen four days ago. I'm guessing Jennifer bumped into this guy at Jessie's hotel and killed him to get him out of the way."

"That would mean there's another body we haven't found," Jack said.

"I don't even want to think about that right now. It's all circumstantial, but it fits. It's why Jessie was killed with a rifle but stabbed after the fact. It's why Stan was killed with a handgun. Jessie's murder was planned. Stan's was impulsive."

"But why did you find the knife by Stan's cruiser?"

"I have a theory about that too. Did you know that the Pritchards live about half a mile from where Stan was killed? On the night he was killed, Will reported that raccoons got into their house. What if it wasn't raccoons? What if it was someone with a grudge against Randy who was dead set on getting a keg pump back? That's who I chased into the forest."

"So, let's say you're right. What now? You can't prove any of this."

"Not yet. But we have something Robin wants. Sedona's money locked in our safe, which she now has the key to." The last bit was mumbled.

"And how'd she get the key?"

Elle waved him off. "That's a really long story."

"Try me."

Elle sighed. She didn't want to go there. Not yet. "It's not important to the investigation. Can I have a rain check?"

Case took the book from Elle's hands and placed it in one of his boxes with all the rest. They stared at each other from across the room. Elle wasn't sure what he saw, but when he smiled, she knew he'd let it go. "It sounds to me like you've got everything handled. I'll just get in the way."

"You're letting them win."

He shrugged. He'd spent most of his life fighting battles that weren't his. Back in Chicago he'd dealt with his share of shithead detectives, asshole cops, police chiefs with sticks up their asses. He'd had more arguments with Bailey than he could remember. Elle had been a breath of fresh air just when he needed it. There was no fight left in him, and he'd known it for a long time.

"Are you sure this is what you want?"

"No, Elle, it's not. But it's time for me to go easy and take some time for myself. Who knows, maybe I'll take up a new hobby. I hear internet dating is a pretty good one."

Elle laughed. "Watch out for those gold diggers. They'll spend your pension before you've even had a chance to cash the check." She turned to leave. At the door, she glanced back to say something else, but he'd already gone back to packing his boxes.

CHAPTER TWENTY-EIGHT

Elle stopped in front of EJ's cell. A light rap with her knuckles got his attention. "Hey, how're you feeling?"

His feet were crossed at the head of his bed. A pile of manga comics Elle had brought from his room sat on the cot next to him. "Just peachy."

At least he was talking to her today. "I want to ask you a few more questions about the eighteenth."

EJ shrugged, leaned his head against the wall, and stared up at his sister, tired, wary. "My lawyer said not to answer any questions without her here."

"Okay, you want me to call Bryce in?"

EJ just shrugged.

"You didn't do this. I know you didn't. But I need to know what did happen that night. Jack tested the blood on your shirt. We know it wasn't human." She crouched so they were eye to eye. "Dan said the two of you were together all night. That you went to pick up his keg pump at nine when you separated from the rest of your friends. What really happened, EJ?"

EJ had thought about it most of the night and much of the morning. He didn't want Elle finding out what he'd done, but he also didn't want to go to prison for something he didn't do.

Still crouched, Elle repositioned herself so she was sitting cross-legged on the basement floor in front of EJ's cell.

"Before I start, you have to promise you're not going to get that look in your eyes. The one where it's like I've done the worst possible thing you could imagine."

Elle sighed. "EJ, the worst possible thing I can imagine is you committing murder."

EJ arranged himself on the cot so he was mimicking Elle's position. He took a deep breath. "Okay, but you're not going to like what I have to tell you."

"If it gives you an alibi for the time of the murder, I'm sure I'll be able to live with it. Whose idea was it to throw the keg party?"

"Dan's. There's this girl, Jessica Reid?" he said. Elle mimed large breasts with both hands. EJ nodded. "That's her. Well, I've been trying to get with her for months—"

Elle rolled her eyes. "And by 'get with,' I'm assuming you mean bring her to a nice restaurant and treat her like the lady she is?"

"Do you want to hear this or not?"

Elle raised her hands in peace.

"Dan thought it'd be a good idea to throw this party. We'd invite the whole school. Show that we're hospitable, fun guys. Give me a chance to impress her." Elle had a lot to say about that too, but she kept her mouth shut this time. "We had planned on grabbing the keg from Finnegan's before heading over. But Dan forgot the pump and said it would be faster if we split up. So I dropped him off in town, which left me high and dry, because as you know, snatching a keg from Finnegan's is a two-man job."

"As I know?"

"Please, like you never swiped one when you were at Flynn."

"Keep going."

"So anyway," EJ licked his lips, "I drove Dan's pickup to the place out on Six and parked in that hidden driveway around the bend. They keep kegs in a cold storage out back. At the time, I thought that would be way easier. There's already a big gap in the chain-link fence. I brought a crowbar to pry the lock off, but they hadn't even locked it up. I guess they figured no one was going to steal kegs. Everything's going fine. I get the keg rolled out to the truck and manage to get it in the back, which was a bitch, let me tell you. But I put the crowbar down to roll the keg out to the truck. It was Dan's, and I know how crazy he is about his stuff. Shit, you saw how mental he went over his keg pump. So I went back to get it." He took another deep breath. He'd stopped looking at Elle, his eyes instead focused on the pile of comics next to him. He kept folding and unfolding one of the corners.

EJ didn't need to continue. Elle knew where this was going. She knew without him going any further that it was the call she'd answered after dropping the money off for Jessie.

"When I went back, I wasn't expecting there to be this giant dog. It was massive." He held his arms out wide. "A Rottweiler or something. I'm not sure, but I must have been making too much noise and he came out of this shed." EJ was quiet for a full minute, trying to collect his thoughts and figure how best to explain to Elle. "He lunged at me and I swung." EJ's eyes when they met Elle's were trimmed with tears. "I didn't mean for anyone to get hurt. I just wanted to impress Jessica. I thought if I showed up with this keg that I'd gotten by myself, she would—It sounds stupid now, but I thought she'd, like, notice me more." His voice cracked. "I didn't mean to." He swiped at his eyes with the back of his hand. "There was just so much blood. And I didn't know what to do, so I stuffed my shirt into that tree trunk and ditched the crowbar down a drain."

The poor animal had been lying on its side when Elle stepped into the backyard. The sight of it had felt like a stab to the gut. She couldn't imagine the person who would do something so cruel. So destructive and devastating. She wanted to find the perpetrator and bring them back to watch as that lonely limp form was loaded into the back of the animal services van. Hearing it from EJ's point of view didn't change that.

Elle reached in and squeezed his knee. "Hey." She shook his knee. "Hey, look at me." EJ met her gaze. He shrugged and his face crumpled. Elle pulled the keys from her pocket and unlocked the cell door. She sat on the cot next to EJ, pulled him to her shoulder, and rocked him as he cried. She had no words for him. She had no idea how to make this bearable for him, so she just held him the way her mother used to. It had always made her feel better, just the intimacy and the knowledge that someone cared.

They stayed like that until finally EJ pulled away. He wiped at his tears. "I was so afraid you were going to hate me."

"How could you think that? EJ, how could you ever think that?"

EJ shrugged, uncomfortable. "It's so hard sometimes. Being around you."

"What's that supposed to mean?"

"I'm not like you, and no matter how much you want me to be, I just can't."

Sometimes she hated how much he was like her. But now wasn't the best time to tell him that. "I don't want you to be like me, I want you to be you."

He peeked over at her, his lashes studded with tears. "If that's true then how come you're always on me about something? You want me to get better grades and stay out of trouble, but you don't understand what it's like. I couldn't do those things even if I tried. I'm not good at school. I'm never going to college, and no matter how much I really try to stay out of trouble, it just happens. All I'm doing is hanging out with my friends doing what everyone else is doing, but I'm always the one that gets caught and punished. It's not fair."

She wanted to laugh. This conversation sounded eerily like one she'd had with her mom once. Her mom had grounded her for skipping school. She'd tried to explain that it wasn't her fault, she'd just been going along with everyone else.

"I'm going to give you some advice Mom gave me once. She said, 'No matter how much you think you have to do something to fit in or be cool, it all comes down to decisions. There isn't anything we have to do. There's only what we choose to do.' I didn't really understand what she meant at the time, but being on the other side now I think I know what she was trying to say. I know what it's like to get caught up in it all. Every little choice doesn't seem that big a deal until you look back and see them all in a long line and all of a sudden you wonder how you got there."

EJ took the edge of the blanket on the cot and wiped the snot from his nose. "You make it sound easy. To just decide not to go along with everyone. But it's not easy."

"When I was younger I didn't really think about the consequences. Life always seemed easy. Until one day it wasn't, and I was faced with a lot of consequences. I don't ever want you to get the rude wake-up I got."

"I wasn't as old as you when Mom and Dad died, but I still remember it all. It affected me just as much as you."

Elle nodded. "That part was probably worse for you in ways. But before Mom and Dad died, I made a couple of decisions. A couple of my choices weren't the greatest and I had to live with them. My last year of high school was a pretty scary wake-up call."

"Does this have to do with why you broke it off with Jessie?"

She stared down at the ground, tracing a small crack from the base of the wall to her foot. "Part of it, yeah." She didn't say anything for a while, too afraid she'd start to cry.

"I'm sorry."

She smiled then. "God, EJ. If anything ever happened to you... I'm the one who promised to take care of you, remember? I have to be able to protect you, and the only way I know how to do that is to be a pain in the ass."

He laughed. "Okay, stop being so fucking cheesy." He wiped his nose with his sleeve. They sat on the cot together, listening to the muted voices setting up the festival outside.

After a few minutes Elle asked. "Hey, you said Dan and you split up. Where did you meet up with Dan after that?"

"I picked him up outside Dell's and we drove to his house so he could get another T-shirt."

"He wasn't wearing a shirt when you picked him up?"

EJ shook his head. "Which I thought was weird at the time when I saw him just standing there on the street. But he said he'd ripped it in the forest or something." EJ shrugged. "I wasn't really paying too much attention. I was scared shitless I was going to get caught for killing that dog."

"Do you remember what T-shirt he was wearing when you split up?"

EJ shook his head.

"Last question. Do you remember if he ever found his pump?"

"Nah, although he stopped bitching about it a few days ago. I figured he'd finally given up on it." EJ picked at a hole in his sock. "Which is kind of not like Dan. He usually doesn't let go of anything. You think he found who took it?"

Elle nodded. "Yeah, I think he did." She squeezed his knee as she stood up, she opened the cell door, and motioned for him to follow.

"What are you doing?"

"I'm letting you go. You didn't kill Jessie. You may be back here very shortly, depending on what happens with the people who own that store, but for now I'm letting you out."

"Just like that, you're going to let me go?"

Elle swept her arm out toward the stairs. "Looks like."

"Won't everybody be pissed off you're letting the only suspect go?"

"I'll handle them. Before you go, I need to know where Dan is."

EJ shrugged. "Who knows. He came by here this morning to say good-bye."

"Wait, what? Dan was here this morning? What time?"

"I don't know. About a half hour ago."

"Okay, I'm letting you go but, EJ," she stabbed his chest with her finger, speaking low, "you stay the fuck away from Dan, got me?"

"Why? Is he the one who killed Jessie?"

"You stay out of it, EJ." She poked his chest one more time to get her point across.

CHAPTER TWENTY-NINE

Dark clouds loomed at the edge of the horizon like an army preparing to attack. The main square of Turlough looked like the American flag had puked on it. The theme of red, white, and blue was everywhere: tablecloths, banners, the clothes draped on every adult and child attending the festival.

The tables with the pies were set up in the middle with every size and flavor of pie imaginable. Surrounding the pies were the brewers' tables. Local brewers came from hours away, counties as far as Effingham and Calhoun. Even the brewers came prepared, producing labels in the colors of the flag.

The only absence of red, white, and blue were the beige uniforms of the state police dispersed among the crowd and the black and tan of Elle's deputies.

Neil watched the crowd from the periphery, one hand on his baton, the other shoveling a piece of cherry pie into his mouth. He leaned forward a few inches to keep any cherry filling from hitting his uniform if some should fall. That's all he needed, Elle on his case for ruining his uniform.

It was that magic hour before the sun fully set just before the street lights came on. It didn't matter. The square was lit up with fairy lights running along lines overhead. Kids ran through the crowd with sparklers, tagging each other and screaming.

It was hard to believe there was a killer somewhere among the crowd. Neil still couldn't believe it. His job was to hold the fort. He wasn't usually one to argue, but he didn't like it. Jennifer Trafford looked innocent enough, but if Elle was right, she was a killer. She'd killed in cold blood. Twice. He didn't want Elle taking any chances. But as she'd pointed out, what choice did they have?

He shoved the rest of the pie in his mouth and unclipped his radio from his belt. "Come in, Elle."

A few seconds later. "Go ahead, Neil."

"Anything yet?"

"Nothing. Have you seen her?"

"Negative. But that doesn't mean she's not here. The place is a zoo." His eyes rose to the sky. "Hope those storm clouds stay away until this thing's over."

"Honestly? I hope it hits something fierce, just to see Brady's reaction."

Neil could hear the grin in her voice and roared with laughter. "I'll take video for you." A beat. "Elle? Be careful."

Her sigh was loud enough Neil heard it through the radio. "I promise."

"No Rambo shit."

"When have I ever?" There was another long pause. He knew she'd do what she needed to do, and that's what scared him. "You worry too much. Keep me posted if you see her."

He had a right to worry. But he didn't say that. All he said was, "Will do. Neil out."

He checked in with the staties on loan before changing his position to another vantage point. It was going to be a long night.

Elle crouched behind a tree. It wasn't comfortable, but then she hadn't expected that when she decided to stake out Jennifer's bike. She'd had Kate return it to where she'd found it earlier in the week.

With the crowd swarming around the sheriff's office, they had very little chance of spotting Jennifer sneaking in to grab the money from the safe. But Kate had assured her there was no way Jennifer would leave this bike behind. It was loved beyond measure. Kate said there must be over a hundred grand in custom parts. So that's how Elle found herself hidden in the brush trying to avoid poison ivy at dusk on Independence Day.

She didn't have much to go on for murder, but stealing a hundred grand from the sheriff's office was a class one felony and carried a max of fifteen years in prison. And who was to say she couldn't find evidence to add two murder charges to that.

The approaching storm electrified the air. Her anticipation was thick.

❖

Jennifer stood on the outskirts of the crowd. She was less than fifteen feet from her goal. The window in the back of the sheriff's office was always left open. At least it had been every time she'd scoped it out. All she needed was to hoist herself up and squeeze through the small opening. Easy for someone her size. With the festival going, they'd locked up the sheriff's office, and everyone was either enjoying themselves or working the crowd.

Usually if she was breaking in, she'd wear something dark and simple, but in this crowd, black would stand out, so she'd opted for jeans and a blue tank top. If anyone noticed her, it would look like she was there for the festivities.

She had her Beretta Nano concealed in an ankle holster just in case the place wasn't as empty as it appeared. Elle had to have discovered that her key was missing by now. She couldn't be sure how much Elle knew, but in her line of work, it was always better to err on the side of worst case scenario. She was alive because she never underestimated anyone, especially a small-town sheriff. Even if Elle looked like she should be sitting behind a desk in the Loop, it didn't mean Jennifer should treat her like that. She was so close to finally getting out of this fucking town. She wasn't going to let impatience screw it all up.

She watched as a man wearing baggy jeans and a tight Confederate flag shirt stretched across his beer belly stumble past. He was holding a tallboy in one hand and a half-eaten corn dog in the other. Every time he tried to take a bite of his corn dog, he missed his mouth. There were gobs of mustard smeared around his lips. Jennifer backed up as he passed. It was now or never.

She kept an eye out for anyone watching, but everyone was too busy shoving their faces with pie to notice. When she reached the back of the building, she met with a dense stretch of trees. She didn't know why this surprised her. Elle was right. You could throw a stone in any direction and hit forest.

In the cooler shadows, the mosquitos began to swarm. Whatever Elle had given her the other night hadn't worked for shit. They still found her skin tantalizing. She trudged to the back window, swatting at any exposed skin. The sooner she was out of there, the better. She groaned when she saw the window. From the inside, it had looked bigger.

"Fuck me."

As she stood there, looking up at the window, weighing her options, she couldn't think of a worse way to spend Independence Day. She'd had some shitstorms, that's for sure. There was the year Bobby invited her out to his yacht party on Lake Michigan and she'd spent the night hiding in one of the heads because some asshole had torn the strap on her dress. Four hours in a space the size of a postage stamp. Or there was the year she'd been coerced into road-tripping with her girlfriend at the time. Stuck in a car with a woman who felt showering ruined the fun of a road trip was not Jennifer's idea of a vacation. Give her a hot shower and room service. Instead, she'd gotten a cold lake and burned hot dogs on a stick. She'd broken up with her the second they got back.

Breaking into a sheriff's office to steal a hundred grand, while exciting, wasn't the excitement Jennifer needed in her life.

Jennifer was thirty-five. Too old, in her opinion, to be scaling walls. After this job, she was planning a much-needed retirement. Bobby had promised her a 10 percent cut of what she recovered, plus her fee. And he didn't even know about the extra twenty-five thousand sitting in that safe. Her take on this would be considerable. She'd also managed to sock away a good nest egg for herself over the years. She planned to take that and get the hell out of the country. The farther the better.

She'd met Bobby at a poker game when she was in college. It was one of those underground high-stakes games where the blinds were a month's rent. He was playing. She was waitressing. One of the regulars had tried to stick his hand up her skirt and she'd broken two of his fingers. Years later, Bobby told her the only reason she'd made it out of there alive that night was because he'd been losing to the guy she'd maimed. If he'd been winning, she'd have ended up in Lake Michigan.

That was Bobby. One day you were in his favor, the next you could be dead. That night, before he'd left, he handed her a business card and told her to call him. At the time, there were only rumors about Bobby Sedona, and they were all dangerous. But she needed to pay rent. The second her parents found out she'd flunked her first term, they'd yank her out of there and she'd be back in Evanston, Illinois. And there was no way in hell she was going home again. The city was everything the suburbs wasn't. Exciting, compact, dangerous, packed with people who looked different, talked different, smelled different. She wanted to be a part of that, and the only way to do that was to make her own way. Bobby was that way. She wasn't naïve enough to believe that it wouldn't have its problems. Jennifer always made sure she stayed in Bobby's favor. Always. It didn't matter what had to go down to make that happen. There was no failure when it came to Bobby.

Through the years she'd worked her way up. She started running errands for him. Little things. Things a personal assistant would do, like getting him takeout from his favorite deli, or dropping off his dry cleaning. When he felt he could trust her, he pulled her in deeper. She began deliveries. She worked with a guy named Frisky. He'd do the driving, she'd to the actual delivery. She assumed it was drugs. Sometimes the packages were significant. Frisky said they weren't supposed to know what they were delivering, but they both knew it wasn't legal.

When Bobby found out Jennifer was in her high school's clay target league he wanted to see how good she was. Turned out she was very good. He took her and a couple friends out on his yacht and they sat around drinking while watching Jennifer shoot down clay pigeons over the lake.

It wasn't long before he had her doing small jobs. Just scare tactics. They were all pretty easy compared to some of the things he'd asked her to do over the years. But by far, this had been the hardest job. Usually, when you do a job you get to leave. You don't stick around to watch the aftermath. It had been unsettling.

Another reason to get out now, while she still had a sliver of a soul left. Forrester hadn't been a big deal. She'd dealt with guys like him for years. If you were stupid enough to fuck Bobby Sedona's wife, then you got what was coming to you. Even the bookie had been an acceptable risk. But that kid in the cruiser was bad luck.

She'd never had to watch what her work caused. Seeing Elle after that had almost convinced her to leave before it got any worse. She'd always considered Jason the screwup in the family, the way he could never hold down a job, keep a place. But seeing how close she'd come to screwing up herself, she'd realized the only difference between her and Jason was that she knew to quit when she was ahead. And that was exactly what she planned to do as soon as this job was over.

The buildings and trees muted the noise from the festival. She could actually hear herself think back here, although the soundtrack had changed to whizzing mosquitos. Jennifer slapped her arm. When she pulled her hand away there was a big glob of blood. Her blood. She didn't take another second to think about it, she began to climb. There was a ledge halfway up that helped get her most of the way, but the window was one of those ones that opened outward, which made it harder once she actually made it up.

It was dark inside. Only every third light was on, giving the place a faded, unused look. With the old computer on the back desk and the shit-brown carpet, it almost looked like she'd time warped back to the early nineties.

Jennifer reached in and adjusted the lever to open the window as far as it would go. She grabbed onto the ledge above and maneuvered her feet through the opening. Before dropping in, she pulled the balaclava she'd brought with her down over her face. She hadn't seen any cameras, and it was unlikely they could afford such a luxury, but she wasn't taking any chances. She landed softly on the faded carpet and crouched down, waiting. Nothing stirred. She circled the desks, keeping low in case someone peeked through the front.

When she reached Elle's office, it was locked. She pulled out her little leather case of picks. She selected her torsion wrench and a pick and went to work. It took all of one minute to break in.

The safe was a different matter. If she didn't have the key and the combination she would've been shit out of luck. As it was, some helpful person had printed the combination on the key.

As soon as she opened the door, a whiff of Elle's perfume smacked her in the face and she stopped. She looked around in case Elle had decided to stake out her own office. But there was no one there. Everything was the same as the last time she was there. A desk piled with stacks of files, a radio charger, and a phone. There was a shelf stuffed with books and an old love seat that had seen better days decades ago.

She approached the safe, still apprehensive of how easy it had been to get in. There had to be a catch somewhere, but she couldn't see it. Maybe they had a spare key and had already taken the money out. It wasn't the first time she'd thought of this.

But when she opened the safe and unlocked the large box, she was a little surprised to see the money sitting in an evidence bag. She lifted it out and examined it for dye packs or any other booby traps but couldn't see anything. She shoved it in her bag and retraced her steps. It didn't pay to stick around after you'd committed a crime. She could worry about how easy it'd been when she was back on the road heading toward Chicago with Bobby's money.

❖

Elle's feet were going numb. She'd been crouched in the same position for over an hour. The sun had set a little over thirty minutes ago. Only the faintest hint of orange lit the west. The east was filled with brooding clouds that obscured the stars.

Her radio crackled and she nearly jumped a foot.

"Elle, come in."

"I'm here. You see her?"

"No, I haven't seen her yet, but I thought you'd want to know I saw EJ heading after the Baker kid. You want me to follow them?"

"No. Stay where you are. I need you at the festival. Shit. I told him to stay away from Dan. He never listens to a word I say. As soon as I get my hands on that little shit, I'm going to ground him for life." She looked over the field. There was no movement. What if she'd been wrong and Jennifer wasn't after the money? What if she wasn't the killer, even, and she'd built this case on nothing? It was possible she'd lost the key earlier.

"He probably thinks he's helping somehow."

"He's going to get himself hurt is what." It only took a second for her to decide what to do. "Which direction were they heading?"

"Elle, you're not going after him, are you?"

"I have to. Dan may not have killed, but that doesn't mean he's not capable of it. I'm convinced he's the one who mutilated Jessie's body. Which direction?"

"The Maverty house."

"Thanks, Neil."

"Be careful. And message me the second you get there."

"I will." Elle clipped her radio and ran to the bike. Kate had managed to cut a new key for the bike by removing the ignition lock and filling a blank. She'd given Elle the key in case the person she was staking out never showed up. Elle hadn't ridden in years and only ever dirt bikes, but there wasn't much difference between the two. With her cruiser parked over a mile away she'd never get to it in time. Plus, this way she could cut across the field and take a shortcut.

She straddled the bike, checked the shifter was in neutral, squeezed the clutch, and pushed start. The engine roared to life. There was a good chance this decision would mean she didn't catch Jennifer, but she couldn't live with herself if anything happened to EJ. Not when she had a chance to stop it. Maybe if her bike was missing, Jennifer would stick around long enough for them to pick her up.

As she tore off into the night, she didn't see the silent figure standing at the edge of the clearing, hidden by a copse of trees.

Chapter Thirty

EJ found Dan stomping through the living room of the Maverty house swearing something fierce. EJ pulled back behind the wall. He'd seen Dan like this before, so angry he'd destroy everything in his path. The last time he'd seen him like this, he'd been whaling on Randy. This was not a Dan he wanted to confront.

He turned to sneak out the same way he'd come—the kitchen window—when he stumbled on a crumpled beer can. He may as well have rung the doorbell.

"Who's there?" Dan shouted.

"It's just me, man. Elle let me go this afternoon." EJ poked his head out of the kitchen entryway. "What're you so angry for?" He shoved his hands deep into his pocket, trying to appear casual. Inside, warning bells were going off.

"It's nothing. I had some pot stashed. Now it's gone. Why'd she let you go?" He pulled out a cigarette and lit it. There was an uncaged energy about him, like a tiger prowling.

"Holy shit." EJ noticed the hole in the living room floor. "What the hell happened?"

"Don't know. It was here when I got here. There's a whole room down there. You didn't know about it?"

"No way." EJ crouched near the edge and peered inside at the cellar below. Moonlight streamed down the stairs leading to the backyard.

"Your sister didn't tell you about it?"

"If she knew, you think she'd tell me about it?"

Dan nodded like this was a good point. "So what are you doing here?"

"I came looking for you." EJ wasn't sure what he'd been planning when he followed Dan out of the square. But if he'd had something to do with Jessie's murder, well, EJ didn't think he should get away with it. And what the hell was Elle doing? Just letting him go? "You said you were getting out of town and I want to come with you."

Dan puffed on his cigarette, leaning against the tattered chair in the living room, flicking ashes onto the ground. "Well, I was planning to sell that pot to fund my departure." He shrugged. "Now that's gone."

"How much pot did you have? An ounce wouldn't even get you to the state line."

"I had enough, okay?" Dan flicked his cigarette at EJ. It bounced off his shoulder, spilling sparks onto his T-shirt.

"Hey, watch it." EJ swatted at the sparks. "What were you really here for? I know it wasn't pot."

"How do you know? You spying on me? Keeping watch over everything I do?"

"No. But I know there's only two people to buy pot from in Turlough and both of them fucking hate you. That's why I always had to do the buying and you know it."

"Who says I got it in Turlough?"

"Fuck off, Dan. Stop fucking lying. I know you don't have any pot and I know you had something to do with Jessie's murder. And you were going to let them pin it on me, weren't you? Some fucking friend. Elle was right about you. You don't give a shit about anyone but yourself."

"That right? Your sister's one to talk, isn't she? Like she gives a shit about you? She locked you up, for fuck's sake. On what? Nothing. She did it to get you out of her hair so she could screw that reporter who's been hanging around town."

EJ went cold. "What are you talking about?"

"I went by your house when you were locked up. That woman's car was parked outside. At three a.m. Seems a little late to be working don't you think?"

"What the fuck are you talking about?"

"Your sister's a fucking dyke. You don't think it's strange she never dates? She likes pussy, man. Get over it."

That was more than EJ could stand. It was one thing to talk shit about him, but his sister was off-limits. He lunged at Dan, ready to rip that smug look off his stupid face. But Dan had been ready for this. Hoping for it. He stepped to the side and redirected EJ's attack toward the banister. His head bounced off the newel post and he collapsed in a heap at the bottom of the stairs, dazed.

Dan grabbed EJ's collar and hauled him to his feet. "You fight like your sister. Like a little bitch."

"Fuck off." EJ swung at Dan's ribs but was easily swatted away.

Dan pulled him toward the hole in the living room. "Come on. Put up a better fight than this."

EJ dug his heels into the warped floorboards. He pulled at Dan's T-shirt, looking for a hold, an anchor of some sort. But Dan had momentum on his side. He shoved EJ toward the hole, and with nothing to grab on to, EJ pinwheeled, falling backward. It was the scariest ten seconds of his life as he slowly fell and landed on the stone floor of the cellar.

He'd tried to twist at the last second and catch his fall, but instead, he landed on his shoulder. He clamped his mouth shut. He didn't want Dan to hear how much pain he was in. But he was sure he'd broken something.

It took Dan all of thirty seconds to climb out the back window and come down the cellar stairs. EJ tried to back up to the farthest, darkest spot in the cellar, but the moon, at a low angle this time of night, cast its glow to the back wall, illuminating most of the cellar.

"So you going to kill me like you killed Jessie?"

Dan stopped on the bottom step. "You trying to get me to confess? What? You got your phone set to record? I didn't kill Jessie."

"Yeah, right. You said he was stabbed to death and they found my knife. The only person who could've taken it was you. That night we had the keg party. It must have dropped out of my pocket."

Dan shrugged. "Tell yourself whatever you want to believe, but I didn't kill Jessie."

"No? Then why you running?"

Dan stepped down into the cellar and walked toward EJ. "I'm not running. This place is a shit hole and I don't want to be here anymore. When I make some money, I'm going to come get Lisa and we'll finally be able to live our own lives without anyone telling us what to do."

"Lisa's better off here where your parents can take care of her."

"Are you saying I can't take care of my own sister?" Dan seized one of the old water pipes running along the ceiling and wrenched it down. "If I were you, I'd worry about your own sister and what she gets up to." The pipe popped free. Dan swung it a couple times. It whistled as it whizzed through the air.

"You're a lying sack of shit who doesn't care about anyone but yourself. I bet Lisa never sees you again."

Dan's first swing landed on EJ's shoulder. EJ tried to block the second, but it was no use. Dan landed blow after blow, screaming the whole time. Each strike was more damaging than the last. Blood from EJ's nose splattered the brick, Dan's shirt, the floor surrounding them both. He lifted the pipe above his head when he heard Elle.

"Drop it, Dan. Or I'll shoot."

He froze and turned. Elle was silhouetted at the top of the cellar stairs, her gun aimed at him.

"You woul—"

The shot echoed through the small space. It missed Dan's head by a foot.

"You missed." He smirked.

"Throw the pipe into the corner."

"You're not going to shoot me." Dan took a step toward Elle, adjusting his grip on the pipe.

She didn't budge. Instead she kept steady aim at Dan. "You think I'll have a problem proving just cause? You've got a sealed record, which probably establishes a history of violence. I've got plenty of witnesses that can testify to your violent temper. I've got EJ to back up anything I say. No one's going to blink an eye if I shoot you right now. So please, go ahead. Test me."

Dan chucked the pipe and raised his hands in the air. The pipe clanked as it hit the stone. Only once he was unarmed did Elle descend the stairs. She stopped when she saw EJ crumpled in the back corner with his face and clothes covered in blood.

"What the hell did you do to him?"

Elle dropped to her knees next to EJ and felt for a pulse. He was alive, but he didn't look good. She unclipped her radio. "Neil, come in."

"Go ahead."

"Call an ambulance to the Maverty house."

"You okay?" There was panic in his voice.

"I'm fine. EJ's hurt, though."

"I'll call it in. It may take a while. There's been reports of flash flooding in Hardin."

"Okay, thanks."

Elle turned to Dan, her eyes dark. "He was supposed to be your friend."

"Yeah? Well, things change." Dan studied his nails, picking at the cuticles.

She wanted to strangle the indifference out of him. She'd never been so sorry to be right. But she'd pegged Dan the second she met him. He didn't give a shit about anyone but himself. EJ had been a distraction for him while he passed the time until he could get out of here. As much as she wished she'd been more adamant about EJ staying away from him, about keeping a closer eye on him, the truth was, she couldn't have done a thing. The harder she pushed against Dan, the stronger his hold on EJ would've become. What she should've done was kept him locked up tonight. But even as she thought it, she knew that was ridiculous.

"Why'd you do it, Dan?"

"Do what?"

"Jessie Forrester."

Dan shrugged. "He was already dead."

Elle took a step back, stunned by the justification. "So that makes it all right in your mind?"

"I wanted to know what it was like. He was dead when I found him. It's not like I killed the guy."

"Let's go, Dan. I'm placing you under arrest."

"For what? He was already dead," Dan shouted. He took a step toward her but Elle stood her ground.

"What kind of sick justification is that? Half his organs had been ripped out of him and just left there. Who does that? What kind of a sick fucking person does that to another human being?" As she said it, Elle tried not to picture the scene in her mind, but it was too late. The nightmare jumped out at her.

"I already told you, he was dead. He wasn't human, he wasn't anything anymore."

"And that gives you the right, to what? Use him as a science experiment?"

"Have you ever seen inside a dead body? The intestines are supposed to be like over twenty feet long. I wanted to see if that was true." He shrugged. And that was the most chilling part for Elle. The shrug. The fact that he still couldn't grasp how horrible his behavior was. "But then I heard someone coming and took off with the money before anyone saw me."

Elle shook her head, disgusted. This was not a battle she needed to fight. Dan was just as warped as she'd suspected. But it didn't make her feel any better to confirm it, only scared for what might have happened if she hadn't shown up in time.

As if to remind her of this, EJ groaned. She looked over to see if he was waking up, but he was still out cold.

The shift in her attention was a mistake.

Dan punched her in the stomach. Winded, she bent over and as she did he elbowed her in the jaw. Stunned, she stumbled back, lost her footing, and fell with a thud on the hard stone floor. Dan pivoted and lunged for her gun.

He landed on top and gripped the gun with both hands. Elle twisted to wrench it out of his grip. As she did he punched her three times in the ribs. The same side that had been injured with a tree branch a few days earlier.

"You son of a bitch." What had only been a hunch before was now as good as confirmed in her mind. She sucked in a couple breaths, steeling herself against the pain, and pulled her knee up to wedge it between her and Dan. He forced her knee down and straddled her, putting all his weight on her stomach, making it hard for her to breathe. With the new height advantage, Dan slammed Elle's arms down above her head. She held tight to the gun.

His face was only inches from hers. This close, she could smell his breath, a mixture of Certs and cigarettes. There was the tiniest hint of stubble on his chin. It was so light it almost blended in with his skin.

The cellar went dark as the approaching storm clouds swallowed the moon. Elle used the distraction to rotate herself and tug the gun from Dan's grasp. The victory didn't last long. He grabbed her hair and smashed her head into the hard stone floor. She blanked for a moment as everything went white then black. The important thing to remember was to hold on to the gun, but she could no longer feel it in her grasp. A second later, she felt the barrel against the back of her head.

"I wonder what the splatter would be for something like this?" Dan's voice was loud in the small cellar.

It sounded so close to Elle's ear. She rested her forehead on the stone floor, afraid to move. She didn't even dare close her eyes. Was this what it felt like to face death? She thought she'd feel terrified, instead she felt panic. She'd let this town get the best of her, the same as when she'd been younger.

"I guess I got the last laugh now, huh?"

But when the shot came, it sounded far away. Before she could figure out where the shot came from, she felt Dan's weight slump forward and roll off her. She scrambled out from under him and reached for her gun.

"I wouldn't." Jennifer stood at the top of the stairs with her Beretta pointed at Elle. "Pick it up with two fingers and toss it into the corner over there." She pointed her chin into one of the darker corners.

Elle obeyed. Dan groaned next to her. She flipped him on his side. Blood had soaked his T-shirt and was dripping onto the floor.

"I didn't aim to kill. But that doesn't mean he won't die if he doesn't get help soon." Jennifer shrugged her left shoulder. "Throw up your radio."

"I'll radio for help myself, thanks."

Jennifer rolled her eyes. "I wasn't offering." She held out her free hand, wiggling her fingers.

Elle unclipped her radio and tossed it up to Jennifer. "Now what?"

Jennifer hurled it into the backyard. "Now you have a choice. You can find the radio and call for help or find your gun and come for me." Jennifer turned to go then stopped. She looked like she wanted to say something. An apology? A good-bye? Elle wasn't sure, but she never got to hear it. Jennifer changed her mind and turned to leave.

That was the last straw.

"You fucking bitch." Elle pulled herself up. "That's it? You rampage through this town with your lies and deceit, ruining lives, and you have nothing to say for it?"

"I didn't lie about everything. I didn't lie when it came to you."

"Are you kidding me? I don't give a shit about that. You killed Jessie. You killed Stan. He was twenty-four fucking years old. He had a whole life to live and you killed him for no reason."

Jennifer backed up off the top stair. "Listen, I could debate this with you and that would be fun, but he's dying." She pointed to Dan. "And I have somewhere to be. I could've just grabbed my bike and left you to die, but I didn't. I saved your ass."

"And what? You want my thanks?"

Jennifer shrugged. "A little gratitude would be nice."

"Go fuck yourself."

"Well, it's been swell. You've got a radio to find and I've got places to be." And just like that, she sprinted away.

Elle rushed toward the corner she'd thrown her gun in but couldn't see it in the dark. After a few seconds, she gave up and charged the stairs, taking two at a time. She climbed through the back window, ran through the living room, and crashed through the front door. Jennifer was already on her bike, about to start it.

Elle lunged for Jennifer. She smacked into her, toppling them both to the ground. Jennifer tried to crawl away, but the bike had pinned her leg.

"Are you crazy? Do you have any idea how much this bike is worth?"

That was the moment the clouds above decided to break open and dump their contents. Thunder rumbled in the distance. Rain drops pelted the dirt, kicking up dust. The onslaught was so intense the world blurred. After a minute, the Maverty house had dulled behind a curtain of water.

Jennifer shoved Elle hard, pushing the bike up as she did. Elle slipped in the mud and her knee hit the clutch. Hard. Jennifer pressed the advantage and slammed Elle back into the ground. Her head smacked and bounced back into Jennifer's fist. She lay there stunned for a few moments.

Jennifer picked the bike up and gunned it. The back tire spun in the mud as she took off down the drive.

The rain slapped the side of Elle's face. She groaned and turned in the mud, slipping as she stood. She stumbled to the edge of the drive, but it was impossible to hear Jennifer's bike over the powerful rain. Elle made a split decision and headed right. With the roads shut down for the festival there was only one way out of town, and she was guessing Jennifer wanted to get the hell out as fast as she could.

The back roads of Turlough were misleading. They zigged in one direction only to curve around and zag in the next. If Elle was lucky, she could catch Jennifer before she made it over the Potawatomi bridge. And she had the weather on her side. Jen would have to be suicidal to go too fast in this rain. It would be next to impossible to see the potholes dotting the road. But then Elle realized she didn't even know Jennifer. She knew Robin Oakes, who was a figment of Jennifer's imagination. While Robin might have been calm and rational, Jennifer might be the complete opposite.

Elle sloshed through the forest, the mud sucking at her boots. She picked up her pace just in case Jennifer was the suicidal type. By the time she made it to the hill leading down to the road, she was soaked through and covered in mud. Her boots looked twice their size. Giant chunks of mud had attached themselves as she slogged over the forest floor. She kicked them against an old oak tree before cautiously skidding down the side of the hill. There was one frightening moment when she lost control and began to free fall. She tilted forward, her momentum carrying her headfirst toward the road. She grabbed onto any brush her fingers could reach. Just as she was about to go ass over teakettle, she snatched some vines and yanked herself to a sudden halt. She cried out as her arm was almost wrenched from its socket.

"And I'm worried she's suicidal." Elle lay there for a moment, panting. After a few more seconds, she reached for the tree the vines were connected to so she could haul herself to her feet, but she heard a sickening crunch and the tree began to lean toward the road. She stopped immediately.

But then she had an idea. Slipping and sliding, she righted herself with another nearby sapling and moved behind the listing tree. The ground around the roots had eroded over time, probably from rainstorms like this one. The roots on the top half were fully exposed. It wouldn't take much to topple it over. If she gave it a little help and aimed it right, she could send it toward the road and create a formidable gate. Her only hope was that Jennifer hadn't passed this way yet.

She braced her feet as best she could and heaved with her left shoulder. The tree swayed but didn't budge. She pushed harder. Nothing.

"Come on, you stupid piece of wood. Fall over." Elle stopped for a second to listen. She wasn't sure, but it sounded like a motorcycle in the distance. "Shit." She couldn't panic. That would be the end of this.

Elle dropped to her knees and began scooping out heaps of mud and earth from under the tree. When she thought she'd gotten enough, she stood and pushed as hard as she could. It gave an inch. She pushed harder. It gave another. She gritted her teeth and gave it everything she had. After a few seconds, the tree tottered out of reach and Elle had to push herself back to stop from going over with it.

Elle scrambled back up the hill and wrapped her arms around a sturdy oak higher up as the tree toppled onto the road. It wasn't a silent affair, which surprised the hell out of Elle. The storm was already so loud, yet the cracking and snapping of old wood tore through the night like fireworks on the Fourth of July. Elle even jumped as the tree crashed in a spray of splintered wood, bounced once, and lay still across the road right before the Potawatomi bridge. It was going to be a hell of a mess to clean up tomorrow. But if it stopped Jennifer, it was worth it. Elle scrambled the rest of the way down the hill, picking out a spot to ambush Jennifer when she came through.

She didn't have long to wait. Less than a minute after the tree collapsed, Jennifer's bike skidded to a stop a few yards from the barrier. She flipped up her visor and dismounted. She pulled off her gloves and tucked them into her jacket pocket while she surveyed the tree. There was no way to get the bike around it and it was far too heavy to lift over. Her only option now was to go back the other way, through the town.

But Elle wasn't going to let it come to that. She'd hoped that Jennifer would take her helmet off. But it didn't look like that was going to happen. She didn't really want to have a punching match with someone who had armor covering their most vulnerable body part. But there was no way it could be helped. Without her gun, all she had was her fists, which weren't going to do much damage to someone in a bulky leather jacket and a helmet. She looked around her hiding spot for anything that could be used as a weapon. There wasn't much, a couple of stones and wet soggy leaves. She dug the toe of her boot into the earth looking for anything under the blanket of leaves. Her foot hit on one of the tree's branches. She scraped the leaves aside and pulled at the branch. It was jammed under the tree. She yanked as hard as she could, but it still wouldn't come out. Jennifer kicked the tree, then walked back to her bike. She grabbed the handle with her right hand and lifted her left leg to mount it.

This was it. Now or never.

Elle jumped from her spot and tackled Jennifer. She had the element of surprise, but it wouldn't last long. And it didn't.

Jennifer twisted, pulling her knee up to wedge between herself and Elle. She pushed as hard as she could. Elle went flying backward and her head smacked the rough road.

Jennifer scrambled to her feet. "You couldn't leave it alone, could you?" She pulled her Beretta from her ankle holster and aimed it at Elle. "I would've let it go. But you're too fucking stubborn." Jennifer shook her head and rain droplets flew off her helmet.

The rain was letting up. Instead of the curtain that closed around them, Elle could see farther down the road now. The sound of sirens behind her made her turn her head. On the other side of the river, she could see the faint glow of red. The EMTs. Too late, she realized that while she might have stopped Jennifer from escaping, she'd also blocked any help from making it to her and EJ.

Elle turned back to Jennifer, who still had her gun pointed at her. There was a strange look in her eyes. Pity? Fear? Regret? Had she been telling the truth earlier when she'd hinted that she'd felt something for Elle? It was the only way to explain her hesitation. Seeing her now, like this, tainted by murder, she looked like a different person. But how different was she really from the person Elle had gotten to know over the past week? If none of it was a lie, what did that say about Elle? Jennifer stepped forward and ripped her helmet off. Her hair, which was still dry, fell.

Elle raised herself up on her elbows. They stared at each other as the rain slowly stopped.

Jennifer swore under her breath and took another step forward. Elle backed up, crab crawling along the road until her back hit the tree. She had nowhere else to go. Elle scrambled through the debris behind her. She found a rock. It wasn't large enough to do any damage, but it might be enough to distract Jennifer.

Elle didn't think Jennifer would shoot her, but that didn't mean she wouldn't knock her out and take off. She hurled the rock at Jennifer's head. It had the intended effect. Jennifer ducked out of the way. Elle scrambled to her feet and tackled Jennifer. In her surprise, Jennifer dropped the gun, which scattered down the road and into the brush at the side. Elle kept that element of surprise on her side this time and followed up with a quick punch to the jaw. She gave it everything she had because she knew it was going to hurt them both like hell.

Jennifer lay there stunned and Elle took the opportunity to turn her onto her stomach. She pulled handcuffs from her belt and clipped them on.

"Hey," an EMT on the other side of the tree called out. "You the one who called?"

"Yeah." Elle stood and looked back down the road behind her. "Do you guys have anything portable you can grab? There's going to be a bit of a hike through the forest."

The guy's eyebrows shot up, but he nodded. "Let me grab our gear. How far is it?"

"About half a mile through the forest."

"Well, shit." He turned back to the ambulance parked on the other side of the bridge. She could hear him telling his partner they had a hike ahead of them.

Elle turned back to Jennifer, whose head was resting against the pavement. Her pale face was splattered with mud. It mixed with a small stream of blood from the corner of her lip.

Elle thought she'd feel relief. When it was all over, wasn't she supposed to feel lighter? But this was only the beginning. She looked at her uniform. It looked like she felt, tarnished and defeated. This was not how she'd wanted this to end. But when had she ever had a choice about how things ended?

She set her hands on her hips and gazed back across the bridge. The rain had started up again. It misted against the red and white emergency lights dancing against the trees. Maybe it was time to change that. Maybe it was time to make some choices for herself instead of living for everyone else. And in that moment, she did feel lighter. It might not have been much, but she knew it was a step in the right direction.

Epilogue

Elle climbed the last few steps, then wavered at the door. It had been a great idea when she'd left her house. Now, standing at the point of no return, she was having second thoughts. Possibly third and fourth thoughts.

The sun dipped low, dusting the tops of the trees in a golden hue. The days were getting shorter again, but they still had a few more weeks before the weather turned.

Elle had spent most of her day training a new deputy, or rather, watching Neil train the new deputy while she offered choice words of wisdom. They'd been through three deputies so far. For some reason, Brady kept bringing up what had happened to the last deputy. After that, they didn't last long. It could have something to do with Neil uploading a video of Brady crying during the rainstorm at the festival. She'd wanted to give Neil a raise, but it wasn't in the budget.

Things weren't back to normal by any stretch, but they were working on it. The biggest hurdle had been Neil and EJ. She'd made a choice to share everything with them. Neil had taken it in stride, like he did everything. EJ had been harder.

Dan had said some things to EJ that made it difficult to move past. It wasn't so much the fact that she liked women that he was having a tough time with. It was the fact that she'd kept it a secret from him. But, as she pointed out, they weren't sharers. They both kept themselves to themselves, something she was trying to change.

Most days, they existed in sullen silence. EJ's anger stemmed from Dan's betrayal more than Elle's.

Dan had survived. Elle had mixed feelings about that. EJ didn't. Even if he hadn't killed Jessie or Stan, he'd still framed EJ. He'd done things EJ would never forgive him for. It would take time to heal. And like Turlough, things would get better.

Things were getting better. Something Jennifer had said to her about leaving now that EJ was graduating made her realize that her fears about coming out, while valid, didn't have to rule her. Sure, there were going to be people who would change their vote when they found out she was a lesbian. But if that happened, there was nothing stopping her from leaving Turlough and maybe going back to Chicago. She hoped that didn't happen. She hadn't lied when she told Jennifer she liked her job and her life. Turlough was her home.

Jennifer had made a deal with the prosecution. In return for sharing her knowledge of Bobby Sedona, they gave her immunity. She was in witness protection awaiting the trial, which would probably take years.

EJ had made it through summer school, barely. He'd spent most of his time this past summer either in school or volunteering at the animal shelter in Mason as part of his three hundred hours of community service. He'd been charged with theft under five hundred dollars and animal cruelty. Elle had suggested the animal shelter for his community service.

Now that he'd graduated, it was obvious to them both that he wouldn't be pursuing an academic career. She'd given him an ultimatum: Get a job or start paying rent. She wanted him off the couch and doing something productive.

He'd told her this morning that he'd talked to McGrath about an apprenticeship at his shop. She was all for him working as a mechanic, but she didn't want him anywhere near that man and his bad influence. She'd had a better idea, which was why she was here. That's what she was telling herself.

Before she could talk herself out of it, she knocked. There was barking, which grew louder and then a loud thump against the door.

A muffled voice behind the door said, "Dirk, you idiot."

The door opened and Kate stood there in jeans and a tank top. She was pulling at the collar of a large bulldog who was trying to break away. "He's harmless, I promise."

Kate opened the screen door and beckoned for Elle to step inside. It smelled like freshly baked bread.

"I can come back if this is a bad time."

"No, stay. It's fine. I just baked some bread for my godfather. It's probably not healthy for him. But as he says, he's made it this long, anything now is just a bonus." Kate's smile was lopsided, indulgent.

Elle could see past Kate into the kitchen and two loaves cooling on the counter. "Your godfather?"

"John Rutherford."

"Mr. Rutherford's your godfather?"

Kate nodded as she beckoned Elle into the kitchen. "Yeah, you didn't know that?"

Elle was stunned she hadn't. She'd thought there weren't any secrets left. But then realized that was a stupid thought.

"I came to talk to you about EJ."

"Oh, yeah? Is he okay?"

"Actually, that's not really why I came." Elle took a deep breath and before she could lose her nerve blurted out, "I'd like to take you to dinner. If you're up for it. With me."

One side of Kate's mouth lifted. "Yeah?"

Elle had gone home and changed out of her uniform. She didn't think it'd be appropriate to ask someone out while she was still in her black and tans. It might give the wrong impression. But now she wished she were in uniform instead of what she'd decided to wear. It was as simple as she could make it without looking like she was trying too hard. She'd chosen dark jeans, a black T-shirt, and a light sweater with the sleeves rolled up. She pushed them up higher and licked her lips.

"Yeah," Elle said.

Dirk whined at Kate's feet and she realized she was still gripping his collar. "Sorry, boy." She let go and he wiggled over to Elle to sniff at her feet. He practically jumped for joy when Elle knelt to scrub behind his ears.

"See? Harmless," Kate said as he licked the side of Elle's face.

Elle laughed. "Gross."

Kate yanked him back by the collar and directed him to his bed, which was littered with several half-eaten chew toys. "Get out of here." She turned back to Elle. "Sorry. We don't get a lot of company."

They stood staring at each other for a few moments.

"So. Dinner?" Kate asked.

"Is that a yes?"

"Absolutely."

Elle grinned. It was a start.

About the Author

CJ Birch is a video editor and digital artist based in Toronto. When not lost in a good book or working, CJ can be found writing or drinking serious coffee, or doing both at the same time. She doesn't have any pets, but she does have a rather vicious ficus that has a habit of shedding all over the hardwood, usually right before company comes. CJ is the author of the New Horizons series. *An Intimate Deception* is her third book. You can visit CJ on social media @cjbirchwrites or www.cjbirchwrites.com.

Books Available From Bold Strokes Books

A Bird of Sorrow by Shea Godfrey. As Darrius and her lover, Princess Jessa, gather their strength for the coming war, a mysterious spell will reveal the truth of an ancient love. (978-1-63555-009-2)

All the Worlds Between Us by Morgan Lee Miller. High school senior Quinn Hughes discovers that a broken friendship is actually a door propped open for an unexpected romance. (978-1-63555-457-1)

An Intimate Deception by CJ Birch. Flynn County Sheriff Elle Ashley has spent her adult life atoning for her wild youth, but when she finds her ex, Jessie, murdered two weeks before the small town's biggest social event, she comes face-to-face with her past and all her well-kept secrets. (978-1-63555-417-5)

Cash and the Sorority Girl by Ashley Bartlett. Cash Braddock doesn't want to deal with morality, drugs, or people. Unfortunately, she's going to have to. (978-1-63555-310-9)

Falling by Kris Bryant. Falling in love isn't part of the plan, but will Shaylie Beck put her heart first and stick around, or tell the damaging truth? (978-1-63555-373-4)

Secrets in a Small Town by Nicole Stiling. Deputy Chief Mackenzie Blake has one mission: find the person harassing Savannah Castillo and her daughter before they cause real harm. (978-1-63555-436-6)

Stormy Seas by Ali Vali. The high-octane follow-up to the best-selling action-romance *Blue Skies*. (978-1-63555-299-7)

The Road to Madison by Elle Spencer. Can two women who fell in love as girls overcome the hurt caused by the father who tore them apart? (978-1-63555-421-2)

Dangerous Curves by Larkin Rose. When love waits at the finish line, dangerous curves are a risk worth taking. (978-1-63555-353-6)

Love to the Rescue by Radclyffe. Can two people who share a past really be strangers? (978-1-62639-973-0)

Love's Portrait by Anna Larner. When museum curator Molly Goode and benefactor Georgina Wright uncover a portrait's secret, public and private truths are exposed, and their deepening love hangs in the balance. (978-1-63555-057-3)

Model Behavior by MJ Williamz. Can one woman's instability shatter a new couple's dreams of happiness? (978-1-63555-379-6)

Pretending in Paradise by M. Ullrich. When travelwisdom.com assigns PR specialist Caroline Beckett and travel blogger Emma Morgan to cover a hot new couples retreat, they're forced to fake a relationship to secure a reservation. (978-1-63555-399-4)

Recipe for Love by Aurora Rey. Hannah Little doesn't have much use for fancy chefs or fancy restaurants, but when New York City chef Drew Davis comes to town, their attraction just might be a recipe for love. (978-1-63555-367-3)

The House by Eden Darry. After a vicious assault, Sadie, Fin, and their family retreat to a house they think is the perfect place to start over, until they realize not all is as it seems. (978-1-63555-395-6)

Uninvited by Jane C. Esther. When Aerin McLeary's body becomes host for an alien intent on invading Earth, she must work with researcher Olivia Ando to uncover the truth and save humankind. (978-1-63555-282-9)

Comrade Cowgirl by Yolanda Wallace. When cattle rancher Laramie Bowman accepts a lucrative job offer far from home, will her heart end up getting lost in translation? (978-1-63555-375-8)

Double Vision by Ellie Hart. When her cell phone rings, Giselle Cutler answers it—and finds herself speaking to a dead woman. (978-1-63555-385-7)

Inheritors of Chaos by Barbara Ann Wright. As factions splinter and reunite, will anyone survive the final showdown between gods and mortals on an alien world? (978-1-63555-294-2)

Spinning Tales by Brey Willows. When the fairy tale begins to unravel and villains are on the loose, will Maggie and Kody be able to spin a new tale? (978-1-63555-314-7)

Love on Lavender Lane by Karis Walsh. Accompanied by the buzz of honeybees and the scent of lavender, Paige and Kassidy must find a way to compromise on their approach to business if they want to save Lavender Lane Farm—and find a way to make room for love along the way. (978-1-63555-286-7)

The Do-Over by Georgia Beers. Bella Hunt has made a good life for herself and put the past behind her. But when the bane of her high school existence shows up for Bella's class on conflict resolution, the last thing they expect is to fall in love. (978-1-63555-393-2)

What Happens When by Samantha Boyette. For Molly Kennan, senior year is already an epic disaster, and falling for mysterious waitress Zia is about to make life a whole lot worse. (978-1-63555-408-3)

Wooing the Farmer by Jenny Frame. When fiercely independent modern socialite Penelope Huntingdon-Stewart and traditional country farmer Sam McQuade meet, trusting their hearts is harder than it looks. (978-1-63555-381-9)

Shut Up and Kiss Me by Julie Cannon. What better way to spend two weeks of hell in paradise than in the company of a hot, sexy woman? (978-1-163555-343-7)

Emily's Art and Soul by Joy Argento. When Emily meets Andi Marino she thinks she's found a new best friend, but Emily doesn't know that Andi is fast falling in love with her. Caught up in exploring her sexuality, will Emily see the only woman she needs is right in front of her? (978-1-163555-355-0)

Spencer's Cove by Missouri Vaun. When Foster Owen and Abigail Spencer meet, they uncover a story of lives adrift, loves lost, and true love found. (978-1-163555-171-6)

Unexpected Lightning by Cass Sellars. Lightning strikes once more when Sydney and Parker fight a dangerous stranger who threatens the peace they both desperately want. (978-1-163555-276-8)

Without Pretense by TJ Thomas. After living for decades hiding from the truth, can Ava learn to trust Bianca with her secrets and her heart? (978-1-163555-173-0)